ATMOSPHERIC
AND OTHER NIGHTMARES

Michael René Dubé

CIP data on file with the National Library and Archives

Paperback edition: ISBN 978-1-55483-468-6
Hard cover edition: ISBN 978-1-55483-472-3

Front and back cover design: Michael René Dubé

Introduction

This book holds thirteen horror stories created to satisfy my thirteen itches. These itches were ideas I had that I did not believe were novel-length ideas but had great short-story potential. All of them were a pleasure to write. Some contain gore, some don't. Some are based on true events I experienced as a child while others are pure imagination. I strive to be as original as I can with my stories. I hope you enjoy them.

— *Michael.*

For Taylor, Randee, Hunter, Chanel,
and my first grandchild, Colton!

Contents

Olive Leaf

1

The village of Olive Leaf was in northern Ontario, Canada. Very few people outside of the village itself had ever heard of Olive Leaf (population 400). The people were friendly, supportive, and carefree. That was until August 2020, when fall stomped summer out overnight.

With the changing colors of the leaves, also came a sudden absence of fish in the Magwan River. Deer and bear became scarce in the area. Even the smaller creatures of the woods seemed to have gone into hiding. Fear was spreading among the villagers. Winters were difficult enough during normal conditions, never mind trying to survive without their freezers stocked.

But there was something else being whispered among the adult population: rumors of someone having settled into the Teatherby shack around the same time the weather changed, and the animals disappeared. Many dismissed the rumors as an unfounded superstition. The occupant had yet to be seen by anyone, but a battered rocking-chair once inside the shack now sat on the decrepit porch. Most believed some of their children had done this as a prank, even though it was forbidden to go near the shack, for safety's sake. Just when the stories had ceased, an incident occurred that proved there was fact behind the fiction.

Chelsea Eckerman was entertaining two friends she'd invited for tea and pie. She was describing how, earlier that afternoon, while gathering the blueberries they were currently enjoying in her pie, she had encountered a scrawny, pale-skinned, sickly looking old man. Although she was afraid of him, he did not appear to pose any threat to her.

"When he saw me, he waved," she told her wide-eyed friends.

"Oh, Chels, stay the hell away from him," said Rose Shepherd.

"Stay the hell away from whom?" Chelsea's husband Tom echoed. He had just returned home from his job at the lumberyard in Karney.

"Oh...Tom. I was just telling the girls about my encounter with the man who's living in the old Teatherby shack," Chelsea explained.

"Someone is living in there?" he said perplexed. "How the hell can anyone live in that thing, it's rotted to shit and falling apart. Who the hell is this guy? You didn't talk to him, did you?"

"Are you kidding? He was creepy. I just wanted to get the heck out of there," Chelsea said, raising her cup of tea to her lips.

"Good. And I don't want you going back out there, either. I will get some guys together and pay our new neighbor a visit. You may think he's harmless, but you never know," said Tom.

"Exactly what I was thinking," said Rose. "I'm sure Ralph will be more than happy to join you, Tom."

"And Jacob," said Mrs. Clark, offering her husband's services.

"Fine," said Tom. "We'll work out a day and time—sooner the better."

2

Three rainy days later, Tom finally hooked up with Ralph Shepherd and Jacob Clark. Ralph was the unofficial head of Olive Leaf. A man in his mid-sixties, he'd lived his entire life in Olive; met and married Rose down in Jolly and moved her into his log cabin. They never had children (Rose was barren). Ralph was an intelligent, kind, and selfless man. His wife was everyone's grandmother.

Jacob was third in command, after Tom. He was a trustworthy forty-seven-year-old woodsman type always dressed in lumberjack apparel, his long black beard oiled and neat. One of the more handsome, brawny men in Olive. How he ever fell for Nancy was beyond Tom's comprehension. Mrs. Clark was at least 300 pounds—without shoes!

They downed the last of their beers in the village hall, tightened up their jackets, each placing their hats of choice on their heads (Tom was wearing his STP cap, Jacob his favorite black toque, and Ralph a well-worn leather cowboy hat) and headed out into the rain. The walk into the woods to reach the Teatherby shack was about 10 minutes (less with Tom leading the way, striding in long steps).

No one spoke it out loud, but there was a palpable grimness in that part of the woods. Even though the heavy rains and wind, the earth reeked of decay to an extreme that forced the three men to cover their mouths and noses. They stopped next to each other, Tom in the middle, staring at the shack.

"Christ. Looks worse than I remembered," said Jacob.

"You certain someone is living in there, Tom?" asked Ralph, talking with his fingers pinching his nose tight.

"Chels said she saw a man here," he said.

"Well, what the fuck. We're here now. Might as well check it out," Jacob said, also speaking through a plugged nose.

"Right. Come on," said Tom, stepping first onto the creaking porch. He looked down at the rocking chair, which was swaying front to back in the wind's grip. Then he looked up at the aluminum porch roof, which hung slanted and bent out of shape over their heads. "Hmm...that looks safe," he mumbled.

The three men shared glances as they stood face to face with the moss-covered door. Tom knocked hard (he meant business). No one answered.

"Hello?" called Ralph, still sounding like Kermit the Frog with his nose plugged. He released his nose and tried again, louder. "Hello! Anyone in there?"

Still no response.

"Should we go in?" asked Jacob, raindrops captured in his beard.

Lightning exposed the eerie-shaped clouds, followed by a monstrous roar of thunder. All three men were startled by the boom. They turned to look behind them, squinting into the haunting woods, and when they turned back, they all three jumped again.

"Shit myself!" Jacob yelled.

Ralph put his hand on his chest, and Tom removed his cap, slapped his thigh with it, and placed it back on his head.

The odor that flushed forth from the puny shack could've melted wax. And standing before them was a little old man whose appearance matched the rank odor. The friends were all taken aback by the sight that greeted them.

"Um. Excuse us for bothering you, sir, but we're members of Olive Leaf's community," Ralph began. "I'm not sure you're aware of the dangers posed by your living here. You see this shack is on its last days and—"

"My propertay," the old man interrupted. His voice was gravely, his tone angry and annoyed. "I have the papers...if you're wantin' to see 'em," he added, his oversized yellow eyes bulging. He seemed to stare directly into each of their eyes as if daring them to do something.

Ralph shook his head, while both Tom and Jacob remained silent, transfixed in awe and disgust by the man.

"That's okay, sir, we'll take your word for it. Just looking after your safety is all," Ralph offered.

"Teatherby's the name. My granddaddy left me this propertay and no one's runnin' me off 'er," the man hollered. Thunder seemed to echo his sentiments.

Ralph had his hands up in a gesture of surrender. He said, "Okay. No problem. We won't bother you again, sir—Mr. Teatherby. Our apologies for—"

The old man slammed the door on them.

"Well, that was most unexpected," said Jacob.

As they walked back toward the village, their boots weighed down with muck, Tom remarked, "Hey, is it just me, or were we just talking to a fucking corpse?"

"Those fucking eyes were as yellow as piss!" said Ralph.

"Creepy, old fuck! We need to warn everyone to keep their kids away from that shack. He's likely to throw a hammer or something," Jacob chuckled.

3

By early September, non-stop rainstorms had placed a gloom over everyone, young and old alike. Olive Leaf was a literal swamp.

"If this is any sign of the winter ahead, you can count me out," Chelsea said, pouring Tom his morning cup of coffee. Not that you could tell it was morning, what with the darkness and rain outside their kitchen window. "Is this weather ever going to let up? The whole house feels clammy; I can't stand it."

"Could be worse," said Tom, reaching for the mug she was handing to him.

"Yeah...how?"

Before he could answer, his cell rang in his pocket. Tom dug it out and looked to see who was calling.

"It's Ralph," he told Chelsea and responded.

Chelsea sat down across from him on their plain blue sofa. She sipped her coffee, listening to Tom's questions and responses to his caller. The news was crushing: Sylvia and Bob Travis' youngest son Archer had vanished without a trace the night before. Now, having been born and raised in Olive Leaf, Archer (11-years-old) was familiar with the area. Him getting lost was not even a question.

That afternoon, Police from Karney and volunteers searched every house in Olive Leaf. Everyone was most cooperative. Many villagers joined the search in the rain, searching late into the evening. Although everyone gave it their best efforts, not even a shred of evidence was found. The entire village was devastated. They even made a thorough search of the river—nothing, not a shoe, not a piece of clothing, not a strand of hair or tooth—nothing.

Ralph took it upon himself to pay Mr. Teatherby a second visit. His was the only house not checked by the police. Once again the old man was standoffish and sharp. And as the door was being slammed in his face again, Ralph thought it queer how the old man's eyes were no longer yellow, but appeared white and clear. Even his stooped posture seemed a little more upright.

A week later, when most villagers had given up all hope of finding Archer (alive or dead), Mitch and Cecile Croft's 13-year-old daughter, Elizabeth, disappeared. Liza (as her parents called her) had last been seen at the Olive Leaf store, buying milk and licorice. The people were in a panic. One child missing is perhaps an accident; two children missing is a warning.

The search for Liza bore as much fruit as the previous search. With two families' lives ripped apart, the villagers gathered in the main hall to discuss what steps would be taken next. The hall was your basic barn filled with picnic tables, a bar, and a small stage for entertainers. Ralph Shepherd tested his microphone and stepped onto the stage to begin the meeting.

"Evening, folks. I wish we were here under happier circumstances tonight," he said, his voice sullen and low. He looked directly at the parents of the two missing children. "Bob...Sylvia. Mitch...Cecile. We are all deeply, deeply saddened by your loss. Words cannot express the heartbreak felt in this building."

Both couples were embracing in tears.

Ralph wiped his own eyes and cleared his throat before continuing. "This is a great and terrible tragedy within our community. We will not stop searching for Elizabeth and Archer—two wonderful, beautiful children—until they are found. We will continue to send search parties out every day.

Heads were nodding.

"I know many of us enjoy our privacy, but we have a real mystery on our hands here. We need to be vigilant with our neighbors. Please. I implore you: If you see anything suspicious, anything at all, report it. Don't brush it aside and forget about it. Report it! Every precaution we take now could save a life, folks. That is all. Thank you for coming and showing your support. All of you," Ralph finished.

4

Every night a heavy fog gushed forth from the surrounding woods and engulfed the village. Menacing, dark clouds loomed over the rooftops, blocking out the stars and moon. A never-ending rainfall was damaging many basements, and road flooding.

Genette Gideon, last seen by her husband four days ago, had left the house to run an errand—she never returned. Five days earlier, Nathan Conrad told his wife he was going to the town hall for a few beers with the guys, he was never seen again, never even made it to the hall. Sisters Meagan and Maxine Scott (13 and 15-years-old) were expected at their Aunt Chanel's house after dinner on Wednesday—they never showed. That was six days earlier.

The number of villagers disappearing was continuing to grow at a staggering pace. No one knew what was happening or what to do. Some suggested aliens were abducting them; others were claiming Bigfoot sightings. It certainly felt like something supernatural was at play, but what?

The villagers gathered in the town hall for another meeting. Everyone was nervous and afraid to leave their homes. Ralph had never seen Olive Leaf in such a state of panic. He had to shout into the microphone to be heard and silence the crowd. All eyes were upon him, some angry, some horrified, most tearful. He cleared his throat and said: "You folks all know me, some better than others. I'm not a religious man...but I've been praying these past weeks. Praying because I'm at a loss here. All our searches for the missing have turned up empty. The good folks of Karney are as dumbfounded as we. We've gathered you here tonight to ask for your suggestions. Any idea is a good idea. Don't be afraid to offer some assistance. I open the floor to you now."

First, the crowd talked among themselves, till the roof was nearly raised from the sound. Then Ron and Randee Taylor stepped up to the stage. Ron spoke in Ralph's ear. He was handed the mic. Ron and Randee were 17-year-old twin brothers, non-identical. Ron grabbed the crowd's attention immediately, his voice loud and deep.

"Scuse me, folks! Hi. I'm Ron and this is my brother, Randee," he said.

"We know who you are!" a voice shouted from the back of the crowd.

"Yeah. Well, anyway. We thought we might have seen something important," he said, scratching his wet hair. "See, this morning, Randee and I were in the woods, trying to hunt rabbit, when we saw the man who moved into the Teatherby shack."

Ralph shook his head. He spoke into Ron's left ear but his voice was picked up by the mic.

"We know about him. We already had a chat with the old man," he said.

Ron looked at Randee, their faces mirroring confusion.

"Old man?" Ron repeated. "He's not old. He don't

look no older than Mr. Eckerman," he said, pointing at Tom who was standing at the foot of the stage.

Ralph and Tom's eyes met with suspicion.

"Then you didn't see Mr. Teatherby, boys. He's at least in his eighties," Ralph explained.

"Well, he came out of the Teatherby shack, so we just assumed...."

"I heard screams coming from that part of the woods the other night!" shouted Jean Hunter.

A hush fell over the hall as everyone turned to look at her.

Tom stepped up and took the mic from Ron. Looking directly at Jean Hunter, with her long black hair hanging loose and wet over her left shoulder, her lips trembling, he said, "Are you sure, Jean?"

"Well, I wasn't at first. I mean, it sounded like it might be the wind, but the more I thought about it, the more it terrified me. Somehow...I just know it was a scream."

"Why didn't you report it when you heard it?" Tom asked, wondering the same thing on everyone's minds.

"I-I was afraid," she admitted, now sniffling in tears.

Several women around Jean moved in to hug her, whispering words of comfort.

Tom turned to Ralph, lowering the mic in his hand for a private word.

"This is insane. You really think that old geezer is capable of murder?" he asked Ralph.

Ralph was lost in thought for a moment, till Tom brought him back.

"Ralph?"

"Tom, that day I went back out to see Teatherby, there was something off about him."

"Yeah. No shit. There were several things off about that old bastard."

"No, no. I mean...different. Different from when the three of us spoke to him. His eyes for one."

"What about 'em?"

"You recall how yellow and bulging they were?" asked Ralph.

"Yeah, yeah."

"When I went back there, his eyes were perfectly normal—healthy!" Ralph described.

"Well, healthy eyes does not make a murderer, Ralph."

"Didn't you feel it when you were there?"

Tom knew exactly what Ralph was referring to. He *had* felt it—something wicked that made your skin crawl and your heart patter.

"You think it's possible those boys *did* see Teatherby and *maybe* he's changing somehow?" said Ralph.

Tom nodded. "I do," he droned.

"So, what do we do?"

"We call the cops and report what we suspect. They'll come down and arrest the fucker," said Tom.

Ralph looked doubtful, but he took a deep breath and nodded.

Tom raised the mic to his mouth and quieted the crowd once again. "People, people," he called. "Listen up. We think we may know who's behind all these disappearances."

"Who?" people shouted. "It's that creep in the woods, isn't it?" someone added. "Let's get him!" came another.

Before Tom could regain control of the situation, the hall's double doors swung wide open, and the riled up villagers stampeded out. Jacob approached Tom and Ralph (he'd just arrived at the meeting).

"What the hell's going on, fellas?" he wondered.

"Shit. So much for that plan," Tom frowned.

Ralph turned to answer Jacob's question, he said, "The villagers have decided that Teatherby is behind the disappearances."

"Oh shit. That can't be good," Jacob realized.

"We have to stop them before they do something we'll all regret," Tom suggested. "Let's go!"

5

Through the rain, the villagers marched into the foggy woods, some armed with baseball bats and hammers, others carrying primitive torches. Lightning tasered the black clouds. By the time Ralph, Tom, and Jacob caught up to the mob, they were already circling Teatherby's sinister-looking shack. Everyone was shouting curses and throwing rocks. The single window next to the front door was shattered to pieces; the stench of death fled from the place as if it had waited centuries to escape.

The three men weren't having any success in calming the crowd. Between the intensifying shouts of the mob and the crackling thunder, it seemed the world was falling apart.

Meanwhile, Abe Walters screamed his way past Ralph, baseball bat in hand, and stomped his way up to Teatherby's front door. Hate burned within Abe's eyes as he demanded Teatherby confess his guilt, his teeth gritting. Just as Abe was about to take a swing at the door, the shack appeared to contract, then expand, releasing a great force that rippled over the villagers. Abe was thrown back about twenty-five feet. Many others were knocked down as well.

Expressions of astonishment swept over the villagers as they shook the burning sting from their bodies. Ralph, Tom, and Jacob rushed to each other at once.

"What the fuck was *that*?" Jacob sputtered.

"I don't know, but we need to get these people out of here!" yelled Tom.

Just then, Teatherby appeared on his front porch. All who were a witness that night would have sworn his appearance coincided with a rumble underground.

"Christ almighty! What in the hell are we dealing with?" Tom said perplexed, gazing in disbelief at the younger Mr. Teatherby.

"It's not possible," Ralph said goggle-eyed.

"The fuck it's not, we're looking at it!" said Jacob, instinctively taking a step back.

No one else (besides the three men) was aware of the physical changes that Teatherby had manifested. Therefore, no one else was as terrified.

"Murderer!" someone shouted.

"You killed my baby!" Sylvia Travis wailed.

Teatherby gripped the crooked wooden railing before him, he shouted to the mob, "I have only done what my nature asks of me!"

"You're a goddamn killer!" someone yelled.

Several rocks torpedoed the shack.

"NO! Stop! Stop it! Get out of here—now!" Tom shouted to deaf ears.

As Ralph and Jacob each grabbed Tom by an arm and began to pull him away from the out-of-control mob, Abe Walters once again approached the front porch, bat in hand. Teatherby was grinning at him, eyes inky black.

"What the hell are you?" challenged Abe, preparing to attack.

"Hungry," seethed Teatherby. The man turned and stepped back inside the shack, the door closing on its own behind him.

Thunder erupted with a vengeance, and the fury of the storm was unleashed above the trees, clawing its way down. The villagers went mad, attacking the shack with their bats and rakes and axes. Every strike against the old wood caused a small tremor.

As Ralph, Tom, and Jacob fled the woods, racing back to the village to collect their wives (hoping their spouses would refrain from asking too many questions, or refuse to abandon their homes), they heard the horrifying screams of the people they'd known for years. As they split up, each running to their own house, Tom yelled, "Fifteen minutes and we're on the road!"

Ralph and Jacob agreed.

Abe swung his ax at the front door. The moment steel connected with wood, he and the rest of the villagers were yanked off their feet and thrown up into the air like confetti—except, they didn't come back down. The wind flung them about, while the rain seared their skin.

At that moment, Ralph, holding Rose's hand in a tight grip, was running in the rain toward Tom's motor home. Chelsea opened the side door for them. Rose was out of breath. She sat down next to Chelsea, who quickly handed her a towel to dry off.

"Are we really doing this?" Rose panted. "Leaving our homes?"

"What choice do we have?" Chelsea replied.

"Fuck! What's taking Jacob so long?" said Tom, rocking in his seat.

Moments after, Jacob came pounding on the door. Tom got up to let him in, but Jacob was alone.

"I can't find her!" Jacob burst. "I searched the whole house but she's not there! I gotta find her. I can't leave without her," he rambled.

"What if she's out *there?*" said Chelsea.

Jacob looked at Tom and Ralph, and said, "Please, wait for me. I have to go get her."

"I'll go with you," Tom volunteered.

"Tom, no!" Chelsea pleaded.

Tom loosened her grip on his jacket and smiled at her, he said, "Don't worry, I'm coming back."

He and Jacob stepped outside, instantly feeling the chill penetrate to their bones. They ran at top speed into the woods, through a wall of fog so thick it held its form even though the heavy rain. The moment they passed beyond the fog the full intensity of the villagers' screams blasted the two men. They halted, their mind's rejecting the reality of the sight before them.

"Noooo! Nanceeee!" Jacob called at the peak of his voice, his hands reaching up toward his hovering wife.

Tom wrapped his arms around his buddy and wrestled him away, just as the trees encircling them snapped to life. Umpteen branches lashed out like whips, piercing the bodies of the powerless, floating villagers. The muddy earth around the shack was frothing with pools and streams of blood. Chunks of flesh were dropping like

— 25 —

wet cakes. Tom couldn't pull Jacob away fast enough, and he witnessed a branch spear right through his wife's doughy cheeks (in one side and out the other).

"Jacob, come on! Come On!"

Traumatized, Jacob was weakened, his legs like noodles, his stomach flip-flopping. He finally gave in to Tom's influence and started to run away. The ground shuddered, uprooting trees that crashed about them. Running blind through the wall of fog, the fading cries raking down their spines, Tom and Jacob cleared the woods. They ran headlong toward the RV, which Ralph was now driving in their direction.

The two men leapt into the camper, out of breath and soaked. Jacob took a seat on the sofa and began to sob. Chelsea and Rose looked at one another, their eyes filling with tears. Tom collapsed in the passenger seat as Ralph sped up the road, leaving Olive Leaf behind them. He glanced at Tom questioningly. Tom shook his head.

Mr. Never

1

Cliff Roberts arrived at 328 Candlewick Drive at 2 pm. His girlfriend, Keira Gracy, had arranged a 2:30 pm meet time with him and the students who were interested in renting out rooms in the five-bedroom house. Cliff was a real estate broker and the owner of several properties. The house on Candlewick was a hard sell because of its size and location. But it was the perfect rental property for students attending Merritt College.

Being a rather busy man, showing the house to all five students at once saved him from making five separate trips to Chatter Falls, from Burlington. He pulled into the long stone driveway, followed its slight curve past the large Maple tree in the front yard, and parked.

He grabbed his folder with the rental forms for the students to sign, and stepped out. Even though it was mid-August, there were already plenty of fallen leaves about the property. The bushes were unkempt, and the mailbox was overstuffed with flyers, some lying wet on the porch from last night's rain. Cliff picked them up, emptied the box, and entered the house.

Kiera had already come the day before to make sure the house was in order. She left the place smelling like cinnamon. He smiled at the thought of her. A door on the opposite side of the large kitchen gave to the garage. He crammed the soggy flyers into a recycle bin and closed the door behind him. Passing through the furnished living room, which had a beautiful fireplace on its centre wall, Cliff entered the dining room (comparable in immensity to the aforementioned) and spread the leases on the grand dining table. Before he could pull out a chair and sit, the doorbell rang. *Perfect. No waiting.*

Cliff opened the door and smiled. There were three females and one male; the last, another male, had not yet arrived.

"Hello! Come on in. Please," he said cordially.

"Thank you," they chorused.

He watched them all brush their shoes on the welcome mat, then head up the set of three stairs which led into the impressive foyer.

"Any trouble finding the place?" he asked.

They all four shook their heads and said no.

"Wow. This is incredible," said Hedy Brook. Her mother was Japanese, and her father French Canadian. She had beautiful features. Choppy bangs drew attention to her professionally applied makeup, having already been certified in the field. "Tastefully decorated," she added.

"I've never seen a house this big before," admitted Niven, his unruly curls reaching out at the top of his head. He was model material, as they say. His eyelashes made every woman jealous, thick and long. Those golden-brown eyes and pouting lips, and that slightly darker skin tone because of his Indian heritage. His sultry voice triggered goose-pimples on Ruby's body. She'd never lived on her own before (none of them had) and was so nervous she could feel her stomach muscles tensing up as if she was holding her breath.

When Niven smiled at her, she quickly looked the other way. Ruby Hunnicutt was still a virgin and intended to remain that way; for how long was a question she did not have an answer to.

"Please. You can have a seat in the living room. As soon as the last renter arrives, I'll give you the—"

(The doorbell!)

"Excuse me. That must be him now," Cliff said, heading to the front door.

"Hi. I'm Redford, Redford Gilbert. Hoping this is the right house," said the bashful young man.

Cliff smiled and opened the door wider. He said, "Sure is, fella. Come on in. You're the last to show."

"Oh. I'm sorry," Redford apologized.

"What for? You're right on time. We're just about to begin the tour."

"Great," said Redford, ascending the three steps into the foyer. "Hello," he offered to the others.

Everyone said hi in return. Hedy turned to Lily, who was closest to her, and whispered, "Wow. *Two* cute guys."

Lily just smiled. She didn't care how cute the guys were, as long as they weren't assholes or perverts or rapists or druggies or all of the above. She was here to make her way through college and move on. She had no intention of getting sidetracked by anything—especially guys! This was a new experience for her. She'd always been a very decisive girl; once her mind was made up to do something, that was it, she was doing it.

Her decision to move to Chatter Falls was one her parents weren't fond of. Without them being around to protect her, they agreed to let her go only because they could not stop her. Though to them she was a tiny girl, she was no different than the other girls her age. Truth be told, Lily thought this Redford guy was a hunk. Thick blonde hair combed back and to the left, the sides of his head shaved. His pale blue eyes blinked a little more than necessary, a shyness quirk. His Clark Kent glasses were sexy, his very pink lips and pale skin. Hedy, she had to admit, was spot on with her assessment.

2

Following the tour of the house (the very impressive house, which boasts five bedrooms, each equipped with its three-piece bathroom), Cliff ran through the 'house rules.' Once his new tenants signed their leases, he thanked them and rushed for the door.

"I hope you all enjoy the house and do well in your studies. You have my number if there are any issues, just try not to call after hours. Good night, and good luck," he said, closing the door after himself.

The five new roommates sat around the dining table, staring and smiling at one another. Lily was the first to speak up.

"Well, I guess maybe we should all get unpacked and settle in. Anyone for ordering pizza and wings for dinner?" she said, smiling.

"Sounds like a plan," said Niven, rising from his seat.

"Hey, how 'bout someone run to the liquor store in town and we can celebrate our new living arrangement," Hedy suggested.

Heads nodded all around.

"Yeah. Sure. I can go when I pick up the pizza, then we don't have to pay for a delivery," Redford volunteered.

"I'll go with you, bud," Niven offered.

"Okay. Cool. It's a plan."

The three girls made their way back up to the third

floor, where their three rooms were located. The boys' rooms were on the second floor. The entire house was fully furnished, and by someone who had good taste. Redford and Niven began to unpack their belongings. The guys didn't bring nearly as much with them as the girls did.

Redford flopped back on the double bed in his blue room. His was the first door at the top of the landing. Niven's door was to the right, his room decorated in multiple shades of brown. He quickly stuffed his clothes into the empty dresser drawers and leapt onto the bed, staring up at the stucco ceiling, and wondering which of the three pretty girls was in the room directly above him. Not that it made any difference, but he hoped it was Ruby. Ruby with her long curly hair and honey-brown eyes (just like her last name Hunnicutt).

On the third floor, Ruby did take the room above Niven as her own. Hedy claimed the middle room, and Lily was more than pleased with the third room; it was her favorite color: violet. All the bedroom doors had locks on them, with each its matching set of keys. Lily put one key in her purse and the other she hid above the closet door, on the edge of the framing.

By the time Redford and Niven were on their way home, walking back from Carla's Pizzeria, it began to rain. Niven was carrying the bottles of Vodka and Rum in a bag in one arm, and several Cokes and Ginger ale bottles in the other. Redford had the pizza box and wings to worry about keeping dry.

"I hope they don't think we're gonna be the delivery

boys all the time," Redford said, blinking the raindrops from his eyes.

"Yeah! They get the next round," Niven added as they turned up the dark driveway to 328. The boys stopped for a moment and gazed up at the menacing-looking house.

"Didn't realize how creepy this place was before," Redford admitted.

"Me neither. We sure we want to go back in there?" Niven said, then chuckled.

"We have to. We already paid," Redford said, laughing. "Come on. Let's get the fuck outta this rain."

When the two boys entered the kitchen, the three girls were gathering plates and glasses. They were surprised to see the guys dripping wet.

"It's raining?" asked Hedy.

"Ya think?" Niven said tartly.

"Wow. This house is so tight we couldn't even tell," said Ruby.

"Thanks for picking all this up, guys. If I'd known it was raining, I would've had everything delivered," Lily apologized.

"Don't worry about it. We survived," said Redford, slipping out of his soaked jacket.

"*This* time," Niven stressed with a smile. He shook his wet curls, spraying the floor.

They settled down at the dining room table, a happy new family. The pizza and wings soon disappeared, and the bottles of alcohol opened. They learned where each of them had come from, what they would be studying, what their goals were, what their lives had been like before, and anything else they might enjoy sharing. By the time midnight rolled around, they were comfortable with each other, and drunk.

Redford was not a drinker. He'd shared a couple of beers with his dad on the odd occasion, but that was the sum of it. Tonight he drank enough Rum and Coke to make him feel dizzy. He stood up as the others rambled on about college sports or something; he wasn't paying attention.

"Hey, where are you going?" asked Hedy.

"I'm done. Finished. Going to bed, people. Yep. I'm already sleeping," Redford sang as he staggered toward the staircase.

The others laughed about him.

"Don't fall down the stairs!" Niven shouted.

"You wish!" came the reply.

Earlier that evening, Ruby had mentioned how she'd been super close to her grandmother on her father's side, and that Nana Hunnicutt (or Hunny as Ruby had called her), had passed away in her sleep two years back. Ruby insisted she still feels Nana Hunny's presence sometimes. Hedy had been involved in a few seances with friends back home. It hadn't occurred to her when Ruby had shared her story with them, but now, with more than enough Vodka and Ginger with lemon in her system, the idea sprang to her thoughts.

"Say. You know what we should do?" she bubbled.

The other three were staring at her, waiting for her to tell them. She brushed her hair over her shoulder and continued, "We should have a seance and call Ruby's nana!"

"What? No," said Ruby. "I don't wanna wake my Nana from the dead or something."

They were all giggling at this.

"Yeah, Hedy. There are only five bedrooms here and they're all taken. Where would Nana Hunnybuns sleep?" Lily joked.

Ruby lightly slapped Lily's hand and said, "Stop that, Lily." But she was laughing, too.

"I'm fucking serious, guys. I've done it before. All we need is a candle," Hedy explained.

"I don't know. Could be fun," said Niven, stirring the ice in his glass with his finger, half dazed.

"What do you know about fun?" said Lily.

Niven looked at the girls and smiled. "I know plenty," he said.

"Come on, guys, it'll be fun. Our first seance together," Hedy insisted.

"Like there'll be others," said Lily.

"Yeah. This isn't the seance club, Hedy. So calm your shit," said Ruby, lightheartedly.

"Well? What do you say? Should we see if Nana Hunnybuns will talk to us?" encouraged Hedy.

"It's Hunny, not Hunny*buns*," Ruby clarified.

Lily pushed her chair back and stood. "Fine. Let's do this," she said.

"Yaaaay," Hedy cheered, clapping her hands.

"But we don't even have a candle," said Niven.

"On my way to get one from my room," said Lily.

After clearing the table off, Hedy set the tall purple candle in the centre. They dimmed the lights down real low. Now in the darkness, they could see the lightning flashes beyond the closed drapes in the large window. Hedy instructed them to hold hands and focus on the dancing flame.

"We are gathered here as friends to call on Hedy's Nana Hunnicutt," Hedy began, her voice low and serious.

The other three burst into laughter.

"Come on, guys, stay focused or it won't work," Hedy pleaded.

"This girl takes her shit seriously," said Niven.

"Shhh" Hedy silenced. "Now. Concentrate on the flame. Let its light penetrate your thoughts. Let its heat burn into your soul."

Moments of silence.

"Nana Hunnicutt, can you hear me? If you can hear me, we are here with your granddaughter Ruby. She misses you and wants you to give her a sign that you are okay. Nana Hunnicutt, give us a sign that you are here."

The very faint sound of rain drummed at the window behind Hedy. There were no other sounds throughout the house, only silence.

Niven yawned out loud triggering giggles from Ruby and Lily, much to the frustration of Hedy.

"Quiet, Niven. List-en," whispered Hedy.

The table seemed to vibrate. Hedy gave Niven a steely

glance.

"What? It's not me. I swear," he said.

"Nana Hunnicutt, is that you?" Hedy murmured.

Suddenly, much to their amazement, the flame of the candle left its perch atop the wax stick and floated upward. Ruby gasped. They all pushed themselves away from the table and stood, watching the impossible happen.

"How are you doing that, Hedy?" asked Lily, petrified.

"Me? I'm not doing anything," Hedy admitted.

"What the fuck, man?" said Niven, now leaning back against the wall.

"This isn't funny, Hedy. Stop it now," Ruby insisted.

"I told you, it's not me!" Hedy shouted.

At once the flame shot up through the crystal chandelier, rocking it so hard it seemed it should fall. Then it disappeared into the ceiling with a sizzle. The girls were all screaming. Following a few moments of panic, a tremor reverberated through the floors, up the walls (paintings shaking from their hooks, light fixtures flashing on and off), and spread overhead for what seemed like forever. Then all at once a thick silence fell over them.

Niven smacked the light switch on the wall next to him, bringing immediate brightness to the room, and giving the girls an extra start.

"What the fuck was that?" Lily yelled.

"Oh my god. That was so cool. That's never happened before," Hedy said breathlessly.

"What the hell, Hedy? Are you insane?" Ruby fretted, running her trembling hands through her hair, over and over.

Hedy's mouth was agape, eyes wide with innocence.

"I don't know about you guys, but I never want to do that again. That was some scary-ass bullshit right there," said Niven, genuine fear in his voice.

"Fuck. I've never been so scared in my life," Lily said, still watching the chandelier sway in circles.

"I can't believe it worked," Hedy gloated.

"It didn't," Ruby corrected. "I don't know what *that* was, but it wasn't my Nana. Couldn't you feel it? It was something...*dark*."

"It's true. It made my skin crawl," Lily gulped.

"Mine too," added Niven.

"Well, whatever it was, it's gone now," Hedy assumed.

They all exchanged looks of uncertainty, then called it a night and retired to their rooms.

3

Saturday morning, Redford was up first. He started the coffeemaker and turned on the kitchen radio. He sat on one of the four bar stools set up along the large island, placing his steaming mug of hot cocoa on the marble surface, and began to eat his buttered toast.

"Hey," he greeted Lily when she entered the kitchen.

"Hey," she said, yawning.

As she poured a cup of the freshly brewed dark stuff, Hedy, Ruby, and Niven crept in, all three looking as sleep-deprived as Lily. Observing the signs of a hangover, Redford chuckled and said, "Geez. You guys all look like shit. What time did you finally call it quits last night?"

Their strange exchange of looks told him something was up.

"Did I miss something?" he asked.

"Something," Niven said mysteriously.

"I hope you guys didn't already break shit. We just moved in. Roberts will be so—"

"We didn't break anything, *Dad*," Hedy snapped.

"No. Worse," said Ruby.

Now Redford's interest was peaked. "Like?" he said, coaxing them on.

Lily sighed. She put her coffee cup down and sat on the stool next to Redford. "Well..." she began, looking directly at Hedy with blame. "...Hedy had this brilliant idea to have a seance and invite Ruby's Nana Hunni-buns—"

"Hunni*cutt*," Ruby corrected.

"Shit, Ruby, no one cares. Long story short, some*thing* answered the call, and we don't think it was Nana," Lily explained.

"Are you serious? You're joking, right?" said Redford, checking their facial reactions. "You *are* serious."

"Oh, she's serious, all right. Whatever it was made the candle flame rise into the ceiling and the whole house shook. Didn't you feel it?" asked Niven, crunching on toast.

"Once I'm asleep, there's no waking me," said Redford.

"No big deal. Geez. Mr. Never's gone," said Hedy.

They all looked at her in shock, Redford because she put a name to their so-called ghost; the others because they somehow *knew* that name.

"Why did you call it Mr. Never?" said Ruby.

Hedy thought about it for a moment, then shrugged her shoulders and said, "I don't know. It just came to me."

"That's creepy as fuck!" said Niven. "I know that name. I think I heard it in my dreams this morning."

"Guys...I think I heard it in my sleep, too," Lily practically whispered.

Redford shook his head as he rose and began to rinse his now empty mug. "Nice try, guys. You almost had me there," he said.

"We're not...it's not a joke, Redford. We're telling the truth," Lily proffered.

"Man, this is some Sam and Dean shit," said Niven.

As Redford left the kitchen, Lily, Hedy, Ruby, and Niven stared in silence at one another, then Ruby said, "So, who the hell is Mr. Never?"

The following Friday night, Lily was in her room lying on her bed with her laptop open, an English essay on the screen. Hedy was in her room, lying back on her bed, chatting with a friend on her cell phone. In her room, Ruby was sitting in front of her vanity, trying different looks with her hair. Redford was in the rec room, studying for Monday's Chemistry exam, the first of many to come. And in the kitchen, Niven was snacking on a bag of chips, his bare feet up on the stool next to him.

And that is when the house shook.

Everyone met in the living room, baffled looks on their faces.

"Holy shit! What the fuck was that?" shivered Redford.

"That's what we felt last weekend, after the seance," said Ruby.

"Could it be an earthquake?" asked Hedy.

"It felt like it came from the basement," said Niven.

The others all looked at him, looked at each other, then agreed to go down together and check it out, with stress on the 'together' part. The relief was felt all around when Niven flicked a light switch at the top of the basement stairs with a resulting bright light. With Niven in the lead, the three girls next, Redford closed up the line.

There didn't seem to be anything unusual about the basement. It was tidy and spacious. No mysterious packages, no rusted freezer, no cobwebs or creepy tools hanging on walls, just your average basement. Just then the house began to moan and tremble, louder and louder, trembling and growling. The only ceiling light, which had been their saving grace, popped! The girls screamed in the dark. Niven and Redford squeezed up close to them.

"Quiet!" yelled Redford.

"Get me the fuck out of here!" cried Ruby.

"Which way to the stairs?" asked Lily, trying her best to see beyond the blackness.

The house continued to rumble as they moved across the floor in a tight huddle.

"Whose idea was it to come down here?" Hedy whined.

"I think we're almost there," said Redford.

"Yeah, sure. How can you tell?" asked Ruby. "I can't see shit!"

"No. He's right," said Lily. "Look up. I think I can see light from upstairs."

They increased their baby steps as one unit. Behind them, unseen in the shadows, was the silhouette of something tall. Long arms were reaching out toward them, tipped with claws like a gardening sickle. Reaching closer and closer, mere inches from the backs of Lily and Niven's heads. Redford led the charge up the stairs, burst through the door and slammed it shut behind them, locking it. At that very instant, the house stopped quaking.

"Fuck me, I'm never going back down there again!" said Ruby.

They all agreed, then laughed about themselves.

4

Throughout the weekend, eerie things occurred in the house. Items disappeared, like hairbrushes and books. And some things vanished right before their eyes, such as Lily's glass of water. She set it down on the table, and not a moment later it was gone, with no one else around to take it. Doors would lock themselves, then open the next moment. And worst of all, they were all experiencing a sense like someone or something was behind them, closing in.

That Sunday, the girls went knocking door to door in their neighborhood, asking people if they had been feeling the quakes, but not one person knew what they were talking about.

"So, you're telling me we're in a house that has its own personal earthquakes?" said Redford.

"Got a better explanation?" asked Hedy.

"Yeah. Maybe we're all just fucking nuts," he said.

"And what about everything else that's been happening here, are we just gonna pretend it's not?" said Lily, sitting on the living room sofa, where they'd gathered to have this discussion.

"Maybe we should call Mr. Roberts and tell him what's going on," Ruby suggested, twirling her curls around her fingers.

"Sure, Ruby. Let's call the landlord and tell him that you guys had a seance that brought a fucking ghost in the house and now it's fucking with us? And you expect him to do what...call Bill Murray?" Ranted Redford.

Niven snickered at this.

"I think she's right," said Lily. "We have to tell someone. This is his house. He has the right to know."

"Yeah. And we'll be lucky if he doesn't laugh his ass off and kick us out," added Redford, shaking his head.

"Well, do we all agree we should call him? Those in favor raise your hand," said Lily, raising her hand.

All but Redford raised their hands.

"Fine," he said. "But just remember, I had nothing to do with your fucking seance." He stormed off to his bedroom and slammed the door shut.

"I'll make the call tomorrow," said Hedy. "Since this is my fault."

"We were all in on it, Hedy. We're all to blame," Ruby comforted.

By 7:30 pm Monday night, Keira Gracy arrived at 328 Candlewick Drive on her Harley Davidson. As she was dismounting her bike, the five students were watching her through the kitchen window.

"Oh...my...god," said Niven. "She is so fucking hot!"

"Calm yourself, big boy, she's already taken," Redford reminded him.

"And I doubt she's interested in little boys," said Ruby.

"Get the door for her," said Lily.

"I'll get it!" Niven jumped into action.

"Hello," said Keira, still pulling her long dark hair out of her leather collar. "I'm Keira. Cliff sent me to see what we could do to help you guys out."

"Yeah. No, come on in. We were waiting for you," said Niven, all smiles.

"Thanks," said Keira smiling to herself about his obvious infatuation with her. He wasn't the first student renter to give her the 'looks'.

After introductions were made, the girls explained the situation to Keira. They didn't leave out any details. Half expecting Keira to laugh in their faces, or blast them for their stupidity, they were surprised when she took their story as genuine. Keira, a follower of Wicca, was no stranger to the supernatural.

"The souls of the dead do not linger. They move on. If you're foolish enough..." she said, pausing to make sure they understood they were indeed 'foolish', "...to call upon a soul's return, only what we call 'ugly spirits' return—demons," she said.

"Great going, guys," Redford put in.

"Can you not," Lily said, annoyed.

Keira then offered to stay and perform a cleansing ritual over the house. This was, of course, more than what was hoped for.

Redford refused to take part. He said, "I didn't bring that thing here so I'm not sending it away."

"I agree," said Keira. "You should keep your distance. You can watch if you like. There's no harm in that."

"Maybe I will," he said.

The others gathered round the dining room table.

Keira set a large white candle on a plate in the centre. She lit the wick and sat down.

"Everyone hold hands, please. These things can be tricky, so I would ask that you not break the circle until I say so, no matter what."

She looked to each one of them as they nodded, making certain she was understood. Taking a deep breath, she closed her eyes (Niven staring directly at her chest).

"I am now speaking to the entity in this house which has made itself known as Mr. Never."

Redford was shaking his head, watching from the living room. He crossed his arms, leaning back against the sofa as Keira continued.

"Mr. Never, if you are here give us a sign."

There was a long pause of silence.

"I am speaking to Mr. Never. If you can hear me, give us a sign," Keira repeated.

The crystal chandelier began to sway and tinkle; they all looked up in awe.

"Mr. Never, you are not welcome here. Hear our request and leave this house at once," said Keira, her voice soothing and haunting.

Redford had taken a few steps closer when the chandelier began to move, watching with keen interest. Suddenly, the house began to vibrate. Keira could feel the reverberations rise through her chair. Swaying lights, shaking floors: What the hell had these kids invited into their house? she wondered. And now, now she was frightened.

"We command that you leave this house at once!"

she said, her voice raised. "Leave...this...house!"

A great rumble seemed to roll from the front of the house to the back, and out. Hedy and Ruby gasped out loud. Lily could see the fear on Keira's face, which did not make her feel at all confident this would work. The house settled back to quiet. They remained seated and holding hands for a few moments.

"I think it's gone," Keira whispered.

"What did you say?" Redford shouted, now on his knees on the sofa, where he had leapt when the shaking started.

"I said it's over!" said Keira.

Keira warned them there may still be aftershocks for a day or two, saying, "Sometimes residue from these things takes longer to dissipate."

As they watched her ride away, they all breathed a sigh of relief.

5

For three weeks things were back to normal at the house (well, almost). No one wanted to say it out loud and make it real, but they all felt the heavy gloom that had befallen them. Physically, they were drained. It was almost as if the gravity in the house had increased, and was pulling them down. Grades were slipping. The fridge and cupboards remained full because no one had an appetite, no one but Redford, that was.

He seemed unaffected by the changes that may or may not have been all in their heads. While he went out with friends, Niven, Lily, Hedy, and Ruby remained in the house, unable to cajole themselves into any activities. As the four of them slouched in their chairs in the living room, Lily said, "I thought I could forget this whole seance business, but I can't get that name to stop echoing in my thoughts at night. Mr. Never, Mr. Never...."

"Same here," said Ruby, pouting.

"You too?" Niven asked Hedy, who nodded.

"Keira said there was sometimes a residue left behind. Maybe that's what this is," Ruby said, twirling her hair.

But Lily was shaking her head. "I don't think so. It's been three weeks and I just keep feeling more and more like shit. I can't concentrate at school. Hell, I can't concentrate when I'm alone in my room," she said.

"So, what are you saying, that you think it's still here,

that we didn't get rid of it?" Niven said.

"Look, I don't know. You really think it's a coincidence that the four of us all feel like shit and keep hearing that thing's name in our heads, while Redford goes unaffected?" said Lily, angered.

"No," he answered simply.

"Guys, I'm scared. Really scared. What are we supposed to do?" Ruby said softly.

"What *can* we do?" asked Hedy.

The question was left hanging.

That night just after midnight, Redford was the last to go up to his room. He left the kitchen stovelight on, as they always did, shut the living room light, and headed up to his room. He had a lot of studying to do before an exam tomorrow afternoon. He thought spending some time with his buddies TJ and Hunter would help clear his mind, but all it did was make him more anxious to get his nose in his books.

Just as he was about to close his door, he thought he felt a slight vibration under his feet, but, no, he must have imagined it. Study. Gotta study, he thought. He closed his door and locked it.

One floor above, behind the first bedroom door, Ruby had just finished brushing her hair. She was wearing her favorite pink nightgown, with a picture of a unicorn on it. She leaned forward, closed her eyes, and inhaled the scent of the yellow rose Niven had given to her. They had been secretly seeing each other for about a week now. She kissed the tips of her right index and middle fingers and touched them to the rose.

"Sweet dreams, my handsome prince," she said.

She then traded the vanity stool for her bed, grabbed the paperback she was currently struggling to read (some romance novel her friend Bridgette had suggested), and leaned back into the pillows. Reading usually helped her to fall asleep, but tonight she just couldn't concentrate. She found herself reading the same lines over and over again.

She dropped the book into the wastebasket next to the dresser and went into the pink washroom. She was so happy Hedy and Lily had allowed her to claim the pink bedroom (pink like her room at home). She tied her hair back with a scrunchy and brushed her teeth. The light above the mirror flickered just as she was finishing up. She waited a moment, but it didn't happen again. Once she returned to her bed, she looked around the room. So quiet.

"Maybe I'll sleep better with the radio on," she said to no one.

She turned the clock radio on, searched for a station that was playing symphonic music, and settled back into her bed. *Yes,* she thought. *Much better.* Ruby clicked her bedside lamp off and sank into her freshly fluffed pillows. She was just beginning to dose, when the male deejay's voice on the radio said: "And there you have the Boston Symphony Orchestra, Sir Colin Davis, Symphony No. 3 in C major..." And then the Deejay's voice became a woman's voice, and it said, "Hello, Ruby, my love. Ruby? Wakey-wakey, my dear."

Ruby blinked and sat upright with a start. Could it be? She wondered. She could have sworn she'd heard Nana Hunnicutt's voice. *Must have been dreaming*, she thought.

"No, dear, you're not dreaming," came the voice again.

Ruby popped up in her bed like a jack-in-the-box, turning toward her little clock radio. "N-Na-Na?"

"Yes, of course, dear. Were you expecting someone else?" asked the radio.

Ruby shook her head. "I-I wasn't expecting...."

"It's perfectly alright, dear. I know my being here comes as a bit of a shock, what with my being dead and all. But I came when I heard you calling. Now tell me, my darling Ruby, what is it you wanted?"

Ruby, so enthralled by the voice coming from her clock radio, didn't notice the creaking of the closet door behind her, or the hunched thing that came out of it.

"I-I don't know why we called you, Nana. I guess it was a mistake. I miss you," said Ruby. "Nana, is it *really* you?"

There was a moment of silence, mere crackles of static coming through the little speaker.

"Nana?" called Ruby. "Are you there?"

And suddenly, Nana Hunnicutt's voice came through loud and clear, but with an evil texture behind it that made the hairs on the back of Ruby's neck stand erect.

"Right beside you, *dear*."

Long fingers folded around Ruby's right shoulder. She whipped round and screamed so loud her voice pierced her ears. (No sounds were heard beyond her door.)

A creature with the subtle features of her Nana's face was staring down at her. It's mouth spread to a smile as big as a slice of watermelon, with black and green needle teeth. Its eyes were large black holes, its nose like Nana's, only longer and pointier. Something like white worms protruded from its elongated head. Before her mind could process what she was seeing, the demon pounced on her, its jaws snapping over her neck and shoulder.

Ruby's eyes bulged as the pain raked through her entire body. The demon yanked back, tearing Ruby's flesh and bone away. Blood vomited on her pink sheets, white vanity, and white carpet. Her piercing screams reached the ears of the dead. Screaming and thrashing about, till red flooded her throat and drowned her. Ruby was then hauled off the bed. She landed on the floor in a dead heap. The demon dragged her across the room, her blood trail a hot thick puddle.

It disappeared into the depths of the closet, taking Ruby's corpse with it. On the vanity, Niven's yellow rose dripped red.

6

Hedy's bedroom door was closed, but her room was empty. One door over, she and Lily were sitting on Lily's bed, taking selfies together and laughing at themselves. They were also in their nightgowns, ready for bed, but unable to sleep, as usual.

"I snapped this when he wasn't looking," said Hedy, showing Lily the picture on her cell phone of Redford sitting on a kitchen stool in his boxers.

"Oh my god, you have to send that to me," said Lily. "He's so fucking hot."

"I know, right."

"I love his feet. They're so small and sexy for a guy."

Hedy laughed and said, "I just wanna run my hands up his hairy legs and kiss those gorgeous lips."

The two girls stopped giggling when vibrations rolled up the bed and rattled the trinkets on Lily's vanity. They looked at one another with worry.

"Resi...due?" said Hedy.

They burst out in laughter.

At once the lights went out, and a red glow flooded the room, bringing a most foul stench of blood with it. On the bed, Lily and Hedy were on their knees, holding each other in a tight embrace. A deafening sound like a factory hammer pounded at different locations around the room, from wall to wall, ceiling to floor—pounding! The girls screamed at every strike. In Lily's room, the closet door was on the right side of her bed. When it flung open, a powerful blast of burning wind rushed in. Hedy and Lily saw the thing they knew at once was Mr. Never—screams tore at their throats! (No sounds beyond the bedroom door.)

The girls squeezed each other tight in a hysterical fit, their minds assailed by the unfathomable. The demon waved his right clawed hand, and in that instant, the girls were stripped of their flesh from the neck, down. Bloodied patches of skin slapped against the walls like discarded waste. At once, Lily and Hedy turned on one another like a pair of fighting dogs, biting into each other's necks with vulgar savagery, delighting the demon with the show.

When the blob of what was once two young women collapsed with a solid thud on the floor, Mr. Never reached down, dug his claws into the meat carcass, and dragged it into the closet. The door closed behind him. The melodic ringtone of Hedy's cell phone was drowned out in the bloody mess of Lily's bed.

Niven cancelled his call to Hedy. He knew she was in Lily's room and was wondering if Ruby was with them since she hadn't responded to his call to her. He put his phone down on the nightstand and opened the top drawer of his dresser. He dug under his socks and came up with a small baggy with a rolled joint in it. Smoking was one of the 'house rules' he didn't think anyone would notice him breaking. He lit the reefer and smoked it while lying back on his bed, hoping this little secret would help him fall asleep.

Something struck beneath the bed; Niven leapt to his feet with a yelp. He leaned back against the dresser, staring at the rumpled Wolverine comforter.

"RA!" yelled Redford, popping up from the opposite side of the bed.

After catching his breath, Niven said, "You fucking asshole! You scared the shit out of me!"

"Then my job here is done," said Redford, climbing to his feet, still laughing and pointing at Niven, whose face was paler than Redford thought possible.

"How the fuck did you get in here?" asked Niven.

"I came in when you went to get a drink. Then I waited for just the right moment to strike," Redford explained, rubbing his palms together like an evil criminal.

"Such an asshole," Niven chuckled. "Paybacks are a bitch, you know," he said, closing his door behind Redford.

"As a hot chick with huge cans once said, 'pleasant dreams,'" said Redford, still chuckling.

Niven locked his door this time and flopped on his bed once again. "Such an asshole," he whispered.

From the opposite wall to Redford's bedroom, he heard a set of knocks and shook his head. "Wasn't even funny!" he yelled.

About ten minutes later, as Niven's eyes were beginning to enjoy being shut, he heard another set of knocks. Without realizing the knocks had not come from the wall adjoining his room to Redford's, he smiled and yelled, "Wasn't that funny!" Refusing to unseal his eyes, he added, under his breath, "Such an asshole."

The third set of knocks—louder. This time Niven opened his eyes wide. Those knocks had not come from Redford's wall; they came from...his closet? Niven sat up, peering at the closet door. His heart leapt into his throat, and he whispered, "Mr. Never."

He hadn't turned his light off before lying down and the room was well lit. Then all at once, the bulb exploded and the closet door whipped open and slammed against the outer wall, the doorknob punching a hole in the plaster. From deep within the inky darkness, Niven could hear what sounded like a waterfall. The flow seemed to be drawing nearer to the doorway, somehow moving.

Niven then saw the curtain of flowing blood reach the very threshold of his closet door. Flashes sketched within the red. Slowly something was poking its way through the bloody shower, something long like a giant spidery leg. Then a second and third leg appeared, creeping forward, their source still unrevealed. Niven leapt from his bed and bolted for the door. He tried to unlock it but it would not open. Screaming and hammering his fists as hard as he could, he called out for help.

"Redford! Ruby! Anyone! Somebody help me! Redford! Fuck! Why don't they hear me?"

He turned and leaned back against the door, panting. The entire room was vibrating, making his teeth chatter. The sound of the blood falls was as loud as if he was standing within them. And then he saw them—those spidery appendages—inching their way closer and closer. There was a clip-clopping sound like horse's hooves on pavement, bouncing around the walls. Then Mr. Never stepped into Niven's full view—Niven screamed!

Two prongs speared into his body, one in the chest (a kiss away from his heart), and one into his abdomen. Blood spewed from Niven's mouth. Thousands of wriggling extensions as fine as hair invaded Niven's inner flesh and bones and blackened his skin just beneath the surface. Niven could still feel the demon's name searing through his mind, when all at once, the intricate webbing tore him apart from the inside out. Buckets of blood slapped the walls.

Mr. Never picked up the only piece of Niven that had been left intact—his face—and carried it back with him through the bloody curtain, the door closing behind him.

7

When the entire house shook at greater length and with greater force than it ever had, Redford was too late to stop his glass of grape juice from falling off the desk.

"Shit!" he said, leaping into action.

He ran out of his room and down the stairs to the kitchen, fetched a hand towel, and raced back up to soak the spill. The house was still shaking. As he scrubbed the purple stain, he cursed the house and its stupid rumblings. He heard Niven's bedroom door open and shouted, "Geez. D'you feel that shit? This place is its own San Fran!"

No one responded. Redford finally gave up on the dulled stain. He got off his knees and left his room, staring at Niven's open door, puzzled. Shrugging his shoulders, he returned the soaked cloth to the kitchen and tossed it into the sink. He rinsed his hands and headed back for the staircase. But before ascending, he stopped at the base and stared up to the third floor. The three bedroom doors belonging to the girls were visible from where he stood. In perfect unison, the three doors opened wide.

He watched and waited but no one came out. Then he looked at Niven's door, which was still open. "Um. Hey, guys? Anyone up?" he called.

No response.

The house moaned a deep and almost human moan;

a shiver ran through his body. Redford tugged on his black boxers with yellow Batman symbols on them. He crept up to Niven's doorway.

"Niven, you up? Niv...?"

Redford peeked around the corner and—nothing. The room was empty. No Niven. He smiled and headed up the second flight of stairs to the girls' floor. Sneaking up to Ruby's door, he jumped into the room and shouted, "Gotcha!"

But he hadn't gotten anyone. The room was empty. Now he rushed into Hedy's room—empty. Lily's room was the same. "Well, what the hell?" he said, now believing his housemates had gone out for pizza and hadn't even bothered to invite him to go along. Just as he turned around to exit Lily's room, the house shook hard enough to cause him to stagger and fall onto Lily's bed. Instinctively, Redford ran for the door but it whipped shut with such force the framing cracked.

The walls rippled and were suddenly like blood, pouring down all around him, splitting the darkness with their glow. The ceiling dripped blackness, and the floor beneath his bare feet became like quicksand, soaking up all the furniture. Redford screamed in terror as he began to sink. Deeper and deeper. When he'd sunken up to his chest, Mr. Never's name wrapped around his mind and began to peel it away, layer by layer.

Right before him, Mr. Never stepped through the bleeding wall and walked across the doughy surface of the floor. Redford couldn't stop screaming as he gazed up at the demon, and worse, the demon was gazing down at him! Although Mr. Never did not seem to have eyes to stare with, he was staring nonetheless. The demon's head was shaped like a giant egg made of bone. Its mouth was like a mummy's mouth, all wrinkled and puckered. Its chest was a crisscrossing multitude of bulging, spiky ribs. With lumpy arms that hung at an extended length, Mr. Never reached down and grabbed Redford under his jaw. Slowly, the demon raised Redford out of the mushy floor, and as he did, Redford could see the faces of his housemates hanging from hooks around the demon's waist—he screamed his throat raw.

Now dangling from the demon's grip, face to partial face with it, Redford gained true perspective of its massiveness. Barely able to kick, he held on to the demon's incredibly muscular forearm. He couldn't understand why he hadn't just passed out from fright (he wanted so badly to).

And then the demon moved him closer to its face; Redford thought, *You can pass out any time now.* The demon's huge head began to tear apart from the top to just above its mouth. Redford wanted to scream but his throat was being squeezed. The bone gave way to bright red flesh, stringy stuff that stretched and bounced like rubber bands. And the flesh gave way to a set of vertical finger-length jaws.

The demon moved Redford's face close to its snapping jaws, then pulled him away. Repeating this motion two, three, four times, it seemed to be threatening him, or warning him. In the end, it raised him at arm's length and gave such a roar, Redford felt urine stream down his legs. Tossing him down on the floor, where he did not sink this time, the demon's head creaked and screeched back together to become whole once again.

With a heavy stomp of its right three-clawed foot, the demon spoke a single warning using the combined voices of Lily, Hedy, Ruby, and Niven.

"NNNEVVVERRR!"

In a dizzying blur, the demon was swept back through the bleeding wall. The room sank into utter blindness. And moments later, with a start, Redford came to, screaming. Lily's bedroom was back to normal. He felt at his throat, which seemed okay, then hopped to his feet. He ran past the other rooms, down the first flight of stairs, and straight into his room. In a frenzy, he gathered up his belongings, crammed them into his backpack, and fled out of the house and into the night.

One week later, Keira received a phone call from Redford. This was the first day since abandoning the house in Chatter Falls that he felt calm enough to articulate whole sentences. This was also the first time Keira was learning of the abandonment.

"Oh my god," said Keira, responding to the news of the events of the week prior. "Are you okay, Redford? Are you somewhere safe?"

"Yes. I'm back at my parent's house. I won't be going back to Chatter Falls, or college. Maybe I'll go back to school in the future, but not right now. I couldn't handle it," said Redford, terror still evident in his voice.

"No. That's totally understandable. Shit. I can't believe the others are all...gone! I don't know what I'll tell Cliff. Shit. And you say there's no sign of them there at all?"

"None. I swear it. I'm so sorry I took so long to call you I-I just..."

"It's okay, Redford. It's not your fault," she soothed.

"Keira?"

"Yes?"

Keira could hear Redford gulp at the other end of the call.

"Aren't you scared?" he asked her.

"Um. Sure. I guess. A little."

"I mean. You had your seance with the others that night. What if...what if it comes for *you?*"

Rattled

1 — October 30, 1975

When the bell rang, another day of grade two ended for Tom Rattle. As his classmates rushed the locker space (which was normally hidden behind a sliding wall on wheels), he was determined to complete the coloring of his pumpkin drawing.

"Hurry along now, Tom. You don't want to be the last one out again," said Ms. Lasovick.

Tom looked up at her and smiled. "Done!" he said.

He lifted the lid of his desk and carefully set the art inside, then added his crayons. It was Friday and tomorrow was Halloween. By the time he ambled over to the ransacked locker, most of the students had fled the room. The cacophony out in the hall was dying down. Tom removed his sneakers to be replaced with his black rubber boots with the red trim.

The left boot fit properly, but when he slipped his foot into the right boot, it was not his boot. Another student, in his haste, must have put on his right boot. Tom was very disappointed at this; he loved his rubber boots. A lot of the boys were wearing them. This was not a great start to his weekend. Feeling quite low Tom left the building. Outside there were plenty of students still running about, but their numbers were quickly dwindling. There was only one bus left boarding because the upper-grade students were always held back at the sound of the bell. This was so the younger students could have a head start.

Tom made his way across the school's front lawn, toward the cluster of pine trees. Students had created a path through the trees as a shortcut to Aqueduct Street. The grass was well worn with muddy footprints. Tom entered the darkness of the path staring down at his right foot's larger boot (which slipped off his heel with every step). The ground was covered with pine needles and exposed knobbly roots.

Suddenly, a pair of blue North Star sneakers with the double yellow stripes stepped in front of him, blocking his way. Tom's eyes followed up the pair of worn jeans, higher up to a ragged jean jacket, and higher still to the face of the teenage boy wearing those clothes.

"RAH!" screamed the teen, raising his arms toward Tom.

Tom froze, his breath held. All he could focus on was the boy's flipped, blood-red eyelids.

"RAHHH!" the teen roared again.

This time Tom's wits woke and he ran wide around the terrifying teen. He could hear laughter as he ran, and could only hope the terror was not giving chase. Surely he would be caught, and then, who knows what? Tom broke through the branches at the end of the path, running into the clearing of the sidewalk. But he didn't stop there (oh hell no), he ran as fast as he could down Aqueduct Street, past the cemetery, and down Church

Street. He ran up his front porch steps, hightailed it inside the house, and landed right in his mother's arms.

"Tom? What's happened, honey?" his mother questioned, rubbing his back to calm and comfort her frightened 7-year-old.

Tom couldn't speak yet; he was doing some pretty heavy panting. His mother crouched down to his level and placed her hands on his red cheeks.

"You're okay, honey. You're safe now. Tell me what happened."

Tom started to relate the story. From that day forward he would avoid the shortcut through the trees. Unfortunately, he would never see his right rubber boot again.

2 — October 30, 2019

Bobby Clak was out with friends celebrating his 57th birthday, and the successful launch of his dark art exhibition at the Henry Gothik Art Gallery in downtown Toronto. They laughed and cheered him with wine over an expensive dinner, showering him with nonstop praises. Bobby was high on life; earlier at the showing, he'd met a very special man. The eccentric writer and owner of a quaint, but very well known, bookstore specializing in all things occult, had also attended the showing. He'd introduced himself (though his name was synonymous to anyone interested in the occult or supernatural) and congratulated Bobby on his captivating pieces.

("Mr. Rattle, it is an honor to meet you, sir," Bobby said, shaking the man's hand and bowing his head in respect.

"Nonsense," Mr. Rattle replied. "The pleasure is mine. I've been watching your career for some time now. And finally, I have the opportunity to enjoy your talent up close. Very excited to be here, Mr. Clak."

"Thank you, sir. I hope I'm not blushing. I've been a fan of yours for many years. I've read all your books. All so very interesting and the inspiration behind many of my pieces. I'd love to chat with you sometime about all things magic and macabre," Bobby said, his green eyes sparkling beneath thick brows.

"As would I, Mr. Clak. Perhaps you would like to come by for a personal tour of my shop and some tea. I make very fine tea. I do realize tomorrow is Halloween and you've probably already set plans in motion; however, if you are able, you are more than welcome to join me at eight o'clock."

Bobby's smile widened, revealing a missing wisdom tooth in his upper left gums. "That would be incredible! I will be there," he said enthusiastically.

"Fine, Mr. Clak. I look forward to seeing you. Now go on and mingle, meet your fans," said Mr. Rattle.

As Bobby turned and was lost in step, overcome with the thought of having a personal visit with one of his idles, Mr. Rattle put his full wine glass down on a counter and left.)

Thursday morning (Halloween), Bobby stretched himself awake, a smile at life on his face. Last night had been incredible, but tonight...tonight with the one and only Mr. Rattle himself, now that was going to be *fucking* incredible! He had phone calls to make, photographs to post online, and he couldn't wait to tell the world he was meeting with *Mr. Tom Rattle!*

After showering and trimming his mostly white beard, he stood before his bookshelf staring at a certain collection, authored by none other than, you know who. He contemplated whether or not it would seem foolish to bring at least one volume with him to have signed by the great man himself. Should I, or shouldn't I? Or maybe I can sneak away with something more personal of his, he thought, then laughed about his adolescent obsession. "I'll just rip out a lock of his hair," he mocked himself. "Or even better, get him to sign my left breast and then have it tattooed."

That afternoon he returned to the gallery. Opening night had been quite a success. His agent had no doubt tonight's showing would be no less eventful. The word was out and Bobby Clak was an overnight sensation. At least that's what his agent swore to him. And why should-n't he believe him, after all, *thee* Tom Rattle was a fan of *his*!

Throughout his day, Bobby could think of nothing other than meeting with the author. He tried to focus on his own business at hand, but it was no use, he just wanted to skip over the hours and get to the meeting. Dawn, a fellow artist who made no secret of her crush on Bobby, took him out for a late lunch.

"So, I said to her, 'Esther, you're really going to leave your gorgeous husband of eighteen years for that hideous thing you call a man?' And she looked me right in the eyes and...Bobby?...Bobby?"

"Oh, yeah," he said, snapping back from his daze.

"You're not even listening to me. Where are you?"

He looked at his watch and grinned. "I'm listening," he lied.

Dawn blinked, giving him an expression of insult and disbelief. "Sure you are," she said. "And you haven't even touched your soup. Usually, I'm the slow eater. What's got you so distracted? I mean, I realize you have the show, and that's a big deal, but you seem to be off in your own little world over there," she observed.

Bobby looked down into his bowl of Thai Coconut Lemongrass Soup, the ambrosial aroma wafting up to his nose. Normally he'd have slurped up every last drop by now. He looked up at her with those green eyes she couldn't get enough of. He said, "I'm sorry. I guess my preoccupation with this author meeting has taken over my brain."

"Him again, huh?"

"Yep. Him again."

"Well, let's talk about him, then. As long as I see you eating your soup," she said.

"Okay."

"Have you thought about what you might ask him?" said Dawn, dipping a small piece of bread into her steaming soup.

"Well, I don't want to make my visit seem like an interview or something. It's not like I'm bringing a notebook and pen to scribble down every word he says."

"Oh, I thought you were."

"Funny."

"So, you're just gonna wing it, with no planned questions or anything? Seems unlike you. Even seems a bit sloppy, don't you think?"

"Dawn, I'm not a fucking journalist. Shit. I'm an artist. I'm sure he's expecting a lot of questions from me but I don't intend to overwhelm the guy. If this goes well, who knows, he might even endorse my work. Do you realize what the support of someone in his position could do for my career? The guy's like fucking Stephen King or Clive Barker!"

Dawn shrugged. "Not sure it would make much of a difference," she said.

"And that's why you're not my agent," said Bobby, smiling.

"Well, I just think maybe you're making too much of this. The man likes your work. He's a dark writer and you're a dark artist. That may be all you have in common with each other. See what I'm saying?"

"I guess."

"Enjoy the visit, take what you can from the experience, but don't put it in your head that he's somehow going to push your career up the ladder just because of a cup of tea and some conversation," said Dawn.

By the look on Bobby's face, shed just ruined lunch for him.

3 — Things In Common

By 7:30 pm, things were just picking up at the gallery when Bobby chased down his agent.

"Trapper, I have to run. I'm sorry, but I have that meeting with Tom Rattle. The minute it's over, I'll race right back here, I swear," he promised.

"I understand how much this means to you, Bobby. Don't worry, I got this," Trapper assured him.

"Awesome. You're the best, Trapper."

"That's what they say!"

Bobby pulled up to the curbside and parked his car. He looked left across the street, smiling at the neon red sign designed in Devil's Handwritten Typeface: Rattle's Books. His heart skipped a beat. This was it. He was actually here and this was actually going to happen.

"Un...fucking...believable," he said to himself.

He turned the engine off and took a deep breath to calm his nerves (it didn't work). He hadn't even noticed until he stepped out of the car that the weather was getting rough. He looked up to the dark clouds as the rain began to blend with the stirring wind. There was the faintest rumble in those clouds. You could smell the oncoming storm in the air.

As he hustled across the street, loose garbage began to gather against the storefronts. He stopped at the edge of the sidewalk to take in the shop's medieval air. Wonderful shit, he thought. With a few steps forward, he was face to face with an amazing old gothic door with intricate ironwork. Not the building's original door, but a special find just for this shop. Because this wasn't just any bookshop, this was Tom Rattle's fucking bookshop!

He reached up and used the iron knocker to announce his arrival. Gusts of wind and rain pummelled him from behind. The door opened none too soon.

"Uh. Thank you so much. It's getting...." Bobby stopped talking when he realized no one was on the other side of the door. It had opened on its own. He thought maybe the force of the wind was the cause, but then thought a malfunctioning lock made more sense. Whatever the case, he entered and closed the door behind him, which seemed to seal shut just fine.

"Um. Hello? Mr. Rattle?" he called.

As he looked around, he whispered, "If Vincent Price was a bookshop..." The scent of old tomes and burning candles instantly brought a smile to his lips. Books lined shelves at every wall and sat in stacks on the floor, but neat and orderly. Everything had its place. He looked up in awe at the three skeleton torso chandelier; each pair of bony hands holding a lit candle. "I have to get me one of those."

There was a unique broom leaning against one set of books, a witch's broom, perhaps. He spotted several unique crystal balls about the room. As he entered deeper into the shop, he came upon a set of tables with chairs for readers to sit at and engage themselves in their dark studies. Upon the tables were several open books of an age he could not guess. He examined the largest of the books, its frail pages smokey and filled with writings he did not understand, drawings of demons and satanic symbols.

"Fantastic," he whispered.

"I see you've found one of the demonology compendiums."

Bobby turned with a gasp. Mr. Rattle was standing in the arched doorway made of human skulls. The haunting glow from the hallway reddened his bearded face. He was dressed in fancy gothic attire: Black long sleeve pleated Victorian shirt and black satin scarf; tight black leather pants with a leather belt and shiny silver buckle in the shape of a five-pointed star; leather riding boots. Bobby had not realized until just that moment how truly striking the man's appearance was.

"Mr. Rattle! You startled me."

Mr. Rattle smiled back to his guest. He said, "Please, Mr. Clak, I much prefer it if you call me Tom."

As he approached Bobby, he held his hand out to greet him. Bobby accepted the hand, offering his in return.

"In that case, you must call me Bobby."

"Splendid. I find all this formal business so stuck up. After all, there is no crown upon my head," said Tom. "Please, if you'll follow me, I've had some tea made fresh in the back room. We'll be much more comfortable there."

"Sure," Bobby said. "This is an incredible set up

you've got here. If I could put myself in a setting like this to do my paintings, I can just imagine the shit I could produce."

"Well, I could never get in the way of creativity. You must come for a weekend. I'll lock the shop up and you can paint till your heart's content," Tom offered.

"Oh my god, that would be a dream. But I wouldn't want to impose on your business," Bobby lied. He was trying to be nice but he wanted to scream for joy at the idea.

"Fuck the business. Shops like mine aren't money-makers. I get on okay, but I do this because it's my hobby and I love it," Tom explained. "So choose the weekend or weekends, and we'll set you up in the reading area upfront. And you can draw on all the inspiration you're able."

"Wow. I am going to hold you to that, sir."

"I hope you will."

4 — Memory Lane

Tom led Bobby down a narrow hall dimly lit by wall sconces (skeletal hands holding candles). They entered a room to their right that was not much brighter than the hallway.

"This is my favorite room in the house. It's off-limits to patrons, of course. I do much of my writing in here," said Tom, offering Bobby one of his modern baroque chairs. Of course, the furniture was all black.

"I can understand why," said Bobby, sitting down. "This room is astounding. I love your sense of style."

"Well, don't let the main floor fool you. My living space upstairs is quite normal, country living by the book," Tom chuckled. "Down here is where I live out my fantasies."

Bobby took in the room's decor as Tom stood over the glass-topped skull head table. He filled Bobby's cup of steaming tea to the rim and handed it to him. Bobby inhaled the blend of jasmine and something splendid he couldn't quite put his finger on.

"Mmm. Smells wonderful," he said.

"Thank you. I have an affinity for tea. My mother was a tea connoisseur. She had a tea for everything. So I got to drink a lot of the stuff growing up. And I have to admit, there were plenty of sleepless nights and anxious times when it did help. I'm just keeping her tradition alive. It's this or alcohol, and the latter is too expensive."

"I like to keep a clear head as well," said Bobby, staring at the large desk behind Tom's high-backed chair. "I can't believe I'm in the same room you create your novels in."

"I'm nothing special. Just a guy with a twisted imagination and the ability to put it all down in writing," Tom said humbly, raising his cup to his lips. "I find what you create to be no less impressive. I always wished I could draw the images that came into my mind. Sometimes words can't express what I've seen in my head."

As Bobby sipped his tea, he discovered the flavor was so intense, so addictive, he had to restrain his urge to gulp it back in one swallow and demand more.

"This tea...is it a store brand?" he inquired.

Tom grinned and said, "One of my mother's recipes. I added an ingredient of my own. It is very good, isn't it?"

"Yes. Very delicious."

Tom picked up a remote control off the table and aimed it at the fireplace; a vigorous flame erupted within the gaping mouth of the skull's face.

Bobby felt the cozy warmth spread up his backside. A set of chimes drew his attention when they were stirred to life by the rising heat. Of course, the chimes were bones dangling from a skull, clicking and clacking.

"Where do you find all this cool stuff?" he asked.

"Travels. eBay mostly," Tom admitted.

"Well, you have some unique pieces," said Bobby, sipping his second cup of tea.

Tom straightened up in his chair and crossed his right leg over his left. "Bobby Clak," he began, "I have a small confession to make."

Bobby's eyes were feeling heavy as he tried to remain focused on his host. "A confession?"

"Yes. When I invited you here I had an ulterior motive for doing so. You see, in truth, I am a huge fan of your work. But I wasn't always such a fan of yours. There was a time when I held nothing but contempt for the boy that Bobby Clak was," he explained.

Bobby was shaking his head. "I don't understand. What are you talking about?"

Tom could see by Bobby's rolling eyes that it was almost time to show his old acquaintance just what he meant. He continued: "Forty-four years ago you were thirteen-years-old, and I was seven. I hadn't discovered the darkness in the world, but you changed all that in a matter of minutes. You might say you woke me up. And now, my friend, I am going to wake you up."

Bobby's eyelids were as heavy as bricks on a kite. He had to let them close. And when he did the darkness spiralled brighter, until he could see the wet pine-covered ground beneath his black rubber boots. He raised each foot, examining the unfamiliar footwear. Nowhere in his memories did he ever own such a pair of rubbers. His vision slowly moved from the boots to the large spidery roots sewn in and out of the earth.

He could hear the pine needles crunching under his footsteps as he unwillingly began to walk. The trees seemed to creep in closer and closer around him, leaning over him like angry entities. Strange as it was, he did not feel like himself. But he did feel small; small like his mind was inhabiting a body much too tiny to be his own. His nerves quivered with trepidation.

As he stepped over the gnarly roots, his focus kept returning to his boots, and he sensed there was something not quite right about them. Suddenly, he stopped dead in his tracks. Someone else was there. Bobby's focus rose up the body of the teenager now blocking his path. The teenager's eyelids were flipped as he gave a laughable roar in an attempt to frighten Bobby, or rather, not Bobby, but the boy Bobby was inside.

And he felt the shock of fear sizzle down his spine, for he had frightened the boy. More than that, he had terrified the boy—the boy—young Tom Rattle! He was young Tom Rattle, and that teenager had been him. And now he remembered what happened next. Young Tom Rattle had screamed and run off through the trees. His cries could be heard heading down the street that day. And teenage Bobby and his friend Vince had laughed their asses off at the prank.

But here, now, the scene changed. Things were not going to play out as they had previously. This time someone else was in the trees. Bobby's ears filled with a sound like a car horn growing louder and louder and louder. Vibrations shook the pine needles on the ground, reverberating up through those rubber boots. A heavy mist plummeted from above, pounded the ground, and spread around him like ghosts.

He knew that someone was hidden in the mist before

him. Bobby the teenager was gone. The mist flushed clear around the small figure: it was Tom Rattle—the boy. The expression on his face was one of sadness. He looked right into Bobby's mind's eye. With sudden swiftness, the mist rolled before him, blocking him from Bobby's view; and when the mist cleared, adult Tom was standing in the boy's place (the same look of sadness on his face).

Though his lips did not move, Bobby heard his voice whisper, "*I never forgot. Now you won't, either.*"

Tom half turned away from Bobby, his shoulders hunching forward. His clothes melted from his body, dripping into a puddle at his bare feet. His ribs popped! His body grew taller, slimmer and slimmer. His shoulders snapped and widened. His arms and legs thinned to mere bones covered in a brownish sleeve of skin. The hair on his head fell away, disappearing into the mist. And then, ever so slowly—slower still—the thing Tom had become turned around.

Acute volts of terror shot through Bobby's body and brain. He was no longer breathing as he stared crazy-eyed at the nightmare come to life. The thing's gold serpent eyes were like fiery jewels. Its nose was long with an extreme curve (as though broken), and pointed at the tip. It was holding something that Bobby could not see from its current stance. And then it gave him the full show.

The demonic beast turned completely around to face Bobby. Hanging limply from its clawed fingers was the blood-soaked body of his friend Vince. A throaty growl rolled off the beast's blubbery, forked tongue and plowed right over Bobby. Its upper lip rose high above gleaming black gums and saliva-dripping fangs. The moment it sank those fangs into Vince's throat with a grotesque crunch, Bobby screamed!

5 — Inspired

The sound of Tom's voice reached out of the darkness as Bobby opened his eyes. He felt like he was going to gasp out loud, but no sound did he make. His cup of tea was in his right hand. He looked about in a half daze, clarity driving to the forefront of his mind.

"One of my mother's recipes. I added an ingredient of my own. It is very good, isn't it?" said Tom. And then, noticing the puzzled look on Bobby's face. "Hey, are you okay? You look a little pekid."

Bobby nodded. "Yeah. No, I'm fine. Think the tea went to my head," he surmised.

"A lightweight, huh? Some of these teas aren't for everyone," said Tom. "Here, let me take that."

Tom relieved Bobby of his cup and set both cups on the table.

Bobby looked at his watch, and although it would appear he'd only been with Tom for about forty minutes, it felt much longer.

"Time to head out, Bobby?" asked Tom.

"Yeah. I think so. I should get back to the gallery. It's my showing, after all. But it certainly has been—"

"Unforgettable?" Tom finished.

Bobby smiled an awkward smile, sensing an underlying meaning behind his host's adage. He brushed it off and shook Tom's hand. He said, "Thank you for having me. I'm sorry I couldn't stay longer. I have so many things I'd like to ask you."

"You're welcome to come and pick my brain anytime. I slipped a little something into your signed copy of my latest book of bullshit," Tom revealed as they reached the front door.

"Oh. Thank you. Really. Thank you, Tom. I'll be in touch," Bobby said, opening the door to leave.

The storm outside leapt upon them like a dog anxious to welcome its master home. Bobby ducked into the wind and raced across the street. Curious to find what Tom had 'slipped' into his copy of *Something So Scary*, Bobby flipped the book open and discovered one of Tom's business cards. He smiled, closed the book, and started the engine.

Back inside Rattle's Books, Tom poured himself a freshly steeped cup of Chai tea and waited for his call to go through.

"Hello?" said the voice of an elderly woman.

"Hi, Mom, it's me."

"Hello, Tom. How'd it go?" asked Mrs. Rattle.

"Splendidly!"

"Oh, that's good to hear, son. No more nightmares, then?"

"Not for me, Mom."

Several months later, Bobby Clak's name was once again the talk of the town. His latest collection of horror art was on display and receiving rave reviews. The piece stirring up the most controversy was a painting of a horrifying demon titled *Rattled!*

When asked where the inspiration for such an incredibly chilling design came from, Mr. Clack was quoted as having said: "Don't know. It just came to me."

The Peddler's Gift

1

While on a day trip in Toronto with my 18-year-old daughter, Carly, we happened upon a street person in the gay district known as the village. I had wanted to visit there for quite some time but was afraid to go on my own. This bus trip was Carly's idea.

So here was this unfortunate man peddling for change, and being completely ignored by everyone who passed him, although his appearance was rather unsettling. He wore a black large-rimmed hat that concealed his eyes and nose. His skin was dark and his lips moved nonstop.

The man's tan shirt looked more like a worn tent draped over him. His bare legs were the topic of discussion on the mouths of passersby, and the subject of their repulsion. To say they were strange was an understatement. He looked like a grasshopper. His knees seemed to be backward, bending in the wrong direction like an insect.

We had no choice but to approach nearer to him because the door to the shop we wanted to enter was right next to him. I must admit, I felt a little silly being apprehensive about getting any closer to him. Carly, on the other hand, grabbed me by the hand and pulled me in his direction.

"Come on, tough guy, I won't let the big scary cripple hurt you," she said.

"Promise?" I teased.

However, I did notice Carly was slowing her approach, but not for the reason I first thought. Suddenly she was turning in his direction and pulling me with her.

"What are we doing?" I asked her.

"Shh," she hushed. "Listen to him. He's singing. And his voice is *beautiful*."

The closer we stepped, the more I could hear his song, and my daughter was correct, his voice was incredibly soothing and emotional. Though he was not singing in English, his vocals gripped you by the heart and mind and tugged with all its might at your emotions.

Now standing a couple of feet before him, Carly and I both noticed that the tin cup at his mangled feet was empty. Carly looked at me and I knew at once what she was thinking. I removed my wallet from my pocket and handed her a fifty-dollar bill. It never even occurred to me that it was a lot of money; it didn't seem like nearly enough.

Carly reached down and placed the bill in his cup as he continued to sing in that amazing voice. Feeling better about ourselves, we started to walk away, but when the man's singing ceased, we looked back at once. His left hand was reaching out toward us. Carly and I glanced at one another, uncertain what the gesture meant. Then the man opened his hand to reveal a small arcane box.

"You think he wants us to have it?" asked Carly.

"Maybe," I said, shrugging my shoulders.

The man gestured in our direction with the box, making it clear to us that he did indeed want us to have it. Carly smiled and accepted the gift, she said, "Thank you. Thank you so much, but it's not necessary. You have a magical voice, you know."

"Un tuteur pours le Coeur Pur" (a guardian for the pure heart), he whispered, then went back to his singing.

Carly and I looked closer at the gift, which was a rather horrible little box. Black and brown, it appeared to be made of thorns, bone, and teeth! Deep purple veins wound in and out its intricate design as if holding it all together. As hideous as it was, one could not look upon it without stirrings of fascination.

I put my arm around Carly and turned us in the opposite direction. Once we reached the shop door, we both turned back for one last look at the strange man, but he was gone. I swear a chill ran up the back of my neck.

"That's weird," said Carly.

"Okay. I've seen enough crazy for one day," I said. "Let's go inside."

Carly slipped the box into her purse, and surprisingly, we quickly forgot about it and its previous owner.

2

Three months later, well into October, the leaves in Moonbeam Lake were clinging to the trees for dear life. The world was colorful and the mood in our house was relaxed and happy. I was working on one of my novels when I heard Carly come in. I looked at the clock. It was 2:12 am. Carly had been out with her friends; her usual Friday night routine.

I heard her go into the fridge, mumbling fairly loud.

"Hey, hon, is everything alright?" I asked.

Carly came into my workroom with a glass of iced tea at her lips, while reaching out to hand me one.

"Thanks. So?"

She took a breath and said, "Oh, these total assholes at the party were harassing me and my friends all night. One even grabbed my ass on my way out."

"What?!"

"Don't worry, I slapped the pig's filthy face."

"That's why I'm nervous when you go out. There's always going to be assholes out there," I said.

"I can take care of myself, Dad."

"People always say that."

"I'm fine. Goodnight, Dad," she said, kissing my cheek and heading off upstairs.

I tried to go back to my work but all I could think of was my baby girl getting grabbed by some punk. My concentration was shot to hell. I shut everything down and went to the front door to make sure Carly hadn't forgotten to lock up.

As I was rinsing my glass under the kitchen tap, I felt a heavy breeze sweep over my bare feet. Turning around, I found the back door ajar. *What the hell?* I thought. *Did Carly come in through the back and forget to lock the door?* The entrance carpet was rumpled and muddied, and clumps of dirt trailed out of the room. A chill ran through me.

Suddenly I heard a loud thump above. *Carly!* I ran for the stairs, not thinking to arm myself first. My only thought was to get to my baby as quick as I could. "Carly!" I called, reaching the top landing. There were shuffling noises, then, "Dad!"

The sting of fear in that cry pierced my heart and drove a spike of terror into my brain. The instant I barged into Carly's room the world slammed on its brakes, and then my vision blurred into a mixture of fast-forward moments, and slow-motion moments. My ears popped and rang from the sound of the gunshot. Fire poked its blazing prong into my left shoulder. The door banged shut as my weight slammed back against it.

Carly's eyes were screaming wide, but one of the three intruders had his hand over her mouth. A second assailant was sitting on top of her, pinning her arms down. Her nightgown was raised above her hips. The shooter was smiling and exaggeratedly chewing gum as I slid to the floor.

None of the attackers were wearing a mask, so I immediately assumed they were not planning on leaving any witnesses behind.

"Looks like Gramps came to enjoy the show," the shooter said in a voice as oily as his stringy black hair.

"Get the fuck off my daughter," I ordered through ground teeth, blood gushing from the hole in my shoulder, and shudders taking over my body.

Carly bit the hand covering her mouth and shouted, "Dad! No!"

The bitten man hauled off and belted her across the face; blood-streaked from her nostrils and lips at once, and still she struggled.

I made an attempt to get up, but the shooter gave me a swift boot in the side of my ribs; excruciating pain zapped through me with the double crack. What else could I do but collapse? The three devils were laughing and joking about my inability to rescue my daughter.

"Leave him alone, you fucking asshole!" Carly cried.

The second man standing next to Carly, who was filming the assault with his cell-phone, punched her right across the left cheek. Oh God, I swear I felt the blow myself. Carly kicked the wall in fury and frustration, causing the shelf on her wall to rattle, and the street man's humble gift to fall on her bed.

The creep on top of Carly picked the box up, examined the thing with a certain amount of interest and disgust, and placed it on my daughter's exposed belly.

"Looks like I get to play with two boxes tonight," he jibed.

His friends guffawed.

"Hold her ass still," he ordered the shooter, who then pointed the pistol directly at Carly's face, grinning.

"Now you don't want to be a dead fuck, do you?" he sneered.

The man atop her rose to his knees and unbuttoned his jeans, unzipped the zipper, and pushed his pants down. He shook his erection at Carly, laughing and purposely drooling on her. The cameraman moved in for a close-up.

"Leave her alone!" I shouted.

"Shut the fuck up or Jake here will put another hole in your faggot ass," said the would-be rapist.

At that moment, a great whirlwind erupted within the room, chirping like a chorus of locust. And though this intense supernatural occurrence was happening, not a thing in Carly's room was budging from the force. Carly and I could see its definite effect on the three intruders, and we could hear its high-pitched song, but we could not *feel* it ourselves.

The three assailants were shouting at one another in total confusion.

"What the fuck's happening?!" the one called Jake yelled.

"You fucking asking me?!" the one between my daughter's legs shouted back.

He then snatched the box from Carly's belly, staring at it as if he somehow knew it was the source of this phenomenon. "What the fuck is this?!" he screamed at Carly.

Carly shook her head as the man tried to loosen the

box from his hand, where it was now attaching itself to his flesh. I couldn't move a muscle; I was glued to the spot just as that box was glued to that bastard's hand.

Red mist appeared within the spinning winds like paint over-spray. Carly and I seemed to realize simultaneously just what that red mist was: Blood was being drawn right from the very pores of the three intruders. They were screaming and thrashing about, trapped in the grip of whatever power had been released from the box. Carly and I were beyond terrified.

Suddenly, the would-be rapist's body rose off of Carly. His back slammed against the ceiling, where he remained like a helium balloon. His right arm dangled beneath him, with the box still attached like some hideous growth. As he screamed in terror, his friends stared up at him in awe. The thorny design on the box lashed out like so many fishing lines, threading in and out of the threesome's bodies like needles and threads.

The two intruders standing were now trapped in the same thorny, threaded cocoons as their leader. At once they were both whipped to the ceiling. The whirling wind was darkening with their combined blood, draining them. But it wasn't just their blood being siphoned, their bodies were deflating into skin and bones. First, the bones snapped and splintered, crunching within invisible jaws. The screams of the intruders almost made Carly and I pity them—almost.

Then only their skin and hair were left, dangling like deflated sex dolls from the ceiling. There came a loud and nauseating slurping sound, and then they were all three of them gone!

I wanted to turn away, but for the weakness of curiosity, I could not. Carly leapt off her bed and came to my arms at the floor. At last, the box dropped to the bed with a mild thud. As Carly hugged me in tears, I struggled to hold onto consciousness, my breath short.

"Oh, Dad," Carly wept.

"Call...an...ambulance," I gasped.

Just then, the box shook in place and the thorny design seemed to expand and contract as if breathing itself. I screamed as the bullet in my shoulder was sucked out of my flesh and popped like a cork! The freed bullet landed in the blood on the white carpet. Carly was hysterical, not understanding that I was being helped.

I screamed again as the exit wound healed and my broken ribs snapped back and were mended. The box ceased its shaking, and the room fell to quiet. We could feel what could only be described as magic, subside. Carly and I hugged one another, long and hard, feeling relieved and safe once more.

For weeks following the events of our house invasion, Carly and I had many discussions on whether or not to return the magic box to its owner or to just dispose of it. It was a difficult decision. In the end, however, we agreed the best course of action was to take no course of action. The box, as wary as we were of it, had saved our lives. It remained in Carly's possession, as it was meant to be.

Jolly

1

The year 1995 had many firsts for 5-year-old Finlay Gunn of Jolly Ontario. He attended school for the very first time, entering the kindergarten class at St. Kevin's. That's where he met his first best friend, Matthew Andrews. And in a couple of weeks, he would be going to Matthew's sixth birthday party (his first-ever birthday party, and a Halloween one at that!)

Finlay was an only child. He lived with his parents at 9 Elgin Street. The house was a duplex and they rented the right side, which was a two-story, two-bedroom. Jerry and Amanda were wonderful parents. They tried not to spoil their little ginger-haired son, but they still did. And why shouldn't they? Finlay was a good boy. He was shy and quiet, always did what he was told. Even as a baby he never fussed much. Sending him off to school had been harder on Amanda than it was on him, she suspected.

Throughout his elementary school years, his teachers would always write that he was a daydreamer on his report cards. But Amanda knew better. Finlay was very artistic with his drawings at home, kept his bedroom immaculate, liked to help her cook and clean, and could hold a mature conversation with her better than anyone she knew. No, her Finlay was not a daydreamer, he was a thinker. She would never say a word about the recurring comment on his reports because she knew better.

October embraced Jolly like it always had: gentle rains that left the stains of leaves on the sidewalks; the smell of firewood on cooler breezes; the streets under the canopy of colored leaves; sunsets that burned like a delicious mango. The neighborhood was a collection of mostly newer, very large houses with a few remaining war-times in the mix.

Pumpkins with jagged smiles greeted you on every porch. Witches and ghosts hung from trees, their accordion arms and legs ruffling in the wind. Giant spiders guarded man-size webs. Finlay loved Halloween, from the very first time he watched *It's The Great Pumpkin, Charlie Brown*, he was hooked. You couldn't ask for a better town to grow up in than Jolly to celebrate everything October.

2

When Finlay brought home his first birthday invitation from Matthew, Amanda's initial reaction was a big—huge—no fucking way am I letting my precious child go to some stranger's house for a birthday party. But the more she stared at the invite (homemade by Matthew himself), with its smiling, orange pumpkin face on black construction paper; well, she just couldn't bring herself to tell Finlay no.

The party was set for 5 pm on Friday one week from that day. So Saturday afternoon, she brought Finlay to the shopping centre to pick out a cheap (but not too cheap) gift for his friend. She let Finlay choose, and he chose a stuffed blue Cookie Monster, with big googly eyes. She wasn't certain if Matthew would appreciate the gift as much as her son would have liked to keep it for himself, but it was something.

Finlay was proud of his choice, smiling the whole time he watched his mother having a difficult time with the wrapping paper. She got him to print his name inside the little card and taped it to the top of the oddly shaped gift. All week at school, Matthew couldn't stop talking about his party. About the balloons and cake and the fruit punch his mother was going to make; and about the gifts, of course!

The only other student from their class who'd been invited was their friend Benjamin; however, Ben's mother sent back a reply that explained her son could not attend because they were going to be visiting his grandmother that weekend, up in Smooth Rock Falls. It wasn't a big deal to Matthew, he liked Finlay best of all. And besides, he had four older brothers at home who would all be there: Mark, Luke, John, and his oldest brother Peter.

Mrs. Gale Andrews was a strict Catholic; her husband, Noble, not so much. Noble worked at the steel factory in Nickle Beach. And when not working, he was drinking beer and brandy. Gale brought her five boys to church every Sunday on her own. She took care of the house the way she believed a woman should. Did the cooking, cleaning, took care of the boys, and lied to her friends about the odd shiner she'd hide behind sunglasses, even on the darkest of days.

Gale was not one to complain. She figured she couldn't ask for a better life. Besides, Noble provided for his family, paid the bills, and even took them out to the drive-in theatre when the mood struck him. Theirs was one of the largest houses on Aqueduct Street. A Victorian built in 1880, with a two-story tower, pediments, fish scale patterns on the upper story, sidelights around the door, black shutters at every arched window. A stand-out home.

Although Gale did have to admit, she'd been noticing some disturbing changes in her husband. He used to take out his frustrations on her alone, usually while in the privacy of their bedroom, and always while in a drunken stupor. But as of late, he'd taken to striking out at the boys. Just the other night at the dinner table, Luke accidentally spilled his glass of juice. Noble, sitting next to him, smacked him behind the head with such force that Luke's face slammed into his plate. Then Noble yelled at him about that mess and ordered him to his room.

And last Sunday, after church services, they'd come home to find Noble sitting in his car with the windows up and the engine running, just staring blankly at the garage door. When Gale tried to talk to him, he screamed at her to leave him the fuck alone. Tuesday morning as Gale was getting the boys ready for school, Noble went off the handle over something he couldn't find. She never did understand what he was looking for. But during his rampage through the house, he punched a hole in the wall leading up the stairs.

3

Come Friday, October 27 Gale convinced Noble to go enjoy a night out with his work buddies. They often gathered for drinks and played darts at the local bar. She hoped that would keep him occupied while she and the boys enjoyed a peaceful birthday party. Early in the day, she baked a chocolate two-layer cake, Matthew's favorite. She made the top into a pumpkin face, just as he'd bugged her to do.

After school that day, it was Peter's job to bring Matty(as they all called him) to the park to play for at least an hour to give Gale a chance to finish decorating the dining room, with the help of Mark, Luke, and John. They taped black and orange balloons all around the room, hung streamers of the same colors from the ceiling, and set the table for the seven of them (Finlay included).

Gale smiled at her accomplishments. Dinner was spaghetti and meatballs (also Matty's favorite), with cake and ice cream for dessert. She set her punch bowl on the table and placed all of Matty's gifts on the corner chair. Her baby was already 6-years-old. My, how time flies, she thought, dimming the chandelier for impact.

"Now, hurry and go get ready," she told the boys. "Won't be long now, Peter will be back with Matty."

Meanwhile, Amanda was helping Finlay slip into his costume for the party. She put black makeup around his eyes so they would appear brighter through his plastic skeleton mask. He wore a full black costume with a skeleton body on it and would carry a plastic scythe.

"What am I again?" he asked his mother.

"A Grim Reaper," she said, wiggling her fingers before his face and making ghost sounds.

Finlay laughed and said, "Hurry, Mom, I'm gonna be late."

"Don't worry, Fin, you'll get there on time. Now go get your shoes on and make sure your bows are tight. We wouldn't want you tripping and hurting yourself before you even get there."

Down in their front porch, Amanda helped Finlay into his coat. She put her house keys in her jacket pocket, picked up the gift for Matthew, which was in a large gift bag, and closed the door behind them. Finlay was already at the sidewalk, anxiously jogging on the spot.

"Hurry, Mom," he pressured.

Amanda reached for his tiny right hand (he carried the scythe in his left), and they headed down the street. At the end of Elgin, they turned left onto Aqueduct Street, taking the same route they used to walk to Finlay's school to get to Matthew's house. It was a beautiful evening, the sun still peeking through the orange, red, and yellow foliage. Amanda took a deep breath, but the scents that filled her nose were mostly that of worms and wet leaves from last night's rainfall. Plus they were approaching the old Church of the Japanese Martyrs

Cemetery.

The cemetery was fenced in by a black iron fence about waist high. It was on Church Street, bounded on the east by Aqueduct St., on the north by Elizabeth St., and on the west by family dwellings. There were very few headstones standing. A circle of trees and half-dead bushes huddled in the centre. It hadn't been in use since 1921. There was already a boarder of fallen leaves gathered along the base of the fence, trapped there by the wind.

About a block past the cemetery, Amanda looked at the invitation from Matthew, which had his address written on the back. She and Finlay stopped on the sidewalk, staring up at the grand white house. Above the red door was number 313 on a plaque.

"Well, it certainly is a large house," said Amanda.

Finlay looked up at his mother, still holding her hand. "I don't like it," he said spooked.

Amanda chuckled as she looked down at her son, his plastic skull face mask attached to the top of his head, his raccoon eyes gazing up at her with worry. Amanda crouched down and smiled at him, she said: "Oh, baby, don't be afraid. It's just a house, after all. And inside is your friend Matty and his brothers, and probably balloons, and I know there'll be cake. And you like cake. But listen, if you don't want to go inside, I'm not going to force you. Okay?"

Finlay looked back at the house, and although it gave him the jitters, he made up his mind that he wasn't going to miss out on balloons and cake.

"Let's go," he said, grinning.

Amanda stood and followed the stone path up to the front door. They climbed three red steps and stood before the red door. Amanda pressed the button to ring the doorbell. A moment later, a tall witch greeted them. Finlay recognized Mrs. Andrews right off. He liked her costume.

Amanda laughed in surprise. "Mrs. Andrews, you gave me a start," she said.

"Please, call me Gale," said Mrs. Andrews, opening the door wider for them to enter.

"Amanda."

"So nice to meet this fine boy's mother."

"Thank you," said Amanda. "And you as well."

They stepped into the foyer which was a large but fairly plain space in need of a make-over. Amanda did not want to look around for fear of seeming snoopy.

"Aren't you just the cutest skeleton," Gale said to Finlay.

"I'm the Grim Reaper," he clarified.

"Perfect," said Gale. "You can head over into the dining room. The boys are all in there. We're just waiting for Matty's big brother Peter to return with the birthday boy. Should be any minute now, I guess. We're going to scream Happy Birthday when he walks in the side door," she explained.

"Sounds like a lot of fun," added Amanda.

Finlay nodded and ran off through the living room. Gale turned back to Amanda and said, "If you come for him by 7:30 pm, we should have things wrapped up by then."

"Great. I'll be here," said Amanda. "Good luck. It was very nice to meet you."

"You also, Amanda. And don't worry, Finlay will be just fine."

As Amanda strolled toward home, she couldn't stop thinking about Gale's last words to her. She knew her son would be fine. But after Gale said it out loud, it just sounded, well, sort of creepy to her. She shook the idea from her head and focused on the brilliant Autumn colors (her favorite season).

4

At 4:58 pm Gale Andrews was sitting at the dining room table with a red Power Ranger (Mark), a blue Power Ranger (Luke), a hairy gorilla (John), and of course, the Grim Reaper himself (Finlay). They all hushed when the side door, which entered into the kitchen, creaked open and slammed shut. Peter purposely hurried inside, slipped into his Freddy mask, and stood next to his mother. The moment Matty crossed the threshold into the dining room, a group of not-so-familiar faces shouted, "Happy Birthday!"

Matty was thrilled. Balloons were tossed his way and party horns were blown till Gale's ears nearly popped. Finlay was glad to see his friend at last. Gale disappeared with the birthday boy for a few minutes, and when they returned, she presented him with a cheerful, "Duh Dah!"

Matty spun in a circle to show off his Batman costume. He'd pointed it out to his mother one day in a drug store, but he had no idea she had purchased it behind his back. Had this been his only gift that day, he would have still been content. As they settled back in their seats, Gale began to serve her spaghetti dinner. She was on a tight schedule.

Meanwhile, Noble had already gone over his limit at the bar. He'd eaten some hot wings and now felt like he had to reload on alcohol to catch back up to his earlier buzz. In his corner, he sat with his friends Gregory Scott, Russo Lance, Drummer Novak, and Colson Wallace. Gregory and Drummer were work buddies. Colson he'd known since he was a teenager and had stood as his best man at his wedding. Russo was a new acquaintance, a fellow he'd met through Drummer.

"So how long were you there?" asked Colson, his mouth full of pizza.

"Two weeks. Weather was great, the ladies were great, the parties even better," said Russo.

"Whereabouts in Florida were you?" asked Gregory.

"Broward County."

"Bring back any...souvenirs?" said Drummer, raising an eyebrow.

Russo smiled and looked at Drummer with an expression that said *you know I did.*

"Like what?" said Colson, not understanding what the meaning behind the 'look' meant.

Russo slightly ducked his head and leaned over the round table, he whispered, "Well, if anyone's interested in a fucking high that makes all other highs child's play, by comparison, I got you covered.

"Yeah?" said Noble. "I call bullshit."

Russo laughed out loud. "Buddy, you ain't been high till you been *this* high."

"Is that a challenge I hear?" said Noble.

Colson put his hand on Noble's wrist and cautioned, "Noble...no. You don't want to do this."

"What the fuck, Colson? Why the hell wouldn't I?"

"You've got five boys at home to look after?"

Noble pulled his wrist free of his friend's grip. Now he looked angry. "Fuck. They're not going anywhere. I got plenty of time. Wife's throwing a party for the youngest boy," said Noble.

Whenever he was with his buddies he referred to Gale as 'the wife' and his kids as 'the boys', never saying them by name.

"I'm telling you, Noble, this isn't a good idea," Colson insisted.

"To hell with you. I do what I fucking want, and don't you forget it."

Colson turned his pleading eyes to Russo, who chuckled and said, "Hey. He's a big boy. Who am I to stop him."

"Yeah. Fuck you, Russo. Fuck you, too," Colson said to Noble as he backed out of his chair and walked away.

"Aff. Forget him," said Noble. "Thinks he's the fucking leader for the war on drugs."

Noble looked at Gregory, who shrugged his shoulders. He wouldn't mind a taste of Russo's souvenir. Drummer nodded his approval when all eyes turned to him. The four men threw back the last of their beers and headed for the door. In the parking lot, they climbed into Russo's 1990 Pontiac Firebird; Noble bitching as he squeezed into the back seat.

"Christ. This thing's tiny as fuck!" he grumbled.

"Yep," said Russo, "she's a beauty."

Sitting in the passenger seat, Drummer said, "So, what's this fucking so-called magic drug, Russo?"

Russo reached under his seat and pulled out a clear baggy with a white substance in it.

"Coke?" groaned Drummer, disappointed.

"Hell no. Better," said Russo. "The guy who sold it to me called it vanilla sky."

"Vanilla sky? You mean...Flakka?" Gregory said with surprise.

"One in the same," Russo confirmed.

"Oh, no way am I touching that shit," said Gregory. "That's the shit they call the zombie drug."

"What the fuck's that?" asked Noble, getting tired of feeling cramped in a car that smelled like pine.

"Don't be such a fucking pussy, Greg. That only happens to assholes who can't handle their shit. Fuck. Teenagers use this shit all the time. Can't be that bad," Russo said defensively.

"Don't care. I don't want any part of it. And you shouldn't either, Noble. You got a family at home to take care of," said Gregory, now echoing Colson's sentiments.

"Fuck off. Not you, too?" said Noble. "Why's everybody always telling me what I can and can't do. Fuck you, Greg, and fuck Colson. Fuck the two of you."

"I'm getting out. Can you let me out?" Gregory asked Drummer.

Drummer opened the door and leaned forward, allowing Gregory to climb out of the back.

"Think about what you're doing, Noble," he said, walking away from the car.

Drummer shut the door. "Fucking babies," he chuckled. "Now are we gonna do this, or what?" he asked, turning to Russo.

"Yeah yeah."

5

"Happy birthday to you...." Gale started to sing as she carried Matty's candlelit cake into the dining room. The boys joined in with her as Matty sat there with a toothy smile. "...with the monkeys and gorillas...happy birthday to you-ooooh!"

"Make a wish, Matty, honey," Gale reminded him just before he blew the six flames out.

The boys all clapped and cheered. Gale began to cut the cake into slices.

"I want an eyeball!" yelled Luke, referring to the icing pumpkin face.

"Me too, me too!" called John, his voice muffled behind his gorilla mask.

"Well, you're gonna have to take that mask off to eat your cake, John," Gale the witch said as she placed his piece before him. She licked some icing off her left thumb and reached for the orange napkins, then handed one to each boy.

By the time she cleared the table of dessert plates, with barely eaten cake messes on them, it was 6:40 pm. The sun had gone down, giving way to rain clouds. The red ranger was wrestling with the blue ranger; the gorilla was jumping on the sofa, imitating monkey sounds; Batman was chasing the Grim Reaper around the dining room table, and Peter was in the kitchen rinsing off dishes.

"Thanks for all your help, Peter, you're such an angel," said Gale.

"Um, Mom, I'm Freddy," he said, turning to face her with his mask on.

"Okay, guys! Come on and sit down, please. It's time for Matty to open his gifts," Gale announced.

It took some hand-clapping and a few attempts, but eventually, she got them where she wanted them. And as Matty unwrapped his presents, a Halloween sound effects CD playing in the stereo, Gale rubbed her forehead, trying to wish her headache away.

At that very moment, Russo and Drummer were in a panic. Noble was in the back seat of Russo's car, writhing spasmodically. He was drooling and babbling incoherently, with the odd Fuck and Cunt spat in the mix.

"For fuck's sake, Russo, what the hell's wrong with him?" Drummer shouted.

"How the fuck do I know. He must've taken too much."

"Ya don't say," Drummer said infuriated. "What the fuck are we supposed to do with him now?"

"Drummer, I ain't gettin' caught with this guy flippin' out. I got enough drugs in this car to put me away for a long fucking time. We have to dump him, man."

"Dump him? Are you fucking mad?"

"You got a better idea, I'm listening," Russo shouted.

"We'll bring him home."

"What? Now *that's* fucking mad!"

Noble was kicking at the back of Drummer's seat now.

"Noble! Noble! Calm your shit, man! Fuck it. I'll drive his car home, you follow. When we get there, we'll dump him in his car and hope he fucking sleeps it off," said Drummer.

Russo was nodding. "That's good, that's good. Yeah yeah. Let's do that."

By the time Russo and Drummer struggled to put Noble in his car, which was now parked in his driveway, the man was burning up, covered in sweat, and wriggling in their arms. It was raining as they shoved Noble into the back seat of his 1982 Ford Fairmont, locked him inside, and tossed the keys on the floor in the front. As they sped away, Noble booted the back left passenger window, smashing it out.

Inside the house, Gale thought she heard something outside. She peered through the kitchen window, which looked out onto their driveway, and was surprised to see Noble's car parked there, and even more surprised to see the back window was smashed. What has he done now? she wondered. There was no sign of him in the driveway, but she heard more clangs coming from the garage. She glanced up at the teapot clock. It was 7 pm.

Heading to the back door, which was connected to the single car garage, she called, "Noble? Noble, is that you?"

As Gale entered the dark garage, Peter entered the kitchen for another glass of punch, the punch bowl now sitting on the counter. Gale flicked the light switch on, giving life to a single hanging bulb. She gasped when Noble spun round to face her; he'd been busy destroying their bicycles with a crowbar. There were tools scattered everywhere, a couple of cans hammered and spilling the last of their thick contents on the concrete floor. Noble himself was covered with the black asphalt sealer, which long ago had been used on their driveway. He looked like the Tar Monster from *Scooby-Doo, Where Are You?*

"Noble? What are you doing?" she said, only stepping in far enough to allow the door to close behind her.

Noble stared at her with wide glazed eyes. There were howling voices in his head, so loud he could not hear anything beyond. And standing before him, all he could see was a hideous creature that was raising its claws toward him. When Noble screamed in a way Gale had never heard before, her heart wrung. She took a step back but Noble was at her in a flash.

He wrapped his dripping arms around the creature with the tall pointed head, squeezing and flinging it side to side. Gale was terrified. She'd never known he was so strong. As she screamed, Noble smashed his face into hers, breaking her green nose, blood immediately running down into her open mouth. She choked.

That's when Peter rushed out the back door to the sound of his mother's scream. He barged into the garage and froze—a man was on top of his mother! They were on the floor which was covered in some black goop; the man was also covered in the substance, and the man was smashing his mother's face in with one of the sealant cans! Peter's brain registered the fact that his mother was not moving, not at all. And then the assailant looked up, his eyes meeting Peter's (Peter's brain registered a second fact: the man was his father!) Peter cried out, "Mmmmom!"

When Noble tossed the pail aside, which struck the heap of scrapped bicycles, he seemed to examine Gale's body for a moment to make sure it was lifeless, and it was. But now a second creature had entered the garage, a shorter, less threatening thing. It turned and ran out, screaming something Noble could not understand. He reached for the short-handled ax that was hanging on the wall near the door and headed after the smaller creature. The howls screeching ever louder in his brain.

When Peter ran into the house screaming, his brother's and Finlay stopped their playing at once, startled by the fear in his cries. Peter fumbled into the dining room, where four of the five younger boys were sitting at the table playing Matty's new Trouble game. Finlay was sitting on the living room floor looking through the pages of Matty's new Batman coloring book, Cookie Monster sitting next to him.

"RUN! HIDE!" Peter yelled hysterically.

At first, the boys all remained still, just staring open-mouthed at their brother. They thought this was some new game he was playing, but they were already playing a game. Peter flung himself over the table and side-swiped the Trouble game clear off the table, once more yelling into his brothers' faces, "RUN! Get AWAY!"

Before Peter (16) could even get off the table, Noble

exploded into the room, growling and roaring like an animal, blood and black goo smeared sideways across his snarling face. Matty, Mark, Luke, and John's faces shocked white as the ax in their psychotic father's hands was embedded in Peter's back, thwacking into the table beneath him. Peter's eyes stared far off as his siblings screamed in horror.

Noble, determined to destroy the rest of these hideous things that were hurting his ears and his mind, yanked and pulled the ax. With a gushing, sickening belch the ax came loose. Mark, Luke, and John scattered from the table. John (13) fell into the legs of his chair when it tipped over. Noble swung the ax (as if he was defending himself from wolves), and chopped clean through John's left leg, just above the knee, and took off the back leg of the chair with it.

John was wailing in agony, blood spewing from his amputated limb. Matty was still sitting at the table (trembling as he sat in a puddle of piss), watching his father chop away at John, till John no longer made any sounds. Blood had sprayed the white walls and was creeping down in thick ribbons. Finlay was watching the live-action horror movie from his hiding place in the foyer closet. From there he could see straight through the living room and into the dining room. Caught up in the sickening clutches of terror, it hadn't occurred to him to run out the front door.

Mark and Luke had backed themselves into the corner between the living room and dining room, where an archway marked the separation of the two rooms. They were locked in an embrace, crying and babbling, bouncing on their toes in a frightened state of paralysis. Their father kicked pieces of John out of his way as he stumbled toward them, reaching out and swinging that ax.

The two boys suddenly found their legs and ran from the corner, going separate ways in the living room. Luke (10) was dashing toward to stairs, but Noble caught the blue ranger by the back of his costume. Screaming and kicking, Noble raised the little creature into the air. Luke bit into his father's wrist. Noble yelped and flung the boy; Luke slammed into the heavy wooded edge of the coffee table. The glass top shattered when Luke's head and shoulders struck. And then the boy no longer moved.

Mark was screaming at the top of his lungs, standing with his back against the television. Inside the closet, Finlay was shaking his head and crying. He thought that was it for Luke, but no, Noble when nuts with the ax and slashed the body and the coffee table to bits. When he was satisfied with the job, Noble looked up at Mark, the creature's whiny cries piercing behind his bulging, bloodshot eyes. Noble's forehead wrinkles deepened, the groove between his eyebrows thickened. Blood dripped from the tip of his nose.

"Daddy. Daddy, don't hurt me. Don't, Daddy," the boy cried (demonic squeals in Noble's deranged mind).

Mark was shaking his head, trying to decide which way to run, which way might he escape his father's reach, which way! Mark (8) fled toward the dining room, hoping to make it through the kitchen and out the side door, where he would run and keep on running. But Mark never even made it to the dining room.

Noble snatched the boy by the hair and yanked him back with such force, he felt the thing's neck snap! Hanging limply in his arms, he smashed its face down on the table, right next to where Matty sat paralyzed. Without looking, Matty knew what his father was doing when he began to swing his arms up and down, Mark's tiny body at his feet. The familiar sounds it made—oh the sounds it made, those horrible sounds.

When he'd exhausted himself on Mark, Noble raised himself, rolling his shoulders back, snorting and spitting blood on the mess. He came up behind the tiniest of the creatures. Stood there breathing heavily behind Matty. Little Batman was shaking in his seat. Daddy's hand gripped the back of his costume and raised him off the chair.

Finlay crept out of the closet just then. He could see Matty's crazy father holding Matty in the air. And before he could stop himself, his five-year-old voice yelled, "Leave him alone!"

When Noble turned around, Finlay knew he'd made a dreadful mistake. And suddenly, he could see that Matty's dad was not Matty's dad at all, but something wicked. It was there on his face, his confused, maddened face. Noble held Matty out toward Finlay like a stuffed toy and began to shake him and shake him, harder and harder. Matty could barely make a sound as his body jerked about. Tears were running down his cheeks.

Before turning to run out the front door, Finlay saw

his friend's eyes were now closed, and Noble's teeth were bared to him in a Joker smile.

6

Just outside 313, the front door slammed shut on Noble's enraged scream as Finlay fled down the porch steps in the rain. He cut across the muddy front lawn as fast as he could go. Moments later, he turned and saw Noble's dark silhouette tottering up the sidewalk behind him, the ax an extension of his right hand. He started to cry out and scream, but there was no one about to hear him.

Somehow Finlay knew he would never make it home before Mr. Andrews caught up to him. He had to hide—fast—because the madman was catching up (the real Grim Reaper). Finlay's little shoes splashed in the puddles along the sidewalk, the stench of worms was in the air. He saw Mr. Andrews stumble and fall, and that was good, he needed the extra seconds to put more distance between them.

His heart was beating in his throat as he came to the cemetery. There was a low rumble of thunder. Finlay ran along the iron gate looking for a way in. He couldn't climb over because there were spears at the top. Then he discovered a pothole under part of the gate, perhaps dug by a dog or other animal. He started to climb into the groove, under the gate. He could see Mr. Andrews quickly approaching, wielding that ax. This made him struggle even harder.

He'd just pulled his feet inside the gate when Noble

reached down for him but missed. He didn't speak any words but instead growled at the boy, profoundly enraged. He swung the ax over the gate in an attempt to strike the creature with the blackened devil eyes. Finlay got up and ran toward the bushes at the centre of the cemetery. He crouched down under the wet canopy of the dying juniper bushes. And there he waited, panting and overwhelmed with terror.

He could hear Mr. Andrews moving along the gate, trying to find a way in, tapping his ax along the iron bars. Suddenly the rain engine revved up and released a heavy downpour upon them. Thunder crackled overhead. Finlay was shivering from the cold and fear. And then he heard something stir to his left. There could only be one thing making that noise, he thought.

Noble's footsteps dragged along the mud and leaves as he drew nearer to Finlay's hiding spot. His arms were no longer swinging about, and his head was down, eyes feeling like heavy sheets. He entered the circle of trees, where the juniper bushes hid the boy. Finlay could hear him mumbling. Noble looked up to the tops of the trees and bellowed like a dying wolf. He swung the ax in frustration, sticking its sharp edge into the trunk of the closest pine. Finlay gasped.

Noble quickly unstuck his weapon and bent over. When he still couldn't see, he dropped to his hands and knees and laughed. He'd found the creature at last, and now he would finish it off. Finlay crawled farther back into the bushes, branches poking out at him as if trying to force him to get out. That's when he recognized the sound of sirens in the distance. Shaking his head to Mr. Andrews, crying for what could be the last time in his very short life, Finlay kicked at Noble's reaching hand.

"No! Leave me alone! Go away! Go away!"

Noble's fingers dug into the ground just before Finlay's toes. "Go away!" he cried.

And then, as the sirens grew louder, something strange happened. Mr. Andrew's eyes sprang wide. He looked as though he could see something scary beyond Finlay. He clutched at his chest and rolled over onto his back. Finlay watched as he jolted and cringed for moments, the rain washing the grime from is roughly bearded cheeks. The madman gasped loud and deep, and again, then expressed a long breath. And then he was still.

Off in the distance, Finlay heard a woman's voice say, "In there! I saw him go in there!"

More footsteps were drawing near. Finlay just sat there in a shiver, gazing at the dead man. Someone was calling to him, but he couldn't understand it, couldn't recognize his mother's voice. His ears were ringing.

"Fin! Finlay! Oh my god! My baby! Fin," she said, crawling into the bush to retrieve her son. She wrapped him tightly in her arms. He could tell she was weeping, but there was a humming in his ears. Police officers helped carry the boy out of the cemetery and placed him in an ambulance. Amanda sat beside him, rubbing his shoulder vigorously, repeating his name over and over, weeping.

Part 2

1

Finlay turned the shower off, reached out for a towel, and stepped onto the peach rug to dry himself. He used the same towel to wipe the mirror above the sink and stared at his reflection: long eyelashes, full red beard, golden-brown eyes, fashionably cut hair. Thirty years crept up pretty fast on him. He was a handsome man (just as his mother always reminded him), but there was something else in that reflection—depression.

He opened the medicine cabinet and removed a bottle of Lexapro. Finding a medication that worked for him was a long process. This one was no picnic, either. He was drowsy all the time, suffered from diarrhea, headaches, and his hands and feet were often swollen. Not the state of health he'd imagined himself in at this stage in his life.

He swallowed the pill and put the bottle back on the shelf, closed the cabinet, and returned to the sorry image of himself. "Fuck it," he said. Entering his bedroom, he immediately opened the curtains; daylight woke the room. Outside the sky was a dark gray, and though it was 9:30 am, it seemed closer to seven in the evening. For Finlay, it all felt appropriate.

Scott Silver, Finlay's boyfriend of eight years, came

up behind him. He set a cup of coffee down on the dresser for Finlay and embraced him from behind, gently feeling up his furry chest.

"Hey, handsome, how are you this morning?" he said, kissing the back of Finlay's neck.

Finlay placed his hands atop Scott's and smiled. "Okay, I guess."

"This is gonna be good for you. Fresh air, the lake, the beach...me," Scott chuckled.

"If you say so."

"I do," said Scott, releasing his hold and reaching once again for Finlay's coffee to hand it to him. "Drink. I'm gonna cook some eggs and bacon. You want toast with that?"

"Sure."

Scott pulled Finlay's towel loose from around his waist and chucked it on the floor as he walked away, spying and smiling, he said, "Dress in comfy clothes, it's a long drive."

Finlay stood there with his cup in his hand, smiling in his nudity, and shaking his head at Scott's toying.

"Don't bust the yokes," he said.

He was lucky to have a man like Scott in his life. Scott was the sweetest person he'd ever known. He stood one inch taller than Finlay. His eyes were blue, lashes thick; his small nose sat above pretty lips, and soft facial hair that never seemed to grow gave him a youthful look. He and Scott had met at a gay bar when Finlay first moved to Toronto. They were both new to the city at the time, Finlay newer by a few months. Eight years later, the topic of marriage was on the table, but Finlay was the one holding back.

He was jobless, and had been for the last two years or so. And it felt wrong to him to enter into a marriage with Scott when he had nothing to offer financially. Scott didn't see it that way, of course. He loved Finlay and understood the mental anguish he suffered. Money was not an issue for him, especially since he'd inherited his mother's family fortune when she passed eleven years earlier.

By early afternoon, Scott came into the kitchen from outside, smiling at Finlay who was on the phone with his mother.

"Yes, Ma. I know where everything is. You and Dad have a great time and don't worry about me. Scott and I will be fine. Yes. And Scott sends his love. She says she loves you, too, Scott. Okay, Mom. Love you. Have fun in Punta Cana," said Finlay, ending the call.

"Car's packed and ready. Are you?" asked Scott.

"Yeah. You know, they're still pushing me to take over the cottage when they retire in Muskoka. Mom mentions it in every conversation," said Finlay.

"I think we should. Why not. It's a great place. I already offered to buy it from them."

"What? When was this?"

"A while ago. They refused to sell it to us, insisting that we just move in and take over. Your parents are amazing, you know," said Scott.

"Wow. I had no idea. About your offer, I mean."

"Yep. We're all waiting on you, ginger man," said Scott, messing the top of Finlay's hair. "Now let's go. Looks like more rain and I hate driving in the rain."

2

With one stop for gas and one for coffee, Finlay and Scott were now admiring the grand houses along Lakeshore Road. Finlay had taken over the driving at their first stop since it had indeed begun to rain. Scott's 2011 mini cooper rolled up the stone driveway to Finlay's parent's cottage. The two-story, five-bedroom, five baths, private lakefront, three-plus acres property was wonderfully treed.

Why such a large house for a family of three, one might ask. Well, Amanda and Jerry had high hopes of filling the extra rooms with grandchildren. They now accepted the fact that that might never happen. They made the best of it by renting out rooms during the summer months. In this way, they were able to pay off their mortgage in less time than anticipated.

"Wow! I always forget just how beautiful this place is," said Scott.

"Not me. When I'm here, I'm reminded of what a huge disappointment I must be for my parents. All those bedrooms for grandchildren they'll never have."

"Oh my god, Fin. We're not even out of the car yet and already you're bumming me out. Get with the program. We're here to relax and love life, not hate on ourselves."

Finlay parked the car in front of the large detached garage. He leaned over and met Scott's kiss.

"You're right. I'm sorry. I'm an asshole. I promise no more negative comments," he apologized.

"Good. Hey, look, it stopped raining just in time for us to unpack the car. See...good shit happening already."

The next day, Finlay took a stroll around the property while Scott put lunch together. It was still drizzling but the breeze felt refreshing, the smell of pine and sand and clean air filled his lungs with happiness. The cottage boasted a wide wraparound deck and a heated in-ground pool. They still had a week to use it before the groundskeepers came to cover it up for the winter.

Inside, Scott had the radio blaring as he chopped up tomatoes for their salad, singing along to "Snow White" by Streetheart. When Finlay reached the backyard, which faced Lake Erie, he walked to the edge of the lawn to where the sand began. He sat down to watch the rolling waves for a moment, the grass wet under his pants. When his cell rang, he thought it would be Scott, telling him lunch was ready, but it was his mother calling.

"Hi, Ma."

"Fin, honey, did you boys make it okay?"

"Yeah. No problems. House looks great. Thanks for the bottle of wine yous left us."

"That was your father's idea. Listen, the reason I'm calling is because I left a newspaper article in your night-stand for you. Did you find it?"

"No."

"Okay. Well, you should take a look at it. It came a

— 126 —

couple of weeks ago. I just thought you'd want to see it."

"What's it about?"

"Better to see it yourself, Fin. I'd better go now, you're father's getting impatient to head down to the beach. The water here is so clear and magical. One of these times, you and Scotty have got to come with us," said Amanda.

"That would be nice."

"Oh and, Fin, I love you, hon."

"Love you too, Mom."

After lunch, Scott and Finlay headed upstairs to change into their swimsuits. Even though the slight drizzle continued and lightning played over the lake, they'd taken a dip in the pool, anyway. Finlay sat on the bed in his bathing trunks and opened the drawer to his nightstand. He removed the folded newspaper and opened it to where his mother had marked the article of interest.

Finlay's eyes widened immediately at the dark photograph of 313 Aqueduct Street. Quickly he read through the short write-up, which described how neighbors on the street were fed up with the haunting presence of the Andrews home:

Following the brutal killings committed by Noble Andrews of his wife and five sons, and the attempted murder of an Elgin Street boy (present during the ghastly crimes), the house remained uninhabited for 25 years. It was finally condemned in 2008. Over the years neighbors have complained of break-ins and, worse, hearing the cries of children coming from the location at night. Whether fact or fiction, the town of Jolly will finally get its wish in the spring of 2021 when the property will be demolished.

Scott smacked his ass cheeks with both hands and called Finlay's attention from the paper. "Hey, you ready? What's that?"

Finlay folded the paper and quickly rammed it back into the drawer and closed it.

"Nothing," he said. "Just something my mother wanted me to see. Let's go."

Scott let him pass through the doorway ahead of him, glancing back at the nightstand suspiciously.

3

Saturday afternoon around 4:30 pm, Finlay jumped at the opportunity to run an errand for Scott. They needed some particular groceries for the dinner Scott was planning for Sunday. He thought they might go together, but Finlay insisted on going alone. Scott didn't question his motives; he was pretty sure he knew what Finlay had in mind. He'd already sneaked a peek at the secret in Finlay's nightstand. He had no doubt Finlay wanted to drive by 313 Aqueduct Street. And if that's what he needed to do, then Scott was not going to stand in his way.

It was almost six o'clock by the time Finlay parked three houses down from 313. He didn't want to park in front and take the chance of drawing any unwanted attention to himself. The air promised more rain, and the street looked as marvellous as it always had in October. He sauntered up the sidewalk and stopped in front of 313. He thought the house might look smaller to him, now that he was all grown up, but it loomed before him larger than in his nightmares.

He debated whether or not he wanted to get any closer, as if the thing might snap at him. The bushes on either side of the front porch had grown into ghastly shapes over the years. He watched their branches move about in the breeze and shivered. Some of the black shutters had fallen loose; he could see one trapped in the right side bushes. The chimney was missing bricks and several windows were broken, smashed in from thrown rocks, he imagined. The house was a perfect picture of neglect.

He took a few steps up the walkway, which was overgrown with weeds, then stopped. Nausea washed over him suddenly. Finlay swayed on his feet for a moment.

"What the fuck am I doing here?" he wondered.

With a sigh, he tried to shake himself free of the strange sensation running through his body. Turning away from the house, he walked back to the coop. Raindrops were splatting on the windshield. As he drove past the house, another shiver. Moments later, as he raced down the highway toward home, that same feeling of nausea came over him again. He pulled off to the side of the road, opened his door, and vomited.

Scott knew something was wrong with Finlay the moment he walked into the house. Though he claimed to be fine, Scott could tell he was lying; he was pale as if he'd picked up some sickness while he was out. That night, Finlay slept restlessly, talking in his sleep and kicking his feet. A patch of darkness, much thicker than the natural dark, hovered over Finlay.

4

The next morning, Scott noticed an even paler complexion on Finlay. His lips were chapped, eyes bloodshot and carrying extra luggage. He didn't even smile at Scott as he passed to use the washroom. Scott was sitting on the bed just after making it up. He noticed the drawer to Finlay's nightstand was slightly open, the newspaper clipping having stopped it from closing. He reached over to correct the problem but discovered the clipping had been shredded.

When Finlay returned from the washroom, Scott looked at him and gasped, flinging himself backward on the bed in fright. He'd managed to give Finlay a start in the process.

"Jesus! What the hell's the matter with you?" he shouted at Scott.

Not only was Finlay's temper surprising, but Scott was still staring at him with his eyes and mouth wide.

"I thought I saw something when you came in," said Scott.

"I know I look like shit but I didn't think it was that bad."

"No. I'm serious. There was a gray shadow behind you, and I swear long arms were dangling at your sides. I'm not joking, Fin. I swear I saw it! And your face looked like a corpse!"

"Do you see it now?"

"Well...no...but—"

"Okay. Then we're good," said Finlay, gathering clothes from the dresser.

Scott looked back at the nightstand drawer, which he'd closed. He took a deep breath and headed toward the washroom.

"I'll meet you downstairs. Need to shower first," he said, still shaking.

After Scott had left the room, Finlay stared at himself in the floor mirror. Everything looked normal to him, and then, for a moment, his image went black as if someone had turned the light out inside the mirror. He staggered back, the image like a splash of ink. And then, in a flash, it was gone, and his normal image was staring back at him; an expression of terror now replaced the sullen look on his face.

"Holy fuck," he whispered. "He's here. How is he here?"

He ran through his visit at 313, and suddenly he realized Noble's spirit must have latched onto him. This was not a conclusion he'd come to by supposition, but rather, by what he could *feel*. He thought he'd imagined the whole thing, but no, it must've been real! And if Scott saw it, he wasn't just losing his mind. His thoughts reeled with horror. What was he to do now? What did Noble's spirit want with him, to live again, to kill again, to kill *him*?! That had to be it. He was unfinished business. He thought of phoning his mother, then thought better of it. No need to make her worry. She'd think he'd finally lost it.

"Time to spill the beans to Scott," he gulped.

As he descended the stairway, he looked out the windows that followed the staircase down to the ground floor. It was pouring rain. Suddenly, Finlay ran for the downstairs washroom and vomited in the toilet. The bowl was filled with a mixture of blood, leaves, worms, and mud! The stench made him gag even more. Scott came up behind him, having heard him coughing and spewing. When Finlay raised his head and Scott saw what filled the bowl, he stepped out of the room, covering his mouth and nose.

"Fuck! What the hell, Fin? That's some fucked up nasty shit! We gotta get you to the hospital."

Finlay, still on his knees with his head over the bowl, shook his head, puke dripping from his mouth.

"What? Are you fucking crazy? You just barfed up blood and half the garden and shit and you don't want to go to the hospital?"

Finlay continued to shake his head. He spat several times, then reached for a towel and wiped his mouth clean.

"Scott, listen to me. They can't help me," he rasped.

Before saying another word, Scott knew Finlay was right. He watched Finlay flush the toilet and wash his face, rinsing his mouth out. When he turned around, he looked cadaverous.

"You look like shit," Scott said aghast.

He helped him to the living room and sat him down on the red sofa. Finlay was glistening in sweat. Scott ran to the kitchen and returned with a tall glass of water.

"Fin, what the fuck is this? And don't tell me you have the fucking flu, either."

Finlay gulped back the entire glass of water, closed his eyes for a moment, then looked Scott in the eyes and blurted, "Yesterday I went to Matty's house."

"Fuck me. I knew it," said Scott.

"Nothing happened. I didn't go in or anything. Didn't even leave the sidewalk."

"Looks like you got close enough."

"Yeah. But I swear that place has been calling me back all these years. I didn't want to go, but I had to," he explained.

"It was calling you back, all right. And now it's got its claws in you. Fuck, Fin, I'm scared."

They were quiet for a few moments, Finlay with his head down, Scott looking about in thought.

"I've been hearing these strange sounds like voices, or singing. I'm not sure, it's always at a distance like I'm fucking schizophrenic. I know they're trying to tell me something, but I can't quite hear them," Finlay explained.

"Is it *him*? Is it that son of a bitch?"

"No. I know when it's him. I feel weak and far away. These other voices make me feel comforted."

"Comforted?"

"I think I know what I have to do," said Finlay.

Scott didn't like the sound of that. He said, "Please don't tell me it involves going anywhere near that fucking house again."

Finlay nodded. "I have to."

"I fucking knew it. Well, I'm not letting you go alone this time. No fucking way. You don't look like you could even stand right now," Scott observed.

"I want you to come. I don't think I can handle going back into that house alone. I doubt it was ever cleaned after the murders. It might be more than I can bear," Finlay admitted.

"When do we go?"

"Tonight...late. So no one sees us enter."

"Right. And we might not exit, either."

5

Scott and Finlay made the drive from Long Beach to Jolly in silence. The day's rain had turned into a storm by 11:30 pm, it was now 12:58 am, and the storm showed no signs of letting up. As they drove past the cemetery, Scott turned to Finlay, commenting, "Shit. I can't imagine having gone through what you did as a kid. What a fucking nightmare it must have been."

"Pull up over here. We don't want to park too close," said Finlay.

"Wrong. I want to park as close as possible so if I have to make a run for it the car is close by," said Scott, chuckling nervously.

"It's okay, Scott. Everything will be okay."

"I'll believe that when I wake up tomorrow."

Scott put the car in park and turned the engine off, the rain drumming on the roof. He turned to Finlay and said, "Are we sure we want to do this?"

"There's no other way," Finlay sighed, opening his door.

Scott hurried around the car and put Finlay's arm around his shoulder to help him along, every passing moment his body being sapped of its strength by the fiendish spirit. The pair were drenched in seconds. The night was so black, Scott was confident no one would take notice of them entering the Andrews property.

"Okay, Fin, which one is it?" he asked.

Finlay was silent for a few moments as they walked, his feet practically dragging through the puddles. When he finally forced Scott to stop and look up, he said, "This is it."

Scott raised his eyes to see 313 in all its horrifying glory.

"You're fucking with me, right," he said. "This is going to be suicide. Have you looked at this place? I mean *really* looked at this place?"

"Yes, Scott, I know how it looks, but it's still just a house," Finlay said, not believing that himself.

"Right. Just a house. Fuck. We're dead, aren't we."

"Come on. Help me inside before we drown out here," said Finlay, coaxing him on.

They made it round to the back of the house, where Finlay remembered Matty's oldest brother Peter used to sneak in and out of the house through a small basement window. "Right here," said Finlay.

"The basement. Of course," said Scott, nonplussed.

Finlay entered first, not willing or wanting to have Scott face whatever they might face first in there. He'd never been in the basement before. So he had no idea what to expect. Once his eyes had a chance to adjust to the darkness, he still couldn't see shit. But as he stood waiting for Scott to join him, he heard the voices again, singing their haunting melody, calling him in the right direction.

The moment he felt Scott's hand take his, he said, "This way."

They found the staircase and ascended with caution,

feeling their way up the cold concrete wall through cobwebs and watery streams. Scott was jumping at every
touch and every sound, especially when thunder seemed
to bomb the house.

"I don't like this," he whispered, his hand trembling
and wet in Finlay's.

"Shh. It's okay," Finlay assured him.

They passed the side door, where a scant bit of light
shone in, spreading shadows across the kitchen floor.

"Not liking this," Scott whispered to himself.

Finlay froze at the border between the kitchen and
the dining room. Being present in that room was suddenly overwhelming and—real! Scott squeezed his partner's hand, hoping to signal his support (though his instinct was to hightail it the fuck out of there). They just
stood there for what seemed like an hour but was, in reality, less than three minutes.

"Fin?" Scott whispered in his left ear.

Finlay stepped forward, crossing into the threshold
of the dining room. Instantly, Halloween sound effects
and music blared out of nowhere. Black and orange balloons came silently through the ceiling and floated to
the floor, drawing their attention down, down, down
to the bloody mess of chopped up chunks of flesh and
clothing and hair and wood.

Scott screamed!

Finlay was awestruck, his body trembling against
Scott's. He remembered it all—and all at once! First Peter, then John, then Luke the blue ranger, then Mark
the red ranger—made redder with blood—and finally

poor little Matty, Batman Matty, in Noble's big strong hands! Blood pumped out of the walls in the dining room and living room, spraying with a force like fire hoses. Scott had pulled Finlay down to the floor and was covering him as best he could, screaming all the while.

And just like a giant's door had been slammed shut, the house fell back to quiet, leaving only the sounds of the storm outside to claw at the windows. Scott and Finlay raised their heads. Together they rose to their feet. There was a thick mist filling only the living room area. Scott didn't want to move, but Finlay pulled him closer with him. They walked past the dining room table, with its visible damage from an ax, and closer still to the living room.

"No. Stop," Scott begged Finlay, not wanting to get any closer to that thickening fog.

Once it seemed to reach its greatest density, the fog appeared to be drawn away, vacuumed back somewhat into a darker realm. And what it revealed made both Finlay and Scott step back. There was a human shape before them hidden beneath a ghostly black robe, free-flowing in a breeze they could not feel. Scott was pulling on Finlay's hand, trying to get him to back up, but Finlay refused.

"It's okay, Scott. This isn't Noble. I think...I know this was Mrs. Andrews," he said softly, his words floating off.

The robed figure began to spread its unseen arms outward, opening the robe to reveal five tiny skeletal ghosts within. Scott and Finlay could barely believe their eyes. They could hear the crying voices that seemed miles away, and somewhere very deep. Finlay was struck with a heavy heart suddenly. Tears rolled down his cheeks. Their sadness sang to him. Scott was hugging him even tighter now.

The ghostly Mrs. Andrews closed her robe around her children just as Finlay felt a vice grip his brain. He cried out as something scratched the inside of his chest! Scott dropped down with him as he convulsed on the floor, kicking and screaming. When Finlay suddenly fainted, Scott stood and watched as the blackness beneath his body crossed the dining room floor and rose into a shadow that reached from the floor to the ceiling, leaning over as if hunching.

All the windows began to rattle, the wooden chairs danced off the floor, making the most terrifying sound Scott had ever heard. He fell to his knees and tried to rock Finlay awake. The entire house was creaking and cracking like its very bones were splintering. Finlay was finally coming to as Scott dragged him toward the front door.

Noble's shadowy image was crossing back through the dining room, slobbering globs of blood and black goo, his fingers wriggling like snakes. He was coming for Finlay, but something was happening with the ghost of Mrs. Andrews. Scott stopped dragging Finlay as Finlay sat up on his own, feeling rejuvenated. They watched in awe as Noble's monstrous demon stopped cold before the robed phantom, and seemed to somewhat acknowledge her.

Behind him, Noble triggered the dining room and kitchen windows to blow out, taking large portions of their wooden frames with them. The dining room table, as large as it was, rose up and smashed against the back wall, snapping in three pieces. The chandelier ripped from its anchor and crashed to bits against the table. Noble stomped his right foot forward in a failed attempt to intimidate the robed spirit. Scott and Finlay, however, jumped to their feet and backed themselves up against the wall, next to the staircase.

The robed spirit raised her arms and peeled back the hood (Scott and Finlay shuddered in horror). The robe fell to her feet in slow motion, ruffling at the floor and spreading outward like black water. And the thing that was revealed hiding beneath that robe was a reflection of the pain and suffering Gale Andrew's had endured. The sadness of having lost her babies, of having been unable to protect them. She was hideous. A thing of mutated bones strung together with thorny flesh and bruised muscles. A thing so full of shame and anger, her head was a giant skull with a fixed open smile of fangs. And atop her misshapen head were large candles alight with flames of fury.

Noble's demon swayed in circles as it appeared to be measuring her up, comparing her possible strength against his own, perhaps. Scott and Finlay kept looking from one unbelievable, horrific vision to the other. Then, bubbling up from the watery floor about Mrs. Andrew's ghost, smaller versions of herself came hissing and burping forth. The stench of putrefaction pumped into the air like a deadly gas.

Each one of the smaller creatures (five in all) scuttled around to the back of the larger and climbed upon its back until they hung forward like some artist's uncanny sculpture of a monster from the pits of hell. Noble's demon charged at them, but his feet sank into the surrounding flood, and Mrs. Andrew's ghastly children pounced on him at once.

Finlay and Scott couldn't see what was happening within the shadowy struggle, but it must have been excruciatingly painful for Mr. Noble's demon. His cries and screams were the sounds of terror one cannot imagine. They were assaulted by thunderous knocking, bells clanging, screaming, roars, beastly snarls, growls, scratching and squealing. Then the sounds held for a few seconds; then exploded again; held longer; exploded, then held for good.

On the floor, amidst the swirling fog, Finlay and Scott were amazed to see the human form of Noble lying on his back, the water rippling halfway up his body. Then the human form of Gale Andrews came into view. She leaned forward and reached her right arm over Noble's chest. His hand reached for hers. Their five sons appeared around them, all of them trying to embrace their parents. And just before they sank out of sight in an instant, Finlay saw Matty smile and wave to him.

One week later, Scott cozied up next to Finlay on the

sand, looking out over the lake. He put his arm around him and leaned his head on his left shoulder. Finlay was on the phone with his mother.

"Yes, Ma. Everything's good. In fact, it's great. And before I let you go, I have some news for you and Dad. Scott and I...we're getting married."

Spirit Bell

1

Wednesday morning five grade eleven students were waiting by the front doors of Norbrook Secondary School. Each had a suitcase stuffed with clothes for a two-and-a-half-day stay at Leadership Camp. Admittedly, not one of them had any idea what leadership camp was, or what to expect when they arrived there. And not one of them cared, either. A three-day get-out-of-jail-free card was all they had to know.

The five of them had been chosen by the staff to represent their school based on grades, maturity, and whatever else they judged the students by. They'd been told it was an honor to be chosen. They'd nodded and smiled, but again, it was all about the time off.

When the bus rolled up and those doors opened, James (or Jim, as he was called) rushed up those steps first, an ear-to-ear smile on his face. Jim Kesek was always smiling. He and Doug Crown had gone to elementary school together. And Doug could not understand why Jim was performing so well in high school (grades-wise) when he was such a do-nothing shit throughout their elementary days. In fact, Doug hadn't liked him before, at all.

Always struggling to do his best in school, good grades

never came easy for Doug. Especially in Mathematics! In grade six, he'd failed every single math test they were given. The stress of that class left him feeling depressed about everything he did. Why couldn't he grasp numbers the way all his classmates seemed to, he wondered.

And then came high school. He was excelling in all his work, enjoying school for the first time in his life. And now this leadership camp! As Doug entered the bus, he was surprised to see it was nearly full of unfamiliar students from other high schools. They were all grade eleven students. He sat down in the seat opposite the aisle, next to Jim, who was bouncing with excitement and already engaged in conversation with the boy sharing his seat.

Non-identical twin sisters Emily and Melody Johnson entered the bus next. Emily a brunette, Melody a blonde, they were like the sisters Doug never had. They sat in the empty seat behind Jim. Red-haired, freckle-faced Darren Richards was last to board; he and Doug were good friends. He took his place next to Doug. The bus driver spoke with Mr. Landry for a few moments. Once Mr. Landry exited the bus, the doors were sealed shut and they headed out.

Their first stop was at yet another high school to pick up one more group of escapees. This was a group Doug wished had never boarded, especially one student in particular: Enio Ricci. The fact that Enio was a good-looking seventeen-year-old (who could have easily passed for twenty-something), made no difference the instant he opened his mouth. He was so hyper, Jim seemed under sedation in comparison.

If that had been his only flaw, Doug would have had no problem with him, but it wasn't. He was downright annoying, obnoxious, loud, arrogant, and a few more descriptive words that all added up to very unpleasant. Students in the seats around him laughed at his half-witted jokes, including Jim! Doug did not find anything he said remotely humorous.

He'd made eye contact with Doug a few times, and Doug was sure to stare back bemused. He was not going to hide his disdain for this buffoon. The drive took them down some long highways. Doug had no idea where the camp was located; he couldn't recall it being mentioned. It must have taken them a good three-to-four hours to arrive at their destination.

When the bus finally rolled up to the campsite, he wasn't even aware they'd left the highway. They were immediately shuffled into a large building, which was quickly filling up with students from all over the region. No chairs. They had to sit cross-legged on the red carpet floor. Once the students were all accounted for, two male teachers from other high schools introduced themselves and welcomed everyone.

Much to Doug's surprise, Mr. Landry was also there. Doug and his friends were not fond of Mr. Landry. He was a tall dark-haired, brown-eyed man; a strict teacher, and according to many, a pervert. His presence at the camp was an unpleasant surprise to all of them. Mr. Berrek and Mr. Moore explained the purpose of Leadership Camp and the basic rules, which Doug and Jim missed out on because Jim would not stop talking.

Everyone was dismissed, allowed to find their assigned cabins and settle in before the first dinner would be served in the main dining hall. As you can imagine, there was a lot of chatter among the teenagers as they filed out. Emily and Melody had to separate from the boys. The girls' cabins were down the hill to the right, while the boys' cabins were to the left, uphill.

Doug, Jim, and Darren carried their luggage past a large building where the washroom facilities were housed. The cabin they were to sleep in was rather large. Inside there were already several boys messing about, setting up their beds. There was nothing in the cabin but bunk beds, six sets in all.

Doug tossed his duffel bag onto the top bunk to his left, Darren took the bottom bunk, and Jim took a top bunk just across from Doug. And very much to their dismay, Enio was assigned to their cabin.

"Fuck. He's in here," said Darren, who'd already been teased for being ginger by the bully.

Doug turned, his smile melting away. He couldn't believe his shit luck. Somehow he knew there would come a time when he was going to have words with this guy. It seemed inevitable now that they were sharing a cabin. He was already dreading bedtime.

"Just ignore him. He's an asshole," Doug whispered.

"Why the fuck did they stick him in our cabin?" Darren whined.

"What's he even doing here? I thought this camp was for good students," came Jim.

"Maybe his school saw this as an opportunity to get rid of his ass for a couple of days," said Doug, his smile returning.

The others chuckled as Enio and two other boys pummelled each other with their pillows.

"Bunch of idiots," Darren mumbled.

2

Doug and the boys caught up with the Johnson twins in front of the large log cabin that was the dining hall. They were all happy to see each other.

"Hey! So how's your cabin?" asked Emily, slipping her arms into a red hoodie.

"We got stuck with that Enio asshole in ours," Darren complained.

"Bummer," said Melody. "Don't feel so bad. There's a group of stuck-up bitches in our cabin. They just stare at us and whisper shit, instead of making friends."

"Yeah. Real mature-like," added Emily.

"What do you think of Mr. Landry being here?" asked Doug, zipping up his spring jacket. The evening in the woods was already proving to be chilly. After all, they were in October.

"Sucks," said Darren. "I feel like he's gonna be watching everything we do."

"I guess every school sent a teacher. Well, let's get in there and find a seat," said Melody.

"Yeah. Everybody's always racing around here," Doug observed.

"I think it's great! I love camping," Jim admitted. "I go camping with my family every summer."

"Like tent camping?" Emily said as she pulled the door open to the dining hall.

Jim giggled in his nerdy way and nodded. He rushed

in ahead of the others, anxious to rejoin the flock.

The hall was filling up with campers, everyone claiming a spot on the long benches on either side of the wooden tables. And this was not a smorgasbord. Dinner was placed equally upon each table. Bowls of mashed potatoes, gravy, vegetables, bread and butter, and sliced up roast beef was placed before the hungry horde.

But before they could even raise their forks, Mr. Landry stood on a bench at the head table and made a few announcements.

"Tomorrow the day will begin bright and early. By 9 am we will all gather in cabin 'A'. Everyone will be assigned to a group, where they will learn about 'warm fuzzies' and 'cold pricklies!'" he preached.

Everyone laughed at this.

"And tomorrow night," he continued, "following dinner and clean up, there will be a dance right here in the dining hall!"

The building erupted in cheers.

"One more thing," Mr. Landry added. "Enjoy your meal!"

The student applause was quickly replaced with the sound of umpteen forks scraping on plates.

That night after lights out was called, the boys in Doug's cabin (cabin 4) refused to settle down and sleep. He and Darren were under the heavy blankets that were provided for them. Doug and Darren kept their backs to the others, hoping they would just leave them alone.

They did not want to get involved in any shenanigans. Jim, Doug could ascertain, was not in his bed, but was screwing around and laughing at every stupid thing that spewed from Enio's mouth.

Whatever they were doing, there was plenty of shuffling feet and wrestling going on. Then Doug heard Darren say, "Stop that!"

Doug rolled over in his bed to see what was happening. Jim and four other boys were standing behind Enio, who had a leather whip in his right hand. He kept snapping it at the boys' asses. They thought it was just hilarious. Enio looked up at Doug and was about to step onto Darren's bunk to snap his whip at *him*! Doug leaned forward, his eyes slits.

"Fuck off!" he roared.

Enio was taken aback by his forcefulness. He stepped down and didn't say a word. Somehow this brought the game to an abrupt end. Doug turned his back on them again as the cabin fell quiet.

Thursday morning, in the misty predawn hours, Doug set his bed, grabbed his towel, and made for the showers. He didn't see anyone at that time. A tall blonde boy named David was the only other camper he came in contact with. He was urinating at one of the stalls when Doug entered the washroom. Doug had not met this boy yet. He had a handsome face and spoke with a slight Scottish accent. The minute he greeted Doug with his pleasant smile, Doug liked him.

Urinating a couple of stalls away from Doug, David signalled for Doug to look up; the ceiling was plastered with toilet-paper balls.

"Holy shit," said Doug.

"Assholes," David grunted. "I know who did this. It was that Enio guy and his friends. Caught them in the act last night," he explained.

"Oh fuck. Yeah. I know the goof. He's in my cabin. Was whipping the other guys in there last night with a leather kink belt. I can't stand him. I told him to fuck off when he tried to whip me," said Doug, now making his way over to the showers.

"Poor you. I'm in cabin six. It was pretty quiet in there. Nobody bugs me, but then again, they don't talk to me, either," David sulked. "I guess I'm too quiet. Nobody wants to get to know the quiet kids," he added, then laughed.

"I'm Doug. I'm from Chatter Falls. You?" (Doug was hoping he was also from 'Chatter'.)

"David. Fort Erie," he said.

Now, by car, Fort Erie was fairly close to Chatter, but when you're teenagers without vehicles, it might as well be another country.

Doug undressed. He turned one of the showers on and stepped into its hot spray.

"Maybe I'll see you later," David said, smiling as he left Doug to himself.

The day passed rather quickly. At certain times, Doug felt like he was being initiated into some low-grade religious cult. With all their teachings about 'warm fuzzies' (saying nice things to people), and their 'cold pricklies' (saying mean things to people), it all felt a bit childish for a bunch of sixteen and 17-year-old students.

By mid-afternoon, Doug had befriended this tiny, sweet Japanese girl named Amii. She had long black hair, bangs, large-framed glasses, and sparkling diamond earrings. She was so friendly and wanted to know everything about him. She thought everything he said was funny, and he was cute.

At dinner time, Doug entered the dining hall with Darren, Emily, and Melody; Jim was already there, sitting with his new friends. As they scouted the tables for a place to sit, Amii rushed up to Doug and hugged him (a warm fuzzy).

"Doug! You have to come sit with us," she said. "Meet my best friend."

Darren and the twins were exchanging confused looks with one another.

"This is Amii!" Doug yelled to be heard above the cacophony of campers' voices. "We met earlier today!"

"Yeah. We met today," Amii confirmed, smiling.

Darren and the twins shrugged their shoulders and nodded, agreeing to follow Doug's new friend to her table. When they got there, Doug and David were surprised to see each other.

"Hey!" said David, rising from his seat to embrace Doug in a warm hug.

Now Amii was confused. "What? How do you know my friend?" she asked Doug.

"We met this morning in the washroom," he replied.

"Amii and I are best buds at our school," said David, laughing out loud.

David and Amii hogged Doug at dinner, seating him in the middle of them, across from Darren and the twins. His old friends didn't seem to mind; they understood that Doug was a likeable guy.

About fifteen campers volunteered to stay behind after dinner with Mr. Landry to move the tables and benches against the walls in preparation for the nine o'clock dance. At seven-thirty Mr. Moore organized a small campfire, encouraging a handful of campers to join him in singing some pretty hokey songs.

Doug, along with his old friends and his new friends, found themselves a quiet picnic table near enough to the bonfire that they could feel its heat. Amii surprised Doug with a small gift. She placed it on the table before him.

"Wow. Thank you, Amii, but you don't have to give me anything," he said.

"I want to. This is special, Doug. It is called a spirit bell," she began.

"Cool," he said.

"What's a spirit bell?" asked Emily.

"You keep it in your house, or bedroom, or wherever. The sound of the bell is said to keep evil spirits at bay."

"Awesome," said Darren.

"But how do you know it keeps them away? Could it call on them, also?" wondered Melody.

Amii shook her head. "Honestly, my mom and my grandma have always believed it works," she said. "Since I was a little girl, I can remember my mother ringing a bell to cleanse the room she was in."

"Yeah," said David. "I've been to her house when her mom does it."

"Well, if you hear the bell ring and there's no wind, you have a ghost. I hope a friendly ghost, like Casper," said Amii.

Doug picked the bell up and examined the silver and black object. There were fine inscriptions all around it.

"So if I think there's a ghost in my room, I just ring the bell and it sends it away?" he wanted to clarify.

"You got it, Doug," said David, Amii nodding in agreement.

"You're very own Ghostbuster," Darren teased.

"Remember, Doug, it's no joke. The spirit bell works," Amii concluded.

3

Later that night, loud music filled the dining hall. All the campers were enjoying punch, chips, pizza, and dancing. The teachers indulged in a little rum and Coke in celebration of yet another successful camp experience. Unbeknownst to them, a group of boys was missing from the dance hall.

Back at cabin four, Enio and two of his friends were sitting elbow to elbow on the floor. Enio had brought an assortment of toys with him to camp (the leather whip he'd already introduced, among them). Tonight he revealed a thick black candle and wooden matches.

"Let's have a seance," he had suggested earlier in the day. "When everyone else is at the stupid dance, we'll come back here and conjure up some good old spirits, like you're supposed to do at a camp-out."

Under the approving gaze of his fellow conjurers, Enio struck a match and lit the reefer he'd been saving just for this moment. He used the flame to light the candle's wick, the reefer dangling between his lips. Passing the smoke to his right, Enio chuckled.

"This is gonna be good, boys," he promised.

"Do you even know what you're doing?" asked Cranston, a pimply-faced boy with braces and thin blonde hair.

"Duh! I do this all the time. Now shut the fuck up and let me concentrate, dickweed," Enio snapped.

"Okay. Now let me see. I call on—I mean *we* call on the spirits of the woods. To all who can hear me, come forth and show yourselves. Make your presence known. We ask of thee."

The boys were snickering as Enio waved his hands above the candle's flame. Their eyes were bloodshot and burning from the smoke.

"Shut the fuck up, guys. How we gonna hear a response? These things take serious concentration," Enio explained.

The boys held their giggles for a moment, then burst into a fit of laughter, falling back and rolling about. Enio was stomping his feet, he was laughing so hard. Suddenly, the floor buckled. The three startled boys sat up, looking at one another in disbelief.

"What the fuck was that?" shouted Brian, the chubby kid stretching his Ozzy Osbourne jersey to its limit.

Before any of them could even speculate, the floor buckled beneath them a second time. They leapt to their feet in terror, backing away from where the cabin's floorboards were jutting upward as if the shark from *Jaws* was crashing through.

Just as Enio, who was closest to the door, turned to run out, the door itself became like liquid. Brown tendrils spat forth and latched onto Enio's legs and arms, and wound around his torso. When he spun around to plea for his friends to help him, they screamed in terror—Enio's face was twisting, the bones cracking.

Cranston and Brian huddled together on one of the lower bunk beds, unhinged with fear. Enio was trying to reach them, to escape the evil that had ensnared him. The closer he came, the less he looked like himself, and the more he was becoming some foul-smelling, unimaginable demon.

Powerful winds whirled around within the cabin, tossing everything about: blankets, pillows, clothes, mattresses. Doug's duffel bag spun into the air and dropped to the destroyed floor. All his belongings tumbled forth from the open bag, including the spirit bell he'd received from Amii. At once the thing that had been Enio snapped back and vanished within the surface of the door, leaving ripples behind. The floorboards popped and cracked as they reversed back to the way they were (when two boys still had their innocence, and Enio was just a mischievous punk).

4

When Cranston and Brian, both of whom Doug recognized from having seen them at his cabin with Enio, barged into the dining hall in what can only be described as a state of hysteria, Doug moved in closer to hear what was happening. Most of the campers didn't even take notice, what with the blaring music and all the raised voices.

He tugged on David's arm to follow him. Amii and the twins had gone back to their cabins a short while ago, tired of the crowd, and just plain tired. Darren was sitting with a group of guys, watching the girls dance. He was content. It didn't matter where Jim was; he'd been doing his own thing all day, hanging with kids who didn't seem to mind his quirkiness.

Doug and David remained in the shadows as they followed Mr. Moore and Mr. Landry. The two teachers had removed Cranston and Brian from the dance and rushed them to the Teachers' Cabin. They kept hushing Enio's friends, hoping not to draw any attention to the situation, whatever it may be.

Mr. Moore unlocked the cabin door. He and Mr. Landry practically shoved the boys inside. Doug and David sneaked up to the window to peek inside. It wasn't difficult to hear what was being said when all four occupants started to shout at one another.

"What the hell are you talking about, Cranston? This

is unacceptable behavior! Where is Enio now?" Mr. Landry shouted at the top of his voice.

Doug was taken aback by Mr. Landry's temper. He didn't peg the man as a fly-off-the-handle type of guy, but there he was—flown!

"We told you, we don't know!" Brian spat, tears running down his plump cheeks. "He turned into this thing, this—"

Mr. Moore slammed his fist down on a dresser. He spoke through ground teeth, trying his best to not take a swipe at one of these boys. "For fuck…. This story is getting old real fast, boys. If you know what's good for you, you'll drop the bullshit and tell us where Enio is hiding."

"It's not bullshit, Mr. Moore. I swear!" Cranston said, sounding more defiant now than apologetic. "It happened just like we said. Enio tried to do a seance and talk to spirits and something answered! Something smashed through the floor and came out the door and it took him—just like that! We saw him! He turned into a fucking monster!"

Doug and David looked at each other in awe.

"Holy shit!" David whispered. "These guys should go easy on the crack pipe."

Doug nodded. "Come on. Let's go check out the cabin before they do," he said.

As the shouting continued between the two teachers and the two campers, Doug led the way to his cabin. As he and David ran along the wooded path toward number four, their minds spun with questions, their hearts juggled in their chests.

"Should we get Amii and the twins? What about your friend Darren?" David said, the fear detectable in his voice.

"No way. Not yet. We don't have time anyway," Doug countered.

"Yeah. You're right."

They ran right up to number four's door and stopped dead. Doug looked at the door, then back up to David, who was biting his bottom lip.

"You sure you wanna go in?" David asked, his hair tousled by the wind.

Doug put his hand on the handle and turned, pushing the door wide open. David gave a little gasp. The cabin was in shambles. There were no holes in the floor, no Enio dripping from the inner side of the door. It just looked like three assholes dumped everyone's belongings and made a grand mess.

Doug grimaced and said, "Fuck. They ransacked the place. Bunch of assholes. My stuff's been dumped out of my bag. If they've stolen anything..."

"Hey! Check it out!" David interrupted him. "It's the candle they were talking about. You think they did have a seance and something happened?"

Before he could answer, Doug, who was stuffing his clothes back into his bag, noticed the spirit bell Amii gave him was on the floor, beneath Darren's bed. He reached for it, and when he picked it up its unique ding gave David a start.

"Shit," he said. "Amii's spirit bell."

"Yeah. It was under Darren's bed. Hey, you think maybe it rang somehow and that's what scared the thing away that Cranston and Brian are talking about?"

David shrugged his shoulders. "Well, they did say everything went back to normal real quick, and they didn't know why," he said, rubbing his arms.

Doug slipped the bell into the right pocket of his jacket. He and David stiffened when they heard something crashed in the lavatory, which was not more than thirty feet to the right of cabin four.

"What the hell was that?" asked David.

"Maybe the dance is over. Could be guys messing around in there again," Doug guessed.

Together they left the cabin and ventured slowly toward the boys' lavatory.

"Why haven't Mr. Moore and Mr. Whatshisname checked out your cabin yet?" David wondered aloud.

"They probably don't believe Cranston and Brian's story," Doug surmised. "Shhh!"

Approaching the lavatory building, the boys realized they were alone out there. The dance was not over yet; they could hear the music. The trees seemed to be chattering between themselves as the wind played among the yellowing leaves. The bonfire must have been recently doused because they could smell the lingering smoke.

David allowed Doug to keep his lead, pulling the door open and giving him the right-of-way. Once the door hissed closed behind them, they tiptoed farther in. The building was normally well lit with fluorescent lights, but at the moment there seemed to be an electrical failure in progress.

A single bulb above the mirror buzzed and flickered. Doug acknowledged David's grip on the tail of his jacket. They were scared.

"Doug?" David whispered.

"Shhh. Do you hear that?"

"Sounds like, like something dripping?" said David, bumping into Doug when he stopped.

Something was dripping all around them. The entire building began to vibrate; Doug and David huddled closer together, practically hugging. The flickering bulb suddenly shone with such brilliance, it should have exploded. When the bulb's light dimmed to a haunting blood-red glow, Doug and David raised their eyes to the ceiling and screamed.

A creature—a demon!—was hanging upside-down from a cluster of thick, red, dripping vines. Its flesh looked like raw meat, painted with a multitude of colors. A large portion of its head was missing so that it had no eyes or nose, but the cheeks rose up like horns. And when it blasted them with the most spine-chilling wail they'd ever heard, its bloody, toothy jaw seemed to unhinge and stretch down to its chest. The boys were scared witless.

Then the demon reached down toward them with its right arm, its extended fingers like wood. Both Doug and David dropped to the floor, trying to stay out of its deadly grasp. Panic-stricken, they screamed and crawled backward, till their backs met the wall where the urinals were mounted. There was a steady bass moan rattling the sinks and toilets. The showers suddenly burst to life, filling the air with dense steam.

"What do we do?" David shouted, tears rolling down his burning cheeks.

Doug couldn't take his eyes from the demon above. He was transfixed by the sheer horror of it.

David elbowed him. "Doug! Doug!"

Doug finally turned to face his friend, his eyes wide, nostrils flaring. He was shaking his head, confused. David refused to look back at the thing he knew he would never be able to erase from his mind—if they survived the encounter! "Doug! What do we do?" he shouted once more.

The pipes began to bang like a huge fist knocking on a steel door. The demon's fleshy cluster was not a separate appendage, but part of its being. And when the creature moved the flexible vines moved with it. And it was coming closer and closer.

As David and Doug slid themselves along the wall, toward the door, the demon's body curved like rubber in their direction. Closer and closer!

"Hurry, Doug! I don't wanna die!"

Doug's eyes popped wide just then. He dug into his jacket pocket and removed the spirit bell. Holding his arm out toward the demon, he clambered to his feet.

"What are you doing?" David called, remaining in a squatting position.

"See this!" Doug yelled at the demon. "Do you know what this is?"

The demon recoiled at once. It gave a bone-rattling

moan so deep and thunderous, several pipes burst, and the ceramic back-splash tiles cracked, falling loose from the wall.

"I banish you, Demon!   Leave...NOW!" Doug shouted, vigorously ringing the bell.

A sound like a ship's air horn blew. This struck Doug to his core, but he held fast and kept right on ringing that bell. The demon squirmed and clawed at the air, slicing designs through the heavy mist. Its body slithered back inside the vine cluster like a snail retreating into its shell. All the while, Doug rang the bell.

A second horn sounded, this time separating one of the three sinks from the wall. Cracks zigzagged in all directions across the floor, up the walls, crisscrossing on the ceiling. When the third horn blew, the last of the demon's extensions were sucked into a black void, wriggling out of sight. The building's vibrations ceased at once. A few tiles still clapped to pieces on the floor, but everything else fell quiet.

David stood up and gently folded his hands around Doug's hand and the bell. He lowered Doug's arm. "It's okay. You can stop now. It's gone. You did it, Doug. You sent it away," he soothed.

Doug looked him in the eyes, and together they smiled.

"That was fucking intense," breathed Doug.

Just then, the ceiling began to expand. A bubble was growing as though being filled with water. Doug and David stepped back.

"What now?" David fretted.

The bubble grew and grew until it was mere inches from the floor. And suddenly, with a loud tear, Enio's body came tumbling out in a wave of brown sludge. The boy slid a ways toward Doug and David and was panting like a dog. Doug and David looked at one another, then rushed to help Enio up.

"You guys saved my life," he said, blubbering.

"Yeah. We did. You're welcome," said Doug.

5

Mr. Moore, Mr. Berrek, and Mr. Landry were none too happy when they discovered the boys' lavatory building in complete shambles. Enio assumed full responsibility, as he should. Doug and David agreed to keep the whole ordeal to themselves. Besides, even their best friends would not believe them, not even Amii.

Friday morning, following breakfast and speeches, everyone said their goodbyes, exchanged emails, cell numbers, and what have you. Amii gave Doug her tightest hug yet. She removed one of her diamond earrings and traded Doug for his scorpion earring.

"You guys have to come to our school dance. It'll be a blast!" she said.

Doug and David had every intention to hang out together, somehow, no matter what. They were as close as brothers now. (Yes, it felt just like that.) While everyone else had learned about 'warm fuzzies' and 'cold pricklies,' Doug and David had defeated one of the coldest pricklies imaginable.

"I'll miss you," said David, hugging Doug.

"Me too," said Doug.

"See ya soon?"

"You know it."

Incident at Mount Garibaldi

1

Ever been lost? I mean truly lost. Not in traffic, or a mall, but out there—in nature—scared to death and wondering how the hell you ended up as lost and misplaced as an angel in hell. Well, I've been there.

It was 2019, and I was riding a bus from Chapel Hill, Ontario to British Columbia. My lifelong friend Reign Grayson had a cottage home at Mount Garibaldi. He'd invited me to house-sit for him while he spent the winter in Mexico. I was eager to write my next novel and the sanctuary his cottage offered was too enticing to refuse.

I'd bused it as far as I could, but an extreme winter storm forced the cancellation of all routes. Thank the cosmos Reign had forewarned me what to expect, so I'd arrived in the proper gear for this weather. When I expressed my desire to leave the depot, the middle-aged cashier working the concession stand bade me not to trek out alone into the storm. She said I could sleep there overnight and hire a snowmobile to take me up into the mountain in the morning. I paid her for my coffee, and as I looked around at the bus-loads of people all trapped there sniffling, sneezing, coughing, whining, their kids running about and screaming, I thought, *No fucking way!*

I ignored her advice (being the impatient, irrational, stubborn type that I am), and slipped out as soon as I'd finished my coffee. I convinced myself I could make it up to Reign's place because I was determined. Besides, I couldn't stop imagining the warmth of the cottage, lying in front of the fireplace, wrapped in homemade quilts, sipping wine all by myself.

It wasn't dark outside when I left; the mountain was fairly bright, nearly aglow in a pinkish hue. Unfortunately, I was fooled by a lull in the storm, for soon after I'd set out, I was trapped in a whiteout. I wasn't certain how long I'd been walking; I guessed about two to three hours, but it might have only been one. I didn't have a true grasp of time.

Plowing my way through several feet of snow, I berated myself for being so stupid. What the hell was I doing? I'll tell you: I was lost, fucking lost in a fucking blizzard on a fucking mountain, searching for a fucking cottage I'd never even been to before. I'd cursed heaven and earth and Reign (for his generosity); the friendly bitch at the station for being right; my lousy extreme cold weather boots that were not holding up to their guarantee; my tingling fingertips, my lousy hat, scarf, parka, snow pants, and my riding-up-my-ass long johns!

Just as I was on the verge of howling, dropping facedown in the snow, and letting myself freeze to death, I spied the faint but unmistakable glow of light ahead. *Reign's*, I thought. I forced my way up to the front door which was practically buried by the snow, and started to dig my way through.

I fumbled frantically for the key in my backpack that Reign had sent me. At last, I stood with my back against the inside of the door. I dropped my pack, whipped my frozen mittens at my feet, and laughed out loud (admittedly sounding pretty nuts). I could hardly believe I'd made it. And to think I was ready to give up. The warmth in the cabin was quickly melting the ice from my burned cheeks. Exhausted, I wriggled out of my gear and left it in a winter-scented heap. There were a few hot embers in the fireplace. Reign had only left that very afternoon. He knew it wouldn't be long before I arrived to take over.

Though my body screamed for me to give it rest, I stoked the fireplace and soon had a wonderful blaze spreading heat to every corner of the place. Its mellowing glow caressed my face as I snoozed on the plaid sofa before it.

2

I slept as though I hadn't slept in a week. The day's trauma sank away from me. I no longer cared how much snow fell. I was safe now; safe, warm, and smiling as I dreamed.

When I woke, the sun was trying to peek in on me from a tiny crack in a boarded-up window on the upper level of the cabin. There was no staircase, just a ladder to climb up to the bedroom. I stretched out the aches in my body; it seemed I hadn't budged a muscle once I'd fallen asleep. I felt great otherwise. It was a fresh day. I would eat, set up Reign's Underwood (call me nostalgic but I love to type on this antique beauty), and begin "Chapter one!" I announced.

Outside, the blizzard continued to pound the mountain. I wasn't worried; my stay was to be a long one, anyway. Whenever a powerful gust of that frozen wind reverberated up and over the rooftop like a wolf trying to blow the house down, a shiver raced through me.

There wasn't much to the interior of the cabin, nothing that would distract me from my work. Still, I'd expected a pack of playing cards, or hunting and fishing magazines, a few books on a shelf, or even a shitty puzzle! But there was nothing. I wondered what the hell Reign did out here to amuse himself. I wasn't sure whether I should thank him or strangle him. I realize he'd offered quiet with no distractions but, well, some distraction would have been nice. At least, as I discovered in my search, he'd left the bar cabinet fully stocked. I helped myself to a bottle of Black Tower wine, sat at the type-writer, my notes covering the entire surface of the table, and set my fingers to work.

About two hours later, I pushed my chair back and stood. Circling the cabin, I stretched my arms above my head and shook the blood back through my legs. Glancing around, I suddenly realized there were no pictures on any of the walls. Not what I expected from Reign, whose profession is photography. I couldn't believe I hadn't noticed this peculiarity sooner.

I checked the fire, but it was still burning vigorously as if someone other than me was keeping it fed. I tossed in a fresh log just to make myself feel better. I guess I must have worked late into the night after that, for I only quit when my stomach complained of hunger.

At some point, I'd finished the first bottle of wine, and helped myself to a shot of sweet rum. Dinner was a can of beef stew with buttered bread and pickles. I didn't have to ration anything, Reign had made sure I was stocked enough to survive an apocalypse. I sipped another glass of wine, watching the hypnotizing flames. The storm rumbled on the opposite side of the walls as though I was surrounded by highways.

That night, when I could finally drag my lazy ass away from the fire, I climbed the ladder and slept in my friend's bed. I suppose the wine and heat must have impressed my subconscious, for I dreamed of ghosts moving about below. Nearly fully shaped human entities rearranged my notes, stoked the fire, and then stared up at me where I slept; all twelve or thirteen of them, just staring at me for what seemed like hours.

Then I heard the clicking of the typewriter keys and the excited chattering of voices. When I finally woke, I sat bolt upright, listening to my heart hammering in my chest; and I swear to you, those voices fading away. It didn't end abruptly with my waking, but faded, as I said, eerily out of range, till the familiar buckling of the cabin replaced it.

Shaking off the dream as nothing more than my mind adjusting to my new surroundings, I got up, showered, and ate spam and eggs for breakfast. I couldn't see out the windows since Reign had boarded up the place. It still sounded rough outside. I frowned when I saw that the fire still did not need my attention. This was a phenomenon that was troubling.

I sat down, ready to pick up where I'd left off in my book the day before, but gasped and spilled my coffee. An entire page had since been typed—and not by me! It was all just gibberish really, bits of sentences running together as if a bunch of people all added a few words. It was nonsense. Things like: Not today, Pa. We're too late. Mama! She's dead, dead, dead, dead, dead.... Too late. God has forsaken us. No God. Daddy, help me! Help me! Help us...!

This shit freaked the hell out of me. I couldn't type a single word all day. I even avoided going near the table. I was scared. Had someone broken in while I was asleep? That had to be it, I told myself (even though there were no signs of someone having entered). And what about that fucked up fireplace with its ever-burning logs? I agonized over these things.

I flooded my body with alcohol, skipped dinner, and finally dozed off in the fetal position, perspiring on the sofa in front of those magical flames. Again I heard the clicking of the typewriter keys, the whirlwind of eerie voices. I dared not open my eyes, though I could feel the owners of those mysterious voices affecting the sweltering air about me.

I waited until the cabin was quiet before I attempted to rise. I rushed over to the table where I found a second typed sheet of paper with more of the same gibberish. This time the typewriter's keys were lightly dusted with glittering black powder. I feared to touch the stuff, not knowing what it was.

Suddenly the hairs on the back of my neck stood on end, goose-pimples erupted up and down my body. I spun round, an attempted scream knotted up in my throat, eyes bulging. The ghostly images of many children (ages two to seventeen), their feet nonexistent, were hovering a foot off the floor in the room before me. At once I knew they were eleven in all. Two taller images behind them (I knew) were their parents. I would have staggered back in terror, had I been able to move. But I was as frozen as a can of beer left forgotten in a freezer.

They did not appear before me as mist wafting about, or as shapes beneath white sheets. They were a frail lot, whose bony bodies reminded me of photographs I'd seen of Australian soldiers after their release from Japanese captivity in Singapore in 1945. The longer they lingered, the clearer I could see them.

Their hair was mangled and missing patches. Bursts of hideous black veins surfaced just beneath the fine layer of their bluish-white skin. They all wore the same sullen expression on their faces, their eyes like black gelatin, reflective and empty. At the forefront of this macabre family was a boy of about four or five years of age. I nearly pissed my pants when he giggled (okay I pissed my pants).

At that moment, the fire instantly died out, bathing the cabin in frigid darkness. A multitude of embers danced through the ghostly family, and as they did, their bodies grew darker and darker, until they were as black as ash. An overwhelming sense of sadness and fear wrapped itself around me and squeezed. I struggled for breath as frost pricked at my lungs and burned within my throat. My vision was blurring, and I knew that soon I would pass out. But before I did, I saw the entire family explode like a ball of fire! At that instant, I was able to scream, and then I passed out.

3

When next I opened my eyes, I lay in a hospital bed. Reign was leaning over me, smiling.

"What the hell?" I croaked.

"I flew back as soon as I heard," said Reign.

"What happened? Last thing I remember was being at your cabin and—"

"No, buddy. Oh no. You never made it to my place, Frank."

"Sure I did," I insisted.

"Search and Rescue found you unconscious in the abandoned cabin two-and-a-half miles from the station, where you should have stayed your dumb ass."

I shook my head with confusion. "Abandoned? No. There were food and all the supplies you left me. And the fire and the—"

"The what, buddy?"

"Reign, I saw a family there. Eleven kids and their parents. I swear the place was...*haunted*."

Reign squeezed my shoulder, he said: "That place is a shell. No one's lived there since the original owners died back in the 1930s or 40s, I think. I mean, you're lucky it's still standing, or you would have froze to death out there."

The next day Reign drove me up to his cottage, which

looked nothing like the previous cabin. I was convinced I'd dreamt the whole thing while in a state of frozen fever. Reign cancelled his return to Mexico, so I spent the rest of November and December with him, and only returned home after we celebrated New Year's Eve together.

About a month later, I received an email with an attachment from Reign. It read: *Nearly shit myself when I came across this at the local pub. It was one of many old framed clippings decorating the walls. Check it out!*

The clipping showed a badly faded photograph of the Elliotte family. It related the story of how this wonderful Christian family perished when their house caught fire during a blizzard in 1938.

I would have preferred to call this clipping a coincidence; however, as I was unpacking my finished manuscript, I discovered two additional pages. I'm not sure what it all means, but if one should visit my house, one will find those two pages framed and on display in my study. And when questioned about their origin, I'll answer by saying that ghosts were the authors. And I'll swear to it.

Midigonstidiger

1

Shane pulled up to the curb, parking in line behind the other parents' cars, and behind the many school buses. He checked the time on his cell phone, hands trembling. He was nervous about this weekend. So many things to worry about, so much to pack, so many bad feelings over the past months. And now this latest blow from his ex-wife with her announcement that she and her boyfriend of only two months were getting married!

The kids pleaded with him to intervene and talk some sense into their mother. This, he knew, would accomplish nothing. He'd spent the last two years trying to talk sense into April, and look where that got him: divorced, broke, depressed, and unemployed for a time. The last thing he wanted was to engage in another pissing match with her. No. Not this time. The kids would just have to sort out their feelings on this matter.

They'd begrudged him over the divorce as if the ordeal was his fault alone. Knowing their mother couldn't care less what mattered to them, or how they felt, they piled all their hostility at his feet. He was the sensitive one; the one they knew would feel their pain. This weekend was all about reconnecting with one another, about putting the bitterness between his children and himself to rest.

Shane checked the time once more. "Shit," he said. "Come on. Ring already."

Meanwhile, inside the halls of Norbrook Secondary School, Roxy and Riley (the school's only twins), were side by side at their lockers. The bell had just wrung and all the students were rushing about, eager to flee the building for the long weekend ahead.

"Hey, can't wait for the party tomorrow night," said Amanda, opening her locker next to Riley's.

"Haven't you heard yet? There isn't gonna be any party. Our dad's taking us on some stupid weekend up north," said Riley, slamming her locker door.

"What? No way. That totally sucks. I had my outfit picked out and everything," Amanda whined.

"Yeah, it's his pathetic way of trying to bring us closer as a family. I'd rather hang myself," said Roxy.

When the girls stepped through the main doors and exited the building, they looked at each other and frowned, having spotted their father waving to them from behind the wheel of his 1984 Chevy Citation, a rusty white four-door.

"Do we have to?" Riley said.

Roxy shrugged.

"I hope no one sees us."

Their brother, Fender, one year younger than they, was already seated in the back seat with his head down, hair dangling before his eyes.

"Hey, girls," Shane greeted as his daughters climbed inside.

Roxy sat in front. She stuffed her purse and duffel

bag on the floor between her feet, grumbling.

"Bad day?" asked their father.

"Bad weekend," Roxy said.

Shane rolled his eyes to himself. He wasn't expecting the negativity to begin so fast. In the rear, Fender was ignoring Riley's fidgeting by turning up the volume on his stereo headset. *Maybe this is a mistake*, Shane thought. Just as he went to pull away from the curb the car ahead of him sped out, cutting him off.

"Geez, Dad, kill us why don't you," Roxy exaggerated.

The next stop was Daryl's school, two blocks away. Shane hoped his youngest daughter would be in a better mood than her older sisters. Daryl was an intelligent 12-year-old. Her grades were always at the top of her class. Not even the chaos at home could bring her grades down. She was always focused on what she had to do. Lately, though, she seemed to follow along with her siblings, acting out against him. It was becoming more than he could take, and that was the reason there would not be a birthday party with friends; that was the reason for the weekend getaway.

After picking up Daryl, they drove home to their three-bedroom apartment on the third floor of a stuffy old building. Shane had sacrificed any hope of privacy by taking the solarium as his bedroom. Two walls were comprised of sliding glass doors, one a large window, and finally, the fourth wall was solid. He didn't mind. It's not like he was planning to bring anyone home to bed with him soon.

He followed his four kids up the three flights of stairs, listening to them bicker and bitch about having to ruin their plans for this stupid weekend. Shane tried to rush them along in as gentle a manner as possible, not wanting to rouse them more than they already were.

"The sooner we get on the road, the sooner we get there. Then you can settle in and we'll have a late-night dinner," he said.

"Can't you just take Fen and Daryl and leave us here?" said Riley.

"Yeah, Dad, we'll be fine by ourselves," added Roxy.

"No. We're doing this as a family," said Shane.

"Some family," Roxy scowled.

"Why can't we just postpone till another weekend?" said Riley.

"Not happening. I've already paid the deposit on the cabin and it's nonrefundable. We...are...going. Now I don't want to hear another word about it. Get your shit together and let's go."

"Mom's right. You're a monster," Riley snapped.

2

Shane had hoped to be on the road by five o'clock the latest; however, with all the delays from arguing with the twins to Friday night traffic in the city, they didn't make it onto the 401 till after seven. The journey was just beginning and already Shane was exhausted. Departure Lake was a four-hour trip. He figured once they reached Highway 11, he'd allow Fender to take over behind the wheel. Sure, he was underage and unlicensed, but the kid could drive anything.

"Are we almost there? I'm starving," complained Riley.

Daryl said, "And I have to pee."

Fender turned the radio up louder to block his sisters out. They'd listened to nearly four hours of nagging, and even though the music was just adding to Shane's headache, he preferred it over the girls' squawking. Just then his cell rang. Shane straightened up, his legs having been squished in the back seat (he'd surrendered the front seat to Roxy's protests of car sickness). His eyes lit up with the news from his friend Paul that a new position he'd applied for within his company was his.

"That's great news, Paul. Best I've heard in a long time. I'll call you when—" the phone went dead. "Paul? Hello? Shit. I lost the connection."

"Great, now *my* phone's not working. This freaking sucks, Dad. Now, what am I supposed to do all weekend?" Roxy whined.

"I don't know, Roxy. Maybe swim, canoe, enjoy a campfire, spend time with your family for a change," Shane bristled.

"Dad, there's the sign," Fender interrupted.

"Finally," Daryl exhaled.

They pulled off the highway and travelled down a weaving, hilly, stone road that darkened and narrowed the farther into the woods they went.

"Welcome to the middle of nowhere," said Shane.

"What do you mean?" asked Daryl.

"Fen, turn the lights off for a second."

When Fender turned the car lights off the outside world slipped under a cover of dense blackness.

"Woh," sang Daryl.

Fender turned the lights on, bringing the woods back into focus.

"Impressive, Dad. Nothing like crashing us into the trees on this stupid dirt road before we even get there," Roxy bemoaned.

"How long is this road?" said Fender, tiring of the drive.

"I don't know. This is my first time coming here, too, you know. I doubt it's much farther now. Just seems long 'cause we're in the dark," said Shane, trying his best to ignore Roxy's bitching under her breath.

"What if we get attacked by a bear or something?" said Daryl.

"You're so fucked," Fender said.

"Fen!" yelled Shane

"Well, why does she always ask the dumbest things?" Fender went on.

"You're dumb!" Daryl snapped.

"It's not a dumb question. I'm sure there are bears and moose and deer out here. We *are* up north in the bush, Fen. Animals have been known to live here," Shane affirmed.

"Swear to God, if I step in any bear shit and ruin my Pumas," said Riley.

"It's not a farm, for Christ's sake," said Shane, shaking his head.

Fender and Daryl laughed at this, making Riley squint her eyes at them in spite. "Ha Ha. So funny."

"Oh my God. How much longer? I'm sick of being in this car," Roxy groused.

"Dad, I really, *really* have to pee," stressed Daryl.

"Do you want us to stop so you can get out and go beside the car?" said Shane.

"What? No. Are you crazy? I'm not peeing out there!"

"She's not a boy, Dad. Geesh," Roxy put in.

"Really, Rox, I never knew. Thanks for filling me in," Shane grumbled. "She wouldn't be the first female to pee in the wilderness, you know."

"I'm not peeing beside the car," Daryl repeated.

"Then you'll just have to hold it a bit longer. It's your choice."

"Mom would never make us hold our pee for this long," said Riley.

"And you know this 'cause you've been camping with your mother lately?" Shane shot back.

Riley grimaced. "Monster," she whispered.

"Call me that again and I'll—"

"Dad. Dad!" Fender broke in. "I think we're here."

Shane ground his teeth, trying to calm himself. The girls always seemed to know just what buttons to push to set him off. Sometimes it was like arguing with April all over again. *Not this weekend*, he reminded himself.

"Cool! I can see the lake," said Daryl.

"Big deal," said Roxy. "Looks like any other lake."

"Where should I go?" asked Fender.

Shane leaned over the front, in between the seats. "Well, I only see one cottage with a light on. Pull up next to it. That must be the main lodge. You guys can get out and stretch your legs, while I go inside to find the Rothmans."

"Can I come in? They must have a washroom," said Daryl.

"If she's going in, so am I," said Riley.

"Me too," Roxy added.

Shane didn't even argue this time. He sighed as he shook life back into his legs. His watch read 11:34 am.

"Everyone be quiet. It's late and I don't want to disturb these people more than we already have to."

Fender got out of the car last. He stretched and yawned and gazed up at the full moon as its luminescence commanded his attention. Stars glittered in greater numbers and clarity than he'd ever seen them before. He breathed in the brisk air and smelled the pine. If not for his sisters' jabbering voices, he swore he'd be able to hear a cricket a mile away.

"This place is creepy," Roxy groaned.

"Quiet. Someone might hear you," said Shane.

Not that he'd admit it to the girls, but he found the cottage unnerving himself. The moon cast a cold glow upon the old place, outlining its unique architecture. Large trees were incorporated into its design with bearded faces carved into their trunks, and candlelight flickered in the windows. As he led the way up to the doorway, he hushed his daughters once more.

"Hurry, Dad, I have to pee," Daryl reminded him.

Shane knocked lightly on the door.

"Like anyone's gonna hear that," said Roxy, squeezing past her father to knock harder.

"I think I can handle knocking on the door," he said, gently pulling her back.

Just then the door opened to reveal the darkness within. They all remained still, waiting expectantly.

"You all just gonna stand there or you comin' in?" said an elderly man's voice.

The girls gasped in fright and made Shane jump. Finally, Mr. Rothman stuck his head into the moonlight and smiled. He chuckled at his joke. "Gets 'em every time."

Mrs. Rothman's voice called from somewhere within, "Pitch, are you putting the fright into our new guests?"

"Come on in, folks. Don't be shy—we ain't! Come on now," said Mr. Rothman.

The girls shuffled in, keeping close to their father. A soft yellow light came into the room courtesy of the oil lamp Mrs. Rothman was carrying. She set it down on the bar counter her husband was joining her behind. Then she lit a second lamp. As the colorful room came into focus, Shane could feel the girls' tensions ease.

The couple's home was neatly cluttered with flowers and feathers. Rugs from India laid one upon another to cover nearly every inch of the wooden floor. The bar and cupboards behind the couple were made by the hands of a skilled carpenter, with delicately carved designs painted in bright green and orange. Though somewhat busy with all its patterns and color, Shane found the decor rather splendid.

The room wasn't the only thing to come into focus, however; Mr. and Mrs. Rothman were also visible to them now. The house and its owners were a perfect match. They were slim and tall, with skin that looked as thick and gray as an elephant's rump. Their clothes were loose-fitting and had the markings of being homemade (simple patterns and material that would last). Shane approached the desk, unable to stare back into Mr. Rothman's piercing green eyes.

The old man could easily portray the creepy guy at the lonely gas-station in any horror movie. His wispy gray hair was combed back and his beard was shocked with white. His big ears leaned away from the sides of his head. His nose was long, thin, and pointed. And his teeth, well, they were fairly new; he kept popping them in and out of place with clacking sounds. He was a larger man than Shane.

"Good looking bunch," he said, winking at the girls.

Roxy and Riley looked at each other and grimaced.

"Cridigeepidigy (creepy)," Roxy whispered.

Riley nodded.

Mrs. Rothman's eyes lit up. She smiled and said, "Oh, how exciting! You girls speak Idig. Widigelidig-come tidigo Didigepartigidigure Lidigake."

Roxy and Riley's mouths were agape.

"That was cool. What did she say?" asked Daryl.

"I said 'welcome to Departure Lake,'" said Thistle, her voice still sounding quite young for a woman who looked quite old. "I learned it when I was your age. We had such fun around strangers, my sisters and I. I'd forgotten about it till now."

"Yeah. The girls like to use it when they don't want me to know what mean things they're saying about me," Shane explained.

"Dad," rebuked Riley.

Daryl was looking around, wondering where the washroom might be hiding. She elbowed her father to remind him to ask.

"It's right around the corner, dear, help yourself," said Thistle, somehow knowing beforehand what the girl was searching for.

"Thank you," said Daryl, and hurried off.

"Oh, me too," said Roxy, following after her, followed by Riley.

"I'm so sorry we arrived late. It couldn't be helped. I hope we didn't wake you," Shane apologized.

"No, dear, you didn't wake us. A couple of night owls is what we are. With no reason to get up early anymore, we started staying up later and later, till it became a habit," said Thistle, shuffling through a drawer that sounded like it was full of keys. "Here we are a special key for a special weekend."

"You have a lot of renters this weekend?" asked Shane, watching Thistle's head shake from essential tremor. Thistle's skin looked worse than her husband's. Her complexion was golden-brown, with deep wrinkles out-lining her cheeks, and thick folds between her eyes. Her neck looked like ripply sand. She wore a purple scarf around her head that hung over her left shoulder. And when she spoke, Shane could only make out a couple of teeth behind her leathery lips. But when it came to her eyes, the brilliance in the light of those green spheres made him think of a powerful soul.

Pitch chuckled at his question. "Just you and yours. This is a very special weekend," he said.

"Yes. So I've heard. What's so special about it?"

Pitch and Thistle looked at one another, then Thistle said, "It's special because *you're* here, dear."

"Oh. Okay. Well, that's nice. I hope it's as special as you two say it will be," said Shane.

Thistle nodded as she took his right hand and gently placed the key in his palm. "It will be," she said, her voice filled with years of use.

3

By the time the girls returned from the washroom, giggling and whispering between themselves, Shane was standing at the doorway waiting for them. They noticed the absence of the old couple and looked about wonderingly. Shane guided them back outside. Fender was sitting on the hood of the car.

"Holy. Took you long enough," he said, hopping down. "What's going on?"

"The Rothmans are gonna boat us across to the cabin we're staying in. I guess it's that one on the tiny island," said Shane.

"Cool," said Fender.

"Why do they have to bring us? Can't we take a boat by ourselves?" said Riley.

"There's supposed to be a canoe over there for us to use. But I'm guessing they only have one motorboat," said Shane, opening the trunk of the car. "Come on. Let's get everything ready to load while we're waiting. I don't want to trouble these poor people any more than we already have."

Fender grabbed his guitar case and set it down against the car door. "I call dibs on the first shower!" he said.

The twins growled in annoyance. Roxy said, "*I* was gonna take a shower."

"And you still can, just not first," said Shane, piling their gear on the ground. "Daryl, you and Riley start bringing this stuff down to the dock."

"Why do we have to do it?" said Daryl.

"Somebody has to," said Roxy.

Daryl stuck her tongue out at her sister when her back was turned.

"I call dibs on the first bedroom!" Daryl called as she descended the hill toward the dock where bare bulbs were strung on a line, reflecting on the black surface of the calm water.

"If you give her first pick of the bedrooms, Dad, I'm not speaking to you for the whole weekend," warned Roxy.

"Promise?" said Fender.

"Shut up, A-hole."

"Rx, I'm not gonna put up with that kind of language. Maybe you'd best *not* speak all weekend if that's how you're gonna talk," said Shane.

Daryl and Riley had raced each other back up the hill and were arguing over who deserved the best bedroom. Daryl believed she deserved it because she'd laid claim already. Riley believed she and Roxy deserved it because they were the oldest, and there were two of them.

"Keep it down, girls. The entire lake can hear you," said Shane.

"Who cares? I'm not sleeping in some cramped, shitty room all because little miss spidigoididigled bridigat (spoiled brat) sucks up to *daddy*," Riley raved.

"That's enough. We haven't even gotten to the cabin and you guys are already fighting. Give me a break for once," Shane grunted.

"Whatever. Not like we wanted to come here anyway. This is all your idea. We wanted—"

"I know what you wanted!" Shane snapped. "Tough shit. We're here so deal with it."

"*Dad*," Fender whispered, giving his father the heads-up that the Rothmans were nearby.

The couple didn't look as friendly in the dark as they neared, more like a pair of zombies. The children were all quiet.

"All set to go, young people?" asked Pitch.

The kids looked at each other for an answer. Shane nodded and said, "Yes. Everything's good. Our bags are down on the dock, ready to load." There was a forced smile in his voice.

Once the boat was loaded there was barely enough room for them to get in. The Rothmans didn't seem bothered by any of this. They were probably accustomed to the number of unnecessary supplies people brought with them on these weekend getaways. Fender sat near the front, next to Pitch and Thistle. They seemed right at home in their old boat with its sputtering motor.

Shane was at the rear of the boat, finding it difficult to take in the beauty of the night with the girls sitting in the centre of the boat, mumbling their disapproval of everything to each other.

"Smells like piss in this boat," Riley whispered.

"Smidigells lidigike oidigld pidigeopidigle (smells like old people)," said Roxy.

The twins giggled.

Pitch and Thistle glanced at one another in the darkness and grinned.

As the boat neared the dock on the tiny island, the trees seemed to part, slowly revealing the cabin perched on the highest peak. Clouds rumbled over the moon, casting great darkness over everything. Pitch tapped Fender's hand as it rested on the edge of the boat.

"Get ready to jump out with the line," he told the boy.

Fender leapt out and landed on the dock. He quickly wrapped the rope around the wooden post to anchor them in.

"Good boy," said Pitch.

"A natural," said Thistle.

"Okay, young ones, time to climb out. This is your stop," Pitch smiled, lending each one a helping hand.

"Thank God," said Riley.

Those clouds began to rumble louder and louder as they unloaded the gear. Once every last bag was sitting on the dock, Thistle turned to Shane and said, "You'll find everything you need in there, except a phone. There's no phone."

"Thank you so much," said Shane.

"Our pleasure. You remind me of Pitch when he was young, so handsome," she said.

Shane blushed in the dark as his children stared at him in awe.

"Well, thank you," he said.

Fender untied the rope and tossed it down to Pitch's waiting hands. The old man sat down and started the boat's engine. As they backed away from the dock, Mrs. Rothman called out, "Edignjidigoy yidigour stidigay (enjoy your stay)!

Roxy sighed out loud. "Cidigan't widigait tidigo gidigo hidigome (can't wait to go home).

4

As the Rothmans faded into the inky night, the island welcomed the Bruce family with a sudden downpour. The children picked up as many bags as they could and ran for shelter under the cabin's porch roof. A startling flash of pulsating lightning was immediately followed by a chilling detonation of thunder. Shane was the last to make it up the wooden steps to the front door.

"Oh my God! Hurry up, Dad! Let us in already," Riley shouted.

"Relax, Riley, you're not gonna melt," he said breathlessly.

Shane fumbled in his pockets in search of the 'special' key. He found it in the front right pocket of his jeans. Shivering and soaked, he unlocked the door. Daryl pushed it open, anxious to see inside their home away from home. Everyone piled in after her, dragging in their luggage. Much to their amazement, the place was quite spacious, uncluttered, and well lit. *And did not smell like old people.*

"Wow! Nice score, Dad," said Fender.

Shane smiled, pleased with the cabin and pleased with himself, for once. "Well, girls, what do ya think?"

"So, it's not a dump. I still prefer to be home with my friends," said Roxy.

Shane shook his head. "You can be with your friends any time."

"I'm starving!" Daryl said, rubbing her belly.

"I hope you don't expect me and Roxy to cook 'cause that's not gonna happen," Riley scowled.

"No, Riley, I wasn't planning to have you do the cooking. Do you cook at home? So, why would you be expected to cook here? Sometimes I don't know about you girls. As soon as we've settled in, I'll make a pizza."

"Yay," said Daryl, eyeing the wooden staircase that led upstairs to the bedrooms.

The girls raced each other up, pushing and shoving one another. Shane closed his eyes to the noise and shouted, "*I'll* be deciding who gets which room! So don't bother fighting ABOUT IT!"

"Why do you bother?" asked Fender. "You know they're not gonna listen."

"Wishful thinking, I guess," he sighed, fingering his long bangs back off his dripping forehead.

Heavy hits of thunder resonated throughout the cabin. Lightning should have been flashing at the windows, but only darkness filled the frames—no one noticed. Upstairs, there were only three bedrooms. Shane took the smallest, gave the largest to the twins, and Daryl was assigned the middle. Downstairs, Fender was thrilled to occupy a small room next to the kitchen, with a bed and a door that locked, providing the privacy he'd hoped for.

Already strumming away on his acoustic hummingbird, Fender happily settled into his temporary settings. His older sisters, on the other hand, though content with their room, just could not bring themselves to let go of their foiled birthday plans. They intended on making their father regret this weekend, even if it wasn't all that bad.

The thunder sounded as if it was closing in around them, tighter and tighter, moaning deeper and deeper, digging under the very foundation of the cabin. Daryl popped her head into the twins' room, and said, "Hey. Can I sit with you guys? My room feels like it's gonna fall apart."

"You mean from the thunder?" said Roxy.

Daryl nodded.

"It feels the same in here."

"Come in," Riley exhaled.

Daryl leapt onto the queen bed the twins were sharing, and sat next to Riley. "What if it rains all weekend? We'll be stuck in here with nothing to do," Daryl frowned.

"If it does, I'm not stepping foot out of this room. And when is the pizza gonna be ready? I'm starving. I think I've lost weight since we've been here," said Riley.

"How long does it take to make a frigging pizza anyway? If I wasn't so mad at Dad, I'd make it myself," Roxy admitted.

"Why *are* you mad at Dad?" asked Daryl.

The twins looked at one another, then back at their little sister. Riley answered, "Are you serious? He *ruined* our birthday party. Hello!"

Roxy added, "Yeah. All of our friends were gonna be there. Now we look like babies cause our dad cancelled it and brought us up here to Camp Creepy Couple."

The girls were quiet for a moment, then laughed at this description.

"Yeah. What is with them anyway? They look like zombies," said Riley.

"Maybe they died and don't know it," added Daryl.

The girls laughed again.

After getting their fill of pizza, Shane slipped into the kitchen for a few moments. He started to sing Happy Birthday as he came back into the living room with a flat, square, chocolate cake on a platter. Seventeen pink and blue candles were ablaze on it (pink being Roxy's favorite color, and blue Riley's). The twins looked at one another unimpressed, Riley yawning.

"To you," Shane sang. "Well, help me out, guys," he said to Fender and Daryl.

He finished the song by himself and placed the cake on the coffee table that was another piece of Pitch's fine craftsmanship. "Come on, girls. The least you can do is to blow out the candles."

"What's the point?" said Roxy. "You already ruined my birthday wish."

Shane slapped his hands at his sides, frustrated. "That's it. I give up. Here I am baking a fucking cake at, like, two-thirty in the fucking morning, and all you two can do is pout like a couple of babies. This is how you want to act—fine!—have it your way. Make your own fun this weekend, 'cause I've thrown in the towel."

Shane blew the candles out in an angry huff and

stomped back into the kitchen. He had a bottle of brandy he was saving for a cozy campfire, but the moment called for an early sampling.

Back in the living room, the twins were looked insulted. Fender was shaking his head and rolling his eyes. Daryl was fingering the icing off the cake.

"I love chocolate," she said.

"Shut Up, Daryl. You're so stupid," said Roxy, leaving her seat.

"What did I do?" Daryl whined.

"Leave her alone, Roxy. You're just flipping 'cause Dad's right. All you guys care about is yourselves," said Fender.

"Fuck you, Fen," Roxy growled.

Now Riley stood, ready to back her twin. "If you weren't so busy trying to kiss Dad's ass all the time, maybe you'd see that we're right, Fen!"

"What? You don't even make sense. I have no reason to kiss Dad's ass, you moron. Just because I'm not acting like an asshole like you guys, doesn't mean I'm kissing his ass," Fender shot back. "All he ever does is to try to please you guys, and all you do is cause shit. You should move back in with Mom 'cause you're just like her!"

The house rumbled. Logs in the fireplace shifted from the vibrations; sparks leaping out onto the floor.

The twins were stomping up the stairs now. Roxy shouted over her shoulder at her brother, "Fuck off, Fen, you think you know it all, but you don't know shit!"

"I know you're acting like bitches!" Fender yelled with

a chuckle in his voice.

"Asshole!" screamed Riley.

The door upstairs slammed shut. Fender shook his head as he watched Daryl picking bigger and bigger chunks out of the cake.

"What? It's good," she said.

5

After several drinks, Shane walked back into the living room. He looked at his son, Daryl's chocolate-smeared mouth, and the empty chairs where the twins had been sitting.

"Go to bed," he drawled.

Fender and Daryl did not question their father. They crept around him, Fender heading toward the kitchen and his room, Daryl up the stairs. Shane gulped back what was left in his glass and pressed it into the centre of the cake. "Fuck it," he said.

Upstairs, Daryl knocked on her sisters' door but was met with a resounding, "Get lost!" She entered her room and flopped on the bed, still licking her fingers clean. The thunder, which she had been able to ignore downstairs, came again to remind her of its grumbling presence. She turned as the door to her room slowly creaked closed on its own, shutting out the light from the hallway's gas lamps.

Shane dragged himself up the stairs depressed, disillusioned, and disappointed. He felt like he'd used up his bag of tricks. What else could he do to satisfy his children? *Nothing*, he thought. He felt the vibrations of thunder surging through the wooden stair railing beneath his hand. Hot and exhausted from a day that had gone on too long, he closed and locked the washroom door behind him.

"I'm so sick of Fen's shit. He never takes our side. He and Daryl are Dad's favorites. He always treated them better than us. And Mom's a fucking bitch for ditching us and leaving us with him. As soon as I'm old enough, I'm moving out, then I won't have to take anyone's shit again," Roxy rambled.

"We should get a place together," said Riley. "Somewhere they'll never be able to find us."

"Exactly."

"I can't believe he thought we would think that cake was, like, amazing or something. As if. We're seventeen now, not twelve, like Daryl. And did you see how she was digging into it as if it was for her?"

"I know, eh. She pisses me off."

Riley growled with anger, and said, "Oooh. I wish we'd never come here. And now that we really pissed him off, Dad's gonna act like a total monster for the rest of the weekend."

"He *is* a monster," said Roxy.

Then together they repeated it in Idig: "Midigonstidiger."

A boom of thunder, louder than any they'd heard so far, broke around the cabin, its rumbling engine trembling on and on. Riley and Roxy leapt closer to one another with a start. The dark walls of their room seemed to ripple for a moment as if from a shock wave.

"Holy shit! That was scary," said Roxy.

Down at the end of the hallway, his eyes closed, face into the rushing spray of the steaming shower, Shane felt something like a burst of fire throughout his body.

He gasped, slamming his palms against the tiled wall before him. Then it was gone. He took a few relaxing breaths and blamed the sensation on the brandy. The pipes knocked when he turned the shower off. He stepped out onto the tiny carpet and picked up the towel from atop the toilet seat cover.

The walls about him appeared to ripple. Shane closed his eyes. *Overtired*, he thought. Simultaneously, thunder and Shane roared the quiet into submission. Shane dropped to his knees in an uncontrollable tremor. Fireworks were set off throughout his body, every joint popping within, searing with fire without. His bones were changing, splitting apart, then mending back together, stronger, bigger. His heart fired fists of blood into his veins, doubling and tripling their size. His arms stretched, hands widened, and fingers dislocated over and over, until their appearance was more like sticks than fingers.

He gripped his head as his skull expanded, his hair withdrawing into the scalp. Veins pulsated up his muscular neck and over his head. His skin formed bruises in large patches, until all of his flesh matched in color. Within his throat, his voice peeled raw. The blue in his eyes burned yellow and orange, and his teeth ached so that he wished them out.

"Idigi hidigeard sidigomethidiging (I heard something)," said Roxy.

"Me too. What do you think it was?" asked Riley.

Roxy shrugged.

"Should we check it out?" said Riley.

"Are you crazy?"

"I'm pretty sure everyone's in bed. What if that old creep is sneaking in?"

Roxy thought about this. "Okay. But you're leading the way," she said.

Together, they opened the bedroom door and peered out into the hallway. The gas lamp left an eerie glow on the walls and floor, and barely revealed the ceiling within the dark.

"Wasn't that brighter before?" said Riley.

"Maybe Dad turned it down somehow. You know, just while we sleep," said Roxy.

Riley stepped out first, as was agreed upon. She tip-toed a few feet forward, then turned back to her sister, and said, "Come on."

Roxy held tight to her sister's nightgown as they baby-stepped toward the staircase. The gas lamp sat tall on the balustrade before their wide eyes. At the top, looking down, the stairs appeared menacing in the dimmer light. Riley looked at her sister nervously.

"You first?" she whispered.

Roxy shook her head. "No way. Together."

They started downward, one step at a time, now holding each other side by side. The stairway vibrated beneath their bare feet. The last dying embers in the fireplace had not the strength left to reveal what may or may not be lurking below in the quivering shadows. About halfway down, they heard the sound of a door being smashed. The girls screamed and hugged each other tighter.

"Holy shit! What was that?" cried Roxy.

"I don't know. Maybe lightning struck the roof," Riley squeaked.

Within the shadows above something moved; Riley gasped.

"What?" whispered Roxy.

"There's something there!"

They watched for the longest moment, holding their breath, eyes steeled on the top centre of the staircase. It moved again. This time both girls gasped.

"See! I told you," Riley said, squeezing her sister's hand within her own.

A gravelly, distressed voice half snarled, half spoke, "Help...me."

"*Dad?* Is that you?" Roxy trembled.

They waited but no reply came.

"Why isn't he answering?" Riley whispered.

Suddenly, the thing at the top of the stairs stomped forward, the gas lamp light splashing up its body till it set its horrific face aglow. It roared at them like a moaning mummy. The girls screamed as they'd never screamed before. The thing struck the gas lamp, sending it right for them. As they turned to flee, Riley slipped and tumbled down the stairs, pulling Roxy down with her.

Without looking up, they struggled to their feet, oblivious to any injuries they might have suffered. Roxy grabbed her twin by the hand and pulled her toward the front door. But when they got there, the doorknob was missing; and not just missing, but the surface was smooth as if there had never been a knob. Roxy started to bang on the wall, screaming, "Help! Help us! Somebody help us!"

That's when Fender came up behind them and said, "What the hell are you guys doing?"

The girls screamed, startled by his voice. They lunged themselves at him, crying and babbling.

"Woh! What the fuck? Get off me. You gone nuts or something? What's the matter with you?"

"It's coming! We have to get out!" Roxy shouted.

"Please, oh please, Fen, get us out of here!" Riley begged him.

"Slow down. I don't know what you're talking about," he said.

"There's no time. We're trapped in here. Look, the doorknob is gone. It's gonna kill us!" Roxy said, bouncing on her toes.

Fender looked where the doorknob should have been. "What the fuck? That's weird."

The girls started to pull him toward the kitchen in a panic.

"We have to go! Please, Fen, come on," said Riley.

Fender was trying to get free of their hands when they heard the roar again, and it was closer. The twins went hysterical, crying and pawing at their brother.

"What the fuck was that?" Fender croaked.

"Oh my God, it's coming, it's coming," Riley whimpered.

"It's a monster!" Roxy insisted. "It's coming down the stairs!"

The girls' fear finally infected their brother and none

too soon. The thing from upstairs had reached the bottom landing. Fender led his sisters through the kitchen and into his room, slamming the door shut behind them.

"Come on! Help me barricade the door!" he shouted.

Together they began to move every piece of furniture in the room against the door. They even threw the blankets and pillows on top. Then they fell back against the opposite wall, waiting and listening. It was difficult to make out any sounds above the nonstop thunderclaps. The twins were struggling to keep their whimpering under control as Fender moved closer to the blockade, hoping to gain some idea of the thing's location.

"Don't get too close," Roxy sniffled.

"Quiet," Fender hushed her.

They waited and waited, but no attack came. Riley suddenly looked at her sister, then at her brother, and said, "Oh shit. Where's Daryl?"

Roxy gasped. "We left her upstairs. What if it's gone after her?"

Fender rolled his eyes in disbelief. "You fucking left her up there...with that *thing*?"

"We didn't know. We didn't know," Riley said, falling to sobs once again as she hugged her twin.

"What should we do?" asked Roxy.

"We have to get her. We're not leaving her alone," said Fender. "And where's Dad?"

The girls exchanged looks of confusion.

"We never saw him," said Roxy.

Riley said, "Maybe he's with Daryl. Maybe they're

safe, hiding somewhere."

Fender thought for a moment and then said, "Well, we can't just sit on our asses. We have to go find them. Agreed?"

Riley and Roxy nodded with uncertainty.

6

Just as the three teenagers began to tear away their barricade, they felt the floor tremble. Glancing at one another suspiciously, Fender guessed, "Thunder?"

The tremors came again, this time rumbling up the walls, causing the hanging lamp to sway and flicker.

"Hurry, let's get this door open," said Roxy.

Fender and Riley agreed, pulling the furniture away from the door. But the rumbling within the walls grew, and cracks spread from floor to ceiling, opening wider and wider to reveal an endless depth of darkness beyond. The twins were holding each other now, whimpering and screaming with every shutter, leaving their brother to clear the entrance alone.

"Come on! Don't just stand there freaking out, help me!" he shouted.

Just then, the ceiling split from corner to corner. Roxy and Riley screamed as a wave of muck came pouring in. Fender leapt out of the way when debris splashed down next to him. The room was flooding quickly, black snakes filling the cracks in the walls, dumping into the room as though being plowed forth from behind.

Slobbering in tears, Riley cried, "Get me out of here!"

"I'm trying," Fender yelled back. "Maybe if you tried helping me...."

"Why's this happening?" Roxy said, wading through the rising slime. "This can't be real!"

"Feels fucking real enough to me!" Fender said, the snakes slithering about him.

Even after they'd removed the barrier, they could not get the door to budge. "It's no use! There's too much pressure against it. We're trapped!" Fender shouted.

"No! It has to open! Please, please open," Riley was pleading with the door.

More muck barrelled in from the ceiling, and the teenagers rose higher and higher, slapping snakes away from themselves while struggling to stay afloat. The walls lit up in flashes as if filled with lightning. Thunder, which sounded more like the collapsing of a skyscraper, roared into the gaping hole above their heads.

Suddenly the door gave in beneath them. One by one they screamed and were wrenched into the current that swept them out through the opening. They sprawled out on the kitchen floor, lying among the rolling muck and writhing snakes. The walls in Fender's room ceased flashing, the water ceased to flow, and only cold, intense darkness remained.

Soaked and panting, Fender got to his feet and helped his sisters to theirs. Such a chill breathed from his room. The floor seemed to drink the remains of the flood, till there was no sign of muck or snakes. It had all somehow vanished.

"You guys okay?" he asked.

The girls nodded.

"What do we do now? How do we find Dad and Daryl?" asked Riley.

"We start upstairs," said Fender.

"No way. I'm not going back up there. What if that monster thing is up there?" said Roxy.

"Well, unless you can think of a better place to start," Fender snapped.

Roxy and Riley looked at one another, shaking their heads.

"That's what I thought. Come on. Let's see if there's a flashlight in these drawers," said Fender, opening the first kitchen drawer.

"I found one!" Roxy grinned.

"Good. Let me see that," said Fender.

He turned the flashlight on and shone the beam around the room, and as he did so, the cupboards and ceiling began to radiate with an orange-red glow like heated iron. Riley put her arms around Roxy, moaning.

"Fen, what's happening now?" she whined.

"What do I look like a haunted house specialist?" he barked.

"So you *do* think this place is haunted," said Roxy.

"Well, duh, how else do you explain all this shit?" Fender responded. "Now keep quiet and follow me."

The girls tiptoed behind their brother as he led them from the kitchen to the living room. The walls were glowing here as well, and an arcane fog was slowly descending from the ceiling. The constant crackling and groaning of the thunder surrounded them as they huddled behind the sofa.

"I'm scared," Roxy whispered. "Why isn't Dad here to help us, and where the *hell* did that monster thing go?"

"Roxy, we're all scared," said Riley.

"Will you two shut up, I'm trying to listen here," said Fender, shining his flashlight into the dark corners of the immense room.

Suddenly there was movement of shadow to their right. The girls squealed with fear. They ducked down behind the sofa, hands over their mouths to keep from making any sound. Fender held his finger over his lips, giving them the *hush* signal. He switched the flashlight to off.

"Did you see it?" Riley whispered.

Fender nodded and said, "Saw something moving."

"It's that thing. It's gonna find us," Roxy whimpered.

They waited for moments, listening, holding their breath. Fender peeked over the back of the sofa, but the fog had fallen and now there was no way of knowing if anything was lurking about. He shook his head to his trembling sisters.

"I can't see shit now. We'll just have to take our chances and head for the stairs," he said.

Roxy and Riley nodded in agreement.

"Okay. Listen to me. Stay low and try not to make a sound. Our best chance is if we can avoid that fucker, whatever it is. Whatever you do, don't...scream," Fender warned them. He took a deep breath to calm himself, and then flicked the flashlight on. "Okay. Let's go."

Just as he and the girls rose from their hiding spot, something very big and very tall stepped toward them, out of the swirling fog. They froze in terror at the sight of it, the glow from the walls slowly bringing its hideous features into focus. Standing just over eight feet tall, its shoulders were broad and abnormally muscular. It had the general shape of a man's body. Its skin was practically transparent, showing off the maze of raised veins beneath.

White fuzz coated its huge round head like rotting fruit. There were chunks of flesh missing from the corner of its mouth, while black blotches covered the left side of its appalling face. Though it was dark, they could still make out its beady black eyes staring back at them. And at the end of its long arms, fingers that were at least triple in length wriggled at its sides. A low growl rose from deep within its bowels and built to a mind-numbing roar. All at once, Riley, Roxy, and Fender screamed at the top of their lungs.

7

Suddenly the floor heaved beneath them, throwing them into a staggering struggle to remain balanced. The monster erupted in gut-wrenching cries. It grabbed the end of the sofa and shoved it sideways with such force that it rose up and slammed into the far wall, where it remained standing on its end. The beast whipped its head side to side and clawed at its chest as if it was in pain.

With the floor rolling in waves, Roxy fell back on her elbows. Riley's next steps caused her to stumble over her sister and land on her hands and knees beside her. Fender crouched-crawled to his sisters. They held each other tight as they watched the beast's skin stretch and tear, then pull itself back together once the muscles had altered.

The thing roared in agony as its jaw unhinged, skin spreading like dough, bones cracking. Several finger-length fangs jutted forth from the newly formed jaws. Dozens of tiny thorn-like horns punctured through the thing's scalp. And then its eyes filled with a fiery charge, setting them aglow in the smoky darkness.

"Run!" Fender yelled, pulling Roxy, who was closest to him, by the wrist. She, in turn, pulled Riley by her wrist.

The floor felt like beanbags underfoot, slowing their escape. Roxy felt a painful tug at her hand.

"NO!" Riley screamed as the monster yanked her

back into its hulking arms.

"Riley!" Roxy shouted, pulling her hand loose from her brother's grip.

Fender turned in horror at the sight of his sister's puny form within the beast's embrace. He charged the thing, using the flashlight as a weapon, striking the creature's head with all his might. Roxy was trying her best to kick the thing's legs, which were solid as tree trunks. All the while, Riley could only think of one way to break free, but she didn't want to try it. With all three kids kicking and hitting, screaming and crying, the thing raised its head and howled in distress.

Riley took that as her cue and bit down into the tough skin of the thing's forearm. She tasted its warm blood and nearly gagged at the thought of it, but before she could think too long the monster released her with a shove. She landed on her hands and knees. Fender and Roxy immediately ran to help her up. Practically tripping over each others' feet, they raced for the stairway, but stopped dead in their tracks when the beast's next roar sounded like *Sha-a-ne!*

Slowly turning to face the thing, they held each other's hands tight, standing shoulder to shoulder, mouths agape, stupefied.

"No way did it just say that," whispered Riley, still spitting with disgust.

"W-what's it mean? Did it...kill...Dad?" Roxy stuttered.

Fender wasn't saying anything. He just stared.

The fog was replenishing itself, flushing in from out

of nowhere, obscuring the monster from their view. Its shoulders began to rise and fall quicker as though it was losing itself to rage once more. Then the deepest growl rose from the pit of the beast's belly and blasted them with the combined roars of a lion and a bear, the fog visibly agitated from its breath.

Without a moment's hesitation, the kids sprinted up the lopsided stairs, fumbling and crawling as fast as they could. At the top, Fender ran to the right, while the twins ran to the left, screaming. Roxy and Riley banged their fists against Daryl's bedroom door, which seemed to be locked from the inside.

"Daryl! Let us in!" they shouted.

At the opposite end of the hallway, Fender stepped over the splintered remains of the washroom door, peering into the empty room as he hurried past. He charged into his father's bedroom, only to find the bed untouched and the room empty.

"Dad! Dad! Where are you? Dad!" he called.

His thoughts were spinning with panic as his sisters' shouts and their pounding fists grew more intense with every moment. Behind them, there were creaks at the bottom of the staircase—the creature was ascending! Fender added his shouts, kicks, and fists at Daryl's door. No matter how hard they tried, they just could not get a response.

"Oh my God, do you think it got her?" Riley cried, her face suddenly as white as her nightgown.

"Shut up! Don't even say that!" Roxy snapped.

Inside the bedroom, Daryl was sound asleep. There were no sounds of thunder above her roof, no rumbling floors beneath her bed. For Daryl, everything was perfectly normal.

Under the beast's weight, the creaks were getting louder as it lumbered up the stairs.

"Enough of this! She must not be in there or she'd have answered by now," Fender deduced.

"What if you're wrong? What if she is in there and needs our help? Are we just gonna leave her there?" Roxy snapped.

"Oh my God, it must've gotten her! I know it. Oh my God," Riley went on.

Like a horde of ghosts, fog crept up into the hallway from the staircase, and shrouded within its midst was the beast.

"Too late!" Fender shouted, pointing at the thing down the hall.

Riley instinctively bolted for the open door of her and Roxy's room. Roxy and Fender followed, slamming the door shut behind them. Roxy placed the hook lock into its eye and then turned to her brother's raised eyebrows. She shrugged her shoulders and shook her head. "What?" she said.

This time they didn't get the chance to barricade the door. The beast was on the other side already, playing at the doorknob and trying to get inside. Fender and the girls hopped over to the other side of the bed, waiting for the door to come crashing in. But nothing was happening. They waited, ducked down behind the mattress. Nothing. And then they heard a knock and a voice calling out, "Guys? What's going on? Are you there? Let me in."

"Daryl!" Roxy gasped.

Fender leapt onto the bed and rushed to unlock the door. Daryl was standing there in her Wonder Woman nightgown, rubbing the sleep from her eyes. Fender yanked her inside and shut the door.

"Hey," she said annoyed.

Fender hugged her and said, "Where the hell have you been?"

Daryl looked at him and her hiding sisters with puzzlement. "What's with you guys? I was in bed, sleeping, duh. Where do you think?"

"Did you see *it*?" asked Riley, covering her mouth with her hands.

"See what?" said Daryl. "Oh, I get it now. You guys smoked some of Fender's pot, didn't you?"

"What? No. Daryl, there's a monster in the cabin! You must have heard something," said Roxy.

Fender stared at his little sister perplexed.

"A *monster*! You're definitely high," Daryl chuckled.

"No, Daryl, it's true. There's some kind of monster in here. And other weird shit's been happening with the cabin," Fender told her.

"Like what? I haven't heard anything," said Daryl.

"Didn't you feel the house shaking?" said Riley.

Daryl shrugged and shook her head. "Where's Dad? He's gonna be pissed off when he finds out you guys are trying to scare me."

The twins looked wearily at one another, and Fender bowed his head.

"What? What's happened? What did you do to Dad?" Daryl demanded.

"Do?" Roxy echoed. "We didn't do anything!"

"Then where's Dad?"

"We don't know," said Fender. "We can't find him."

Daryl looked from one solemn face to the next, then said, "Well, I'm going to look for him."

When she turned for the door, Fender grabbed her by the arms. He shouted, "No! You can't go out there. It's not safe. That thing's out there. You're safer with us."

"Let me go, Fen. You're scaring me."

"You should be scared. Can't you see we're telling the truth? That thing may have already gotten to Dad. We don't know."

"You're lying! Stop this!" Daryl shouted, tears running down her cheeks.

Behind her, the doorknob was suddenly being jerked right to left. Startled, Daryl flung herself into her brother's arms. The twins were chirping in fear. Fender started to back him and Daryl away from the door. He directed her to climb over the bed and join her sisters, and then he followed. The doorknob stopped moving, and there followed the first complete moment of true silence.

At once thunder coughed three times then boomed! The bedroom door exploded inward, splintering in all directions. Everyone screamed, eyes wide, ears ringing. Daryl saw the thing step into the room and she peed a little. The bed was the only thing standing between them and it. The beast moved forward, its feet dragging, claws twitching at its sides, jaws drooling and snapping at the air.

Fender was looking around, frantically searching for a weapon, a way out, something—anything! With his sisters crying and screaming beside him, his mind swelled with confusion. This was it, there was no weapon and there was no way around the monster.

8

The girls backed themselves into the corner of the room, holding their brother in front of them, their grips on him so tight he could barely breathe. The beast leaned over the bed, reaching out towards them. "Mon-s-s-ster-r-r!" it gurgle-spoke.

The girls hadn't understood, hadn't heard the beast above their shrieking. But Fender's eyes grew round with understanding. The thing's arms were raised to them now as if begging them for something, but what?

"Quiet!" Fender yelled to his sisters. "Quiet! Listen! It's trying to tell us something!"

The girls muffled their whimpers, gasping in tears. They couldn't help but squeal when the beast shook its head and snarled, "M-m-m-mon-s-s-ster-r-r!"

Then the beast staggered and slammed into the left wall, plaster crumbling at its feet. It put its clawed hands to its head and growled in pain. As it fumbled around the bed bellowing, the kids dashed out of its path. Sprinting for the door, Roxy and Riley in the lead, they were thrown off course when the entire room shifted sideways. The twin's luggage spilled forth, scattering about the rocking room.

Tumbling over one another, they struggled in terror to stay away from the beast, which was now mingled among them in the chaos and undergoing some strange metamorphosis. The box-spring and mattress flipped on top of them as the room performed a 360° roll. Fortunately, the room had no dressers to crash upon them, only built-in shelves in the closet.

While helplessly being tossed head over heels, each one of them caught glimpses of the beast's unmaking: Flesh fell away in crimson chunks; muscles popped and split like overcooked wieners, and then their father's raven tattoo on the left side of his chest began to appear on the beast. Daryl spotted it first, then Roxy and Fender, and finally Riley took notice as she rolled right into it. In an instant the room ceased its spinning, leaving the children in a dog-pile, with the beast buried under the bed-sheets. They shook the dizziness from their heads and quickly moved away from the breathing white heap.

"Did you see its chest?" said Fender.

The girls nodded in unison.

There was a moan from the heap, a moan that sounded very familiar. The kids looked at one another. Fender sneaked closer, reached out, and slowly pulled the sheet down.

"Dad!" Daryl cried out.

Shane opened his eyes, the blurry images of his children coming into focus. Fender helped his father to sit up. Shane checked himself mentally; physically he was naked under that sheet.

"Holy fucking shit! Was that real?" said Shane.

Roxy and Riley fell to their knees and hugged him. He hugged all four of his children at once.

"What the fuck, Dad? What happened to you? How

did you turn into that, that...*monster?*" asked Fender.

Roxy and Riley looked at each other, the sudden realization that they might have been the cause of their father's mutation, or at least contributors to the fact, finally hit home.

"Is everyone all right? I don't know what happened. I could see you guys, but I couldn't stop myself. It was like I was watching from outside my body," Shane described.

"We have to get out of here, Dad. This place is haunted or possessed or something!" said Fender.

Just as they started to help their father to his feet, the sheet now wrapped around him, the house gave a disapproving rumble. They looked at each other with foreboding.

"Dad?" said Daryl, taking him by the hand.

"Okay. Let's stay together, make our way down the stairs, and get the hell out of here," said Shane.

"But the door!" said Riley.

"Yeah! There's no way out. The handle is gone!" said Roxy.

"What do we do?" said Daryl, trembling.

"Stay calm. We'll figure a way out once we get down there," Shane said hopefully.

But the rumbling arose again—meaner.

Having never felt more vulnerable in his life, Shane attempted to bury those feelings and be the father his children needed him to be.

"Listen to me! Hold on to each other and don't let go, no matter what happens!" he ordered.

The children nodded, terror etched on their faces.

"Ready?" Shane shouted.

Again the children nodded.

"I love you!" said Shane, leading them through the shifting doorway. In the hallway, deafening breaths whipped about them, and a knocking sound echoed high and low, near and far. They reached the top of the landing, looking down the staircase into the living room. "Come on!"

Quickly, they began to descend the steps, which were now like rubber, making every movement perilous.

"Dad!" Daryl cried.

"Hold on tight!"

By the time they'd made it halfway down, the roof and walls and every part of the cabin became like cotton sheets and ruffled into the great nothingness surrounding them. So there they huddled, stranded on what was left of the staircase, floating within the vastness of this unfathomable space. Everyone was screaming, including Shane, trying desperately to maintain their balance on the rocking platform.

"I'm sorry, Dad!" Riley shouted. "I'm sorry!"

Shane couldn't understand what his daughter was apologizing for, but he held her closer anyway, saying, "It's all right, baby, it's all right!"

A streak of lightning danced around them like a giant cowboy's lasso, blinding them with its scorching fury. And with a sudden pitch, Daryl and Roxy fell into the darkness.

"NO!" Shane cried out, dropping to his knees and

reaching down. "Daryl! Roxy! No No No!"

Their tiny island pitched again and again. Though they tried to hold onto one another, Shane was next to fall from the bucking platform. Fender and Riley screamed as their father's voice faded below. Riley's eyes were round with shock. When Fender caught a glimpse of her face, he knew she'd given up. Just as he leapt to stop her from falling, the platform crumpled out of existence. Both he and Riley plummeted into the depths below, splashing into horrifying darkness.

Meanwhile, Shane was struggling within the watery tomb, arms stroking up and down, legs kicking. The bed-sheet was coiled around him now, restricting his efforts. With the all-encompassing blackness swallowing him up, Shane felt a pang of loneliness like never before. The last of his breath bubbled forth with a gut-wrenching, lung constricting heave. Suddenly, hands gripped his arms and he felt his body being pulled upward. He gasped and choked in the cool air, sunshine glaring in his eyes. Fender and Roxy were towing him to shore. He wanted to help them, but his body was limp.

"We gotcha, Dad. You're gonna be okay," Fender assured him as they swam.

Daryl and Riley helped them drag their father out of the lake and onto the flat rock surface. The kids were hugging him even though he was just lying there. But as the moments passed, Shane was rapidly regaining his strength and his senses. He sat up and found he was somehow still in the same clothes he'd arrived in.

"Are you guys okay?" he asked.

The children were nodding.

"Anyone hurt?"

Heads shook.

It was a beautiful day: clear sky, warm breeze, birds chirruping. Behind them sat the cottage, as warm and inviting as when they'd first set eyes upon it.

"Dad, what the hell did we just experience here?" asked Fender.

Shane shook his head. "Son, I have no fucking idea, but I'm glad it's over," he said, smiling.

The kids once again closed in and hugged their father, and each other. And then they heard the faint sound of an engine and the gurgling of water.

"Hey there!" Pitch called, waving.

"Morning!" Thistle chimed.

Shane and the kids looked at each other perplexed. The boat drew nearer, its happy occupants grinning ear to ear.

"Hello, young people. Enjoying the sunshine are we?" said Pitch, tossing the boat rope to Fender.

"Eager to head home, I see," Thistle nodded, lending a hand to the girls as they climbed aboard.

The family remained speechless as they took a seat and waited to leave the island of horror behind them.

"What about our stuff?" Daryl whispered to her father.

"That's all taken care of, honey. Your car's been packed since dawn," said Pitch, gunning the motor as they headed across the lake. "You all packed it. Don't you remember?"

Heads shook, but no one spoke.

"But how did you...? How did you know to come and get us?" asked Fender.

Pitch looked at the boy and cocked an eyebrow, his eyes glimmering in the sunlight. "Why, the weekend's over, son. You must have had a real fine time to forget the days like that."

Fender looked back at his father and sisters, all mouths gaping.

"You mean.... Are you saying it's Monday?" asked Shane.

Thistle giggled, "Of course it is, dear. Boy, you folks certainly did lose track of time. How nice for you."

The rest of the boat ride was quiet, except for Thistle's humming. She smiled and stared at them, and hummed. The minute they reached the shoreline, Shane and his children were clearly in a hurry to depart from Lake Tomahawk. They stumbled over their insincere thank-yous, rushed up the hill, and practically climbed over each other to get inside the car.

"Oh, Mr. Bruce!" Thistle called.

Everyone watched the old gypsy waddle toward them.

Shane's hand was on the key, ready to turn the engine over. Thistle approached and stuck her face into his window. Pitch was right behind her.

"Yes?" said Shane.

"The key, Mr. Bruce," said Thistle.

Shane looked at the keys at his fingertips. He looked to his right and met his son's frightened eyes, his head subtly shaking.

"Just go, Dad," Roxy whispered from behind.

"Gotta have the key, Mr. Bruce," said Pitch.

"Try your pocket, dear, it's probably there," Thistle suggested.

Shane felt his front pocket, shaking his head as he stared into the old woman's eyes.

"The back pocket, dear," she said.

Shane maneuvered to reach into his back pocket, and there he felt something. He pulled it out and gazed upon the 'special' key, dumbfounded. Thistle took the key from him and smiled.

"There it is our special key," she sang.

"You all have a nice drive back to the city. Watch out for the deer on the path, they can put a scare into ya and cause an accident," Pitch warned as he and Thistle backed away from the car.

Shane simply nodded, too unnerved to respond verbally. He turned the key and the engine revved. Relief smiled on the faces of the children. Putting the car in drive, he tried his best not to spin the tires and fly out of there like his ass was on fire. The Citation crept down the path, out of the Rothmans' view.

"Works every time," Thistle said, elbowing her husband in the ribs.

Pitch chuckled. "Can't dispute the results," he said. Then, placing his arm around Thistle's, "So, who's next?"

Winterthorn

1

In the Fall of 1968, Mrs. Dianna Elizabeth Winterthorn (wife of the self-made millionaire, antique collector, highly sought after artist and somewhat recluse, Daniel Valor Winterthorn) died as a result of hemorrhaging after giving birth to the couple's only son. (Or so the infant's father was told.)

Having chosen to home birth in the comfort of their Chatter Falls manor, Dianna's nursemaid was her younger, and only, sibling, Victoria London. Heedless of her sister's jealousy of her marriage to the handsome millionaire, Dianna died more of shock and heartbreak than that of suffocation under the pressure of the pillow Victoria smothered her with!

Amid Daniel's collapse into sorrow, Victoria offered to help raise her dearly departed sister's newborn. Of course, there was much more boiling in the cauldron of deceit Victoria was brewing. Taking advantage of Dianna's trusting nature, she'd managed to pry Daniel's most guarded secret from her. Her first reaction to this revelation was a delayed burst of laughter. When Dianna hadn't joined her, she realized her sister had been serious.

Dianna (crossing her heart and swearing to God)

claimed that her true love's mother had been abducted by aliens. In the winter of 1986, seventeen-year-old Violet Winterthorn was abducted from her parent's home in northern Ontario, Canada. She'd been missing for several days before finally reappearing at their doorstep, looking as if she'd just crawled out of a swamp. She was hysterical. Gasping in tears, drenched in sweat, and in the throes of labor!

Violet's father carried her up to her bedroom, where he gently set her down on her bed. Her mother worked quickly to undress her, ordering her husband to lock their doors, fetch warm water, cloths, towels, a sterilized knife...and to hurry the hell up!

Lynn and Jake Winterthorn had no time to question anything that was happening, their daughter (whom they were almost certain was still a virgin when she vanished three-and-a-half days ago) was now giving birth! There was so much blood-loss, red pooled beneath Violet.

The baby, with its white-blue eyes wide open, was a seemingly normal male child. Jake cut the umbilical cord. His wife placed the baby in Violet's weak arms. She held him only long enough to name him Daniel. "Mom...Dad," she exhaled and was dead. Lynn and Jake looked at one another in a state of disbelief, overwhelmed with grief, and numbed to their cores. In Lynn's arms, an enigma.

In the years that followed, Daniel grew into a beautiful boy; a sweet, loving, and incredibly intelligent boy (and, oh, so much more). Lynn and Jake could not keep track of their grandson's uncanny talents, or 'tricks', as they came to refer to his amazing (and more than not terrifying) abilities. They were thrown head-first into an existence of secrecy and solitude. There was no subtle introduction to their grandson's inhuman traits; it came right out and smacked them square in their faces!

Shortly after his fifth birthday, on a rainy Tuesday afternoon, Lynn and Jake were sipping their peppermint tea in the dining room, enjoying the lightning show outside. Thunder had been booming steadily, but when the next peel came it sounded as though it had exploded within the very walls of their house. Both Lynn and Jake jumped in their chairs. Lynn put her hand against her chest.

"Oh, my, Jake, is that normal?"

Jake shook his head. His eyes squinted suspiciously as he listened to the sounds about them. Lynn began to tune in herself. "Jake?"

Together, they tip-toed through the living room and found themselves gazing up the staircase. Jake put his hand on the railing and was surprised to feel a tremble beneath his palm. He took Lynn's hand and placed it on the railing below his. He read the fear in her eyes. Lightning flashed in the window behind them, shortly followed by another boom, this one even louder and more heart-stopping than the last.

Lynn snatched her husband by the hand. "Daniel," she said, realizing that if they were afraid of the storm it only made sense that poor little Daniel would be. Jake rushed up the stairs with Lynn right behind him.

Daniel's bedroom was to the right of the landing, his door closed. A strange queasiness befell the couple at once. Jake placed his hand on the doorknob.

"Jake," whispered Lynn, her expression mirroring the same fear he knew was pasted on his face. The same fear that was tingling from his head to his toes. A fear neither of them could account for. They looked down as cold air and water rushed under the door at their feet (Lynn's in knitted slippers; Jake's bare as usual). Lynn took a step back. Jake opened the door.

"Je...zus...Christ!" Jake shouted.

The pressure released from the other side of the door was tremendous. Wind and rain pummelled the couple as they stood transfixed in shock. In the centre of the boy's room, Daniel had his yellow rubber boots on, his yellow raincoat, the hood on his head, and he was dancing in the growing puddle on his carpet, happy as could be.

The ceiling in his room had not collapsed in on itself, nor had it disappeared; but to say that it existed would not be fully or completely correct, either. It was there and not there. Lynn and Jake could see the dark sky above; the heavy rains were coming through the roof, along with the powerful winds. There were glimpses of the ceiling at moments.

Although he'd never once raised his voice to his daughter or his daughter's son, Jake raised his voice now, as surely as the roof was somehow raised.

"Stop it! Stop it now!"

Little Daniel ceased his playing, staring with surprise

at his Grams and Gramps. They had caught him red-handed (or wet-handed).

"Turn this off, Daniel!" Jake shouted. "Please!"

And all at once the entire flood at their feet reversed back up to the sky, taking the wind with it. The ceiling reappeared like a hologram. Jake and Lynn were both gasping. They had no words, not for Daniel, not for each other. Finally, Lynn forced a smile to her grandson, and said, "Daniel, get out of those wet clothes and into something warm, please."

Jake backed out of the room after his wife, closing the door once more. They'd always known there would be something *different* about Daniel; they just didn't expect it to come on such a grand scale. Jake whispered to Lynn on their way back down the stairs.

"Christ almighty. That was some trick."

Victoria had enjoyed her sister's story, but she did not believe for a second that Daniel was an alien offspring. She arrived at her own conclusion to explain away his so-called tricks; something she was already familiar with—witchcraft! Daniel, she figured, was keen on his wife's innocence and knew better than to reveal the true nature of his successes. And whatever magic he had tapped into, she wanted it for herself. Taking Dianna out of the picture was her first step. With the help of three men as mad as she, she was going to take his powers, his wealth, all of it!

Valor hugged his father as tight as he could (Daniel called it the bear hug).

"Can't I come with you?" the eight-year-old begged.

"Val, you'd only be bored. Besides, no other children will be there. This is a grown-up thing. Important people are coming to see Daddy's work, and if they like what they see, they may even purchase one or two," his father explained about the art exhibition.

Valor looked over his shoulder at Victoria. If only he could be alone with his father for even a minute, then he could tell him about the strange men who often came to the manor while he was away. But Victoria never left Daniel's side; the opportunity to tattle had yet to present itself.

She gave Daniel her usual assurances of Valor's safety and well-being during his absence. Valor, even at such a young age, wondered why his father could not see through her over-the-top performances. Daniel kissed his son on the top of his black hair (like his father's).

"Be good, Val," he said, winking to the boy, who winked back with both white-blue eyes (also like his father's).

Valor stood in the open doorway and watched his father descend the concrete steps that widened from top to bottom. Daniel waved to his son as he slid into the back seat of the limousine; Valor waved back, his hand getting caught up in Victoria's red-as-apples hair. He swiped it away with disgust. Victoria's golden eyes narrowed as she watched Daniel's ride wind its way down the lengthy driveway, disappearing round the bend. He'd be returning around midnight. She and her coven had work to do.

Victoria slammed the front door shut, spun on her heels, and pointed in Valor's face.

"Your room...now!"

Valor gave her as miffed a stare as he could muster.

"Fine," she said through ground teeth. She grabbed the boy firmly by the wrist, her long, pointy nails jabbing into his skin.

"Ow! Let go," he said, struggling to break free. But he was no match for his intolerant aunt.

She proceeded to drag him down into the basement, forcing him to fumble down those old steps. He could feel the warm dryness of the upstairs giving way to the cooler dampness of the basement.

"Let go. You're hurting me," he complained.

"Shut up, you little pain in my ass!" she snapped. "I should have smothered you like I did your..." she caught herself just in time. After eight years of this little shit's whining, she'd had quite enough. Tonight was a game-changer. She didn't care what happened with the boy now, as long as her plans came to fruition.

Valor always sensed the darkness in Victoria, and at the moment he could see it like sludge creeping down her body. It was a wonder she could breathe or speak as the blood-streaked goo passed over her lips. Valor understood that no one else could see this but he alone, and that was no comfort.

Still cursing under her breath, Victoria shoved the

boy into the wine cellar. She swung the heavy door shut and placed the 2×4 back into the two braces that held it in a locked position. A rather primitive mechanism that for some reason had never been replaced with a much simpler lock and key.

"Hey!" Valor cried. "What are you doing, Aunt V? Let me out! Dad's not gonna like this, you know."

"Keep your fucking mouth shut for a while and I might let you out!" he heard her shout, the sound of her heels click-clacking back up the stairs.

"Hey!" he called, waited, and nothing.

Valor looked around the dark room. The stench of fermentation clung to the walls. A chill grabbed and shook him where he stood.

Victoria showered and slipped into her favorite dress (black, of course), which fit like a wet-suit. She squeezed her feet into a pair of black heels; accessorized her ears, fingers, and neck with sterling silver jewellery (stars, moons, and the like). Ruby lipstick, black mascara, false lashes, smokey eyes, and topped off with a long, approving smirk at her reflection. She was more than ready for this.

Around 9 pm a single vehicle crept up the driveway, its three occupants playing the caution game. The 1960 Ford Thunderbird rolled up to the front door, then rolled on a little farther and parked. Victoria was watching through a window in the foyer. She smiled. Her coven had arrived.

Coming first up the walkway was Roman Straud: handsome, muscular, gay. A sharp-tongued, twenty-four-year-old DJ with a freshly shaved head, well-groomed beard, and tailor-made suit (deep purple). Roman was the kind of guy who didn't bother to wait till your back was turned to stab you; he enjoyed the look on your face when you felt his blade. And that's why Victoria loved him like the brother she never had.

Next came Jonas Haze (28-years-old). He'd inherited a small fortune from his parents who died in a mysterious house fire. He reckoned himself a cowboy rock star, donning snakeskin cowboy boots and matching hat, oversized belt buckles, tight jeans, and pirate fashions like white shirts with ruffles. Perhaps he attempted to draw attention away from the fact that he measured at just under 5'4—with a tall hat!

All three men were dangerous, but the last in line most of all. Twenty-nine-year-old Tane Mathews was the proud owner of the black beauty they'd arrived in, and more importantly, Victoria's lover. Tane had spent the latter half of his life as a member of several covens. He was quite knowledgeable in dark magic, spell-casting, and conjuring. He and Victoria had met during a coven meeting with the Black Stars Chapter. Victoria had suggested that she and he were much greater than the halfwits running the Black Star's shit show. Tane concurred.

Victoria's heart fluttered when she saw him, his black hair hiding his black eyes. He was dressed in a black velvet and leather, high-collared, tight-fitting long coat. His black leather pants were tucked snugly within his black skull and bone buckle, mid-calf boots. Victoria quivered between her legs.

She composed herself before opening the door. Greeting her on the other side was not Roman, but Tane himself. He reached for her hand, raised it to his lips (large silver punk rings on his fingers), and kissed. Victoria licked her lips.

"Princess," he said.

"Tane. Boys," Victoria said, looking over Tane's shoulder to the others. "Welcome."

"Are we all set for this evening's service?" asked Tane, his smooth voice trickling down her spine.

"Yes, we are."

Tane peeked inside the immense foyer. "And what about the little bastard?"

"I put him where he won't be a bother," she said. "Come in, gentlemen. Our guest of honor should be returning any time now. We wouldn't want him discovering you on his doorstep. And besides, I'm quite anxious to sample his Armand De Brignac."

"Champagne? Now you're talking," said Roman.

The sound of Victoria calling his father's name woke Valor on the concrete floor. At first, he'd forgotten where he was. As he rose, his left shoulder aching and stiff, it all came back to him. Victoria called out a second time, shouting just outside the wine room door. Valor stood and staggered over to the door, a fraction of light shining underneath.

Upstairs, Daniel was already suspicious of the car parked in his lot. He was exhausted from the exhibition and eager to kiss his son goodnight before retiring himself.

"Victoria? Victoria, where are you? Whose car is parked out front? Do you have a guest? Victoria?" he shouted.

Valor began to pound on the locked door, calling, "Dad! Daddy! Down here! Help me, Daddy!"

"Valor?" called Daniel. He followed the sound of his son's voice to the basement door, wondering what the hell was going on. At this hour his son should have been in bed. When he opened the basement door, he could see light flickering from the opposite end of the darkness. "Valor?"

"Daddy!"

Suddenly fearful for his son, Daniel raced down the stairs and stopped at the wine room door, which was boarded.

"Val?" he called again.

"Dad!" the boy said with excitement.

Just as Daniel was about to raise the 2×4, he felt an intense crack at the back of his head. He turned around, wavering, his memory failing to recognize his assailants; then he whispered incoherently, his eyes rolled up, and finally, he went down hard.

"And the motherfucker is out!" said Roman, laughing.

"Dad?" came Valor.

"Shut your fucking mouth, kid, or you'll be next," Tane threatened.

"Leave him alone! Leave my dad alone," Valor cried.

"Leave my dad alone," Roman mocked. He and Jonas laughed at the joke.

The boy could hear the sound of his father's body being dragged off to the left, toward the room Daniel used for storage. There was some commotion for about ten minutes, then silence snaked through the basement. Valor got on his belly and put his ear to the crack under the door. He could hear Tane's voice muttering. The others responded in singsong gibberish. Valor could not understand what they were up to, but if he could see them, he'd probably see that strange, sickly goo running down all their bodies.

"Nothing's fucking happening," Jonas complained, bored with Tane's cheap sideshow performance.

"Yeah, what the fuck, Tane? You said this spell was foolproof. Well, look at us—a bunch of fools," Roman said, setting his candle on the table.

"Is he still breathing?" asked Jonas. "Fuck. I think you struck him too hard with that fucking brick."

"Goddammit, Tane, did you have to hit him so hard? He's supposed to be alive for this to work. Killing him before gaining his power was not part of the plan," Victoria sneered at him.

Tane grabbed Daniel by his hair and raised his head; when he let go, his hand was covered in blood. "Ahh fuck. Fuck!" he shouted.

Roman stepped up and felt for a pulse at Daniel's

throat, then at his wrist. "Shit. This guy's as dead as Pete Burns."

"What?" said Jonas. "Already? Some power."

"Oh, shut up, Jonas," Victoria said, then turned her angry eyes to Tane, who was leaning back against the brick fireplace. "Well, fine job of just knocking him unconscious. Do you know how much fucking planning I put into this? Do you?" she screamed.

"Oh, and here we go," Tane sighed.

"Fuck you, Tane. I killed my sister for this night. All you had to do was get him in the fucking chair, say the goddamned words, and we'd all be on our way to great wealth and happiness! But no. You whack the fucker like you're up to bat (she struck the burning candles off the table with a wide swing) and fuck the whole thing up!"

"Oh, shit!" came Roman, stepping away from where the candles landed and caught the old, fraying carpet on fire.

"Shit. Does that fireplace run on gas?" Jonas wondered.

The four of them looked at one another. Tane growled under his breath, eyeing Victoria. He then grabbed her by the wrist and hurried out of the room, followed by Jonas and Roman. As they rushed past the wine room door, Jonas asked, "Hey, what about the kid?"

"You want him?" asked Tane.

"No."

"Then shut the fuck up and move your ass."

At the end of the hallway, flames spread up and

around Daniel's body (Valor was screaming in his prison). Upstairs, the front door was left open to the night. Tane drove a safe distance down the driveway and stopped the car. They all four stepped out to watch Winterthorn Manor's final moments of existence.

"Shouldn't we be hightailing it out of here?" Jonas said nervously.

"You worry too much," said Roman.

Inside the wine room, Valor faced the door. His eyes were glowing, the air humming about him. Corks began to launch from the bottles in the racks lining the walls. Valor stared at the door, the door, no more door, no more door.... The 2×4 and the door itself began to stretch outward. And just like the water balloons he had had at his eighth birthday party, the rubber gave, exploding into liquid!

Valor hurried out of the room, the hallway a tunnel of smoke and heat. He raced up the stairs to find the front door ajar, and he could see his father's murderers in the distance. Quickly, he ran for the back door and headed across the lush grass toward the wooded area. Just as he reached the edge of his father's property, a great explosion rocked the earth. Valor turned with a start; his home was gone.

Shaking her head with bitterness, Victoria climbed back into Tane's Thunderbird. "Great. Just great. Now what?" she said.

Tane drove on. "Now, princess, we find out who is

next in line for Valor's inheritance," he said slyly.

With a self-assured smile on her face, Victoria settled into her seat.

2 — Fifteen Years Later

Locating Straud couldn't have been simpler. All Valor had to do was look up Martini bars in the local yellow pages, where he found Roman's Martini Bar on 3rd Street, downtown Thunder Bay. Bringing an end to Roman Straud was as easy as ordering him a Dirty Bloody Martini (a hint of the evening to come) and winking when he nodded to thank you.

Roman had been ruffling his feathers all night in a brazen attempt to seduce one of the young men in his establishment. He'd had plenty of hits, but none of those were what he was looking for. Valor, however, knew exactly what he was craving, and so became his burning desire. And if his favorite martini wasn't enough to snag him, the wink locked him in.

Roman rose from his seat, brushed the circle of delicious young meat out of his way, and slithered right up to Valor.

"You know your way straight to a man's heart," he said, raising his glass in a cheering motion. "Welcome to my humble venture. I'm the owner of this place. Roman. Roman Straud. And the pleasure to meet you is all mine."

Inside, Valor was cringing at the sound of his voice. His hatred toward this man was immeasurable. He wanted to tear him apart in ways that would horrify the Devil himself. But that would have to wait. The game had only just begun.

Valor gave him his very best bashful smile. He said, "Wonderful place, Mr. Straud. You seem to have done well for yourself."

"Thank you. And, please, call me Roman."

"Sure thing, Roman," Valor said, slowly placing his straw to his lips to drink from his tall glass of lemon-lime water. (A clear mind was necessary for the many tricks he was going to perform on this night.)

Roman could not stop staring at this handsome conquest. His black hair was styled somewhat like a Japanese anime character. A rough beard showed off the perfect jawline and brought out the ruby in his plump lips. He was wearing a black Steampunk fashion, mid-length coat, with the collar open just enough to reveal a tuft of dark chest hair. And for the benefit of keeping his identity hidden, Valor's white-blue eyes appeared dark to Roman.

"Say, uh, would you like to join me for a nightcap at my house? Perhaps if the mood so strikes, we might even indulge in a little hot tub time," Roman offered.

Valor sipped the last of his water and placed the glass on the bar. He turned to Roman and said, "Ready when you are."

Oozing with pride, Roman gulped back his martini and slid the glass over the bar, giving a (look what I'm going to fuck) wink to the moustached, shirtless bartender. Valor followed him out the back doors to the private parking lot behind the building. Roman pulled his keys out of his pocket, eager to show off his 2019

Belize Blue McLaren 720S Spider.

Valor nodded and smiled his approval of the ride. *Part of my inheritance*, he thought.

"As you can see, business has been good, *very* good," Roman bragged, climbing in behind the wheel.

As they drove, Roman slipped a disc in the car's stereo. Rave music instantly pounded through the speakers.

"I love this stuff!" he shouted. "So alive!"

He kept glancing in Valor's direction, his head bouncing to the heavy bass beat. "Say, you from around here?"

Valor shook his head, purposely licking his lips when he knew Roman was watching. *Keep him hungry.*

Thirty minutes later, on a dark back road, they pulled into a hidden driveway and were met by a monstrous wrought iron gate. Roman punched a code into his cell phone and the gates opened inward. The path leading up to his not-so-humble abode was edged by towering bushes on either side, giving one the sensation of being in a maze.

Roman pulled up to his house and put the car in park, allowing its headlights to shine up at his colossal mansion. It was exactly the type of sybaritic piece of real estate Valor expected it to be. When he cut the engine and the headlights went out, blackness solidified around them. Roman couldn't help but lean in for a quick (and very wet) kiss. The instant he opened his door, a startling crack of thunder and blinding flash of lightning signalled a torrential downpour. (A trick as simple as finger-snapping.)

They raced under the shelter of a large veranda. Standing there drenched, Roman moved in for a quick second kiss on the lips. They smiled at one another. (Valor wanted to bite his face off!) With the flick of a single switch, the house came to life with several artificial candle sconces along the walls and leading up the winding white staircase.

Roman signalled Valor to follow him upstairs, quickly stripping out of his slopping wet clothes. Valor followed in the same manner, littering the stairwell, right up into his bedroom.

"Light," said Roman, and his room lit up with soft light.

When Valor stepped into the doorway, he couldn't help but giggle under his breath. The room was the first aspect of Roman to catch him off guard. There was no black gothic style here. There was no black anywhere. The room was completely white, with a hint of red in pillows, a large carpet, and an oil painting. But so much white.

"Oh, we're going to make a mess in here," he whispered.

Roman grabbed hold of the white covers on his king-size Japanese style bed, roughly tossing them down. Then he threw himself on his back diagonally, grinning from ear to ear at his reflection in the mirror on the ceiling. The house began to tremble; Roman didn't even notice. Valor slowly stepped up to the bed and stopped, staring down at the unsuspecting thirty-nine-year-old.

Roman spread his legs wide, allowing Valor room to

place his knee as he moved on top of him. Valor could feel the heat of his body, smell the anticipation, hear his unbridled heart racing. He kissed him, and the kiss was full of emotion—a goodbye kiss.

Valor reached down and gently cupped Roman's balls in his left hand, Roman sighing with pleasure, and then he squeezed.

"Woe," Roman said surprised. "Easy there."

"What's the matter, Roman, I thought pain was your forte?"

Roman's eyes shut in agony as his guest squeezed again, a little tighter. "What the fuck, man?"

"I know it's been a while, fifteen years to be precise. But surely you haven't forgotten me already...Roman."

Roman's eyes shot wide open, staring directly into Valor's now white-blue, glowing eyes.

"No," he said in disbelief. "You died. You died!"

Valor squeezed him again. "Does this feel dead to you?" he growled.

Squirming and groaning, Roman spoke through ground teeth. "It wasn't me. I swear. Tane killed your father. Tane! It was all his and Victoria's idea. I swear to you, Val."

"Don't call me that! Only my father called me that. I know what you did, what you took part in, what you gained from my father's death...and mine."

"You can't prove anything," Roman grunted.

"Prove? You silly fuck. I'm not here to get proof of what I already know."

"Then what? What do you want from me...money?"

Valor guffawed. "All this already belongs to me! No, Roman, I'm here for revenge. I'm here to take back my life! The life you and your conniving friends stole from me."

"Let go of me and get the *hell* out of my house!" Roman shouted.

Valor released him and crawled back off the bed. Roman struggled but could not move a muscle under Valor's gaze.

"Funny you should say, because hell *is* in your house tonight," Valor sneered. He took a step back. "For my father, you black-hearted *fuck*."

Roman raised his head (the only part of his body he had control of) as the sensation of many fingers reached up from beneath him. He screamed and pleaded as he felt himself rise off the bed, slowly at first, and then...

"No, Valor, please."

...he was launched upward and bashed into the mirror with such inconceivable force, his bones crumbled like potato chips. Shards of glass rained down on the bed.

Eyes glowing, Valor spun the man around, mid-air, so that now he was looking down upon his bed. Bloodied and barely conscious, Roman still pleaded.

"Valor, don't. I'll give it back. I'll give it all back."

"Can you give my father back?"

No response.

"Then you have nothing to bargain with. Oh, and one more thing, Roman. Fuck...you."

The sheets on Roman's bed began to ruffle and move

on their own—alive! He was aware just enough to acknowledge the impossible happening. It did occur to him that Victoria had been right about Daniel's powers all those years ago. Except this was like no witchcraft shit he'd ever seen.

The sheets rose and were manipulated into a bed of blades. And with the same unseen force that had introduced him to the ceiling, Roman was now swinging side to side in a reverse position to the blade in Edgar Allan Poe's *The Pit and the Pendulum*. Valor stood there just long enough to see the first slices spray the white walls, then he backed out of the room and the door closed. He entered the extravagant washroom, where he soaked in the Jacuzzi, washing the night from his body. Once he was dressed, he took Roman's keys and exited the mansion.

The storm had subsided, as he'd desired it to do. As he sat in the McLaren, he checked the glove-box and discovered a little gem—Roman's address book. He spun the car around, gunned it down the driveway, and out through the gates. And as the gates closed behind him, the mansion erupted in flames (famished flames, unnatural black and blue flames) that ingested the building in no time at all. And when the feeding frenzy was over, nothing but chalky powder remained in its wake.

3 — Moonbeam Lake

Jonas Haze was the first name Valor found in Roman's address book. It appeared that the little man had a big weekend cottage on Moonbeam Lake, less than a four-hour drive from Thunder Bay. Valor arrived there on Thursday morning. All he had to do now was wait.

The cottage was conveniently secluded, the surrounding property meticulous. Gorgeous flowers were in bloom. No sign of the presence of children. Another bachelor. Valor strolled up the walkway, which led him to a stone staircase. And looking up, he was face to face with a stunning log cabin.

As he rose, he could see there were three peeks to the building, each growing higher than its predecessor. No expense was spared in its construction (his expense). Valor could feel his body stiffening with hatred. He placed his hand on the door's lock and at once it gave to his will.

Inside, the cottage was no less stunning. The first thing to catch his eye was the two ceiling-to-floor aquarium pillars on either side of a drop-in-the-floor living room area. The furniture throughout the cottage was 1950s styles, and turquoise seemed to be Jonas's preferred color choice. The main feature was the retro fireplace. There was even a retro jukebox.

At the top of the spiral staircase with its transparent steps, Valor stared intently at a large photograph hanging on the wall. There they were—his father's murderers—all of them: Straud, Haze, Mathews, and his Aunt Victoria. In the photo, they had wine glasses raised in a cheer. He understood at once what it was they had been celebrating. The frame rattled against the wall, and then it crumpled up like a ball of paper, glass and all, and dropped at his feet.

There was quite a collection of framed photographs on the upstairs walls. Valor examined them all with great scrutiny. By the final frame, he'd come to the wonderful conclusion that Jonas Haze did not know how to swim. There were dozens of pictures showing the lake and the grand pool in the backyard. And in all of those photographs, not once was Jonas in the pool, not even near it, or the magnificent lake.

Valor went down to the poolside. The water sparkled in the afternoon sun. A large stone waterfall majestically emptied into the pool. He stripped naked and dove into the water. Splashing through the surface, he laughed to himself. "I think it's time you earned your water-wings, dear little Jonas," he spoke to the day and laughed some more.

Friday night around 10:13 pm, Jonas Haze was cruising down Forkes Road in his shining, white 2015 Cadillac CTS Sedan, religiously following the 50km speed limit. Forkes Road was a treacherous route, with hairpin turns, a wall of stone to your right, and a steep drop into Moonbeam Lake to your left. Jonas loved his cottage, but he loathed the drive down Forkes Road. He'd tried to leave sooner to make it up before full dark, but one delay after another set him exactly within the hour he'd hoped to avoid.

Still in high spirits, he'd had a good week in stocks, and was now looking forward to a couple of carefree days on his own. Subtle raindrops began to patter against his windshield.

"Shit. Not now. I'm almost there," he said to the weather.

He butted his cigarette out and gripped the steering wheel with both hands. He even turned his stereo off to better his concentration on the road. "Fuck my luck. And fuck you, weatherman. Sunny weekend my ass," he mumbled to himself.

At that very moment, Valor was standing at the end of the dock. His mesmerizing white-blue eyes were staring up into the blackening sky. He was as still as a statue. The rain was falling around him but not on him. And it was coming down with greater force by the minute.

Jonas's Cadillac started to pick up speed. He tried to slow it down, but that only caused the vehicle to fishtail and increase its speed.

"Christ! What Da Fuck! Slow down, bitch!" he yelled.

"It's not going to listen to you, you know." (Jonas jolted in his seat.) "It's just a car," came a boy's voice from the backseat.

Jonas tried to look over his shoulder. The Cadillac fishtailed round the next bend, shooting stones over the edge. The rearview mirror adjusted itself to place the boy clearly in Jonas's line of sight.

"Who are you? Where'd you come from? How'd you get in my car?"

"You can let go of the wheel now, I'm controlling the ride," said the boy.

"What?" said Jonas. "Are you fucking nuts, kid?"

Suddenly the boy occupied the passenger seat next to him. "Let go now," he drawled.

Jonas was in shock. He did as the boy instructed just as raindrops began to strike the windshield like bullets, some penetrating right through the glass. Jonas shielded himself as he stared in horror at the ghost passenger.

"Try to relax. It will all be over for you soon," said the boy, then grinned.

"Who the fuck are you? This isn't happening. This isn't real!" Jonas screamed.

"It's real. As real as the day you murdered my dad."

Jonas lowered his arm from his eyes and stared hard at the boy. Subconsciously, he'd known who he was from the first glance. But to accept the truth was unthinkable. Now he had no choice. Reality struck home and it was terrifying!

He turned and fought with the door handle, hoping against hope it would open and he could fall out of this nightmare.

"Nope. You're not getting out this time," said the boy image of Valor.

Jonas whipped back round to face him, more bullets ricocheting off the leather seats, shredding the flesh from his cheeks. "It was a mistake!" he admitted.

The boy turned toward him and growled like a demon, his face contorting horrifyingly. Jonas couldn't push himself back far enough from the apparition. A moment later, the boy looked like Valor once again. He motioned for Jonas to focus on the road ahead. The headlights illuminated the sign that read: Dangerous Curve.

"No," said Jonas. "Please. I can't swim!"

He turned and read the next and last warning sign in the glow of the headlights. Bright letters shouted: SLOW DOWN. Jonas wished he could, as he always had before. He saw the guardrails leap into view as the Cadillac hammered on through. He grasped the wheel and screamed his throat raw, glancing from what he believed was Valor's ghost, back to the oncoming blackness of the lake.

The world gave out beneath them, the Cadillac hydroplaning over the surface of the lake as if it was never going to sink. He screamed so loud his ears plugged. Suddenly the impact of the Cadillac's nose slamming into the lake triggered the airbag. Jonas was barely conscious. He raised his head, dizziness swirling in his brain. The ghost was gone, but he was sinking into the blackness.

Moments past before he fully realized his situation, remembering where he was. He tried to open his door but it was jammed, as was the passenger door. Hopeless, he sat back in the seat, and the ghost reappeared just outside the windshield. It was knocking on the glass as if it wanted to come in. But that wasn't it. It didn't want in, it wanted to let the water in!

Jonas was shaking his head, sobbing, as he watched the smile grow on little Valor Winterthorn's pouty lips.

"No. No. Please don't. Please. I'm sorry," he whimpered.

He was soon to be a fish in a bowl in a lake. Valor waved goodbye to the pathetic man. His ghostly image backed away from the car, his smile fading to a look of fierceness, head lowered. The windshield burst inward, tiny shards of glass attacking Jonas's body like a swarm of stars. His screams drowned within the flooding bowl.

Above, the rain ceased at once. The image of the boy rose from the lake like a patch of fog, danced its way to the dock, where Valor stood, and faded over him. Valor shook the cool night air from his body. Inside the cottage, the jukebox blared one of Jonas's favorite tunes, loud enough to echo around Moonbeam Lake. Valor smiled and danced off the dock to the sounds of The Diamonds singing "The Stroll."

4 — Saturday evening, downtown Toronto

Valor stood on the sidewalk across the street from the Shangri-La Hotel, gazing up at the sixty-six story glass tower. Once again, thanks to Roman's address book, locating Tane and Victoria (now Mr. And Mrs. Mathews) was as easy as killing them would be. He'd been hoping to catch them together, but as fate would have it, Tane had just exited the hotel. Valor's eyes narrowed, a wicked grin on his lips. Tane pulled out a cigarette, lit it, and inhaled with great satisfaction. He held his breath for a long moment before exhaling, then quickly took a second drag. He studied the rain clouds scuttling overhead, darkening the sky.

Same old Tane, Valor thought. His hair was shaved around the sides, leaving a spiky Mohawk at the top. New was his sinister black goatee, separated into two braids. He was wearing a gray mid-length coat, fashioned after Nosferatu himself; and a pair of red leather ankle boots.

As he walked east up Adelaide Street, Valor followed. He didn't seem to be in a hurry. Valor suspected this was nothing more than a smoke break. Raindrops began to fall, but Tane didn't seem to mind; he was thoroughly enjoying his second cigarette now. Valor crossed the street, on course for the man directly responsible for his father's death.

The rain fell a little harder with every step closer to his prey. Valor's pulse increased. Tane was looking down when they bumped into one another.

"Oh. Excuse me," said Tane.

"I can't do that," said Valor.

Caught by surprise, Tane smiled awkwardly at the young man. He said, "Pardon me?"

"Can't do that, either," said Valor.

Now with a look of agitation, Tane rolled his shoulders back. "Do we have a problem here, friend?" he sneered.

Valor stepped a little closer, making Tane feel more uncomfortable than he already was.

"We're not friends, Tane."

The agitation was replaced with confusion. Tane attempted to step back without it being obvious that he wanted more space between himself and this stranger.

"You know me? I don't know you. Maybe you should refresh my memory," he said in a cocky tone.

Valor looked him right in the eyes, his own eyes (darkest brown) suddenly brightened to white-blue.

Tane staggered back in a hurry. His hands were trembling, his jaw slack. "Impossible," he said stupefied. "No. How could you have escaped that explosion?"

"You murdered my father, Tane. You and the others. And you've been living high on the hog on my inheritance, and my father's works. And for you, that all ends today," Valor said, the glow of his eyes glaring out the rest of his features.

Tane laughed an uproarious laugh. He said, "Poor

little Valor. Come for revenge, have you? What are you gonna do, report us to the police?" he guffawed.

Valor did not flinch. He watched Tane shaking in his red boots. "That knife won't help you," he said.

Tane wondered how he could know he was carrying a knife. No matter. He reached inside his coat pocket for it anyway, releasing the switchblade like some wallet thief in an alley. His toothy grin was maniacal. And then, from out of nowhere (No. Not nowhere. From him. From Valor!) a force like a ball of wind barrelled into him. Tane was thrown back about eight feet. The switchblade had come loose from his grip, and Tane didn't bother to pick it up. He clambered to his feet and started to run down Adelaide, turning right on University Avenue.

Under the heavy rainfall, Valor followed. He knew exactly where Tane was headed: St. Andrew Subway Station. He was easy to spot, running through sidewalk traffic dressed like a character from *Interview With A Vampire*. Valor could smell the fear radiating from him like a mixture of flowers and ashes.

Tane ran down the stairs into the station. He stopped, spinning in circles, unsure what to do. Pulling his cell phone from the inner pocket of his coat, he quick-dialed Victoria's cell.

"Pick up, pick up, pick up!" he panicked.

Valor was now standing about fifteen feet from him, listening to him scream profanities into his phone. Valor held his right hand out and at once the phone slipped right out of Tane's grasp and was in Valor's in a flash.

Victoria's voice was yelling through the speaker. Tane rushed onto the subway train the instant the doors slid open.

"Victoria. Victoria!" Valor shouted.

The phone went silent, and then a whisper, "Valor?"

"Yeah, Aunt V, the one and only. Listen, don't wait up for Tane, he's taking a ride on the subway and won't be coming back...*ever*," he hissed. "I'll see you soon, Aunt V...*real* soon."

As the train began to pull away, Tane was staring at Valor through the rear window. He grinned and waved. Valor chuckled about him as he let the cell phone drop to the ground and crushed it underfoot. Tane watched him step up close to the tracks, and it made him increasingly nervous.

As the train sped away Tane breathed a sigh of relief. Behind him, the passenger doors whipped open. People hurried to distance themselves from them. Malfunctions did not happen often with the train doors, but they did occur now and then. However, one passenger understood perfectly well that this was not a malfunction; one passenger whose feet were moving him closer and closer to the open doors and the world blurring past beyond, understood.

"Hey, pal, you might not want to get too close there," an old man warned Tane.

"I can't help it. He's making me do it," he ranted.

The old man glanced at his fellow passengers, giving them all his version of crazy eyes. Surely, this guy was a nut job. No one was making him do anything. Passengers seated nearest to the doors began to scooch away. Tane's body jerked as he wrestled with his unseen puppeteer. Step—*pull!* Step—*pull!* Step—*Step!*

"Hey, man, you should back the fuck up," said a teenage boy, his backpack on the floor between his feet.

"It's not me, you fucking assholes!" Tane shot back. "Help me!"

Passengers shook their heads, insulted and angry. As Tane seemed to be performing some bizarre mime stunt, moving ever closer to the threshold, a young woman who'd had enough of his antics huffed and said, "Oh, why don't you just sit down, asshole."

Many around her agreed, shouting, "Yeah! Sit down!"

When Tane ignored their suggestions, an elderly lady with a grocery bag held snug in her arms shook her head.

"Huff. There's one on every ride," she complained.

The old woman gasped in surprise when Tane screamed, his legs violently yanked out from under him, his body sucked out the open doors like lint into a vacuum.

"Holy shit!" yelled the teenage boy. "The asshole jumped!"

The sliding doors sealed shut.

Tane was now riding the outside of the train, held against the steel snake like a magnet. He tumbled and dragged along, moving toward the nose of the train. Passengers in the other cars gasped and screamed as he rolled by, blood smearing the windows. Not a sound escaped Tane's throat, his lungs stuffed with air and pressure.

The train's conductors barely caught a glimpse of Tane as he speared past their windows. His body torpedoed a great distance ahead of the train; and then, suddenly, like a yo-yo, the invisible string yanked him back again. Tane's eyes were wide open when he shot back and kissed the oncoming train.

Cherry pie all over the tracks.

Feeling quite satisfied, Valor turned and headed back toward the hotel.

5 — Victoria

There was such a profound feeling of hatred toward his Aunt, Valor's temples throbbed. His parents were not her only victims. He knew this from the choppy images that ran through Tane's mind as he 'road' the subway. His inheritance had not been as easy for Victoria to claim as she and the others had hoped it would be.

Several lawyers and six years past before she finally attained what was rightfully his. And during that interim, she and Tane had recruited several new members into their schemes. No longer did they pretend to be affiliated with the Devil. Stripped of those beliefs after the botched ceremony with Daniel, and the destruction of his property, there was no reason to continue with the whole witchcraft charade. No need for pretense, when you're thieves and murderers.

The killings were unnecessary, of course, but Tane and Victoria thrived on them. Why take a chance leaving witnesses alive, when you can just as easily slash a couple of throats, set a couple of fires, and go on a shopping spree the following afternoon. Even after his inheritance was in their pockets, they continued with the madness.

These were the images running through Valor's mind as he rode the elevator up to the 47th floor of the Shangri-La. It occurred to him that Victoria had received an early enough warning from Tane to have made a run for it. But the second those elevator doors opened, he knew she hadn't budged. She was not about to hide from her puny—recently risen from the dead—nephew. She could not understand why the hell Tane had fled to the subway. She was not afraid of Valor, and if he did show up at her door, she would handle him.

Though the door to her condo was locked, it clicked and opened inward, slowly revealing Valor, who was standing in its frame. Easy-listening music was playing throughout the room. There was an open bottle of champagne on a glass table, a used crystal glass next to it. As he looked around, he gasped under his breath at seeing one of his father's abstract paintings above a white fireplace.

Valor touched the painting with his fingertips. A vision of his father in deep concentration, the brush in his right hand, laying gentle blue strokes of paint across the canvas, rippled through his mind's eye.

"Ah. I see you're admiring your father's work," Victoria interrupted.

Valor turned to face her.

"Not one of his better works, I'm afraid. Still, I suppose it'll go for a few thousand, regardless. Not a complete waste," she said, her prissy attitude fuelling his anger.

When he did not respond, she reached for the champagne bottle and poured herself another glass. She was visibly nervous.

"I see you're alone. My husband didn't return with you. Rather rude of him."

"He sort of went to pieces when he saw me," said

Valor. "Just as Roman and Jonas did."

This was news to her.

"Allow me to skip the trivial bullshit and get right to the point, Val."

"Don't call me that. My father was the only one who called me that," Valor snarled.

Victoria rolled her eyes with irritation, and continued, "What exactly is it you hope to gain from this pointless reunion? A little closure? A chance to get your grubby little hand in the cookie jar...perhaps?"

Valor's eyes narrowed as he watched her step around the gray sofa. Her black floor-length cocktail dress, with flowing chiffon sleeves, and sexy slit in the skirt, made a swishing sound as she moved. With her back to him, the dress opened in a V down to her dimpled ass, she glanced over her left shoulder at him, waiting impatiently for an answer.

"Well, are you ever going to enlighten me on what the hell you're doing here, or are you just going to stand there, intruding?" she barked. "And another thing: how the *hell* did you escape that explosion? You were locked in the goddamn cellar!"

"Yes. Locked in the cellar, where you and your friends murdered my father," Valor said solemnly.

Victoria poured herself another glass of champagne, spilling most of it on the glass table. She slammed the bottle down in anger.

"Oh, Valor, don't be so melodramatic. That was ages ago," she said. "No one cares."

"I care," he seethed.

Victoria's nerves were jangling. Why hadn't Tane returned yet? Her piss-ant nephew was beginning to frighten her. She was feeling vulnerable, and that was unacceptable.

"Look. You can have the fucking painting. Just take it and get out," she ordered.

Valor shook his head. His intimidating grin reaffirmed her fears—he wanted something more.

"I'll write you a check. How much do you want?"

And just then, she swore his white-blue eyes enhanced in brilliance like a flashlight with fresh batteries.

"You don't get it," he said, the furniture sliding away from him, moving in opposite directions across the floor.

Victoria stumbled back, closer to the fireplace, eyes wide, mouth agape.

"The power! I knew it. I was right all along."

A fantastic flash of lightning zigzagged around the windows of the condominium; thunder vibrated the thick panels with pelting rain, jump scaring Victoria.

"Not quite. You see, my mother was no liar. Dad was born half-human, half-alien. You just didn't want to believe it. You could have never taken his power and used it yourself. It's not a fucking magic wand, you stupid bitch! It was part of his makeup, just as it's part of mine."

"I don't believe it," Victoria said astounded.

"Tane isn't coming back because he's dead, scattered on the subway tracks, rat food."

"No!" Victoria shouted.

"Jonas and Roman met similar fates. You won't be hearing from them anymore."

"Liar!"

"But I know some old acquaintances of yours who you *will* be hearing from," said Valor. And in his eight-year-old voice: "Say hello, Aunt V."

Valor's head leaned back, his hands flexed open at his sides, and what first appeared to be misty wings sprouting from his back, Victoria realized were spirits. Though her eyes could not discern any true features, she knew precisely who they were.

"Fuck you!" she screamed.

The wraiths surrounded Victoria, a creeping, coiling horde of green-black shapes, with misty tentacles and eyes that sparked green. They embraced her from her neck to her toes, her name echoing off their invisible tongues. Victoria spun on the spot, screaming in unhinged terror.

All at once, she felt the impact of her bones being crushed; droplets of blood dabbled the hardwood floor. Her body fevered with shock. Valor watched as the tornado of death swept Victoria's ragged corpse up, and passed right through the main window wall. He approached the window for a closer look, but the satisfied spirits of Victoria and Tane's victims had vanished beyond the fierce storm.

Taking a deep, relaxing breath, Valor felt relieved for the first time since his father's death. He turned and walked up to Daniel's painting to admire it further.

"It's beautiful, Dad. I'll cherish it always," he said.

He then returned the furniture to its original placement and sat down, exhausted. He could rest now, but not for long. There were still other members of Tane and Victoria's family of murdering thieves to track. He would locate and dispose of them all, one by one!

Came Back Haunted

1

Sean Valentine held his cell phone between his right cheek and his shoulder as he tied his brown Slater boots.

"No. I told you. I'm not staying overnight. I'm hoping against hope to be back here before it's dark," he explained to his younger brother, Zachary.

"But you're gonna leave a key, right?" said Zach.

Sean chuckled. He snuggled into his dark brown corduroy jacket and buttoned it up.

"Zack, it's already in the fake rock outside the door. You worry too much. There are a couple of frozen pizzas in the freezer, so help yourself. Get settled in and, for god's sake, bud, relax," said Sean.

"Okay. Good. Well, tell Mom I'm sorry I couldn't make it today for Dad's birthday. Give her a hug and kiss for me."

"Will do. Okay, I'll see you tonight," said Sean.

"Later," Zach squeezed in just before the line went dead.

Sean slipped his phone into the inner pocket of his jacket, grabbed the keys to his motorcycle, checked himself once more in the mirror, adjusted his tie, then headed out. It was a warmer day than they'd experienced recently. The clouds were scarce, the sun bright, and the colored leaves looked alive and happy in the trees. His ride would take him from Moonbeam Lake to Tobermory, where his mother resided with her new boyfriend, Gaetan.

It was his father's birthday today, and every year he and his brother accompanied their mother to the cemetery where he is buried. It's a simple ritual. They place flowers at his grave, wish him a happy birthday, watch Joan shed a few tears, then leave. This would be the first year Zachary is a no show. Joan understood that his absence was not a choice. She was fine with it, as long as one of them came.

It was just after noon when Sean rolled up into his mother's driveway. He remembered the years when she would run out the front door to hug and kiss her boys. These days, at seventy-nine, she no longer made leaps off the porch steps to greet them. Gaetan answered his knock at the door, a friendly smile on his face, his matching white beard, eyebrows, and hair shining white.

"Sean!" he piped, taking his hand in a vigorous handshake. "Come in, come in. Joan's anxious to see you."

"Good to see you, Gaetan," said Sean, closing the door behind him.

"Lovely day, isn't it?" Gaetan bubbled, still quite fit for an 80-year-old. The man was what gay men would refer to as a silver daddy (in shape and handsome). He led Sean through the foyer, passed the living room, and into the kitchen, where Joan was busy putting the finishing touches on lunch.

"Hi, Mom," said Sean.

"Oh, there's my handsome boy," she beamed, hurrying to wrap her arms around him. She squeezed him tight and kissed his cheeks. He recognized that glare in her eyes that said *Looking more like his father every year.* She gently caressed his furry right cheek, but only for a moment, because on this day every year thoughts of Paul could easily bring tears. She didn't want Gaetan to see her cry for her deceased husband, even though he fully understood how deep her love for him ran.

"How was the ride down?" she asked him.

"Beautiful. I couldn't have asked for a finer day. The wind was warm and the roads were perfect," he described.

"If only I was a few years younger," sighed Gaetan.

"You just never mind," said Joan, placing a steaming bowl of creamy carrot soup under Sean's appreciative eyes.

"What if it had a sidecar for you?" Gaetan went on.

"Sit down, old man," Joan joked.

Sean was happy to see his mother and Gaetan so happy together. They'd both lost their first loves: his father to heart disease at sixty-four, and Gaetan's wife, Maria, from breast cancer at sixty-two. They'd lived together now for the past five years, following a long courtship (Joan was reluctant to cheat on her husband, dead or not).

After the soup came strawberries with whipped creme.

"That was wonderful, Ma," Sean complimented, dabbing the corners of his mouth with a napkin.

"Thank you. You missed a spot," said Joan, collecting

the dishes from the table. "Let me get these in the dish-washer and I'll be ready to go," she said to Sean.

"No hurry. I'm just gonna use the washroom for a minute," he said, leaving the room.

Gaetan remained at home while Sean used the man's pickup truck to drive his mother out to the cemetery. As far as graveyards go, Gulch Cemetery was surely one of the most overcrowded in Ontario. Sean parked the pickup at the rickety iron gates that signalled the entrance to the dreadful place. He and Joan smiled at one another. She patted his hand and opened her door.

"Come on, Sean. I know you boys never liked coming here. Can't say I blame you. This place has always given me the jitters," Joan admitted.

"What? I never knew you felt that way, too."

"Who wouldn't? If there had been another choice at the time of your father's death, he certainly wouldn't have been buried in this godforsaken place. I'm surprised the dead remain," said Joan, leading the way.

Sean guffawed as he followed, carrying a small pot of orange Chrysanthemums. The narrow stone path quickly dissolved into no path at all. Sean wondered how his mother could even locate his father's tombstone among the nearly stacked graves grown over with wild greenery. The brilliant light of the afternoon barely filtered through the canopy of trees.

"Should be right around here," said Joan, cautiously weaving through the maze of headstones.

"Geez," said Sean. "This place is disappearing into the landscape. Doesn't anyone care?"

"Most of the people buried here no longer have any living relatives. They're a forgotten bunch, I'm afraid," Joan answered sullenly.

"That's pretty sad," said Sean, nearly bumping into his mother when she suddenly stopped.

"Can you read his name on there, Sean? I think this might be it. Gets harder to tell every year."

Sean crouched down and brushed dried mud from the epitaph. He smiled and nodded. "Yep. I don't know how you managed it, but you found him."

"He draws me to him. I'd be lost without his guidance here."

Sean set a place for the potted Mums at the base of the tombstone. A smaller tombstone was leaning against the left side of his father's. Many of the tombstones were leaning on another. Sean stood next to his mother and put his arm around her. He joined her in quietly singing the happy birthday song. Paul would have been eighty-one.

"I still miss him so much. Gaetan is a good man; he would have liked him, I think," said Joan.

"Dad would have wanted you to be happy, Mom. That's what you have to be...for him."

"I know. And I am. The missing never goes away, you know. Sometimes I wish it would, but then I think that would mean forgetting, and I never want to forget him."

"Aww. You're the most beautiful person I know, Mom."

"We'd best get going. I don't want to leave Gaetan by himself for too long. I know this day can't be good for him. Me running off to see another man, and all," Joan quipped.

By the time Sean started the pickup, Joan suddenly gasped, checking around herself.

"Uh oh, what's missing?" asked Sean.

"Oh, I don't believe this. My purse. I set it down at your father's grave and must've forgotten to pick it up. I'm so sorry, Sean. Such a stupid old lady," Joan chided herself.

"It's okay, Mom. Shit. Don't worry. I'm sure it's still there. Wait here and I'll fetch it. Only take a minute," he said, slipping out.

Sean hustled into the trees, hoping to recall the path his mother took. "Come on, Dad, help me find the way. You do it for Mom. Make me a believer."

He stopped when he reached what appeared to be the centre of the cemetery. A moment of vertigo spun around his head as the tombstones all seemed to lean in his direction. "Shit. Dad, I'm feeling lost here," he admitted, standing there squinting, the target of myriad rays of sunlight.

Suddenly an urgent thought screamed *Get out of here!* The chill of fear enveloped him, or was it a chill in the air, perhaps both! Sean looked around as the feeling of being watched grew too intense to brush off. He took a few steps forward and spotted his mother's purse on the ground. "Fuck! Finally," he said, rushing to pick it up. "Thanks, Dad," he said, turning to leave.

Darkness swept through the woods as if a heavy cloud had blocked out the sun's light. Sean started to back away from his father's grave, then turned to run back to the pickup, and his awaiting mother. Suddenly he heard the loud knocking of several tombstones tumbling over behind him. When he looked back all was quiet; he continued on his way.

More knocking tombstones. Sean froze in his tracks. He found it extremely odd that not one stone fell when his mother was out here. Slowly turning to look behind him, he tuned his hearing to every sound. He sensed that something dark was present. At once invisible energy shot toward him, smashing right through the tombstones on a direct course like a fired cannonball! Sean ran in a panic, striking his legs against several tombstones in passing.

He couldn't get up to full speed in the maze. It occurred to him in a flash what a sight he must be: A grown man running for his life with a purse in his hand. There was no time to laugh about it now. The thought was obliterated when a heavy grip wrapped around his ankles. Sean went down hard, landing with his arms upflung, his mother's purse still in his right hand. It was like he'd been tackled in a game of football.

Stricken with terror, Sean leapt to his feet and charged out of the cemetery.

When Joan saw her son come running into view, his face red, expression full of horror, she climbed out of the pickup to meet him halfway.

"No no! Get back in the truck!" Sean yelled.

Confused and frightened herself now, Joan did as she was told, even locking her door beside her. When Sean hopped into the pickup, she didn't try to ask him what was wrong. He reversed the pickup away from the Gulch Cemetery gates, then floored it out of there. Ten minutes down the road, he seemed to get hold of himself.

"Got your purse," he said.

"But, Sean, what...?"

"Please, don't ask me. Don't ever ask me," he said.

2

Sean was relieved to see the Welcome To Moonbeam Lake sign. His journey home from Tobermory was plagued by an increasing weightiness on his back and shoulders. He couldn't stop thinking about the cemetery incident, wondering what in the hell attacked him. He hoped his mother wouldn't be too upset with him, but next year he planned to wish his father a happy birthday from the safety of his own home.

He always enjoyed the ride down Crescent Road to his secluded cottage. Along the way, he passed three neighbors, vast property spaces between them. His was the fourth property, followed by two others. They all respected each other's privacy. As Sean rolled up the stone driveway to his cedar-sided home, he felt as if he would collapse from relief.

He parked his bike in the garage and entered the house through a connecting door. Though he was anxious to see his little brother, his first thought was to fill the tub to the rim and soak the day's tension away. Not five minutes inside the kitchen, he felt the strange weight he'd been burdened with since the cemetery slide down his body. It was like the force of gravity loosened its grip on him. Home sweet home, he thought.

"Hello? Zach? You here?" he called, removing his coat and boots.

"Boo!" Zach shouted, leaping into the doorway, smiling with his arms out wide.

Sean yelped. "Jesus Christ! What the fuck are you doing, trying to induce a heart attack or something?"

Zach was giggling but he could tell the scare might not have been the best way to greet his brother. He hugged him, patting him on the back. He said, "Sorry, old man, didn't mean to make you shit your pants. Did you miss me?"

"Oh yeah. How long are you staying?" Sean joked.

Sean described his experience with his brother over pizza. Zach raised his brows a few times, rolled his eyes, but in the end, he believed every word. Growing up together meant that Zach knew when his brother was bullshitting him, and when he was telling the truth. There was no doubt in his mind now that the truth was what he was hearing.

"Strange part is that I felt like I was being borne down upon the entire ride here, but the moment I walked in the door...normal again," Sean described, reaching for his Cola.

Zach looked around the room suspiciously, he said, "You telling me you brought something home?"

"What? No. I mean...oh, shit. No. You don't really think....?"

Mach's brows were raised again. "Yeah, I do," he said.

Both brothers were silent for moments, then guffawed.

"That would not be funny if it were true," said Sean.

"We'd be fucked. My vacation would be ruined," Zach added, laughing.

"Well, you could always offer to have 'it' go fishing with you," said Sean.

"Yeah, and you could finally get someone to clean your filthy house," Zach teased, tapping his brother's shoulder.

Sean stopped laughing. "Very funny. I keep a clean house, thank you very much, Marty (Sean used to tease his brother when they were younger by calling him after Michael J. Fox's character in the *Back To The Future* movies because he resembled the actor). "Anyway, enough about today, I just want to forget it happened. How's work been?"

That night as Zach watched TV and munched on cold left-over pizza in the living room, Sean was snoring in his bed upstairs. Behind Zach, what first appeared as dust on the floor darkened into charcoal, then rose like a cloud ever-shifting and fidgeting. The phantom shimmied closer and closer to Zachary, where it lingered for a time, then ascended the staircase. Zach turned at once, sensing the change in the air too late.

Upstairs, as the whispering phantom wafted down the hallway, Sean dreamed he was back in the thick of Gulch Cemetery. Blackness surrounded him. And as he walked headstones would appear suddenly, glowing. Tortured, sombre voices assailed him from the bloated depths, asking, "Wwwwhy? Wwwwhy?"

In reality, the phantom now entered Sean's bedroom. The room grew stifling hot. Lying stiff on his bed, the sheets kicked down to his feet, beads of perspiration rolling off his naked body, Sean came to with a start. His eyes darted around the room as he found himself paralyzed, his tongue pillowy. All he could hear was the sound of his heavy breaths and a rhythmic humming like the thrum of crickets.

And he felt a pressure at his feet, rolling up his legs (just like the pressure he'd felt during his ride home, only much heavier now). Sean quelled a scream as the phantom sketch inched over the fringe of his vision. Closer and closer. Sean looked into the darkness of it, which was like staring into a void of space.

The thrumming intensified. Sean could feel the thing's burgeoning hatred as it hovered next to him, its quivering inducing nausea. It seemed to linger forever. Sean was struggling to find his voice. He began to salivate, frothing at the mouth until, finally, he managed a few low grunting sounds. His ears were ringing as he worked his way up to a throaty scream.

Zach started at the sound. In a trice, he had bounded up the stairs, down the hall, and froze at the threshold of his brother's bedroom. Eyes full round, mouth agape, Zach just stood there in consternation. His mind raced to answer the question: What the hell am I looking at? Sean continued to scream, unable to free himself of his paralysis. The phantom appeared to turn in Mach's direction, its movements suggesting its awareness. Zach finally stepped into the room, shouting, "Go away! Go away! Get out of here!"

The phantom's shape suddenly grew larger like a cobra's hood expanding in self-defense. Zach staggered back in terror. The phantom, efficacious in its effort to shackle him in fear, bolted upward and spread over the ceiling. The entire house seemed to rumble in protest of the parasite's presence. Several smoky tendrils darted down toward Sean's face, stopping mere inches away. Then the obsidian patch stormed out the door, raking the walls as it disappeared down the hallway and out of sight.

When the house fell back to quiet, Zach raced over to Sean as he leapt from his bed, swiping at his body as if to remove the feeling of invasion.

"Holy shit, Sean, are you okay?" worried Zach, grabbing him by his shoulders.

Sean fell into a raucous coughing spell. Zach ran to the washroom to fetch him a glass of water. When he returned Sean was pulling his boxers up. He accepted the water and gulped it back. Zach took the empty glass and pulled his brother out of the room. They headed downstairs and flopped on the sofa, next to each other.

"What the fuck, Sean? What was that fucking thing?"

Sean shook his head tremulously. "It's what attacked me in the cemetery," he said, breathlessly. "I didn't imagine it, that thing's real!"

"Yeah, real fucking scary!" Zach shuddered. He got up and pulled the flannel blanket from the back of the Lazy-boy chair and threw it around Sean's shoulders.

"It's not a spirit," said Sean.

"Would do you mean? Then what the hell is it?"

Sean spoke in a half daze, he muttered: "So much sadness and anger. It was crushing my chest. I couldn't breathe. At the cemetery, I thought it was a ghost. You know, like someone in that graveyard come back from the dead, sorta thing. But it's not. It's something else. It was attracted to the cemetery by the spirits themselves. Their sadness and, even greater, their anger must have been like a beacon. And this thing, this entity or whatever it is, answered their call. It felt like it was made of them, of their deepest emotions. And none of it good."

"Fuck me," said Zach. "And you brought the fucking thing home like a stray puppy."

3

The next morning, Sean woke from a night of restless sleep on the sofa. He sat up feeling ragged as he rubbed his rheumy eyes. Zach was snoring a few feet away, curled up and looking none too comfortable in the Lazy-boy. Sean stood and used his blanket to now cover his little brother. He wished last night's events had been a dream, but he knew better.

The house was quiet, no different than any other normal day. It made him wonder where the hell the phantom was presently hiding; where these things go when they're not busy inflicting nightmares upon us. He wanted his housecoat and slippers but wasn't too keen on going back up to his bedroom. Then he determined not to allow this thing to influence him this way. This was, after all, his home.

Later that afternoon, the brothers happily left the house to make a supply run to Emsdale, the nearest town. They hopped in Sean's Jeep Wrangler, staring up at the house as they backed out of the driveway.

"Is it just me, or does it somehow look menacing?" wondered Sean.

"Yeah. I never saw it before, but now that you mention it...yeah," Zach concurred.

Around two o'clock, Mrs. Elinore Frank from down the

road drove up Sean's driveway in her little pickup truck, her precious pug, TicTac, panting in the seat next to her. TicTac started to bark the moment the house came into view.

"Now, TicTac, you settle down. You've been here plenty of times," said Elinore.

When the dog wouldn't stop she decided better to leave him in the truck. She grabbed her basket full of eggs and made her way up to the front door. Sean had designed her and her husband's cottage for them, and they'd been returning the good deed with fresh eggs ever since.

TicTac was pouncing at the dashboard and barking hysterically at his master, for he could sense what she did not. Elinore rang the doorbell once, twice, a third time. She tried knocking, using the iron knocker, but still, no one responded.

"Hello?" she called. "Mr. Valentine? Sean? Hello?"

Just then, what sounded like the powerful spray from a fire hose rushed the opposite side of the door! Elinore jumped back in fright, dropping the basket in her hands. She stood there baffled, staring at the door. A moment later, she attempted to pick up the basket (which now held several broken eggs). The concrete porch quaked beneath her. Hairline fractures started at the base of the door and bolted outward. Elinore squealed! She left the basket and ran down the driveway.

TicTac assaulted her with happy wet kisses as she climbed into the pickup, threw it into reverse, and hammered the gas pedal. TicTac fumbled about as they fled the property at high speed. Down the road about a mile, Sean waved at Mrs. Frank's pickup as it zipped past.

"Christ. Somebody's in a hurry," Zach observed.

"Yeah. That was weird. Didn't take Mrs. Frank for a speeder."

When Sean and Zach approached the front door of the house, they discovered the basket of eggs left by Mrs. Frank.

"Oh shit," said Sean. "Well, now we know why the poor thing was flying down the road like a madwoman. Something scared the shit out of her. She would have never left me broken eggs."

"What do you think happened?" asked Zach, afraid of what the answer might be.

"I don't know," said Sean, picking up the basket.

Neither of them noticed the cracks in the porch landing.

4

Needing to catch up on the sleep they were deprived of the previous night, Sean and Zach were in bed and asleep by 10 pm. Snores echoed back and forth, up and down the hallway, from Sean's room to Mach's. They'd left the hallway light on for a sense of security, and now that light was flickering.

Somewhere far off in the distance, both Sean and Zach could hear the thrumming of crickets, just beyond the edge of their dreams, it seemed. The song grew louder and louder, drawing nearer and nearer. It rose from the depths of slumber and awakened them at once. With both men now sitting upright and alert in their beds, Sean called out to his brother.

"Zach? Are you awake?"

"Sure am," came the reply from down the hall.

The hallway light continued to buzz and flicker as the song rose in volume. Sean had a clear view of the entire hallway; Zach could only see the portion visible through his open door.

"Are you hearing what I'm hearing?" asked Sean.

"You betcha!" said Zach.

Sean dropped his legs over the edge of his bed and padded toward his door. At the opposite end of the hall, Zach stuck his head out and peered round the corner, making eye contact with Sean. Slowly they entered into the hall, looking about for the source of the thrumming. Suddenly, feathery fronds sprouted out of the floor at the very end of the hall, passed Mach's position. He turned and gasped at the sight, turning back to his brother to confirm that he, too, was seeing this. Sean nodded and slowly stepped forward, while Zach backed away.

The fronds grew taller and taller, wavering as if from a gentle breeze. Once they were about five feet tall, an abstract head and shoulders rose into view, followed by arms, body, long legs, and in place of feet more fronds rooted to the floor. Its completed form resembled a horrific pencil sketch come to life!

"Zach," Sean called with a quavering voice, reaching out.

Backing away from the demonic vision and its dancing feathers, Zach steeled himself as he moved toward his brother. More of the lively feathers began to sprout all around the hallway, from the floor, up the walls, and out of the ceiling, silent and horrifying. "Zach, a little faster, please."

The deafening moans of myriad voices overtook the house, rattling dishes in the cupboards, cracking windows, shaking the plaster loose from the walls and ceilings. And all at once the phantom shot toward Zach, transforming into a black ball in the air and striking him square in the face. And the moment it struck him, wrapping around his head, the shape continued to shoot out toward Sean, stretching the length of the hallway and opening with a flourish like an otherworldly flower. With no less than six extensions snapping the air just out of reach of Sean, he fumbled back and landed against the foot of his bed.

"Leave us alone!" he screamed.

The bed shook against his back, thumping on the floor. The phantom petals, which were like living strands of silk, were vibrating like threatened serpents. And as sudden as its attack had been, its retreat was just as swift. The flailing petals withdrew into the translucent wrap suffocating Zach. Instantly, it charged toward the far wall and vanished beyond. Zach collapsed on his back as the extended feathers retreated.

Sean vaulted from the floor to his brother's side. Zach wasn't breathing! Sean performed mouth to mouth resuscitation. Zach burst awake in a panic. He sat up wheezing and coughing. Sean tried to assure him he was okay, but Zach rushed to the washroom, turned on the light, and stared nose to nose at his reflection (seeing is believing).

"Fuck fuck FUCK!" he shouted.

Sean rubbed his back as he splashed his face with cold water.

"That fucking thing almost killed me, Sean. It almost killed me!"

Sean scratched his head nervously. He observed, "It seems to be getting stronger. I don't know why. Why's it getting stronger?"

"Who fucking cares? It almost killed me, the son of a bitch! We have to do something. Get help or something. Tell someone, tell anyone! My fuck!"

"Who? Who do we tell?"

Water was dripping from Mach's chin. He turned to Sean and said, "I know who."

5

Zach entered the living room at the close of Sean's phone call, catching the "Love you too, Mom." Sean sat in quiet contemplation for moments before acknowledging his brother's presence.

"So, did she laugh and call you insane or was she understanding," asked Zach, sitting on the sofa with a steaming cup of coffee in his hands.

"She knows I would never bullshit her, Zach."

"Yeah, I know. I was just kidding. So, is she gonna do it?"

Sean nodded and said, "Yeah. She's gonna call back when she has the details for us. I hope this fucking works cause if it doesn't...."

Zach sighed.

The evening arrived with a thunderstorm in tow. Heavy rains blackened the house's already dark exterior and drummed against the windows. When thunder reverberated throughout the foundations, Sean and Zach were made to wonder if the groans came from within or without. Still waiting by 7 pm for their mother's call, the pair were growing ever anxious.

Subtle hints of the presence toyed with them about the house: Taps turning on and off by themselves; the washer and dryer in the basement rumbling to life for moments, then shutting off; the coat rack falling over; the radio in the upstairs washroom playing on its own; kitchen cupboard doors and bedroom doors slamming. Needless to say, the occurrences kept them on edge, until they were pushed over it.

8:30 pm

Sean stood with an aggravated huff. He grumbled, "That's it! I can't take it anymore."

"What do you mean? Where are you going?" Zach puzzled.

"Down the basement to unplug the washer and dryer, I can't stand listening to them turn on and off every fucking minute!"

"Wait for me," said Zach. "I'm not staying here alone."

He hurried to catch up to Sean as he charged toward the kitchen. Sean grabbed a flashlight from under the sink, checked to make sure it functioned properly, then opened the door to the basement. Flicking the light switch to the ON position, he turned back to Zach with a grim expression.

"What?" said Zach.

"The light isn't working."

"So, forget it."

The machines kicked on just then. Sean's eyes narrowed. He hesitated a moment, staring down into the inky darkness, then growled and said, "Fuck this." And so began his descent, followed reluctantly by Zach.

The beam from the flashlight gave little comfort as they stood at the bottom of the stairs. Wherever the beam shone only made the surrounding dark—darker!

The lids of the two machines began to open and close, making a thumping sound like footsteps, faster and faster, then stopped in an instant.

"Hurry, Sean, unplug 'em and let's get the hell outta here," prompted Zach, holding onto his brother's waist as he led the way.

They moved in the direction of the beam, toward the visible cords plugged into the wall. Zach tried to see beyond the darkness to their left and right and behind them. "I can't see shit," he whispered.

"Got 'em," said Sean, and just as he yanked the cords free from the sockets, they started at the sound of someone mumbling, giggling, and whimpering to their left. Sean slowly moved the beam of light along the concrete wall in search of the source.

"Sean?" Zach said tremulously.

The beam illuminated a bubbling pool of honey-colored goo on the floor, and rose higher, to the source of the mewling.

"Oh fuck!" Zach blurted. "Sean?"

Sean could not reply just yet, so entranced by the thing in the spotlight. It looked like a cancer-stricken boy with no hair on its pale blue head, too many ribs to count protruding beneath its tight skin, twisted limbs and broken neck, head leaning on its risen chest, and worst of all was its bleeding eyes and denticulated Cheshire grin. Then the ghastly thing heaved and vomited a surge of sludge that filled the air with the stench of excrement. Sean and Zach both screamed at the sight. They turned to flee, only to come face to face with the demon phantom blocking the top of the stairs, and screamed again.

Sean spun the beam round to where the first sighting had been, but it was gone. He jerked the light back up the stairs, unfortunately giving them a clear view of what was now coming down. The thing filled the doorway and looked like a tall skeleton, only with an extra-large rib cage and spidery extensions of bone.

"Is there another way out?" yelled Zach.

"No. We're trapped!" Sean declared.

"Fuck me!"

They started to back away as the thing's many extensions crept down along the walls on either side of the staircase, creaking and cracking, scratching a path into the panelling.

"Run to the back! Find something to fight it with!" yelled Sean.

"Like what?" came Zach, unable to see without the aid of his brother's flashlight. "I can't see shit!"

"Here! Use this!" said Sean, handing him a golf club.

"Oh my god, are you serious?" said Zach.

"It's all I could find," said Sean, raising his club as proof.

The demon's claws scraped along the floor as it descended the stairs, chunks of concrete blasting outward from the walls below. Every step boomed, every breath screeched. Sean and Zach climbed up on the washer and dryer, striking ineffective blows at the claws. The door at the top of the stairs slammed shut. Sean's flashlight began to blink off, on, off, on, off...on, off....

"Oh shit!" he cried.

The sound of the scratching claws rose up the wall behind them. They could feel the machines wobbling under the attack. All they could do was swing into the darkness and hope to connect with something, without knocking each other out. But suddenly the claws retreated like anchors being towed in, carving deep grooves into the floor.

"Something's happening!" yelled Sean.

The brothers screamed at once when the phantom creature's body lit up, glowing as if filled with a hundred flames. The light pulsed, shining in between its crooked bones. Every pulse grew brighter and brighter as the phantom twisted and jerked violently. Screeches assaulted their ears and made their teeth vibrate.

"What the fuck's happening?" Zach shouted.

Sean watched intensely for moments before he understood, and shouted, "It must be Mom!"

The phantom's bones splintered and snapped! Its black mouth spread wide with a loud Pop!, and a multitude of mimicked souls disgorged from the pit like smoke billowing from a smokestack. With a final burst of flames, the phantom dispersed, leaving behind the smell of wet leaves and worms. Sean gasped when the flashlight in his hand came back to life, shining its beam at his face.

"Holy fuck, man! Is it gone? Is it over?" asked Zach, still crouched on top of the dryer.

"Yeah. I think it is. Now get the fuck off my dryer," said Sean, smiling.

Sean's ringtone was sounding upstairs. The brothers raced up to the basement door and burst out into the kitchen. Sean rushed into the living room where he reached for his cellphone on the coffee table and answered it.

"Hello!"

Zach flopped into the Lazy-boy with exhaustion. He watched his brother roll his shoulders back, bend his neck side to side, and sigh with relief.

"You saved our lives, Ma. You have no idea. We can't thank you enough. And I'll send our thanks to Father Marvan for saying a blessing over the graves. I wouldn't have believed it could work if I hadn't experienced it myself. We love you too, Mom. Thank you so much."

Sean put his phone down and crashed into the sofa.

Atmospheric

1

Blood oozed from the cut above Saffron's swollen left eye as she ran terrorized through the catacombs. She tripped in a pothole, staggering awkwardly before collapsing on her elbows. Overcome with panic, she clawed choking strands of her hair away from her throat. Then, something gripped her by her right foot, snapped it to the left with a crack (Saffron screamed!), and forced her to flip onto her back. Although she couldn't see in the darkness, she knew it was staring down at her, delighting in her suffering.

"Please," she whispered tremulously.

A heavy waterfall suddenly splashed down on her. Saffron squirmed under the burning hot flow, turning her chin up to avoid being hosed in the face. The stench of urine was repulsive, causing her to cough and gag. A powerful hand locked around her neck like a snakebite and yanked her off the ground. Her assailant was silent, not even a breath could she hear passing over its hidden lips (lips she knew must be grinning).

She felt its hot breath melting down along her neck, then teeth like jagged glass sawed into her shoulder. Saffron screamed and screamed as the excruciating pain sent violent shocks throughout her body. She could feel a thick layer of skin and muscle tearing as the teeth ripped away, blood guzzling forth, the stretching and stretching, and then the final—Snap!—when the piece came free. She could hear it chew and swallow. As if to toy with her, the thing shook her about, then flung her with an apoplectic roar. She lay on her side half-naked and tortured, panting, and bleeding.

Get up, Saff, she coached herself. *I still feel your heart beating. You're not dead yet. Get up, get up!*

She gathered her fleeting strengths and rose to her feet, teetering as a drunkard toward a speck of light in the ceiling ahead. She thought she heard laughter behind her, or perhaps a growl, whatever the case, she was determined to get away with what little life she had left. The closer she drew to the light, the larger the spotlight became, filling her with hope for safety. "Help me! Somebody help me!" she shouted, reaching out.

There was a rumble. A tremor shook the walls and addled Saffron. She stumbled, bumping against the wall to her right, where a gluey substance caught her hair. She yelped as if she was being poked at. *The light!* she remembered, pushing herself forward. She kept glancing back, but now the tremors had left cracks in the walls, where light spewed forth. And behind her, her assailant's dark figure seemed to drift, ponderously passing through the beams of buttery light. Saffron shuddered.

Her only route of escape lay at least five feet above her, out of reach. Another tremor. Both Saffron and her assailant were tossed about. But a ledge in the wall created by the shifting cave presented an opportunity to her. She climbed up at a speed which was not her choice but her last strengths and began to push up on the final barrier between herself and the outside world.

She heard it again—the laughter or the growls. As the ledge began to crumble out from beneath her, Saffron screamed, struggling furiously to get the cap off her escape hole. She didn't sense her attacker was below her yet. (She'd know, she was certain, if it was.) It's very life filled the surrounding air around it with an electrifying pulse. And there was that smell, a gag-inducing blend of sweetness and excrement.

Above Saffron's groaning and forcing, the hole she was trying so desperately to escape through was only the size of a hubcap and was covered by an entangled group of rusted shopping carts, leftovers from a world she did not even know. "Somebody! Please! Help!" she cried weakly. As her footing disappeared, crumbling out of existence, the ground above was also undergoing changes. The carts began to roll and topple down the hilltop under the force of the wind. Saffron thought she felt the lid giving way, then not. "Come on!" she yelled, and the carts tumbled over.

She came up out of the ground, red light beaming up behind her like some hellish entity. But at once everything seemed to move in slow motion. The fumes and smoke from below spiralled up into the storm. The darting snowflakes rendered her as sightless as the cave's darkness had. Saffron crawled out on her hands and knees, palms slipping out from under her in the muck and slush. She slid down the hill and crashed into the mess of carts. Frantically, she fought to free herself from the puzzle, her mind finally surrendering to the madness it had been keeping at bay.

As she crabwalked away from the carts, the beast was not in sight, but she knew it was out. "Help me!" she tried again, praying fervently for someone to come to her rescue. She got up reeling, wondering which direction to run. And then, without another moment of thought, she was zigzagging around mountains of garbage, freezing and petrified, fumbling over hidden lumps under the snow.

Thunder gave her a start, while swarms of lightning set many sections of the already beaten city ablaze. Close to the water, where angry waves pummelled the rotting beach, Saffron could carry her fractured ankle no farther. She belly-flopped, sliding up to the edge of the cliff Home Run-style. Glancing up, she saw lightning spread across the sky like so many white veins shooting to life, her pupils shrank.

When she turned over, the beast once again snatched her by the throat with such speed, her scream was cut off before it reached her lips. Sapped of strength, Saffron hung there in its arms, face to face. Belting snow sketched the air white between them. "Just...kill...me," she uttered. The beast's eyes traced her purple bleeding lips. It leaned forward, and from a distance, their silhouette against the flashes over the ocean gave the impression of lovers about to kiss.

Saffron was burning up as she felt teeth and tongue revisiting her shoulder wound. Her jaw was jerking as blood escaped her nose and mouth. She was giddy and barely conscious. She felt her entire body float backward and down to the cold, slushy ground. Dull color sprayed before her eyes as her soft belly filled with teeth and over-anxious claws. Blood pooled over her sides and made the night a devilish artwork.

And the killer loomed over the corpse, captivated by its gutted prey, gazing intently at the brightly colored entrails. Crouching down at Saffron's head, the powerful hands that had invaded every part of her, pulled and twisted and severed the head. A careless kick sent the head rolling over the cliff and down toward the beach where it landed with a gushing splash in a pot of mud and oil. Then, as the storm looked on, no more appalled than a blind man, Saffron's mutilated body was dragged out of sight.

2

Jett cursed his very existence as he battled discomfort for a moment of rest in the overturned scrap of a dump truck. He wiggled his frozen hands into the damp stuffing of the seat, through the torn leather covering. A short time later, he awoke, the sound of hail on his shelter.

As he moved to sit up, his hair sounded like Velcro as it came unstuck from the frozen rear window. So many mornings had he known like this: cold, hungry, and alone. He kicked at the door with both feet, forcing it open. If he'd slept any longer there's a chance he may have become trapped in the makeshift shelter. The hail ceased just then; Jett's brow furrowed. The ocean raged below as he stretched out into the cold, his breath mystifying before him. Steam rose from cracks in the hills made during last night's tremors. Although it was definitely morning, no sun shone on the day. Darkness entombed the world. No one born in the last thirty-six years had known it to be any other way. Disease and decay plagued humanity and all life alike.

Jett climbed up the hill, over piles of yesterday's world turned to trash. He now stood with his back to the ocean. An ocean that may or may not be there when next he stood on this spot. Before him, about half a mile away, lay the designs of yet another levelled city. Having spent a lifetime travelling the globe in search of some form of peace and purpose, and having no luck, Jett looked upon this as just another stop along the way.

He rubbed his arms, his stomach growling. The final stretch to the city's gates was marked by two rows of scrap vehicles piled one on top of the other. Many had fallen from their perch, but a 100-foot piece of roadway in the middle made the path obvious. Jett expected some sort of welcoming committee, whether bad or good. However, he saw and heard no one. When he reached the entrance, a great rumble of thunder galloped overhead, glowing acid rain came crackling down. Jett hurried under the gate and searched for shelter. Powerful winds raked through the open street as he ran into a trash tunnel. There were still no signs of life. The shelter was an amazing structure. He'd never seen an entire city built from garbage and built well.

As Jett headed deeper into the tunnel, thunder followed above him like a giant's footsteps on the roof. Feeling pretty confident that the tunnel would hold up in the storm, his pace slowed to an easy tourist-like stroll. The ground was dry, except for the odd puddle where rain had burned its way through weak spots in the ceiling. Blue steam lingered around these areas like guardian ghosts.

In the distance, blowing out of the wall, a red silk scarf stood out brightly in contrast to the rusted steel and rubber. Jett reached for the scarf, its color twining softly about his hand. He started to smile. Something new. But there were softer things he would come to know yet, and soon. A haunting whisper of wind slipped past him, drawing his attention forward once again. The squeaking of an old pram buggy placed him on alert at once. Before him, the tunnel began to turn toward the left.

Once he passed the buggy and rounded the bend, a pack of rats scurried across his path. Jett watched the rats, knowing that if there was a way out, without venturing into the storm, the rats would know it. He quickly followed the rodents until the tunnel narrowed. Here, iron rods protruding from the walls were meant as a deterrent for stragglers. Jett's eyes sharpened, his fingers curling into fists, his back arching. The tunnel was like a snake, withering side to side. Then it dealt him a steep hill, its peak in full darkness.

Jett crept upward, thunder simulating the sounds of Earth splitting in two. When he reached the top a surprised raven seeking shelter flapped its wings and screeched at him. The wind rattled and rolled an aluminum coffee pot between them. "Easy, friend. I'm not here to bother you," he said, the nervous raven bobbing its head and hopping.

Beyond the tunnel lay the remnants of a train bridge, and just beyond that was a set of shining steel doors, which appeared to be the only entrance into the city of trash. He stepped back, away from the pecking rain, and began to search for something to use as protection to make the trek across. Everything he managed to loosen from the tunnel walls was too small, too heavy, or too decrepit to withstand the acidic rain. As he paced back and forth something buckled underfoot. Jett got down on his hands and knees and dug out an assortment of twisted metal shapes.

Among the buried trash, he uncovered an aluminum pole. Jett yanked the pole free from its position in the collage of trash—a table umbrella! He hurried back to the tunnel's exit, the raven keeping a curious watch. He forced the rusty ring up the pole, causing the faded, flowered umbrella to unfurl with crackling stiffness.

As he started across the bridge, stepping with caution over the mushy wooden boards, holes burned wider and wider in the polyester. Before long, beads of rain were attacking his right shoulder. Trickles rolled down the pole and burned his gloved fingers, but Jett did not falter. He quickened his steps and wiggled his fingers, teeth grinding. Then he saw the final stretch between him and the opposite landing was void of boards. Jett looked up; his canopy was collapsing. Without hesitation, he whipped the umbrella sideways, using it as a balancing pole. One foot after the other, he crossed the right rail like a balance beam, charging ahead.

A few feet away from the opposite landing, Jett slipped. The pole landed across both tracks, surprising him with his luck. He looked miles down below his dangling feet, then up toward the doors before him, where he caught a glimpse of a face staring back at him. "Help! Help me!" he shouted, the sizzling rain forcing him to bow his head. When no one came, he replaced his grip on the slippery pole and began to swing his legs back and forth. The eyes peeking through the slight crack between the doors watched him curiously.

Jett swung harder and harder, higher and higher until, much to the amazement of his one man audience, he performed a 360-degree spin with great agility. Once around, twice around, and on the third spin, Jett somersaulted into the air. He landed on all fours, jabbing the umbrella pole firmly into the ground, his eyes glaring up at the eyes watching him.

"Slam dunk! If that weren't the bestest stunt I seen in thirty years uh watchin' over this bridge!" came a chuckling voice.

The doors began to open wider. Jett, panting hard, his body steaming, stepped inside nonchalantly, despite the burning. The heavy doors sealed shut behind him with a hiss. Smoke bellowed from splits in the ground. The air was thick with rust and ash. Overhead, the rain pattered the aluminum roof. Jett turned on the chuckling man, infuriated.

"Now slows down there," said the toothless, grubby man.

Jett grabbed a fistful of his garments. The man's eyes were wide and frightened, but he did not resist Jett in any way.

"Why didn't you help me, you son of a bitch?" Jett fired.

The man laughed, his odd sense of humor further enraging Jett. Then Jett eased off a little; the stench of this laughing fool was making his eyes water.

"Friend, I do wish I could have lent a hand," the man said as Jett began to see more than just eyes and nose, and suddenly understood the joke. "But hands is somethin' I ain't got."

Jett released his grip and rubbed his blistered hands together through what little leather remained of his gloves. The man offered his soiled right foot as a greeting; Jett ignored his offering.

"Anyhow," the man continued, "people call me Scissors, on account O' my missin' danglies. And what people call you, friend?"

"I'm not your friend. And where the hell am I?"

Scissors laughed and said, "Never seen anyone make that bridge way you did, friend. Slam dunk!"

"Cut the chitchat and tell me where I am, or arms or not, I'll beat you bloody...friend," Jett warned.

Scissors chortled, then stopped the instant Jett looked back at him with nefarious intent. He staggered up to Jett, looked him right in the eyes, then dropped his chin to his chest. Jett looked down.

"Here's where you at. And there ain't no place like it nowheres."

Jett read the rubber mat. "Welcome?"

"That's it! You says it like you been here forever. Must mean you here to stay, friend."

Jett's eyes narrowed.

"Sorry," Scissors said as he sat down on a car tire, next to a bonfire set in a steel rim.

"Can you show me how to get inside?" Jett pursued.

Scissors nodded, flashing him that rotted smile, his brown bloodshot eyes looking past Jett.

"Follow them fellas. They knows the way in", he sniffled.

Jett turned to see the rats waddling away from him. He looked at Scissors, shook his head, then started after the rats. "Keep you wits, friend!" he heard Scissors yell, then laugh and laugh.

"Shit," Jett cursed, following the rats on his hands and knees through a sewage tunnel, the smell of which he found to be less appalling than the stench of Scissors. "I'll kill that fucking freak if this is a dead-end."

He kept his eyes on the shimmering gray hair of the rats running ahead of him, their heavy bodies wadding through the gunk. From somewhere in the inky distance, he could hear faint sounds of music and voices growing louder with each sloshing movement forward. A small round grill door appeared before him, its spray-painted skull and bones logo was all that remained between him and the mysteries of the garbage city called Welcome.

3

The grid door refused to open, inward or out. Rats crawled over Jett's legs as he kicked at the door, but still, it wouldn't budge. Then he heard a click-clunk sound as if a lock had been opened. Jett waited for moments in the icy sewage water, his teeth chattering. He crouched forward and forced the door open with surprising ease. As the door opened downward and out, music like pipes clanging and bizarre vibrating tones echoed into the tunnel.

Jett stepped out under the gaze of obstreperous crowds where stifling fog lingered in the air. Many among them began to point and laugh, laughing above the intense volume of industrial music and cheering. Jett failed to see the joke his presence made. Such behavior he was not accustomed to, nor likened to. Was it that he was dripping of sewage? he wondered, stepping forward.

Fires burned in barrels everywhere he looked, sparks and smoke dancing toward the ceiling over the street. By now he'd had enough of this secret joke and finger pointing. A short man with homemade weapons donning his uniform stepped up closer to Jett, hatred in his glaring eyes.

"We don't need you here. Leave," he ordered.

Jett approached him, looking down at him. "I think I'll stay," he said flatly.

"Go back where you came from, you piece of shit!" a

woman's voice yelled. Laughter drowned out the music. When Jett finally turned around, there it was: the sewer door he'd crawled out of was the rectum of a giant asshole painted on the wall. "Piece of shit!" someone shouted to him.

Jett studied the painting, ignoring the mob's attacks. His eyes darted up and down, side to side, quickly calculating the course of his intentions. With a swift spin, he turned and snatched several of the oddly shaped blades hanging from the short man's belt.

"Hey!" the man shouted as Jett sent each of the blades on separate courses. One whizzed past the stunned faces of people to his left, straight toward its target with the accuracy of a bullet, and pierced the side of an oil drum near the painted wall. A second blade, curved like a half-moon, boomeranged over the head of the junkies sitting on the ground with needles in their arms. They looked on in awe as a fiery torch in a sconce on the wall shattered upon impact.

And finally a third blade, jagged along its edges and at least a foot in length, seared the air as it passed under the noses of some who were still laughing; the hair on the backs of their necks stood on end. This blade took more sconces, igniting the entire wall ablaze. As the crowd separated in panic, Jett looked at the short man's startled expression, then stepped past him, bumping him out of his way.

"Assholes," Jett said to himself.

As the bustle of the crowd was left behind him, Jett remained, as always, calm about himself. He roamed the maze of Welcome's claustrophobic streets in search of anything edible to cure his hunger. Every corner and every step of the way presented strange activities. He stopped to watch a gang of people engaged in an orgy on a chain-link fence. They saw him staring and just stared back. Their orgy drew little attention from anyone else. This didn't surprise him since everyone else was too busy with their games.

As he walked away, a woman involved in the orgy opened her legs to him. "Hey, baby, where you goin'? I got some hot places you can put your tongue. Hey!" she called, but Jett kept right on walking. "Hey, you cockless fucker! You son of a bitch! Fuck you, asshole!"

"Maybe you're into this," came a voice from Jett's right. And out of the shadows stepped a mutated man, his jaw connected to his chest, his left arm hanging out of his hip. He was stroking the erect deformity between his legs. Jett quickly turned away and rounded the next bend, where a group of people huddled around a fiery barrel. Some were mutated from birth, others mutated by choice. They watched and waited for their turn to be branded with burning irons like cattle. Presently, the man being served was screaming in pain.

Sparks from live wires sprayed the ground, sizzling maggots in a heap of fresh garbage outside a place where deafening music was being performed live. Jett recognized the sounds of banging steel barrels and applause. Two naked men ran by him, whooping like rodeo cowboys. Many people, oddly dressed or not dressed at all, staggered past him with bloodshot eyes. He shoved his way through the horde and proceeded toward the music.

At the foot of the inn, Jett met Siamese hookers. They were slow to move toward him, having each their luggage of fat rolls to carry. Jett looked them up and down, never the glimmer of indifference on his face. The twin on the right reached out and touched his shoulder with her chubby fingers.

"Two for the price of one, you handsome treat."

"We'll show you what foreplay is all about. Make you come for days, treasure," said the other.

"No thanks, ladies," Jett said, trying to get around them. The twins grabbed hold of his waist and pulled him against them, their hands gripping his buttocks.

"Ooh. A gentlemen type. You're not a resident of Welcome, that's for sure," said the left twin.

Jett forced them back, saying, "Maybe I'll think about it if you can first direct me to the nearest eatery."

Another hooker came forward and stepped between Jett and the twins. She said, "Watching you has given me a heart-on, sweet lover." She opened her leather bra to reveal two heaving breasts and a large heart beating between them.

Jett rolled his eyes. "Look. All I want is some food," he said.

"You can eat me," said the hooker. "For half the price of those raunchy bitches."

"I need real food," Jett stated, and shoved the hookers aside with frustration. He walked up to the door of the inn.

"Only the favored are allowed in there!" the hooker

warned him as she snapped her bra back together.

Jett entered through the door, its loud slam unheard inside the hotel called The Furnace.

4

The moment Jett stepped inside The Furnace, he'd triggered the start of something horrific, something undreamed of in all his thirty-one years. Jett had never seen such sights before. So much confusion, yet all was in order (systematic chaos). Sex was everywhere: men fucking women, men fucking men, women fucking women; gangs of people in scanty outfits lying on tabletops, feasting on each other's bodies like mad beasts at play.

There were so many people, he couldn't move but one step every few minutes. Hands groped at him. He was unable to focus on one sight at a time. People were walking around on stilts, dressed in colorful strips of silk and satin, their bodies tattooed and painted. Some waved torches about. Jett saw a mutated man with piercing eyes and teeth sharpened into fangs, pissing on the dancing fools below him, and they were cheering!

Women were wearing tight-fitting outfits, with collars as high as three feet above their heads. Every freak he could imagine was present, and some he couldn't. He pressed deeper into the crowd, into the mosh pit. Elbows, shoulders, and hips shoved Jett back and forth. He spun around, ready to take on any one of those freaks. But he soon realized that all this hitting and pushing about was meant with only playful intentions. So he elbowed left and right, and even threw a couple of direct punches until he crossed the room. And as he did, one set of eyes followed his path from the point where he entered, to where he ended up.

Jett no sooner squeezed into a chair made from torn-up sofas and bricks, when a very angry-looking man came charging toward him through the crowd. The man slammed an unopened can of beans on the table before Jett. He leaned over the table until the heat of his foul breath warmed Jett's face.

"Eat! Then leave!" he ordered, with no if, and, or buts about it.

Jett stared unblinking into the man's black, daring eyes. Then the man turned and lumbered back into the crowd and disappeared. There were several other tables around Jett, but only the disparate gang at one of them seemed interested in him. He knew he was being watched, but he was too hungry to care at the moment. He removed one of the dozens of darts attached to his leathers, which he used for weapons like throwing stars. This particular tag he used to open the can of beans, and in seconds he'd shaken the entire contents of the can into his mouth. But it wasn't enough; he was still famished.

The screeching of the band's microphone cutting in and out drew his attention back to the stage. The band members were throwing themselves about the stage as if water and electricity were involved in the act. No one gave a damn that each member seemed to be soloing at once, or that nothing they played even came close to actual music. The only words Jett understood was vulgarity at its crudest. The audience thrived on the blasting sounds and bathed in the sweltering heat of the place.

As Jett shifted in his uncomfortable seat, the six thugs who'd been observing him stood and were making their way toward him. Here it comes, he thought. The gang circled Jett's table and waited for him to make a move. Jett looked up at their repulsive faces. Their leader, who faced him directly, placed his scarred hands upon the table and gave it a shake. The empty can of beans rolled off the edge, but Jett caught it and put it back.

"Scared?" the leader asked, leaning over the table.

Jett remained still, staring unblinking back into the man's yellow eyes. He wore a tall, crooked top hat that looked like it had been kicked around some, and a long tattered black coat with the collar raised high. Only one side of his face was bearded, the other thickly scarred. With gray skin and rotten teeth behind blackened lips, he seemed perfectly cast for the role of leader.

"You deaf, motherfucker? The man asked you a question," a voice said in his right ear. Then the man behind him flicked Jett's left ear; Jett's eyes narrowed.

"Nice getup. Your name wouldn't happen to be Tinkerbell, now would it?" said the bloated-faced member to the left of the leader.

The leader was the only one, along with Jett, who didn't laugh at the joke. He shook his head and brought instant silence back to the others.

"What's your business here?" he snarled.

Jett showed him the empty can of beans, thinking his reason for being there was quite obvious.

The two men behind Jett pulled back on his shoulders, yanking his chair away from the table. But before matters could worsen a beautiful woman, who seemed to suddenly appear out of thin air, sat down on Jett's lap. Jett was stunned. The gang leader ground his teeth as he shook his head, eyes narrowed.

"No! Not this one!" he raged.

The woman said nothing as she wrapped her arms lovingly about Jett's shoulders, cradling his head into her breasts.

"Damn you, Pretty."

Pretty turned to look into Jett's eyes. He was at once taken by her beauty. Her skin was heliotrope, lips full and dark, eyes resplendent violet, and her lengthy purple hair brushed in around her cheeks. As the band pounded out marching rhythms, Jett's would-be assailants stomped back to their table like scolded children.

"Just who are you?" she asked Jett, running her finger over his lips.

He kept silent, gazing into her eyes.

Pretty looked him over and smiled, finding him very much to her liking. "Come with me."

Jett allowed Pretty to guide him through the crowd and up to one of the many freestanding staircases. The gang members were not the only ones watching them ascend.

Pretty led Jett across a short swinging bridge and down a long dark hallway. At the end of the hall, they climbed another set of stairs. Pretty's long purple dress trailed behind them. Finally, at their destination, she unlocked a door and they entered a large room. Pretty sat him down on the mattress on the floor. The room was heavily decorated with multicolored fragments of material, Moroccan style. Her collection boasted some of the finest pieces to be found in these times.

From a wooden crate, Pretty removed an assortment of canned foods. She tossed them one by one very quickly to Jett, who caught them just as quick.

"For the road," she said.

"Thank you," he said with a bow, placing the cans in a leather satchel.

"Who are you?" she asked him again.

"My name is Jett. I'm just passing through, hopefully without trouble."

Pretty giggled. "No one can look as good as you do and not command attention, and that usually means the wrong kind of attention—trouble."

"Those assholes down there, who are they?"

"Speaking of 'trouble.' The one who got up in your face, that's Villain, their leader. He's a real piece of work. The others are a bunch of crazed maniacs. Beez is the one with the puffed-up face. He and Gutter are Villain's right-hand men. Gutter's the green loose-skinned bastard with the patches of black hair on his warped head. They'd die for him. They've killed for him.

"Then there's Massacre, that big mutated dumb fucker who cut his fingers off his left hand because he thought it would instill fear in someone—it did."

"Dicks."

"The other two are Fright and Stealth. If you haven't

figured it out, Stealth is the one with no mouth...on his face. That stretched putty face gives me the chills. I don't know how he eats, and I don't want to. And Fright, that silver-eyed, monster-looking motherfucker; listen, as long as you are in Welcome, do not let your guard down for a second. They will kill you."

"So why did you help me, and why did they let you?"

"This is my place. In here my word is law. They know better than to fuck with me," said Pretty.

Jett suspected there was more to it than just management, but asked no further questions. Pretty was finished talking, besides, as she allowed her dress to slip from her shoulders.

"Do not fear me, Jett. I can see right into your soul. Can you see beyond my skin?" she whispered seductively.

And as Jett gazed upon her nakedness, one after the next, violet and hypnotizing eyes were revealed all over her body. But not frightening eyes. Utterly sensuous, mesmerizing eyes. She turned and stepped silently between his legs.

5

Jett was nearly dressed when he and Pretty heard footfalls coming up the stairs. Pretty unveiled a hidden passage that would lead him outside The Furnace. Jett flung his satchel over his head and shoulder.

"Thank you, Pretty, a name never more deserved."

She kissed him on the lips and smiled as a knocking came to her door. Jett crawled through the hole in the wall. He could hear more knocking as he slipped away.

"I'm busy!" Pretty shouted. "Leave me be!"

The door creaked open, but looming in the doorway was not Villain or one of his goons, it was the gaunt figure an old man. Pretty smiled at him and said, "You can't afford this visit, old man. Now kindly shut my door and be on your way."

The old man grinned, his sunken cheeks revealing the skull beneath. The length of his black robe swished across the floor as he approached her, despite her obvious discontent with him.

At that moment, Jett was climbing down a rope ladder in an alleyway. When he jumped the final distance, he drew the attention of Joy, the oldest living black man in Welcome. Like so many of the day, Joy was learning disabled, disfigured, and hearing impaired. He was so named because joy was the only word he could speak.

He watched the tall lean man in black pass him by and understood that he'd come from that secret place where only the most beautiful men could come.

Meanwhile, Pretty was losing her patience with her uninvited guest. "Who sent you? Was it Villain? Well, you can go back and tell that piece of shit I'm not playing games with him. Joke's over. Now get the fuck out. Don't make me force you," she warned.

As the man stepped closer the door swung shut on its own. The umpteen strings of lights around the room began to flicker, bulbs popping. Pretty stared at him in silence. He stopped advancing and stood perfectly still in a patch of darkness left by the popped bulbs. Fear swelled within Pretty.

"Do not come any closer. All I have to do is scream and twenty people will rush up here to take you down, Mr.," she lied, knowing no one would hear her screams above the downstairs ruckus.

The old man stepped closer until she was pressing her hand against his chest to stop him. She stared into his glimmering eyes as blackness bled into the sockets. Pretty gasped! More lights popped until only a few remained lit and flickering, immersing the room in an eerie glow.

The old man's right hand touched her tiny waist and slid up under her left arm, then his left hand slid under her right arm. Pretty trembling, transfixed by his bewitching eyes. With shocking strength, he flung her onto the mattress. Snapping out of her trance, she scrambled away from him, fumbling onto the floor.

"Who the fuck are you?! What do you want?!" she shouted, her back up against the wall.

The old man's head jerked left, and at once the entire room tilted to the left. Pretty lost her balance, screaming as all the contents of her room were tossed along with her. But the man never budged, as if his feet were rooted to the floor.

"Help me!" Pretty yelled, crawling over the clutter piled about her.

The old man then jerked his head to the right, and the room followed suit. Pretty slammed into the opposite wall, her mattress half on top of her. She kicked it off and began to crawl along the edges of the room, trying to make her way around the intruder.

His fingers sprouted long claws. Opening his arms to her, Pretty felt herself whip through the air and land within his fierce embrace. In a flash, he severed her right arm at the elbow. Her cries reached no other. Her myriad eyes twitched and blinked uncontrollably.

The old man held her severed arm above his head and drank the flowing blood. When he tossed it aside, Pretty heard the dull thud of it hit the wall, then the floor. The devil gargled with her blood, letting it gush over his chin. And suddenly, a zigzagging slit like a pumpkin's smile was carved across her throat!

The killer fed savagely on Pretty's flesh. He dug out every eyeball from her corpse and placed them in a circle around himself on the blood-drenched mattress. The aching in his belly was slowly being subdued. When there was nothing left of Pretty's head but a skull with mangled hair, he held it under his gaze and grinned nefariously.

So much blood. Solid red from his fingertips up to his elbows. He now sat slumped against the wall, panting from fullness. The once frail little man had grown prodigiously fat. His brow furrowed at the sound of footsteps and voices drawing near. Too soon his pleasure was disrupted. Without a moment to spare, he rushed to the hidden panel. Glancing around the room at the mess he'd created, he then closed the panel behind him.

"Come on, Pretty! We know you're in there. Open up!" Fright growled. "You best let us in, bitch! Villain won't stand for no bullshit!"

When no reply came, Stealth body-slammed the door in. Fright charged in and immediately slipped in a pool of blood. While he struggled to rise, Stealth looked around the room confused.

"Oh fuck! Shit! Well, don't just stand there, dummy, help me up!" Fright shouted.

Staring at Pretty's head bewildered, Stealth lent Fright his hand without looking down.

"Fuck me," Fright drawled. "That skinny motherfucker done this. Fuck. Villain's gonna be fucking pissed!"

As they hurried back down to inform Villain, Joy was watching a curious sloppy fat man climb down Pretty's rope ladder. This made no sense whatsoever. The fat man was not even halfway down the ladder when it began to rain. This section of Welcome was exposed to the elements, so Joy retreated deeper into his trash pile, taking his eyes from the man for only a moment. When he looked up again, the fat man had become something far more menacing.

Joy wondered if he wasn't dreaming as the shape hovered above the alley. As if in slow motion the figure in black descended to the street. Joy instinctively covered himself with more trash to keep from being seen. Acid rain began to set fire to flammable garbage, shedding some light on the figure as it approached.

The lengthy cloak worn by the stranger whipped and snapped in the wind. And as he strode past, Joy could see two large clawed feet, covered in long white hair. There was a sudden beam of fierce red light too brilliant for Joy to look at, and just as suddenly, the darkness returned.

Joy scanned the alley, scratching his scarred head, but the figure had disappeared without a trace.

6

Jett awoke to the irritating cacophony of a hundred Welcomers beating on makeshift drums. The air was damp and bitter tasting. Having slept under the shelter of an overturned aluminum boat near the edge of town, he crawled his way out. Too curious to pass up a chance to see what all the commotion was about, he headed toward the inner streets.

It wasn't long before he joined the crowds not participating in the inharmonious activities. It appeared that all of Welcome had come out for this event.

"What is this? What's happening?" he asked a one-armed woman. Her eyes were large balls, having no eyelids. When she spoke her lips flapped and her jaw cracked.

"Mourning for the slain one," she hacked.

"Must've been someone important, huh?"

The woman just stared at him.

Jett stepped back and watched the parade pass them by. Thunder seemed to drop from the sky and boom just above their heads.

Less than thirty feet away, half of the Siamese hooker spotted Jett. They hurried to a closer location where one could point him out to the other. Their fleshy cheeks jiggled as their heads shook, mouths moving excitedly. Rushing through the crowd, they ran to the end of the parade where Villain and his gang were carrying all that remained of Pretty in a makeshift coffin, which bore no lid.

The instant Villain received word about Jett's presence, he ordered his men to split up and surround the suspect. As Jett stood unaware, Beez and Gutter closed in on him from his right, while Massacre and Stealth approached on his left.

Jett felt something hard ram into the back of his knees! He crumbled under the impact as a strong arm grabbed him around the neck from behind, cutting off his breath. Stealth was the owner of that strong arm; he forced Jett to his feet. Massacre appeared in front of Jett and pool-cued him in the abdomen with a steel pole. Jett would have doubled over, if not for Massacre holding him up.

The parade's drumming ceased as the crowd parted to allow Villain a clear path to his men. By now, Stealth held Jett's arms behind his back, threatening to break them if he struggled. Villain stood before him now, looking very smug.

"Either you're very fucking stupid, or you have balls of brass. Which one do you think it is?" he asked, looking at Fright.

Fright cockpunched Jett; Jett's pain was evident by his tearing eyes and reddened face.

"Stupid!" Fright demonstrated.

"Just as I thought. Didn't I say he was a stupid motherfucker, boys?" said Villain. "Show him why he's about to die a painful death."

Stealth forced Jett over to the casket and shoved his

face right into the box for an up-close visual. The stench made his head reel, but he opened his eyes anyway. There was a mess of ripe meat and bones under his nose, nothing he could distinguish as anything *but* meat. When Stealth pulled his head back a little, he was able to discern certain objects among the slop—eyes! These were not just any eyeballs, they were washy violet eyeballs.

"Pretty?" he choked.

At once he began to struggle, trying to force himself away from the horror. He and Stealth staggered back. When Stealth once again forced his grip on his arms, Jett held still.

Villain marched right up to him, gobbed in his face, and growled, "Today you die, motherfucker."

He then turned, removed his top hat, raised it into the air, and addressed the crowd: "We have here the filth who murdered, nay, *slaughtered!*, Pretty after she'd so generously opened her house of fire to him! I put before you not a question of *should* he be put to death, but *how* we shall perform such a duty...*our* duty as the citizens of Welcome!"

The crowd was cheering and hissing. Villain looked into Jett's eyes and grinned with wicked delight.

"What say you, Welcomers?!"

People started shouting, "Post! Post! Post!"

Villain threw his hat up once more and silence swept over the throng. "My fellow Welcomers, you have spoken! It is my pleasure to pronounce the Post as his sentence! To the Post!"

The gathering went wild with excitement. Stealth released his stronghold on Jett, shoving him forward. Gutter, Massacre, Fright, and Beez all took to punching him, kicking him after he'd fallen, and gobbing on him in turn. They then dragged him up the street. Jett could barely open his eyes for all the blood and swelling. His head hung low as they slammed his back up against an old hydro pole, which managed to remain standing firm after so many years. They tied him to it with rope, leather straps, and even barbwire. Villain ordered the dumping of Pretty's pieces at his feet.

"Die with your victim at your feet so you remember in death what you did!" he shouted. Then, leaning in to whisper to Jett, he added, "If it had been my choice, you'd have been skinned and left for the rats, motherfucker!"

With all the commotion, no one had paid attention to the change in the weather. The air had become sweltering hot almost instantly. People suddenly began to run about in hysterics.

"It's a blazer!" Fright identified.

Although Jett was unfamiliar with the term, he was certainly acquainted with the symptoms. All of Welcome was screaming with unbridled panic, scrambling for shelter. The sky seemed to bubble bright orange, shining golden on Villain's face.

"It's coming!" shouted Beez, pointing to the clouds.

Everyone fled the scene, except Villain, he remained to the last minute.

"Enjoy the ride!" he jeered, spinning on his heels with mirth.

The wind sounded mechanical like the screeches and squeals of heavy machinery. Fiery dust spun trash into deadly weapons all around him. Even larger scraps like car doors, bumpers, tires, furniture, and the like pitched to and fro. Surely, he knew, if he couldn't manage to free himself from his bindings, he would die.

He attempted to wriggle his hands loose, his arms, but he could not budge. Though he couldn't yet see it, he knew the blazer was closing in. Waves of devastating heat bowled over him. Pretty's pieces were long scattered far and wide. The monster's roar was deafening—terrifying! Flying debris zippered past him. One object came spinning out of the storm like a Frisbee, dancing upward to his right, then swooping down to his left, then up again. The silver disc suddenly shifted directions and shot straight into the post, just missing Jett's face! Planted halfway into the wood, he'd nearly been decapitated by the hubcap.

The post creaked, cracked, and collapsed, dragging him along the ground until it jammed into something unmovable. Jett was now able to wriggle his way free. He ran pell-mell in the opposite direction of the flaming twister's path. The blazer seemed to give chase, leaving everything in its wake blackened and in flames. Anyone foolish enough to still be running about was made into charcoal to feed the hellish beast's insatiable appetite.

Startling explosions erupted all about him as he fled toward the ocean. He ran and slipped, rolled and fumbled his way down a hill slick with mud. Jett was unsure of where he was going, so long as it was away from the threat. Everything before him appeared to already be in flames or crashing down into rubble. But one structure remained intact, and that was precisely where he headed.

He struggled to push the stone door open, its bottom edge scraping along the inner floor. Jett managed to squeeze through the narrow opening. He forced his weight against the door to reseal it; the flaming hairs brushing in along the door's edges snuffed out with a banshee shriek.

So now he stood in pure darkness within this veritable oven. He was safe and trapped at once. The heat radiating off the four walls was unbearable. He crawled to the centre of the room where he lay on his side, curled up in a ball, and passed out.

7

Fires still burned in the defeated streets of Welcome. Black smoke filled the air. Blazers were a regular occurrence, a shitty part of life; however, everyone knew that one day Welcome would be wiped out of existence. Welcomers were out in the early morning rain, trying to salvage what they could for repairs. Many had missing to wonder about, dead to clear off the streets.

Meanwhile, unknown to him, someone watched over Jett as he slept. Light shone through a hairline fracture in the ceiling, casting a faint yellow glow upon his face. As he stirred the other took advantage of this light to scrutinize his features.

His livid skin appeared greenish under the yellow beam. Long stringy black hair lay sprawled on the ground behind him. His eyebrows were thin, but with long hairs forming pointed peeks near the ends. A dark moustache hung past his jawline, matched in length by the vertical stripes that were his strange beard design. He looked a bit sinister due to this feature.

He stirred once more, licking the blood on his lip. The silver darts attached to his clothing tinkered when he moved. The throwing stars hung from his shoulders, down his forearms, his legs, and were attached to the knee-high boots he wore. As he turned his head, he revealed the burned and gluey skin on his left ear and neck. The skin stuck to the floor, stretching until tearing.

His deep breaths were raspy.

Mutated from birth, Jett's inflated ribs were on display through the open circle in his outfit. Wires kept his black gloves secured at his wrists. Around his waist, he wore a black leather skirt, which lay spread out behind him. As he stretched his reedy body out of its ball, he felt a kick at his right foot, then another. A third and harder kick behind his already bruised knee succeeded in waking him. Jett leapt to his feet, eyes burning as he leaned back against the wall. He couldn't see beyond the ray of light.

"What is your intent?" a stern female voice inquired.

Jett was rattled and groggy. He shook his head.

"I can kill you in an instant," said the voice.

"What have I done to you?" he asked.

"Nothing, and that is the way it will remain."

Jett stepped forward, and out of the darkness a flash of gold and orange swept his feet out from under him. "I warned you, you son of a bitch!"

Jett rubbed his left elbow and said, "I won't harm you. But I won't leave, either. I can't. There are people out there...people who want me dead."

"Why?"

"They think I killed someone."

"Did you?"

"No."

"They must have reason to believe you did."

"I was the last one to be seen with her," he explained.

"Her? Huh. I should've known."

"I am guiltless," Jett maintained as he stood.

The flash of gold and orange speared out of the darkness, and once again Jett found himself hitting the floor.

"You haven't answered all my questions yet," said the voice.

Jett leaned against the wall. "You won't catch me off guard again, woman."

A silence followed, then, "Who are you, if not a murderer?"

"My name is Jett. I was merely seeking food and shelter in Welcome, not blood and war."

"Why should I believe you're innocent? Why shouldn't I tell those maniacal heathens where to find you?"

"I didn't have to tell you anything, but I did. Does that not merit trust?"

Another moment of silence, then a tall dark woman stepped into the light. She was swathed in golden cloth like a mummy. Her shoulders and washboard abdomen were bare. Her long bright orange hair was tied into a ponytail, with colorful beads braided among its thick strands. She was shapely and sexy, with brilliant green eyes. She reached out to Jett with her right hand and he accepted it.

"You have my trust. But break it and I'll kill you myself," she said.

"You know who I am, now who the hell are you and what are you doing here?" he asked.

"You're weak. Here...sit. I can't do anything about those wounds, but I do have food and drink."

They sat face to face in the centre of the room, an overwhelming pong of decomposition wafting up through the cracks in the crumbling floor. The light shone on their heads as Jett slowly chewed dry bread, his jaw sending jolts of pain with every movement.

"You haven't told me who you are yet," he said, rubbing his jaw and wincing.

"Halo," she breathed. "Like you, I am just passing through this shithole. Hid in here from the damned blazer and then saw you come in, and here we are. That's my story. What's your next move?"

"I'm gonna find whoever killed Pretty and make them pay," Jett said bitterly.

Halo chuckled. "You go back in there and get caught again, you might not survive this time."

"I was caught off guard. That won't happen again."

"Like I caught you off guard...twice!"

Jett ceased his chewing for a moment, then said, "She was a good person. I will find her killer."

The earth trembled as if to punctuate his vow.

"We'll go in together and find this killer of yours, as soon as you've regained your strength," said Halo.

Jett looked at her, baffled. "Together? What are you talking about? This is my bullshit. No one said you had to get involved."

"Well, I have no other plans."

"Fuck that. I don't need your death on my conscience as well."

"I'm coming. I can help. *Trust* me, Jett."

"No fucking way."

"You need me."

"I don't need shit."

"Maybe. But I'm still coming."

Jett sighed. "Don't blame me when your pretty little head is mounted on some post."

"Good. It's settled. We go together. So...you think I'm pretty?" Halo teased.

8

Joy was creeping through the dark tunnels beneath Welcome. He was following the same mysterious figure he'd seen leaving Pretty's on the night of her murder. This time the figure was dragging three corpses behind it, all victims of the blazer. The tunnels emitted dizzying heat, lava springs bubbling through cracks in the uneven path.

Joy tracked the figure downward, deeper and deeper underground. He walked with his back against the steaming walls, along narrow ledges where certain death awaited in the boiling bowels below. But Joy's mind did not comprehend fear, only curiosity. So he kept on after the stranger, never giving a second thought as to how quickly death could take him, or how brutally!

The sound of rushing water and wood knocking against wood drew nearer. After struggling to keep up with the Reaper-like figure, Joy entered into total blackness, engulfed by the stench of putrefaction. He bumped into the frame of a rusty bicycle and was thrilled. If only he could get the darn thing to the surface. He spat a glob of saliva into his palm and smeared it along the handlebars, claiming it as his own.

Moving on, he stumbled into myriad objects strewn across the path: dolls, paint cans, broken dishes, sections of pipes, an old store sign he could not read. It wasn't easy to navigate through all the clutter, but Joy was unstoppable.

Hearing noises to his right, Joy rounded a sharp bend. He'd caught up to the stranger, who was at that moment dragging the bodies, one by one, through a pool of steaming black liquid. As the bodies came sliding out of the pool, the figure's extra-long fingers left tracks in the thick goo glistening on the skin. The bodies were then tossed with indifference atop an existing pile of corpses.

Joy sneaked closer as the hunched figure stepped around the pile and out of sight. As the old man crept on his tiptoes, his right foot slipped into the pool. Joy yanked his wet foot out, shaking chunks of slop from his warn boot. He got down on all fours to get a closer look. He poked at the lumps of spoiled meat floating in the slime, some with patches of hair still intact. His queer smile twitched.

A new tremor nearly sent him headfirst into the sludge. He staggered back and braced himself until the shaking subsided, just like his smile. Sturdy on his feet once more, he circled round the mountain of castrated and decapitated cadavers. Joy found the brightly colored gore rather decorative. Having no teeth, his pointed tongue was able to lick the bottom of his bristled chin whenever he became aroused—he was licking vigorously.

Around the other side of the heap, the cave was like a burning jungle. Thick vines hung from the toothy ceiling, illuminated by scattered pits of fire. Each taking its turn, the pits blasted a steady fountain of flames for about forty seconds, like rocket engines firing up. Where the ceiling was not high enough, the flames spread across its surface, spilling over like splashes from a waterfall.

Joy crouched down as he made his way through the maze of fiery pillars, moving vines aside as he went. Skulls dangled from the vines. Joy found this intriguing and fancy – his tongue slithered out. How wonderful, he thought, using bones to make such pretty things. He wished he'd thought of it, especially about nine days ago, when he'd discovered the skeleton of a rat in the alley.

As he crawled on his hands and knees through a curtain of clanking bones, Joy spotted Beez. He stopped to look at the moist red goo that smeared under his palm, then licked it clean with one hard stroke. That's when Beez saw him. His eyes widened and his hands clenched into fists.

"Help me!" he shouted.

Joy could see Beez's mouth moving, but he couldn't hear anything.

"Why don't you fucking help me, you goddamned monkey?" Beez cried, his hands tied high above his head, his ankles strapped together with hair and vines. He was naked. Hanging before his face was his genitals. A lump of burned flesh was all that marked the spot his reproductive organs had once occupied.

"Untie me! Help me, you stupid fuck!"

Just then, razor-sharp claws trailed down Beez's sides. He screamed as Joy's tongue worked overtime, his head shaking with elation.

"No! Get the fuck away from me!" Beez screamed,

wiggling helplessly.

Another tremor rolled beneath them. Bellows of smoke puffed from the fiery pits. Beez screamed and screamed as the killer's jaws shred up and down his back like a shoal of piranhas. Screaming and screaming and—red pudding spilled from Beez's throat. In an orgy of overkill, pieces of Beez scattered like a one-year-old's birthday cake!

When the left side of Beez's face landed with a splat on Joy's foot, he reached down to touch it. Suddenly alert to the intruder, the feeding beast ceased its gorging and froze. Curious, it rose to its full height of nearly nine feet. As the beast's head turned in his direction, Joy understood that it was time to leave. A slab of meat dropped from the killer's hand as the old man backed away.

When the killer commenced its feeding, Joy slipped out. He ran back through the tunnels, his arms swinging at his sides. Leaping over the lava streams, he sang, "Joy, joy, joy...."

9

Freezing rain cascaded over the edges of the Mausoleum's roof above Jett and Halo as they slept. Nightmare visions of Pretty haunted Jett's dreams. When the rain turned to hail as large as baseballs, its knocking awoke the pair.

"What is that? What's happening?" Halo asked, nervously rising.

"Sounds like hail," Jett said as the tomb vibrated.

"No. I'm not talking about the weather. Listen. Don't you hear that? It's getting louder," she said as the scraping sound intensified.

Now Jett could hear it. At that instant, pockets in the weakened concrete floor crumbled like chalk, allowing the gut-churning stench to flood their shelter. Dozens of rats scurried to the surface. The foundations shook and the ceiling crunched inward. Powder clouded the room.

"Will it hold?" Halo shouted, glancing from the collapsing ceiling to the mischief of rodents at her feet.

"I don't think so!" Jett said just as a chunk of ceiling dropped, spraying their boots with splattered rats.

The hailstones came rocketing down, bouncing off the floor and walls about them. Jett covered Halo's head, ducking his own as they huddled together. Then all at once, the hail ceased; the ground quaked as if an army of tanks were passing by. They looked up through the growing hole in the ceiling as lightning scratched frosty channels across the sky.

"This doesn't look good!" Jett yelled, watching the ceiling crumble away.

"It's not gonna hold!" said Halo, her grip on Jett's arm tightening.

Wailing winds dove into the tomb, whirling smaller hailstones about them like shotgun pellets. The ground suddenly shifted, throwing the couple off-balance. Together they struggled to open the door but it was jammed, raised by the quake.

"We're trapped!" Halo shouted.

Jett looked up and pointed. "That way!" he said.

He boosted Halo up through the ceiling, then sprang up and held onto the edge, until Halo could help him climb out. Just as they leapt from the roof the tomb collapsed into rubble. The wind tossed them to and fro, slamming them into one another. "Run!"

They headed up the cliff, toward Welcome, their only hope for shelter. Another round of icy baseballs assaulted them. Jett looked ahead and yelled, "Shit!" The nearest roof was not near enough. Ice balls were striking at them and bouncing off the ground. The loud echoing thuds on the aluminum roof ahead made them run even quicker.

Jett felt the ice balls like fists hitting his back. Halo was a few steps behind him. He grabbed her by the hand and sling-shot her ahead of him, into the shelter, then dove under the roof behind her. Panting heavily, they stared at one another for moments, then burst into laughter.

"I swear I've never had to run so fucking fast in my life!" said Halo.

"I have," said Jett, thinking back to the blazer. "I've been doing a lot of running lately," he added, cringing at the pain in his back.

An ice ball bounced in at them. Jett picked it up and threw it back out, yelling, "Fuck you!" He then stood with a groan. "Come on."

"Where are we going?"

"Well, I figure since we're already here, we might as well search for the evidence that's going to clear me of murder."

"What if someone recognizes you and we get caught?"

"Not a chance. I won't be fucked with again," he said confidently.

As the pair headed deeper into the tunnel of trash, a young woman named Soda crawled her way up the hill behind them. Bloodied and beaten, she caught a quick glimpse of the two just as they disappeared around a bend. Thoroughly exhausted, she was unable to call out to them, ice balls slamming into her body. The moment she was about to pass out, her horrific pursuer's clawed fingers clamped onto the back of her head. Soda gasped!

10

The heavy beating of the weather drummed throughout the trash tunnels as Jett and Halo sneaked along the darkest corridors, trying to remain incognito. They ducked behind a large freezer and watched the junkies and hookers go about their routine lives.

"No one knows me. Let me snoop around and ask questions. I can talk to those bitches and see if they know anything," Halo suggested.

"Okay. But watch your ass out there."

"Why don't *you* watch my ass out there," she said, putting extra sway in her hips as she walked away.

As Jett observed Halo mingling with the disorderly crowd, sudden clattering behind him gave him a start. He pivoted on his heels, ready to face just about anything, keeping his guard up as he'd promised himself he would. But all he saw was an old black man rummaging through the trash, probably searching for a bite to eat.

Jett watched him suspiciously. The old man shovelled his way through the street's garbage until he found himself at Jett's feet. He stood up in surprise, a busted-up set of dentures in his hands. He smiled at Jett, then rammed the dentures into his toothless mouth. He reeked like a corpse dipped in shit.

He just stood there, staring up at Jett, now smiling with those brown chomps.

"Joy," he blurted.

"What?"

"Joy, joy," the old man repeated.

"What the hell is that supposed to mean?"

The old man's head tilted side to side like a confused puppy. Jett had a strange feeling he'd just been recognized. He glanced to his left to see if Halo was still in sight, but she'd already gone inside The Furnace. When Jett grabbed the old man by the shoulders, he went into a hysterical fit, drawing unwanted attention.

Sitting within earshot, the hideously disfigured hunchback, Fright, was basking in the euphoric effects of the drugs he'd taken. He peered around the corner of the wall where he was sitting and grinned devilishly.

"He's *alive!*" he whispered, drooling. He ran inside The Furnace to deliver the news to his leader, but when he saw Villain sitting at his usual table, happily fondling some hooker's heaving breasts, he made up his mind to capture Jett on his own. Surely, Villain would praise and reward him for it.

Meanwhile, about a block away from The Furnace, Massacre and Gutter were enjoying a moment together, lying naked in their private shed. The loud thudding of the ice balls had finally quieted to pellets. As the two tongue-wrestled, the sudden slamming of the door gave them a start. A great figure of a man stood silently staring back at them, his head twitching.

"Who the fuck are you?" Gutter said, exasperated.

"Someone who wants to die," Massacre answered for him.

The stranger removed his black robe to reveal a physique of near perfection. A body unlike any they had ever laid eyes upon devoid of mutations, scars, or any signs of wear. Muscles flexing, shiny and beautiful. And a trail of hair leading down to a pulsating delight the size of which the couple could not refuse.

"Woh," Gutter said in awe.

"Looks like it's fucking meal time!" said Massacre, rubbing his hands together, tongue tracing his black lips.

Back at the Furnace, Fright had taken so long in deciding whether or not to play the hero of the day, Jett and Halo had time to find each other and were long gone. Fright looked but could not find them anywhere. He knew that if he reported this to Villain now, he'd certainly be in for the beating of his miserable life.

"What do I do? What the fuck do I do?" he muttered to himself, his voice gravelly. "Villain will kill me. Shit."

Just then, the answer came to him, when he spied Joy scouring through the trash. Fright galumphed across the street and grabbed Joy by the arm. Joy began to shake and moan, louder and louder.

"Shh! Quiet, you fucking idiot! I just want a favor from you," he explained.

"Joy," the old man said, smiling.

"Yeah, yeah. Joy. I saw you talking to the guy with all

the tags on his suit. Where did he go?"

Joy kept smiling, swaying his arms front to back, front to back. Fright looked over his shoulder at the door to The Furnace. He snagged Joy by the throat and shook him.

"You'd better talk to me, shit for brains, or I'll shove my boot up yer ass—way up!"

He threw the old man down and kicked him in the side of the head. Joy's new teeth went flying and shattered on the ground. And for the first time in a long time, there was no smile on the old man's face.

Fright picked him up, yelling, "Where'd he go?"

Joy stared into Fright's queer narrow eyes (one silver, one black), then turned and looked down the dark street.

"Yeah," Fright droned. "That's more like it, shit for brains. Now show me the way."

Joy hurried along, glancing back at Fright now and again. Fright kept shoving the old man, laughing as if it was a game. At the end of Welcome's longest abandoned street, they climbed over a wall of rubble. Joy stopped and began to dig through a junk pile.

"What the fuck's this? I ain't got time for treasure huntin', shit for brains."

But Joy kept digging as Fright shook his head with frustration. Suddenly, beams of red light filtered up between Joy's fingers. Fright then shoved the old man aside, shouting, "Move it, asshole!"

He rushed to uncover the hole no larger than a bicycle tire. Fright knelt and dipped his head inside. "Well, tongue my ass hole! This must be where the bastard's been hiding. And I'm gonna be the one to nab the cum-chuggler. Get back," he said, dropping his legs down the hole. "Stay here. I don't want him to hear your dumb ass coming a mile away. Besides, you smell like fucking shit, old man!"

Joy watched Fright's hands release their grip on the edge of the hole. He looked inside. Fright was looking back up at him and pointing. "Stay!" he whispered.

As he started down the dark path, Joy began to seal up the hole above. He placed the heaviest objects he could find over it. And when he was finished the job, he smiled and returned to his rummaging.

"Joy joy joy...."

Below, Fright held his homemade blade in a firm grasp as he headed deeper underground. He was more confident than ever that he'd soon have Jett's head for a trophy. The streams of lava replaced the oxygen with heat and smoke. Fright's eyes were burning, his lungs crackling. Curious sounds echoed throughout the tunnels, but Fright was well-practiced in good listening.

He edged his way along a rocky shelf, staring down into a black river. The river soon disappeared into the mouth of another cavern. Wood debris was gathered at the entrance, unable to pass through the narrow opening. The pieces knocked together, forced back and forth by the currents. With no alternative route, he leapt from the ledge and landed just below the mouth of the next cavern. His footing gave way beneath him, leaving him clawing for solid ground.

Pulling himself up to safety, he looked back at the

wild rapids and hammering boards, and grumbled, "If this leads to a dead-end, I swear I'm coming after you next, shit for brains."

11

Villain looked around himself, his men were all missing. Stealth alone remained by his side, as usual.

"Stealth!" Villain called, shoving a drunk whore off his lap. The crowd moved aside, allowing Stealth through. Villain looked up at him, brow furrowed. "Where the fuck is everyone, huh?"

Stealth was motionless.

"Find 'em...now!"

Stealth immediately turned and headed for the door. As he watched him leave, Villain decided that he was bored.

"Wait!" he called again.

Stealth waited.

"I need to stretch my legs. We'll look together," he said.

Just outside the door, they passed a whore with her head between the legs of a mutated man, his head shaped like a licorice twist, his mouth on the left side of his face.

"Fucking whores. They'll blow anything with a cock," Villain complained.

He and Stealth made their way through the daily street orgies. They reached the end of the block where Massacre and Gutter were shacked up.

"Fucking juice-swapping queers. Nobody shows me any respect anymore. When I want something done, they'd better be ready to jump at my say so. Fucking useless cunts," he babbled as Stealth nodded in agreement.

By the time they reached the shack, Villain had talked himself into a fit of rage. They knocked on the door but received no response.

"That's it. Kick it in," he ordered Stealth.

Stealth obeyed, kicking Massacre and Gutter's door in, then quickly moving out of Villain's way as he charged past him.

"Put your fucking dicks away, assholes, we got...."

Perhaps Stealth's mouth would have been open in awe as well, had he a mouth to open. But his reaction to the scene before them seemed dulled. Lurching in the doorway, he remained emotionless as Villain moved in for a closer examination of the atrocities.

Massacre and Gutter were nothing more than lumps of glistening flesh. In a state of shock, Villain quavered, "What in the fuck is going on?" As he came round to face the front of Massacre, he doubled over to vomit. Stealth slowly surveyed the room. It seemed as though buckets of blood had been tossed at the walls. Droplets still fell from the corner of the ceiling. The two bodies were subjected to sexually perverted mutilation and dissection.

Villain stared at Gutter's face, which stared back at him from inside Massacre's ripped open abdomen. Villain was hypnotized by disbelief. There were no genitals on either body. Villain quickly looked about but could not see any sign of them, nor did he want to know their exact whereabouts. Gutter's headless corpse was trussed with ropes on the floor, with its buttocks in the air, blood oozing from the rectum.

"This is fucking insane!" Villain blurted, turning away from the pile of body parts entangled on the bed.

Stealth crouched down.

"What the hell are you doing? Don't touch anything!"

Stealth looked up at him.

"What? What is it?"

Villain carefully stepped around the bed, blood caking under his boots. He leaned closer to Gutter's arched back. "No! Son of a fucking bitch!"

Gutter's spine had been sliced open, and the weapon used to do the deed was protruding from his neck. Villain pulled hard to yank the weapon free. Holding it up, he ground his teeth, "We find him...and we *kill* him! I want this *cock*sucker's nuts roasted on a shish kebab!"

As they left the red room, Villain tossed Jett's throwing star into the pool of blood on the floor. "Burn this bitch down. And where the *fuck* are Beez and Fright? Can you answer me that?"

Meanwhile, Fright had come to another bend in the cave, where light flickered and crackled from sconces on the walls. He smiled, expecting that this was where he would find Jett.

"Time to die, asshole," he snarled.

He readied his weapon and crept down the corridor. When he heard what sounded like scuffling noises behind him, he reacted with a sharp half-spin of his body, blade pointing toward the darkness. He couldn't see anything except his shadow dancing on the wall.

As he continued onward the third sconce back lost its flame. The blackened wall was glowing, breathing, stretching outward like bubblegum. Slowly, the killer tore itself free in the form of wriggling tentacles, snapping loose, and solidifying in the centre of the path. Fright was completely unaware.

The stench in the air intensified as Fright fought his way through the vine jungle. Whatever he may have imagined finding on the other side, he was not prepared for the reality of it. An arcane laboratory was full of equipment unfamiliar to him. Large drums were bubbling with colored liquids, with multiple tubes running from one to the next, until the last spilled into a large tub. Fright was baffled. He stepped cautiously, feet scraping along the uneven ground. Human remains were dangling from chains and ropes and hooks of different shapes and sizes, some dried out and rotted beyond identification, others dripping with freshness.

"Wait'll Villain gets a load of this. He's gonna shit himself," he whispered.

Natural pockets in the cave wall had been utilized as shelves for an assortment of glass bottles and candles. Fright stooped forward to see what was soaking in the bottles. He stared for moments until he realized the object awash in the yellow fluid was male genitals!

"What the fuck's this asshole up to? Shit. Shit!" he said, accidentally knocking a bottle off the shelf. When it crashed at his feet, human tongues spilled forth.

"Fuck!"

Fright staggered back, reeling, his grip on his blade overly tight. Different body parts flashed into focus around him as if their spirits were calling out to him now, frantically, desperately.

"Fun's over, motherfucker! You hear me? Come out and face me, asshole!"

Out of fear and rage, Fright began to knock more bottles off the shelves. He shoved several drums over, blood spilling over his boots in waves, rolling into the grooves where lava nestled. "This is nothing compared to what I'm gonna do to you when I find you, dead man! You hear me?" he shouted, knocking more drums over. When he stood back to admire his work, he snorted and spat. And with a sudden jerk round, he gulped.

"What...the fuck...are *you*?" he drawled.

The killer's right hand snatched him by the throat with immense strength, squeezing slowly, until Fright's gray face turned blue. Fright was staring deep into its heart-shaped throat as its fetid breath passed over him, its jaw quivering, dripping goo like a rabid animal. As it straightened its posture, Fright thought he could hear its ribs cracking. He was beginning to see spots from its tightening grip. It took great effort, but he managed to swing his blade and slice across its bulging abdomen.

The killer released its hold and dropped Fright to his knees. Fright was coughing and gasping as the killer dug into the gash and came up with a handful of green pus. It stared down at Fright, licking its lengthy fingers with a serpentine tongue. Fright backed away, watching mesmerized as the wound healed within a matter of minutes.

At once Fright turned and fled from the killer. His erratic pulse beat at his temples, his loud breaths mixed with panicked hums. The killer was pursuing him, its high-pitched growl-laughter instilling a terror in him he'd never felt before. It's footsteps thumped and dragged, thumped and dragged, and then didn't!—toying with him. Fright stumbled into the same rusted bicycle Joy had discovered leaning against the wall. He threw it between himself and the killer and charged onward.

Just ahead the path dropped out of sight. Below was the thrashing river, with its deadly wooden jaws steadily champing. With the killer less than fifteen feet behind, Fright took his chances with the river. As fast as he could, he ran to the end of the path, sprang out, and swan-dived out over the boards below. Splashing into the black waves, he disappeared.

When Fright's head finally broke through the surface, he could no longer see the killer above. He swam vigorously against the current, barely able to keep his head above water. The river dragged him under again and again, seemingly as determined to take his life as the killer was!

Closer and closer he bobbed toward the wooden jaws, gasping and screaming, his strength depleting. This time when he was pulled under it seemed like he was tossed in the depths forever. And the moment he decided it was better to drown than die at the hands of the killer, he resurfaced. He swam toward the dark rocky shore and finally managed to crawl out. Lying on his back, chest rising and falling in rapid breaths, he chuckled weakly and closed his eyes. He'd made it.

PAIN!

Something sharp and jagged plunged into his abdomen. Fright screamed as he arched forward, grabbing the killer by the leg. The killer's right hand folded around Fright's and squeezed until all the bones were crushed like garlic cloves. Fright threw himself back in agony. The killer's claws whistled past his face. For seconds Fright did not realize he'd been cut until the warmth of his blood began to ooze from the four gashes. He continued to strike with all his might at the killer's legs as its foot dug deeper and deeper under his ribs.

Blood erupted from Fright's mouth as the killer worked his insides like a bicycle pump. When at last it realized its victim was dead and the fun was over, it pulled its foot free from the meat shoe. Red paste gushed between its clawed toes as it dragged Fright's corpse into the darkness.

12

Jett jumped from sleep when he heard shuffling noises behind him.

"Just me," said Halo, sitting opposite to him.

The rain fell hard behind her, thunder competing with the rumbles beneath them. "We got trouble, Jett. A couple of Villains hoods have vanished into thin air, and two others were found murdered, and I hear it wasn't a pretty scene, either."

Jett shook his head, perturbed. "I gotta find that old bastard again. I'm almost positive he knows what the fuck is going on."

"There's something else," said Halo. She flicked one of the stars on Jett's thigh. "One of these was used in the murder."

Jett's eyes shrank to angry slits. "Someone's setting me up. But why?"

"I don't know," Halo said, rubbing her arms over the fire. "But Villain's working the people into a mob. It's only a matter of time before their search leads them out here."

Jett was in deep thought.

"What are you thinking, Jett?"

"I have no choice. I have to get back inside Welcome and find that old man. He's the answer. I know he is. If I can goad the killer into making another move, maybe I can make it be his last."

"Yeah. Or *your* last!"

"If I don't try, this thing will follow me wherever I go. I can't live that way. I won't," he finalized as the wind suddenly blew in colder, changing the rain to snow. "They'll be guarding the gates. I have to find another way in."

"Done. Follow me," Halo said, heading out of the collapsed silo.

Jett kicked the dying fire out, watching Halo's silhouette amidst the whiteout.

They walked against harsh winds, snow swirling into funnels around them, thunder accompanying its lightning counterpart. In no time at all the ground was under a foot of snow, and the temperature dropped far below freezing. Halo led Jett around to the north side of Welcome where a handful of buildings of a former city remained standing.

Jett was impressed. "This makes no sense. Why has this section been abandoned for the garbage side? There's plenty of decent shelters here, and plenty of room, I'd imagine, for all," he said, following Halo into one of the buildings.

Inside, there was a subway car jutting out of the ground floor, rising through several stories.

"Disease," said Halo.

"What?"

"Disease. That's why no one lives here. This area is contaminated. Only the dying live here," she explained.

"Is it safe for us to be here?"

"Sure, only long exposure has any kind of effect."

No sooner had she unveiled the mystery of Welcome's north side, when they came across small groups of people huddled together in the corridors. Their bodies were racked with suffering, and deformities that prevented speech, or movement. Some were moaning sullenly, others crying.

"They won't bother us," said Halo.

"I don't doubt that," came Jett.

"So, where do you think that old fool is keeping himself?"

"He'll be searching for food. Seems to be all he does."

"Then let us hurry. This way," said Halo, leading him down the hall to the back of the building.

Once they'd reached the invisible border, where the north and south sides of Welcome seemed to meet, where trash took the place of concrete, they tried to stick to the darkest alleyways. Another blizzard was battering down on them.

"I don't like this! We're putting ourselves at risk," Halo reminded her partner.

When Jett did not reply, she moved in closer to him. "What is it?"

"I thought I heard something," he said, looking around and up.

"Like what?"

Jett shook his head, breathing warmth onto his fingers as he peered silently into the impenetrable storm. Then he heard it again, and this time, so did Halo. Something in the clouds.

"You hear that?" he asked Halo.

"Yes!" she said, trying to look up.

Suddenly, something rather large came plummeting out of the sky and landed with a hard thump before them. The pair jumped back. Joy's body lay sprawled out in the white as if he was attempting to make a snow angel. Blood was quickly spreading beneath the old man. His eyes had been gauged out, then jammed back into his sockets. His arms had been stripped of all flesh, and another one of Jett's stars was sticking out of his chest.

Jett and Halo looked at one another grimly. He reached down to remove the star just as people were coming out to see what happened. Blood burped from the old man's neck, which had been hacked at till the head was nearly severed from the body.

"Great. How do you intend to explain this one?" asked Halo.

"This isn't mine. It's an imitation," Jett examined.

"Well, well!" broke a familiar voice.

Jett and Halo turned to face Villain. A gabbling, shocked crowd began to surround the body.

"Fuck," Halo whispered to Jett. "I'm ready to run when you are."

"What is it with you psychos? You haven't got the fucking sense to quit while you still have your heads on your shoulders?" Villain sang to the crowd. "We failed to kill you the first time. We won't this time," he hissed.

Stealth was snuggling a sledgehammer, his black eyes reflecting the orange of Halo's hair. The people began to dig for sticks and pipes to use as weapons against the pair, hurling catcalls and profanities at them. Halo followed Jett's eyes up to the low rooftop, signalling a possible way out.

"Kill them!" Villain commanded.

With fantastic speed, Jett reached for the weapon attached to his right leg—his whip snapped the air! He spun full circle, the star at the tip of his whip sliced across the throats of the first line of attackers. Some bodies fell at once, while others staggered before falling. Villain was enraged.

"NO! Kill him! Kill him!"

Jett's whip rolled back into his hand like a yo-yo. He drop-kicked another attacker, sending the mutated man stumbling back into others. His fists cracked many jaws, while Villain and Stealth remained back and watched, amused. They turned their attention to Halo, who was quite capable of defending herself as well.

"Cunt. I want them both dead. Understand?" he said to Stealth.

Stealth nodded.

Knives and clubs flew through the air, missing Jett and Halo's faces by mere inches. Blood was shooting up like geysers from writhing bodies. Two men grabbed Halo by the arms. They'd had no luck trying to cut into her unique limbs.

"Hold her!" a third attacker called, his hand groping his genitals.

Before he could make his play, red veins like wires shot out from the corners of her eyes, wrapped around the man's neck—pinched!—and in that second, his head was severed from his body. The two men at her arms were shocked and horrified. But before they could make up their minds about what to do next, Halo's optic antennas, waving about like live electric wires, wound themselves about their necks! Two more heads plopped at her feet.

Jett was taken aback when he saw this and was impressed. "Nice trick!" he yelled.

"I've had enough of this shit if you have!" she said.

Villain had also been impressed with Halo's skills. "You see that, Stealth? Bitch can hold her own. Now I want to see her bleed!"

At that moment, a deformed woman weighing no less than three-hundred pounds, came screaming at Jett with a piece of pipe in her pudgy hand. Jett kicked her in the throat. But as she stumbled back, another man lunged at him with a large blade. Jett grabbed hold of the man's wrist, spun him round, using the momentum of his attacker to stab another attacker in the chest. And while still in motion, he then turned the blade on its owner, planting it firmly in his forehead. Finally, he reeled round to face Halo and shouted, "Now!"

Halo followed behind Jett as he ran through the crowd. He used his whip to lash out and snag a man about the neck. Then, pulling the man to his knees, he stepped on his shoulders and used him as a springboard to leap onto a slanted rooftop. The instant before his whip released its stranglehold, Halo propelled herself off the man's shoulders and landed next to Jett.

Villain's face burned red with rage. The mob was

throwing anything they could find at them: jugs, bottles, knives, cans.

"Son of a bitch! He isn't getting away from me this time. They're headed into the north side. We'll cut 'em off there," Villain seethed.

Meanwhile, Jett and Halo continued to fumble over unsteady rooftops. At the end of the line, they climbed down and continued back in the direction they'd come, hoping to lose anyone who may have been tracking them.

"Don't worry," said Halo. "There's no way they'll follow us. Living so close by, they're all more susceptible to catching their death here than we are."

"Yeah, but are you sure *they* know that?" said Jett.

"Believe me...*they* know."

As they hustled toward the buildings, Jett ground his teeth. "Well, that was a fucking waste of time."

"Jett, we tried. Seems like this killer is always one step ahead. And can you please tell me where the fuck that man fell from. People just don't fall out of the sky!"

"I can't explain any of this. This fucking thing, whatever it is, is smart."

"Then we'd better get smarter, and fast!" Halo stated.

13

Jett and Halo were practically tossed inside the crumbling building from the sheer force of the storm. The snow was building up in the doorway. It was dark. They wanted to get out of Welcome as quickly as possible, but first, they needed immediate shelter. Besides, they were certain no one would bother to hunt them as long as this weather persisted.

Inside they were faced with a hoarder's dream. Over time, it appeared that everything that could gather between the front and back of the building did so. They had to climb over walls of garbage, corpses included! Steam puffed from their breaths. They'd only just gotten over the pile when Villain and Stealth appeared at the far end of the hallway.

"Got you now, motherfucker! I'm gonna rip your balls off and ram 'em down your fucking throat!" Villain hollered.

"Split up!" Jett yelled to Halo.

He ran down the adjoining hall to their left, while Halo headed down the right. As he'd hoped they would, Villain and Stealth pursued him and not Halo. Reaching a dead end, Halo entered through the only door available.

"What the hell, bitch? You outta your fucking mind?" a woman shouted, coming at her with a glass bottle. "Who the fuck you think you are, barging in here all—"

Halo punched the woman square in the face, busting her nose. The woman screamed as blood gushed between her fingers. She covered her face as a second woman took up shouting at Halo.

"Fucking bitch! I'm gonna cut your ass!" she threatened, searching for something to carry out the deed with.

Halo ignored the two and made her way around a circle of beaten furniture. She pulled a sheet of plywood off the wall that was covering a small window. As the two women continued their verbal assault, Halo dipped out.

Meanwhile, Jett had run up two flights of cluttered stairs. Villain was determined not to let him get away this time. He and Stealth were right on Jett's heels and closing.

"Why you runnin'? There's nowhere to hide!" Villain shouted.

And he was right. Jett stopped suddenly when he reached the end of the hall. He tried the doors to his left and his right, but both were secured.

"Tough break, asshole," Villain smirked, standing about twenty feet away, Stealth looming over his right shoulder.

"I didn't kill anyone," Jett tried.

Villain guffawed. "You think I give a fuck," he growled, slipping his trench coat off his shoulders. "I'm gonna enjoy killing you."

Villain started marching toward Jett like a cowboy, arms at his sides as if he was going to draw his invisible pistols. Jett readied himself for battle. With a swift and subtle movement, he threw a star in Villain's direction. Villain howled, pulling the star from his chin. Blood ran from his half goatee, dripping on his boots.

"Mo...ther...fuck...er," he said, teeth ground.

Villain charged at Jett. He swung left, then right, missing both hits. Jett grabbed his wrists, but at once an extra set of hands grew from Villain's forearms, subsequently grabbing *him* by the wrists.

"Surprise!" Villain sniggered.

Jett head-butted Villain, which caused all four of his grips to loosen. He then leapt into a double kick, hitting Villain in the chest. Villain flew into the apartment door behind him, breaking it down. Jett jumped over him and searched for the nearest window. But as with the rest of the building, clutter was stacked chest-high.

As he dug a path through the room, Jett could feel strong winds from the other side. A few feet farther and he could see there was no wall in the next room and snow was piling in.

"There's no way out!" Villain yelled.

But there was, and Jett was standing before it now. However, there was a two-story drop between him and freedom. *I've made it through worse*, he thought.

By the time Villain and Stealth stood at the edge of the room, looking out over a white scenery, Jett was nowhere to be seen.

"Motherfucker! Cocksucker! Son of a bitch! I want that fucker's heart on a platter when I sit down to eat my dinner tonight. You got me!" Villain raged, pointing his bloodied finger in Stealth's face. "Tonight!"

Once the two had gone, Jett's head popped out of the heap of snow in the room. He stood at the open wall and shook his head, then turned and left the building.

As Jett headed toward his and Halo's rendezvous point, which was the remnants of a vertical-lift bridge, he could smell acid clouds rolling in. The snow turned to ice pellets, then turned to rain. He ran as fast as he could to make it under the shelter the bridge. Once there, and alone, he wondered where Halo could be.

"Miss me?"

Jett spun on his heels. Halo was sitting higher up in the darkness. When the lightning flashed, he could see her smile. He made his way higher and sat next to her, without a word.

"What's the matter? We got away, didn't we?" Halo said as she started to gather flammable items to build a fire.

"I risked our lives for nothing," he said.

"Listen, hero. Those fuckers decided long before now that you were guilty. Even if the real killer were to come out of hiding now, they'd still want your ass in several pieces. Best thing is to forget it and move on."

Jett looked into her eyes, new flames shining on her cheeks. "Back there. That thing you do with your eyes."

"What of it?" she said defensively.

"It's amazing. Why didn't you tell me you could do

that?"

"Figured you'd learn my secrets soon enough," she said, her voice softer.

She began to unravel the linens from around her arms. "You want to know *all* my secrets?"

Jett watched her unwrap her legs, which were a creamy yellow color like her arms.

"This is all of me," she said. "I don't have skin like most. Parts of me are flesh, but most are something like bone."

Jett's eyes moved up her legs, over her thighs, her firm breasts, up to her brilliant eyes. He reached for her hand, pulling her close to him. As they kissed, the ugly world around them fell silent, then disappeared.

14

Jett snapped awake, only to discover a hideous woman sitting on his chest, her hands covering his mouth and nose to suffocate him! He struck her across the jaw, throwing her off of him. She rolled, then leapt back to her feet at once. Jett was on his feet now, still gasping for breath.

His attacker's skin was cracked and peeling, gray and purple. She looked like stone, with bleeding eyes and nostrils. No heart beat within her zombie chest, and no thoughts drew ideas in her mind. She only knew to attack and kill her target—Jett! The walking corpse was Soda. Someone had reanimated this poor woman. Jett knew Villain, though wicked himself, was not artful enough to pull off this trick.

Soda growled with a voice that had been stripped of its force before she died. She dove for Jett, wrestling him to the ground. Her claws dug into his arms and back, leaving deep grooves of blood. Jett tried to hold her face away from his own, as she attempted to bite him with a mouthful of beastly fangs.

They struggled like wild dogs, fumbling and snarling, rolling down into the ditch. Soda's straggly hair hung down around her gruesome face as she pinned Jett on his back, his head underwater. He kicked his legs up, overthrowing the zombie once again.

"Come on, bitch!" he challenged.

Soda's eyes were exposed like painted golf balls. She hissed and growled. Jett charged, drop-kicking the creature in the chest. They both went down. Before he could get up again, the zombie was crawling up his legs. Despite her decrepit appearance, she was extremely strong and agile. He booted her in the face several times before she finally let go of him.

Jett dashed toward the bridge tower. Soda was right at his heels as he climbed up the cross-section of slimy beams. Jett kicked at the zombie, trying to knock her off, but she was unstoppable. Nearing the top, he spotted a heavy cable swinging in the wind. He climbed one beam higher, then somersaulted through the air like a trapeze artist.

Coming out of his final spin, he reached for the cable. Swinging far and wide around, he came back at Soda at full force. Soda screeched as she fell. Once back on the ground, Jett approached the zombie in disbelief. She'd landed across a steel beam, her body snapped in two, but in no way was she dead. Jett picked up a rod and struck Soda's head again and again, until he'd bludgeoned it apart from her body, granting her true death.

He tossed the rod and wiped the sweat from his brow. The heat was making him giddy.

"Halo!" he called, choking.

She was nowhere to be found. He jerked at the sound of scuffling behind him. Hiding behind a concrete block, he spied a frightened child of about nine or ten years of age.

"You there. Did you see where the dark woman went?"

he asked.

The boy nodded, his face black with dirt.

Jett crouched down before him. "What's your name?"

The boy shrugged his shoulders.

"Can you take me to the woman? Her life is in danger."

The boy nodded again, this time directing Jett's attention to the ocean. Jett watched as dozens of funnels were combining into one. The blazer of blazers was coming, and this time there would be hell on Earth!

The boy led Jett to an underground tunnel in an area he had passed a dozen times since he'd been in Welcome. Loud explosions erupted to their right. The moment they leapt into the hole, flaming tentacles shot down toward them. Jett shielded the boy as the rumblings above rose to terrifying volumes.

Deep into the tunnel system, Jett stopped the boy.

"You sure you know where you're going?" he asked.

Following a few moments of expected silence, the boy said, "I know these caves by heart."

Jett's eyes squinted suspiciously. "So, you can speak after all, huh?"

The boy turned and continued on his way, leading Jett to a section of the cave where mutilated bodies were strewn across the trail. As they stepped in between the corpses, they passed a hole in the wall. Jett looked inside, where he could see a river. They were opposite to where Fright had leapt to his inevitable death.

The boy tugged on Jett's arm, saying, "This way."

Mauled, bloody corpses met them every step of the way.

"Shit. Half the population of Welcome must be down here," Jett observed. "Are you sure Halo's down here? I don't have time to fuck around."

The boy just kept nodding in response.

"We must be pretty deep underground. I can barely hear the upside anymore."

The boy stopped suddenly and looked back at Jett. "That's the way in," he said.

Jett watched the boy get down on all fours and scuttle into a crawlspace. "Fuck," he mumbled, squeezing himself into the tiny hole, behind the boy.

One minute the boy's silhouette was moving ahead of him, and the next he was gone. An orange flickering glow filled the void. Jett peeped his head out and glanced around; the boy had abandoned him. "Little fucker," he cursed, dragging himself on his elbows through the tight exit.

Here, vines dangled from the ceiling, fires burned in pockets in the floor and walls, and the stench of death lingered heavily in the mist. Jett parted his way through the vines toward a slurping sound. Human skeletons cluttered the way. Suddenly, he gasped. There were several arms attached to vines by large hooks, and beneath them was the twisted, half-eaten corpse of Villain.

Villain's head was facing him, eyes wide. Jett shuddered. The man's head had been beaten into ugliness. The sludge of decomposing flesh and viscera was stewing in iron pots set around Villain's torso. It was a ghastly vision.

Just then, Jett's ears alerted him to a familiar sound— cutting air! He ducked and spun round to face Stealth's failed attempt to sledgehammer his skull in. Instead, the powerful blow struck Villain's head, launching it across the room, slapping its way through the vines. This enraged Stealth even further. He stepped back, raising the hammer for a second strike.

Jett back-flipped and kicked Stealth in the face. The man barely flinched. Stealth swung his hammer side to side, its head whizzing past Jett in near misses until one swing finally connected. Jett was knocked to the ground, bone chips cutting under his palms. Stealth's eyes looked like two black holes in his face. He raised his arms over his head and swung down between Jett's legs, jamming the hammer's head deep into the ground.

In a flash, Jett hurled two stars, taking out both Stealth's eyes. The man reeled in agony, still beating the air about him frantically. Jett circled low behind him and jumped up into the vines. He hung there, waiting for the right moment to strike. Stealth's hammer whizzed through the air, chopping vines, his eyes frothing red. Jett secured his legs around the vines. He swung upside down and wrapped a vine around Stealth's neck.

With every last ounce of strength, he pulled the noose tighter and tighter. Stealth tried desperately to land a hit on his enemy but to no avail. Jett managed to tie Stealth's left arm, but his right swung up and down, never weakening, never slowing. He shook his head violently, his struggles tightening his binds.

Giving up on Stealth's right arm, Jett dropped from the vines and rolled to a safe distance. Stealth heard the scuffle and attempted to strike out, inadvertently pulling the noose to its limit. Jett stood back and watched as the jerking body fell limp. The hammer thudded at Stealth's feet.

"Easy for you to say," Jett quipped, relieved.

He then whipped around at the sound of vines creaking. Jett sighed, then began to shout. "Where the fuck have you been? And where's Halo? You said she was down here! So help me, kid, if you're dicking me around, I'll kick your ass all over creation!"

Slowly, the boy seemed to float out of the inky darkness. But there was something not right about him. His eyes were blank, face drooping. As the orange light bathed up his body, Jett could see the long claws dug into the boy's head. And out of the shadows, the killer's flowing white mane came writhing forth. As the gruesomeness of its face was revealed, Jett could make out a bulbous forehead, riddled with large, pus-filled boils.

"*You!*" he said exasperated.

Now he could see that the boy who'd led him to this god-awful trap was nothing more than another disguise, a piece of magical flesh. Cackling, the killer stepped forward into the light, wiggling the dead flesh of the boy at him, mocking him. Jett stood his ground as he measured her up—yes, *her!*

Her face was long and narrow; her white eyes bulging and jelly-like; her nose a lumpy protrusion that hung over a missing top lip. Bucked, long, rectangular teeth overwhelmed her face in a V shape. Her drooping black breasts were tightly strapped to her body with leather bindings. Her arms were extremely long and muscular, with human bones tied from her elbows to her wrists.

"Where's Halo, witch? What have you done with her, you fucking cunt?" Jett shouted.

The witch took another step closer, the sound of the long black skirt she wore swooshing on the ground. There were bones tied about the strands of her hair, and he could now see the large hump on her back.

"You hear me, bitch, or can't you talk with those fucking atrocities you call teeth?"

A tongue that looked more like an octopus's tentacle came slowly slithering out her mouth, coiling at the end.

"That's what I thought...*bitch!*"

The witch suddenly whipped the boy flesh at Jett, knocking him off his feet. He heard the swish of her skirt as he struggled to separate himself from the slimy, rubbery suit. Then the combined snarls of three zombies came revving out of the tunnels about him. Jett leapt to his feet just in time to meet the first zombie's attack.

The creature flung itself at Jett, but he dodged out of its path and came face to face with a second male. This one's head looked like a fallen meteorite, with glowing splits emitting steam. It hissed a mouthful of needle teeth at him. Jett punched it in the face, which felt like hitting a wall. The thing wobbled a bit as the third zombie, a female, came screeching at him from his right.

Jett leapt into the air, throwing his legs around the female's neck. He pulled himself and the zombie to the ground, snapping her head around so that now her face was behind her, eyes, ears, nose, and mouth oozing with bloody pus. She didn't move again.

Before he could shove her aside, he felt a heavy kick to his back. Jett rolled over and turned on one knee, sending several stars into the zombie's chest. The creature ignored its wounds, coming at him with clawing hands. Jett spun and kicked its feet out from under it. Then he jumped on its chest, screaming. He yanked the stars out of its chest and jammed them into its eyes, rancid blood spraying back at him.

At that moment, the third zombie's arms wrapped around him, raising him off his feet in a squeezing embrace. Jett kicked the creature's legs with the heels of his boots as it whipped him side to side. The smell of it was intoxicating. The other male staggered blindly into them, knocking all three of them down. But the stubborn, embracing creature would not release its hold on him. As Jett struggled in its grip, the blinded zombie clawed at them both, tearing chunks of flesh from its fellow-creature. Before it could scoop a fistful of his flesh, Jett kicked it in the jaw. The creature's head jerked to the left, its neck cracking like wood. Like a toy that's battery has run down, it dropped beside them.

Still trapped in the last zombie's hold, Jett began to bash the creature's face in with the back of his head, over and over, again and again. Wiry worms came snaking out of the thing's face and head. Jett pounded harder and harder until he could finally feel its skull give way to mush. When the creature's arms, at last, went slack, Jett rested for a moment, his head soaking in the warm pillow of face soup.

15

Now that he was alone once again, all the sounds in the tunnels Jett had unconsciously shut out were breathing back to life. Blasts of steam, bubbling lava, whistling wind racing through the darkness, were all becoming increasingly clear to him. He raised himself out of the mess of dead pudding, dizziness swirling around his brain for moments.

"Halo," he said, worriedly.

He shook himself free of all negative thoughts, and hurried down the passage he was certain the witch had fled. The walls closed in around him, constantly shrinking, constantly heading downward. Darkness enveloped him completely. Suddenly, Jett screamed! He fell a great distance, until splashing into the hot water of an underground lake.

As he swam for the surface, he could see bright light rippling above. Within moments, he was breathing the thick, heated air. He was astounded by what he saw. Staring back down at him was a giant stone head. White eyes glowed above a mask of what appeared to be streams of blood. And behind the streams was a wall of fire.

Jett could see a shoreline to his right, but just as he began to swim toward it, something wound round his right leg and pulled him under with great force. Down he went, spiralling deep under the surface, till the light no longer penetrated the depths. He was taken on a chaotic ride as if he'd been hooked to the tail of an unsuspecting shark. But this was no shark, it was much worse!

In a flash of horror, Jett realized he was next on the menu for a monstrous creature. All he could make out was a set of jaws the size of a house, with something like shimmery neon-blue flower petals surrounding them. All about him was a crazy forest of snakes that were this thing's tentacles. And there were dozens of human bodies snagged in among the tentacles, like flies in a web, dead, and waiting to be devoured at the creature's leisure.

Jett was determined he was not going to be a snack for this beast. With his unique lungs, he was able to hold his breath much longer than any human could. Using one of his stars, he began to cut at the tentacle. But as he worked, the creature instinctively tightened its grip, threatening to break his lower leg bones!

The beast jerked him about. Then he crashed into another body and quickly held onto it, wrapping his arms and legs around it. The tentacle attached to this corpse was wound around its neck. Jett felt up and down the body, looking for weapons. He was about to give up hope, losing his grip as he slid down to the corpse's feet when he discovered a knife strapped to the dead man's ankle!

He sliced clear through the tentacle on his leg, free at last. Blood tainted the water as the creature reeled its injured tentacle in. Meanwhile, Jett swam for the surface. The instant he breathed air again, he made a mad dash for shore, crawling out on hands and knees. Looking back at the giant blood-spewing stone face, he said, "Fuck this place."

Ahead of him, there was an archway embellished with ornate designs. Bluish light radiated from beyond. Jett's legs felt like rubber for a few moments when he first stood. He took a deep breath, then entered under the archway. He passed through a long tunnel made of bones, which seemed to come alive under the eerie, flickering glow.

The tunnel opened into a great cavern, where black stalagmites and stalactites glowed fiery red from the lava within. A mere few feet inside, Jett spotted Halo! He ran to where she was suspended from the ceiling by her hands and feet, her head hanging back. Her orange hair gently swayed in the slight breeze that circled the cavern. Jett reached up to touch the underside of her head. There was a substance like webbing covering her eyes.

"Halo?" he whispered.

When she stirred slightly, he sighed with relief. "It's okay. I'm gonna get you down," he said, though he didn't have any idea how he was going to accomplish this. Her hands and feet were somehow buried within the rock as if at some point it must have been soft. Only the witch's magic could have achieved this.

Jett looked about for something, he wasn't sure what, but something—anything—to use to break her free. As he scouted the area, he suddenly realized he might be able to heat the molds and melt the trap. He kicked the tip of a stalactite, breaking off the tip. Then, using a leather strip from his left arm, he wrapped the piece of rock so he could grip it.

Next, he slid a large stone block beneath where Halo was hanging. Standing on the rock gave him enough height to reach the ceiling, and begin his attempt to melt the molds around her feet and hands. Halo was moaning now as he pressed the piece of stalactite against the trap. Much to his surprise and delight, the idea was working. He pulled her left foot free and placed her leg on his shoulder, so as not to have her weight pulling on her wrists.

He worked as quickly as he could, freeing her right foot, then her wrists. Halo was slumped over his shoulder, free at last. As Jett set her down, strange screams echoed about them. Jett tried to remove the globs on Halo's eyes, but it was as if they were part of her face.

"Halo. Halo, can you hear me?" he whispered.

Halo attempted a nod. She was weak. She slowly reached up to touch her eyes, wondering why she couldn't open them. When she felt the gluey patches, she panicked. Jett pulled her hands away, hushing her.

"Shh. It's okay. Whatever it is, we'll get it off. Just be still. I'll figure it out," he promised.

And then, *she* was there. The witch had returned to her lair. By her angry, snarling hiss, Jett could tell she had not expected him to make it this far. He felt Halo's cheek to reassure her she would be okay, then turned to face the bitch.

Jett moved as far away from Halo as he could to keep the fight away from her. He approached the foot of the imposing stone staircase where the witch was descending.

Her lengthy skirt dragged behind her, her white hair was alight. Midway down, she opened her extended arms, flexed her gnarled fingers, and shrieked!

"Oh yeah," Jett said to himself. "She's pissed."

He shot several stars in her direction, one after the other, at least a dozen within a moment. Every star hit its mark. The witch looked down at her chest, blood trails leaking from every puncture. She pulled one of the stars from her leathery skin and examined it. Looking back down at her adversary, she hacked with laughter, her voice creating a forever echo.

This only made Jett more determined to take her down. "Well, if you thought that was funny, wait'll you see this," he said, teeth ground.

Jett pulled the blade he kept from the corpse in the lake and charged up the steps, which were more like giant stacked blocks. The witch screeched as she heaved herself at him. He sidestepped out of her way as she landed on the same level as he, her skirt ruffling about her. She shot her tongue out toward him like a viper. Once it retracted, she snapped those teeth like brick hitting brick.

Jett threw more stars at her and charged. When the witch raised her right arm to block the stars, Jett leapt into the air and kicked, snapping the bone tied to her arm in two. He came again, somersaulting over her head. And as he passed over her, he reached for her hair and pulled with all his might, forcing her down to the ground with him. But the witch spun on him, crawling low like a lizard. She climbed right up on top of him!

Before she could pin him down, Jett kicked her in the face and rolled backward, away from her. She screeched at him, her body suddenly rising in one swift swoop to the upright position. Jett headed higher up the stairs, somersaulting over the final distance to land with enough time to turn and face her next strike.

At the top, vines dangled from the ceiling and thousands of insects like fireflies blinked in and out of sight. Behind him, he'd seen another tunnel, which stood out all the more amidst the fiery fissures in the surrounding walls. Jett cartwheeled over the witch's left shoulder and kicked her in the back. He reached for his whip and snapped it right in her face, tearing a good chunk of flesh out.

The witch was losing patients. Her tongue was slapping about her face, dabbing her wound with green saliva. Her breathing was loud and raspy and angry—very angry. She lowered her head, fingers twitching at her sides, black eyelids narrowing over those jelly spheres. Jett threw his arm back and shot the whip at her once more; this time the leather tail wound around her neck.

She grabbed hold of the whip and suddenly rose into the air, dragging Jett along the ground as he held his end. But it wasn't a leap she'd taken—the witch was floating!

"What the fuck?" said Jett, struggling to keep his grip.

Her skirt hung to its full length, shimmery and shredded at its edges. Her white hair danced about her revolting face. She was cackling again, spitting the blood that was running down her cheek. Jett pulled back in this strange tug of war, his feet sliding along in her favor. When he felt his grip slipping, he tried the hand-over-hand technique to try and regain some ground.

At that moment, Halo was finally coming to her senses. She sat up, recognizing Jett's voice somewhere in front of her. She also recognized the chilling sounds of the witch. Feeling the globs stuck over her eyes, she realized just how cunning the witch had been in blocking her main form of defence. Try as she might, she could not tear the substance off. Feeling helpless was not something she was familiar with. In blindness, she began to crawl toward the commotion.

As Jett was losing his grip, and the rope war, he blinked hard in the heat, making sure his eyes were not playing tricks on him. From behind the witch, several bright red barbels sprouted forth. As they snaked outward, dozens more followed, wavering about the witch with what looked like large thorns along their lengths. Slowly, the red snakes were winding downward, closer and closer to him.

Jett released his hold on the whip, but he was too late. The snakes lashed out and coiled about him, from head to toe! When Halo heard Jett's scream, she increased her speed and felt the bottom step in front of her. Jett was right above her, she knew, and in trouble.

"Jett!" she yelled out of fear.

"Halo, get back! Get back!" he shouted.

She heard Jett's voice choke as the red snakes squeezed his throat. The witch cackled victoriously as her snakes pulled Jett closer and closer below her. Jett's whip was still hanging from around her neck. She pulled it loose and let it drop before him. Jett was struggling in the ever tightening grip of the snakes, their sharp thorns digging into his flesh.

As the witch began to descend, Jett began to rise. He felt the earth give way under his feet as he swung off the ground, entangled in the clutches of the red extensions. The witch was gloating as her skirt settled back on the ground about her. She drew Jett nearer to her like a human balloon. And out came that black-green tongue of hers, first licking her wounded cheek, then slobbering up and down his face. Jett felt nauseous from the stench of her. Her lively tongue withdrew in an instant; Jett wondered how it fit within her mouth. Seeing her eyes up close, he could make out the green veins like lightning tracks, pulsating over the globes.

The witch blinked, which made a sticky peeling sound. Her mouth stretched into an ever-widening smile to show off a second set of needle teeth behind the first set. Jett knew exactly what she intended to do with those meat grinders. She tilted her head and spread her maw wider and wider.

"Not today, bitch!" Halo screamed.

The witch was shocked to see the orange-haired female standing behind Jett. Just as she shrieked, Halo's thread-like eye tendrils shot round the witch's neck and pinched! For moments it seemed like nothing had happened. Then the witch's body gave a quick tremble. The red tendrils lowered Jett back to his feet, then slipped loose, piling on the ground.

The witch's body wavered, then collapsed. Her head rolled over the edge and landed with an ugly thud on the next step. Jett stepped out of the dead snake pile and walked up to Halo. The air sang with the sound of the flickering flight of the strange insects. Halo smiled at Jett, and he smiled back. Silently, she fell into his arms.

"I had things under control, you know," he said.

Halo looked into his eyes, stunned, then she laughed and replied, "Yeah. I could tell."

Jett swept her hair out of her face and kissed her forehead. She leaned forward and kissed him on the lips. They looked down at the witch's corpse, steaming blood pumping from the severed neck. Jett put his arm under Halo, and together they limped into the tunnel he'd noticed earlier. They soon made their way through a blockage of jumbled roots and exited onto the befouled beach. The ocean's toxic waves slammed the rubbish along the shoreline. It was the most gratifying sight in their eyes.

The air was as fresh as could be expected. Drizzle tackled them on gusts of wind still heated from the blazer. Even without seeing it, they knew there was nothing left of Welcome.

"Clever bitch. She had it made here. All the food she could eat, all the blood she could drink. Then I came along, a stranger in town, and gave her the perfect alibi to go on a killing spree," said Jett, holding Halo's hand.

"Look," said Halo. "We're right back where we first

met."

"Thank you, Halo."

"For what?"

"Saving my ass back there."

"We saved each other's asses, Jett."

"I guess we did. So, how did you ever get that shit off your eyes?"

"Spittle," she explained. "And just in time, too."

"I wouldn't have thought of that. Where do you want to go now?" he asked as they walked.

"As far away from this shithole as possible!"

Vicious

1

"Whatever you do, try not to disturb your neighbor, Dr. Coffin," said the Realtor in a hushed voice.

"Coffin?" Sophia echoed.

"Yes, dear. A rather unusual name, I know. Doctor Garnet Coffin. He was a pediatrician, I believe. Long since retired now. Lives in that big ole house all by himself, and most definitely does not like to be disturbed...from what I hear, anyway. Who would at 91-years-old," said Doris Vecherson, stopping herself from scaring the shit out of the young new homeowner any further.

"I'm sorry, dear, listen to me, gossiping about your neighbor and you haven't even moved in yet. Here are the keys: two sets for both the front and back doors. You go on in and enjoy your new home."

"Thank you, Mrs. Vecherson, for everything," said Sophia, taking her son Arie by the hand, and trying not to make it appear so obvious that she wanted to run from the older woman. "Thanks again," she said, pulling Arie along.

Mrs. Vecherson waved as they disappeared through the front door. She had a creepy sensation of being watched. When she turned toward her car, which was parked on the street, she spied Dr. Coffin peeking at her through his heavily draped living room window. She forced a smile to him, but could not see if he'd smiled back, his features hidden within the shadows. The drapes closed.

Inside her new house, Sophia was also peeking out the living room window, watching Mrs. Vecherson leave.

"She sure does talk a lot," said Arie.

Sophia turned with a start. "No kidding. You hear what she said about the man who lives next door?"

Arie nodded.

"Good. So you know not to go anywhere near his house. Last thing I need is for some miserable old man banging at my door to complain about you messing up his garden or something," said Sophia, knowing Arie was not the type to cause any trouble. She wanted to be certain to avoid Dr. Coffin at all costs.

"Can I see my room now?" asked Arie.

Just then the front door banged shut. Heavy-footed steps came into the living room.

"Hey. Sorry I'm late," said Navy Sauer.

"Hi, Dad," said Arie, running up the creaky staircase.

"Slow down, Arie, you'll trip and fall," Sophia called after him. She walked into her husband's open arms and hugged him. "It's not just a new house, it's a new start, right, Navy?"

Navy was a handsome man. His blue eyes and movie star looks had been what first attracted her to him. Then he'd poured on the policeman's charm, even impressing her father, before they were married. He stood head and shoulders above Sophia, the perfect knight in shining...well, this knight's armor didn't shine anymore. Navy had a temper. And when Navy became angry, he became physical.

Sophia was a stunning thirty-two-year-old Spanish/French beauty. Her hair was a shiny blue-black, her eyes almond brown, and her lips full and red. She began a career as a teacher when she was twenty-six, but after the birth of their son, Navy refused to allow her to return to work (Arie was her job now). That was seven years ago.

"Why do you do that?" asked Navy, pushing her away from him.

"Do what?" she said.

"You know what. Every time we're having a nice moment, you fuck it up by saying something you know is gonna piss me off."

"Baby, I didn't mean anything."

"You want me to get cross at you, that's what you want. You fucking do it on purpose. Then you cry the blues after the fact like it's all my fucking fault. We had to move here just to escape the fucking rumors you spread about me in Jolly—my home town! Can't even show my fucking face there without people pointing and glaring at me," he rambled on.

Sophia stepped farther away from him. "I'm sorry. I said nothing to anyone in Jolly. They just figured it out," she said nervously.

"Bullshit!" Navy yelled in her face.

"Dad?" came Arie's voice from the top of the staircase.

Navy looked up at him with narrowed eyes. "Come down here," he said in a firm voice.

Arie crept down the stairs, afraid to approach his father.

"Navy," Sophia said, raising her hands to him, her head shaking, eyes watery.

When Arie was near enough for his father to reach out and touch him, Navy messed the boy's hair and said, "Did you find your room okay?"

Sophia slouched with relief.

"Yeah. I think so. Is it the blue one?" asked Arie.

"Must be," said Navy. "Let's go for lunch. I'm treating," he added.

As they headed for the front door, Arie looked up at his father. "Dad, the house lady said we shouldn't bother the old man next door."

"Oh yeah. She did? Well, don't bother the man, Arie. Remember, he was here before us," Navy reminded him. "Keep your ass in our yard and we won't have a problem."

"Yes, Dad."

2

By the second week of October, Sophia had the house in order. She'd torn down the old wallpapers in the bedrooms and painted. She wanted to repaint the living room and kitchen, but Navy restricted her spending. She counted herself lucky to have made over the bedrooms. Navy didn't concern himself with what the house looked like; they never had company over (he did not permit it), and he was barely there himself.

Every day Sophia walked Arie partway to school, met him at the same point to walk him home for lunch, and back again. This was her routine. In between walks to meet her son, she did laundry and house cleaning and prepared lunches and suppers. If not for Arie's company, Sophia would have become quite lonely, and in fact, she did, often.

Thursday afternoon saw perfect fall weather in Chapel Hill. The sun was shining as a warmish breeze whooshed through the trees. The aroma of leaves surrendering to death and dampened earth, combined to create a comfort that can only be conjured this time of year. Sophia was sitting on the wooden steps of the back porch, sipping her pumpkin spice flavored coffee. She winced at the pain the hot drink caused when it touched the cut on her swollen bottom lip (a result of too much sugar in Navy's coffee last night).

Around the side of the house, Arie was playing in

the dirt with his collection of construction toys. He'd made hills for his excavator and bulldozer to dig into and fill his dump truck with clumpy dirt, and used his road roller to smooth out the new make-believe roads. As he was dumping another load into the dump truck's box, he turned with a start at the sound of branches cracking behind him, and gasped!

"Oh. I didn't mean to scare you, young man," said Mr. Coffin, his voice about as scratched as an old cat pole.

Arie was speechless. This was the oldest human being he'd ever seen. Mr. Coffin was very slender, his blue pants about an inch or so too short (but if you knew him, you knew he wore them that length on purpose, to show off a bit of his fancy colored striped socks). He had a white long sleeve shirt on with fine gold print on it, red and white striped suspenders, and a large bow tie the same color as his trousers capped off the look.

"Saw you out here and thought I might pop over to introduce myself," he explained. "Combed my hair and everything," he added with a grin, his white handlebar moustache curled into fine points at the ends.

Arie was staring at his perfectly bald head with its large brown age spots.

Mr. Coffin chuckled at the boy's confusion. He said, "That was a jest, young man. I was joking about the hair. Say, you have a name so I can stop calling you young man?"

"Arie," said the boy, at last.

Mr. Coffin reached down to shake Arie's hand. Arie

just stared at the thin, wrinkled fingers for a moment, before he finally offered his little hand up.

"It's very nice to meet you, Arie. Is your mother home? I would very much like to introduce myself and say hello."

Arie nodded, then thought to speak up. "Yes, sir, she's out back having her coffee break."

"Perhaps you would be so kind as to lead me to her?"

Arie wondered what his mother would think of him talking to the 'stay away from him' neighbor. Mr. Coffin's eyes, though darkest blue and bloodshot, looked upon him with kindness. He decided it would be okay.

"Sure. Follow me," he said, and without thinking, he took Mr. Coffin by the hand and led him round the back of the house.

Indeed, Sophia was surprised to see her son appear before her, hand in hand, with the creepy old man from next door. She nearly spat up her coffee. Wiping a few small drips from her chin, she stood up to greet them.

"Don't be alarmed, Mrs. I'm quite harmless. Garnet's my name, Garnet Coffin," said the old man, now reaching to shake Sophia's hand.

"Sophia. Very nice to meet you, Mr. Coffin."

Garnet found the young lady's hand felt as soft as she was pretty; Sophia found Mr. Coffin's hand felt like she could stretch the skin for days.

"Oh no, dear, don't call me that. Garnet is fine by me. After all, it is the name my lovely mother gave to me," he said, his big ears rising when he smiled.

"I was told you were a doctor?" said Sophia.

"Yes, that's true. But that was another lifetime ago. I haven't been a doctor for over thirty-five years now. It was a wonderful career, but I can't say I wasn't glad to call it quits," he said with a chuckle.

"Would you like coffee, Mr...I mean, Garnet?" asked Sophia. "I have a fresh pot."

"That's very kind of you, dear, but I gave up coffee around the same time I retired. Perhaps you can offer me tea some time, and I would accept," he said, his shoulders slightly slouched.

Sophia smiled. "I'll be sure and do that," she said.

"Well, I've taken up enough of your time."

Arie had been standing next to them up till this point, then he decided his mother was safe and he could return to his work site. Once he disappeared around the house, Garnet looked at Sophia's lip and said, "I see you cut your lip there." He winked as if to let Sophia know he understood the lip had not been an accident.

Sophia reached to touch her lip again but stopped herself. She said, "Oh, yes. I'll be more careful next time."

"I don't mean to stick my big nose where it doesn't belong, Mrs."

"Please, call me Sophia."

"Sophia. Such a lovely name for such a lovely lady. My door is always open, dear. I know what it's like. My father wasn't the kindest man to my mother when I was a boy. I just hate to see that kind of thing. Just hate to see it."

Sophia couldn't help herself. Though she just met

this man, she felt she could trust him. She placed her hand on his once again, holding back the tears.

"Thank you. Thank you so much. I won't forget," she said.

Garnet nodded. He smiled and said, "That's a beautiful son you have there, Sophia. Watch over him. I can tell he loves you very much. Now, off with me before I bore you to tears."

Sophia watched him walk away, his feet dragging gently along the concrete pathway between their two houses. She sat down on the porch steps once more and wiped away her tears. What a sweet man, she thought. Better not to mention him to Navy. She would remind Arie to keep quiet about him as well. She'd always taught him that keeping secrets wasn't nice, but sometimes it was necessary.

3

In the weeks that followed, Sophia, Arie, and Garnet became very good friends. Garnet enjoyed walking to the nearby park on weekends with his neighbors and watching Arie run about the playground. He shared some of his deceased wife's recipes with Sophia, happy to receive a share of the baked goods that came of it.

Garnet's house was a large red brick, two-story home. His yard was maintained by a professional gardener, and once a week a house cleaner took care of his laundry and dusting. He was very self-sufficient for a man of his age. Sophia and Arie spent many Saturdays listening to the stories of his life. They learned that having never had children of their own, Garnet and his wife used to foster children from the children's aid society until proper homes were found for them.

They also discovered that Garnet's favorite hobby was collecting bow ties. He had a small room dedicated to his collection. Bow ties of every color and every pattern you could imagine, enough to wear a different one twice a day, every day of the year.

"Why do you like them so much?" Arie asked one day.

"I guess because they make me feel happy. And they always bring a smile to people's faces. Oh, I know sometimes they're laughing at me, but any time I can put a smile on someone's face for whatever reason, it's a win for me," Garnet explained.

"I think they're all very cheerful," said Sophia. "Now, we'd better get home. It's getting late and I don't want Navy to walk into an empty house. He wouldn't like that," she said.

Arie nodded in agreement.

As they walked back downstairs, Arie sniffed the air and said, "Your house smells funny, Mr. Coffin."

"Arie!" Sophia scolded, even though he was right.

Garnet laughed about this as he followed behind the pair. "That's the scent of Old English furniture polish you smell. I like a nice shine to my tables and banister," he explained.

When they stepped outside, Sophia was surprised to see how dark it had become. Garnet's house was dimly lit inside, and she hadn't realized night had fallen already. She took Arie by the hand and rushed through the backyard, passing between Garnet's tall bushes that acted as a fence. They stepped lightly on the back porch steps and entered the house through the kitchen. Sophia was calming down because the lights were all still off, which meant Navy hadn't come home yet—or so she thought.

"Quickly now, Arie, up to bed," she automatically whispered.

As they were tiptoeing through the living room, the small lamp by the bay window clicked to life. Both Sophia and Arie gave little yelps to the shock. Next to the lamp, Navy was sitting in their rocking chair, slowly swaying front to back, front to back. Since he wasn't saying anything, Sophia spoke up, her voice full of nerves.

"Navy. We didn't see you there. You frightened us," she said.

"I bet I did," he replied, his words underscored with anger. "Where the hell have you two been?"

"Go on up," Sophia whispered to Arie, gently ushering him up the first steps. She turned back to answer Navy. "We were just in the backyard, looking at the stars," she lied.

"Were ya now. You sure about that?"

Sophia had to think fast. Had he checked the backyard and knew they hadn't been there or was he bluffing?

"Yes. It's a clear night. Arie's learning about stars at school so we were trying to name the constellations." She said it with such confidence, she almost believed it herself.

Navy was quiet for a few moments. He suddenly stopped rocking and stood. He turned the lamp off, unzipping his pants in the near darkness of the room. Sophia gulped; she knew what he wanted. He kicked his feet free of his boxers and unbuttoned his shirt as he approached her. Sophia just stood there. She didn't undress because she knew he liked to tear her out of her clothes. Sex was never pleasurable for Sophia; Navy was rough and selfish, and he treated her like a stranger he'd picked up off the street every single time.

He leaned up against her, the weight of his body forcing her to lie back down upon the steps. Rubbing his throbbing cock against her soft belly and down between her legs, he pressed his lips to hers. His beard was prickly against her skin. Feeling around inside her mouth, his tongue forceful and gagging, he bit down on her tongue. Sophia couldn't move. She felt his teeth digging in and soon tasted her blood.

"Next time you lie to me, bitch, I'll bite it right the fuck off. You got me?"

Sophia nodded, tears rolling back into the sides of her hair. Beneath her, the edge of the steps was causing her great physical pain. But Navy wasn't finished with her yet. He placed his hands on either side of her head and fucked her, groaning and drooling on her. And when he was finished, his hairy chest heaving, he stepped over her without a word and went upstairs to shower.

Sophia grunted as she peeled herself off the stairs. She fumbled her way to the kitchen and poured herself a tall glass of water. After drinking that down, she splashed water on her face, silently crying.

4

The next week Sophia tried to avoid Mr. Coffin. She was too ashamed to let him see her limping and worse, unable to talk normally till her tongue heeled. Arie decided that since they couldn't visit with him, they should do something nice for him. He and Sophia sat together one night after school and designed a special bow tie, a one-of-a-kind bow tie, just for Mr. Coffin.

Come Saturday, Sophia didn't feel right about avoiding Mr. Coffin. After all, what was he thinking about them, that he'd done something wrong? She wrapped the bow tie in a box and walked over to his back door with Arie in tow. They'd stopped knocking before entering, but today she felt it better to knock and show some respect.

Garnet answered the door to them, his usual smile on his face. He was overjoyed to see them and invited them in at once, insisting they just enter from now on.

"How have my two favorite people been?" he asked, guiding them into the dining room. He had three glasses waiting on the table next to a pitcher of juice, a bowl of chips, dip, and cheeses.

"What's all this?" asked Sophia, her mouth still sore. "Looks like you were expecting us."

Garnet blushed, "I was hoping."

Sophia leaned over and kissed him on the cheek, whispering in his ear, "I'm sorry."

"Don't be."

"We brought you a gift. This is just like it's your birthday!" said Arie, handing Garnet the wrapped box.

They pulled out chairs and sat around the table. Garnet opened his gift, his eyes lighting up as if he'd just been given the secret to life eternal. He removed the bow tie from the box, feeling it with his fingertips. Tears welled up in his eyes.

"I don't know what to say. This is the most beautiful bow tie I have ever seen," he said.

Arie smiled ear to ear. "We made it ourselves," he said proudly.

Garnet reached up and yanked the bow tie presently around his collar. He set it down on the table and proceeded to apply the new bow tie in its place. Sophia helped him readjust his collar. Then he stood and made his way over to the large antique mirror hanging above the dining room fireplace. Sophia and Arie smiled at each other as he admired his reflection.

"Just beautiful," he said, still stroking the red bow tie with a tiny stuffed heart at its centre. "I can now stop my collecting because I will never find a finer bow tie than this one."

Arie giggled.

"We're glad you like it, Garnet. It was Arie's idea," said Sophia.

"Like it? I love it!" he said delightedly.

Later that same evening, Sophia was upstairs sitting on

the edge of Arie's bed, listening to him read from Cullen Bunn's *Crooked Hills: Book One*. As they were enjoying the story, they heard Navy call out from below.

"Soph! Soph, where are you?"

Arie shook his head at his mother and whispered, "Don't go, Mom."

Sophia forced a smile for him, kissed his forehead, and said, "I have to. Finish up the chapter then lights out. Okay?"

Arie nodded.

Just as she was about to close his door behind her, the boy called, "Mom?"

Sophia hated to see the fear in his eyes. "It's okay, Arie," she assured, just as Navy screamed out for her to come downstairs.

Next door, Garnet had just come out of his garage where he'd placed a garbage bag (his gardener would transport it to the roadside for him in a couple of days) when he also heard Navy yelling at Sophia. His eyes narrowed with anger. Though he was no match physically for Navy, perhaps he could cause a distraction and spare Sophia from another beating. Determined to do just that, he went into the house and fetched a small crystal bowl from his kitchen cabinet.

Meanwhile, Sophia was now wearing the meal of mashed potatoes in gravy, peas, and baked ham she'd heated up for her husband. Gravy and potatoes fell from her face in globs at her bare feet.

"You fucking call this food? I wouldn't feed this shit to a goddamned pig!" Navy shouted.

The truth was, Navy always ate big meals while on the job. He was never hungry by the time he got home around 10:30 pm every night. Bitching about what she'd made was just an excuse to terrorize her.

There weren't tears yet in Sophia's eyes, so Navy punched her in the abdomen. She folded in half with a loud groan, then collapsed on the floor. Navy reached down, grabbed Sophia by the back of her hair, and pressed her face against the floor, smearing her around in the slop like a mop.

"Now you can eat that shit up just like the fucking pig you take me for," he shouted venomously.

Just then, he froze when he heard the knocking at the front door. Navy released Sophia's hair, knocking her head down on the floor. "Keep your fucking yap shut or so help me...."

Navy adjusted his uniform, puffed his chest out, and opened the door. Immediately Garnet could see the look of despise on his face (he didn't try to hide it).

"I'm so sorry to bother you, young man."

"Then why are you? It's late. Shouldn't you be in bed by now," Navy growled.

Garnet kept his smile and his cool. He raised his crystal bowl and said, "I was just wondering if I could borrow a bit of sugar. I seem to have run out and I always take sugar in my tea before bed at night."

Navy wanted to knock the old man off his porch, but instead, he snatched the bowl from his hands.

"Wait here," he said.

Navy gave the door a slight shove to close it, but Garnet put his foot in the way and stopped it from sealing. He peered into the house, around the wall's edge, and could just make out Sophia on her hands and knees. She was cleaning the floor and was covered in food. She happened to look up, her eyes connecting with his, and at that moment you couldn't be sure who was the sorrier.

Navy flung the door wide open and rammed an un-opened bag of sugar against Garnet's chest, practically knocking the senior off his feet, then capped the bag with the crystal bowl.

"Here!" he said. "Now get your feeble ass off my property before I arrest you for trespassing."

And before Garnet could say a word, he slammed the door in his face.

Navy watched Garnet amble down the sidewalk toward his own house. He turned back to Sophia and said, "Fucking nosy bastard. You have been talking to him about me, haven't you?"

"Never," said Sophia, finally on her feet again.

Navy stormed up to her and was about to backhand her in the face, but he stopped in mid-strike and guffawed. "Get your ass cleaned up and in bed before I get up there. You fucking reek," he snarled, shoving her from behind as she passed him.

5

The following day, Navy was called into the office by the Chief of Police himself. He sat down facing Chief Brian Hicks. The Chief put down the file he'd been reading and smiled at Navy.

"Officer Sauer," he started, "how's life in your new house treating you?"

Navy thought it was an odd question but responded nonetheless, saying, "Good, Chief. In fact, very good."

The Chief nodded. He tented his fingers and leaned over his desk. "Listen, Navy, I'm going to be as blunt as I can be with you. Get...help," he said sternly.

Navy's brows arched. "I'm not sure I follow, Chief."

"I think you do. We received an anonymous call last night from a very concerned neighbor of yours. This person claimed they knew for a fact that a certain Officer Navy Sauer was physically harming his wife Sophia. Does this sound familiar to you?"

Navy kept silent, but for his grinding teeth.

"If you don't do something about this, I'm afraid I'll be forced to take matters into my own hands. Do we understand each other, Navy?"

Navy nodded reluctantly.

"Good. Then we're done here."

Navy left the office, left the building, got in his squad car, and screamed at the top of his voice, pounding on the steering wheel.

That night around 11:30 pm, when Navy was certain his wife and son were asleep, he sneaked out of the house. Without turning the car lights on, he backed out of their driveway and pulled into Garnet's. Before he could run from his car to Garnet's back door, he was drenched from the pouring rain. Garnet's kitchen light was on and the back door not yet locked for the night. Navy was surprised the old bastard was still up.

He crept inside and closed the door with barely a sound. Leaving a trail of muddy footprints, he made his way through the dining room and stopped at the threshold to the living room. He could see the old man sitting in a recliner, reading a thick book. Garnet didn't take notice of him until he was standing right before him. He let the book fall loose on his lap, his eyes wide.

"Surprised to see me?" said Navy, water dripping from his fists.

"Here in my house, unannounced...perhaps; but not especially, no," said Garnet, unable to keep the fear out of his voice.

"You've got a hellofa pair on you. Sticking your business where it doesn't belong, making phone calls. Get up! We're gonna take a little ride, you and I. And one of us...ain't coming back," Navy said, reaching for Garnet's left arm. He yanked him from his chair, the large book thumping on the floor. The old man was so frail, Navy felt empowered by his ability to whip him about. "Move it, you son of a bitch!"

"You're making a mistake," Garnet whined.

"*You* made the mistake when you called my department!"

"I was only trying to protect Sophia and the boy."

"Protect? Don't make me laugh. Who's gonna protect you now?"

"You're just a bully, beating on your own 'cause you get off on it, that's all you are," accused Garnet.

Navy tossed him off his back porch; Garnet felt his right arm break when he landed on the pavement. He moaned as he lay there, his clothes instantly soaking up the rain. Navy grabbed a fistful of Garnet's shirt and set him back on his stocking feet. He shoved the old man into the back seat of his cruiser. Garnet continued to moan in pain, holding his arm against his chest as they sped down Bishop Road. Navy turned right onto Cross Street where he slammed on the brakes and threw the car into park.

Garnet was pulled from the back seat by a man whose eyes shone with madness. Navy shoved him along, forcing him to plow through the wet trees that bordered the section of the Chapel Hill River cut off from the main flow. Here they struggled to keep their balance while edging their way down the slippery slope that led down into the green, stagnant pool. Garnet winced in pain as he struggled down to the mucky landing. His feet were sinking into the slop as Navy loomed over his shoulder. Once they were face to face again, Navy looked at the polluted water, then back into the old man's squinting eyes.

"Get in!" he shouted.

Garnet shook his head as he trembled uncontrollably.

"But I can't swim," he said.

Navy removed his gun from its holster and pointed it at Garnet's chest. "I said...*get...IN!*"

Garnet shook his head again, mumbling, "No, no, no...."

Navy rushed Garnet, placing his Glock 17 to the man's forehead. "Your choice, gramPA!"

A look of calm washed over Garnet's face. He turned and began to wobble into the water, the thick, slimy surface spreading around him. Deeper and deeper he stepped until the green was just under his armpits. He turned back to face Navy, his face was expressionless, eyes unblinking. Navy shook his gun at the man, silently telling him to continue with his demise.

Garnet let himself fall back into the depths; the water rippled over his head; and just like that he disappeared. Navy scanned the edges of the pool for about fifteen minutes afterwards, making sure the old man didn't crawl out. When he was positive Garnet was lying dead at the bottom of the pool, he climbed up the hill, got back in his car, and drove home. He raided the fridge, feeling famished all of a sudden, then headed upstairs to shower. And as he stood under the gentle spray, he replayed the moment when Garnet's head sank below the green surface in his mind. Feeling incredibly aroused by the memory, he grabbed hold of his engorged cock and pleasured himself to orgasm.

Soon he was crawling into bed, next to Sophia, smiling in his contentment.

6

Three weeks later, when teenage friends Tim Rogers and Cooper Martin stopped to throw rocks off the Cross Street pedestrian bridge, they discovered the body of Garnet Coffin on the muddy bank below. They rode home as fast as they could on their bicycles and gave Tim's mother, Gracie, a gruesome, detailed description of what they had seen. Gracie dialed up the police at once, and within half an hour, she and the boys met an ambulance, the fire department, and Chapel Hill's Chief of Police at the scene.

Hicks would later detail in his report that there was no identification found on the corpse. The victim appeared to be in his late seventies or eighties, roundabout. The right arm had sustained a fractured ulna. The discovery was called in by a Mrs. Gracie Rogers, whose son Tim Rogers and his friend Cooper Martin (both fifteen-years-old), could not speculate on the victim's identity. As of this day November 7, 2020, no missing persons report had been filed.

But a person was missing, and two people took immediate notice. For several weeks now, Sophia and Arie had been knocking on Garnet's back door. Under normal circumstances, the door would be open to them, but it was locked! Arie kept telling his mother to break it down, that something was wrong with Mr. Coffin.

"What if he's hurt, Mom? What if he needs our

help?" the boy persisted.

"I know, I know," said Sophia. She rose to her tiptoes and tried to peek through the little window on the door, but it was made of thick yellow glass, and all she could see was a blur. "Come on. Let's go home. I'll try and come back tonight when I'm alone. Hopefully, Garnet is okay. Hopefully, we're worrying for nothing," she said.

But as they returned to their backyard, Arie shook his head and mumbled sadly, "I don't think so."

Later that night, Sophia was anxious to get Arie off to bed. She wanted to run back to Garnet's and find a way inside. She wanted to call the police, but she knew that would carry a beating with it. She would just have to investigate herself. The moment Arie's light went out, she slipped into her shoes and went silently out the back door. She figured she had at least another hour or two before Navy would return.

There were three small windows at ground level at Garnet's house: two in the back, and one on the left side. All these areas were well hidden from view. She tried the two back windows first, but they were both secure to break-ins. At the third window, she discovered a small break in the glass, probably from a rock kicked by Garnet himself as he walked past. Might as well complete the job, she told herself.

She found another rock and tapped on the surrounding glass; much to her surprise, the aged seal around the pane gave easily. The window was just big enough for her to squeeze through. She had not been in Garnet's basement before, and it held its own in the creepiness department. At first, she wasn't even certain she could locate the stairs to go up, but in a few minutes, she'd crossed the dark, damp basement and was ascending the wooden steps.

This was Garnet's house; she'd felt right at home here; and yet at that moment, reaching for the doorknob to the upstairs, she'd never felt more frightened. She knew it was not a fear of Garnet himself, but of what she might find up there. The door gave into the kitchen. There was a faint glow of light from beyond the room. She recognized that glow as coming from the lamp with the painted glass shade that Garnet had beside his recliner chair.

The house was so quiet, she thought she could hear it breathing, but that was just the wind sneaking its way through a window somewhere in the house, sneaking in the way she had sneaked in. Her nerves were jangling as she moved forward, making her way through the dining room and toward the living room. Indeed the lamp was on, but no one was sitting in the recliner.

A large tome was lying prone on the floor. She picked it up and flipped it open to where several of the pages to Edgar Allen Poe's *Complete Tales and Poems* were crumpled and damaged. She unfolded the pages, pressing them flat, then closed the book and placed it on the table next to the chair. This wasn't right. Garnet was a stickler for organization and cleanliness. He'd never purposely cause damage to a book, of this she was certain.

She turned and scanned the room for any other signs out of the ordinary, but everything seemed to be in place. Moving a little quicker now, she made her way upstairs to check Garnet's bedroom. His bed was still made up. It was as if he'd just vanished into thin air. Next, she found herself in Garnet's bow tie room.

A smile crept across her lips as she touched the bow ties, remembering how much joy the silly things brought to Garnet. And that's when she realized the one bow tie not accounted for was the one she and Arie had made for him. Since giving him that bow tie, he hadn't worn another. And it wasn't here. She wasn't sure what to make of any of this, but none of it sat right with her.

As she was passing by Garnet's bedroom on her way back toward the stairs, strong arms reached out and pulled her inside. Sophia screamed, her voice echoing down the hall. Navy tossed her around and flung her onto the queen-size bed.

"What the fuck you think you're doing here, bitch?" he shouted down at her.

Sophia put her right arm up before her face, anticipating the blow to follow his question. Instead, he forced her legs apart and leaned in over her. "Answer me, you fucking cunt! What the fuck are you doing in the old guy's house, snooping around? I should arrest your flabby ass for a break and enter," he snarled, placing all his weight upon her now.

"Navy! Get off me! Get off me!" she screamed, struggling fruitlessly.

Now the blow—Navy's fist plunged into her left side.

She lost her breath as she attempted to coil under his hold, and lost her fight as well. He tore her T-shirt open right down the middle, snapping her bra free. Sophia was still coughing in agony from the hit as he kneaded her breasts. If not for the unexpected clang from the kitchen, she guessed he would have raped her again.

Navy grabbed her by the left wrist and whisked her out of the room. He dragged her down the stairs in his haste to reach the kitchen. When he barged into the room, he discovered a crystal sugar bowl sitting atop its emptied contents on the floor. He looked around suspiciously, then down at Sophia and shook her by the hand.

"You bring the boy here too?" he huffed.

Sophia looked up at him, confused. "No," she whimpered.

"Arie? Arie, you in this fucking house? You best answer me if you are, boy?" he yelled.

No response.

Navy reached down and picked the bowl up. As he examined it, the crystal cracked and cut his forefinger. He gasped and tossed the bowl aside, yelling, "Fucking shit!"

He then forced Sophia to her feet and exited through the back door, locking it. And as he hauled his wife from one backyard to the other, he scoffed: "Stupid bitch. Your wonderful Mr. Coffin died a couple of weeks back. Guess it slipped my mind to tell you. So you can stop going over to his house 'cause he's not gonna be your sugar daddy anymore!"

7

For several days Sophia could not bring herself to tell Arie that Garnet was dead. She hid away from him and spent long hours crying. He knew something was wrong with his mother, and he was old enough to guess that that something had to do with Mr. Coffin's disappearance. On their walk home from school Friday afternoon, Arie put the question to her: "He's never coming back, is he?"

Sophia was very emotional these days; her spirit had been broken by Navy's abuse and by Garnet's death. She looked down at her son's sad eyes, hers welling up with tears, and said: "I'm so sorry, Arie. No. He's not coming back. Mr. Coffin was very old. I guess it was his time. We just have to be thankful for having had the chance to know him. And keep him in our hearts."

"I miss him," said Arie.

"So do I, honey."

That night a heavy rainstorm bowled through Chapel Hill, stripping the tree limbs clean of any straggling leaves. Lightning blazed above the houses, accompanied by intense cracks and booms of thunder. Arie lay awake in his bed, unable to fall back into sleep after the crash of thunder that awoke him with a start. He sat up with his back against the headboard, peering into the dark recesses of his room. A sound like buzzing static was growing louder by his closet. And Arie had the strangest feeling that something (or some*one*) was there.

"Hello?" he whispered.

The rain was rushing his window in alternating soft and hard waves. When the next explosion of lightning illuminated his room, Arie could see wisps of mist sneaking out around the frame of his closet door. The static sound was drawing nearer, creeping across the floor toward his bed. Arie sat up straighter, pulling his blankets up under his chin. "Hel-lo?" he whispered once more.

The closet door creaked wide open, an entire cloud of mist rolling outward. Arie was transfixed by the phenomenon. Within the cloud, he could see tiny bursts of light mimicking the storm outside. Riding on the static came a whispering sound from what seemed like a far-away place. The whisper slowly grew louder and louder, until Arie could finally understand that it was a voice he was hearing. And not just any voice, but the voice of Mr. Coffin.

From out of the sparking cloud an image began to glisten into view. The whispering voice said, "Don't look at me, Arie. I'm not how you remember."

But Arie surprised even himself when he spoke. "I'm not afraid, Mr. Coffin."

Emitting green steam like something doused in toxic chemicals, a body starved of flesh crept forward. The body was mere bones covered in stretched leather, blackened and purplish. The shoulders were hunched forward, causing the arms to appear much longer, from the bony shoulders to the twig fingers. Arie couldn't quite make out the facial features hidden within the thickness of the green murk.

"Is that you, Mr. Coffin?"

Garnet's voice road in from a great distance on static and whispers, and when it reached Arie's ears it seemed to emanate from the entire space of his closet.

"Yes, young man, it's me."

Arie let his blankets fall loose at his waist, he said, "What happened to you, Mr. Coffin? Mom is really sad that you're gone. She won't stop crying about it. I'm sad too. I miss you."

The voice seemed to sigh, and it sank deep within Arie's chest, and he understood the sorrow there.

"It's okay, Mr. Coffin. Don't be sad. We still love you," said the boy.

The voice spilled from the closet once more. "Arie, you and Sophia are in danger. Listen to me now. I'm going to give you something for your mother."

Arie was nodding.

"You must NOT tell your father about me. Not a word, Arie. Do you understand?"

"Yes, Mr. Coffin, I understand."

"Good, Arie. I must go. Remember...not a word to your father."

"Not a word," Arie repeated.

This new incarnation of Mr. Coffin seemed to float backward, the cloud in the room chasing after him into the closet.

"Wait! Will I see you again?" asked Arie.

There was no verbal response, but the boy was certain he saw Mr. Coffin's head nod.

Arie wanted to get out of bed and rush into his mother's room to tell her everything, but he couldn't move. His eyelids felt heavier than usual, and he just had to close them. So he did, and sleep stole him away at once as the rain eased against his window.

8

Saturday morning, Arie waited in his bedroom until he heard his father's angry shouts end with the slamming of the front door. He raced to his window and watched his father's car reverse out of their driveway and speed off. Unable to stand another moment of keeping his secret, he ran down the stairs and burst into the kitchen, taking his mother by surprise.

"Mom! Mom! He came to see me last night! My room got all smokey and he came out of my closet! I was so scared at first, but then I wasn't—"

"Arie! Calm down. What are you talking about? Who came to see you?" asked Sophia, holding him by the shoulders.

"Mr. Coffin!"

Sophia let go of him and stood upright, her face flushed. "Are you telling me someone was in your room last night, Arie?"

"Not *someone*! Mr. Coffin."

Sophia took her son by the hand and led him to the kitchen table to sit down. Holding both his hands in hers, she leaned in close to him and spoke softly.

"Arie, you must have had a dream last night. Most likely the thunderstorm caused it, but you know you couldn't have seen Mr. Coffin in your room. You know he's gone now, right?"

Arie grunted with annoyance. He said, "Mom, I'm

not a baby. It wasn't a dream. He really came to see me, but he was different. I couldn't see his face cause he said he didn't want me to see him. He didn't want me to be afraid. I told him I wasn't scared."

"Oh, Arie. I know how much you miss him, honey. I know you wish he could come to see you still, but that's just not possible," said Sophia, running his bangs back with her fingers.

Arie pushed her hand away. "He was *real*, Mom. He told me not to tell Dad that he came. And he gave me this to give to you," he said, producing something from the pocket of his pajama bottoms.

Sophia gasped. In Arie's little hand was the bow tie they'd made for Garnet. Possible means by which he might have attained the bow tie ran through her mind, but nothing short of a miracle came back as the answer. Sophia reached for the bow tie; feeling it with her own hands made it surreal.

"Arie," she said, "how did you get this?"

"I told you, Mr. Coffin gave it to me last night when he came out of my closet."

"What else did he say to you?"

"He said we were in danger," Arie frowned.

"What kind of danger?"

"Mom, he didn't tell me everything."

"Okay. I believe you. Go get dressed and I'll make you bacon and eggs for breakfast," said Sophia.

Arie headed out of the kitchen, then turned back to his mother and said, "Mom, I'm glad Mr. Coffin came to see me. I missed him."

Sophia smiled at him.

She could hear her son trampling up the stairs as she gazed at the bow tie. And just as she was about to stand, she felt as if she'd been slammed between two colliding walls. Blackness entombed her. And suddenly she found herself standing in the pouring rain. She could hear someone talking, faint at first, becoming more clear. She recognized that voice—Navy.

She wanted to move but she couldn't. All she was able to do was watch the scene unfold before her. She could see her husband from behind. He was talking to someone but she couldn't see around him. The rain looked green and sometimes red. She was breathing heavily. Instinctively, she knew who Navy was talking to; she knew, but she didn't want to be right.

Navy took a step forward; and Sophia screamed in her mind—Garnet!

She could see the gun in Navy's hand. Then she watched poor Mr. Coffin stroll into that swampy pool. She saw him turn to face her husband, then down he went. And the instant Navy turned around, Sophia was catapulted back to reality! She dropped the bow tie and raced to the sink to vomit. A chill swept through her body from head to toes. Sophia turned around and looked at the bow tie on the floor (the red bow tie with the little stuffed heart), and wept.

All day she wondered what she should do, what she *could* do! If she telephoned the police, what would she tell them, that Garnet's ghost told her her husband murdered him? She had no proof. It would be her 'abused wife's' word against a fellow officer. No. Going to the cops was out of the question. And that left...what?

9

Eleven-thirty, Saturday night. Sophia had just unplugged the bathtub and wrapped herself in a towel when Navy pulled up in the driveway. She didn't hear him come in, but she somehow sensed his presence. Not wanting him to find her undressed (her nakedness would only make him want to have sex with her), she tiptoed into the bedroom and gently shut the door.

Quickly, she rubbed her hair as dry as she could with the towel and slipped into a knee-length nightgown. She thought she heard the creaking of the bottom steps as she shut the light and crawled under the covers, turning her back to the door. New creaks, higher up the staircase now. Sophia closed her eyes and listened. She then heard the heavy flow of his urine in the toilet bowl. For sure he would know she'd just gone to bed by the lingering steam in the washroom. She wondered how she would ever fall asleep again, next to a man who was a murderer.

By now he should have entered their room, but he was still lurking in the hallway for some reason. This made Sophia's nerves shrink. Curiosity almost convinced her to get out of bed to see what the hell he was up to, but fear kept her where she was.

And where he was, was standing just outside Arie's bedroom door, listening to his son talking to himself. After a few moments, he opened the door wider and stepped in, startling the boy. He crouched down and moved his face real close to his son's.

"Just who the hell are you talking to in here?" he asked, his voice serious.

Arie was gripping something in his hands at his chest. He shook his head, afraid to speak. Navy noticed the boy's hands.

"Whatcha guarding there, son?" he asked.

"Nothing," Arie whispered, tucking his hands deeper under the covers.

Navy reached into the blankets and pulled Arie's hands out into the open. The boy had a tight hold on the object, but Navy pried it loose. In the faint light shining from the hallway behind him, Navy examined the bow tie with keen interest. Suddenly it came to him—where he'd seen this thing before—and if he was not mistaken, which he knew he wasn't, this object should not exist. His eyes sparkled with confusion and rage (mostly rage).

Grabbing a fistful of his son's pajama top, he raised him off the bed and held him up, his feet just able to touch his bed.

"Where the fuck did you get this?" he shouted.

Arie started crying at once, holding onto his father's arm.

"Where, goddammit?"

"Mr. Coffin," the boy cried.

Navy's cheeks flushed red, the lines on his forehead deepened, his eyes went wide round, then narrowed. He whipped Arie against his closet door and turned to rush out, slamming right into Sophia and knocking her off her feet. While she was still recovering from the blow, Navy reached down and grabbed her by the throat.

"Come here, you *bitch*!"

"Navy, no!" she shouted.

Arie came out of his room and leapt onto his father's back, yelling, "Let her go! Leave her alone!"

Navy reacted as though he was defending himself against a grown man; he hammered himself back against the wall, in effect banging his son loose.

"Arie!" Sophia screamed. She pounded on Navy's wrist until he let her go, then struck him on the left side of his face and split his lip open. "You leave my son alone!" she said with a mother's fierceness.

Navy laughed in her face. He was still holding onto Garnet's special tie when he squeezed it within his fist and struck her in the mouth. She felt an incredible shock of pain. And when she spat, two teeth came out in a glob of blood.

"Mom!" Arie screamed in horror.

Navy shoved him aside and snatched Sophia by the hair. He pulled her down to the floor and dragged her to the top of the staircase. Sophia was struggling to break free as Arie screamed for his father to stop hurting his mother. Running after them, Arie reached for Navy's hand and was tossed against the wall.

"No! No! Navy! You're crazy! Let me go!" Sophia pleaded. And then the accusation slipped from her tongue, "Murderer!"

Navy suddenly stopped. He dropped to his knees,

grabbed her by the hair on either side of her head, and pounded her head against the floor.

"What did you call me? What did you call me?"

Sophia dared not repeat the word as she cried.

Arie attacked his father from the side, hitting him on the shoulder and the head as hard as he could, his mind overloaded with hatred and terror. And down the hall, where the assault began, Mr. Coffin's bow tie lay on the floor next to Sophia's bloodied teeth. The three Sauers were too preoccupied to notice the special tie dissolve into a red puddle, then slime its way up the wall.

With Sophia's head between his knees, Navy spat in her face.

"How did you find out? Were you following me that night? Tell me, you fucking cunt!" Navy removed his gun from its holster and placed its nose between Sophia's breasts. "You'd better tell me before I blow your fucking heart right outta your chest. Where...did you get...that fucking tie from?" he said, drooling.

"Daddy, no," Arie cried as he now sat balled up against the banister at his mother's feet.

By now the patch of red had made its way to the ceiling right above Navy. Arie looked up in amazement as the thick paste began to take form. He suddenly realized that the hum of static had been buzzing in his ears for a few minutes, but he hadn't acknowledged its presence. A loud hiss of breath filled the hallway as mist spilled overhead, across the ceiling. Sophia saw what was coming, her eyes widened. Navy followed his wife's focus to the ceiling; he stood at once.

Suddenly, the top half of Mr. Coffin's leather-skinned skeleton dropped out of the mist, green strings swaying from his body. His face was a stretched-out version of what it once was, his eyes beady green lights. He opened his mouth to the size of a football and shrieked so loud their ears popped! Navy screamed in terror just as Mr. Coffin's long arms swung out toward him and pushed him backward, sending him tumbling down the stairs.

Sophia rolled over, screaming as she watched Navy's descent. Arie raced to his mother's side. By the time Navy lay sprawled out on the floor at the base of the steps, Mr. Coffin had disappeared. The red bow tie was on the floor a couple of feet from Sophia. She reached for it as Arie helped her to her feet. Her entire body was racked with pain.

They started slowly down the stairs. Sophia picked up Navy's gun on the fourth step. Her hands were shaking. She held Arie under her right arm, close against her body. Only now did she realize it had been raining outside. Lightning lit up the living room, casting a chilling glow on Navy's body. Was he dead? she wondered.

They stepped with caution from the final step onto the landing, where Navy's right foot was. As Sophia began to lean in closer to his face, Arie grew nervous for her.

"Mommy," he whispered.

"Shh. It's okay, honey," she said, leaning in even closer.

Navy suddenly spoke, his menacing voice sending frosty fingers down her spine. "I'm going to kill you both."

Sophia looked at her son's horrified face. She thought for only a moment, then said, "Arie, fetch me the extension cords from the bottom drawer in the kitchen. You know where."

Arie nodded and ran off, returning with three cords. Sophia took them from him and proceeded to tie Navy's wrists together, despite his groans of discomfort. She then tied his ankles in the same manner.

"Now...help me," she said to Arie.

Together they dragged Navy out the front door, then struggled to get him into the back seat of his car in the icy rain. He was in and out of consciousness, hardly aware of what was happening. "Now go back into the house, lock the front door, and don't let anyone in but me. Understand?" Sophia asked her son.

"Yes," said Arie.

Sophia waited for him to close the front door. He waved out the window to her. She waved back, then started the engine. With the wipers swooshing and thudding side to side, Sophia backed out of the driveway and sped down the street.

10

Sophia pulled up to the pedestrian bridge on Cross Street. She stepped out of the car and closed the door, standing in the downpour for what seemed like a lifetime. There were so many aches crying out from her body, but she ignored every one—she had to. Gathering her strength and will to do what she was intent on doing, Sophia turned and stared through the rain-blurred window at the body lying in the back seat.

She opened the door. Navy was presently unconscious. Good, she thought. She struggled to pull him from the backseat, till all of him was lying in the puddle at her feet. Closing the door, she reached for his feet and began to lug him inch by inch, foot by foot, toward the trees lining the drop into the polluted aqueduct.

While Sophia was struggling to make a path through the prickly bushes, behind her Navy had awakened. He sat up and scanned his surroundings. It didn't take long for him to figure out what his wife was planning to do with him. Reaching into his right boot, he removed a pocket knife and quickly cut the cords binding his ankles, then his wrists. And just as Sophia was ready to make her descent with Navy in tow, the full weight of his body barrelled into her.

Together they tumbled down the hill, a bundle of moans and groans, their combined injuries protesting further abuse. They stopped rolling when Navy's weight sank into the mucky shoreline. Sophia was fighting back in a frenzied hysteria, any ounce of sanity she had left was knocked out of her at the top of the hill. He was going to kill her, she knew, and then return home and kill her baby. She could not—would not!—allow that to happen.

Wearing nothing but her flimsy nightgown, she was covered in slime and mud in an instant. But this was working in her favor, as Navy could not get a fixed hold on her. She felt along the ground for something to defend herself with, but the best she could do was a rotted stump that crumbled when she struck him with it. Amid her adrenaline working overtime, and the blinding darkness of the rain, Sophia didn't even see Navy's fist coming at her – *Boom!*—right in the forehead. She thought she was going to pass out as she seemed to float backward in slow motion. But when she landed in the steaming water, alertness charged back to the forefront of her mind.

She'd only just surfaced for air, when she felt Navy's strong hands on her shoulders, shoving her under again. *He's trying to drown me*, she thought. *I'm going to drown here in the same swampy shit as Garnet.* And the moment his name came to her thoughts, Sophia felt his presence.

Above her? Below her? Behind? Everywhere!

Navy's grip on her shoulders let loose. Sophia rose slowly

to the surface. She took the foul air into her lungs, but it was far better than the alternative. When she looked around, she found herself nearer to the shoreline than Navy was. He was staring right at her as if he'd been waiting for her to come back for more. Sophia started to swim toward shore, with Navy following.

Ten feet. Eight....

And there was a sound like a submarine rising from the depths. Sophia stopped and turned around, facing Navy. He then turned around, putting his back to her, and watched as the green water began to rise like a growing waterfall. The ripples streaked into the details of a face on its side (the top half clear while the bottom half was smeared like falling sand).

Sophia could not hear anything above the angry moan of the giant face. It continued to pull itself up from the surface of the water until the full head rested with only its chin buried beneath the watery horizon. The giant's mouth roared open. Navy turned from it and swam in full panic mode toward shore. But it was too late. The face resembling that of Garnet Coffin swept toward him and swallowed him whole!

All this was just too much for Sophia. She felt her eyes close. The giant head collapsed into the water, pushing her up onto shore in one great sweep. When she woke from a crack of thunder, Sophia sat up in the bed of muck. There was no sign of Navy or Garnet's giant face. She forced herself to climb the hill and returned to the car.

On the seat next to her was Mr. Coffin's special bow

tie.

When Sophia pulled up to her house, several police cars were already there. Their spinning lights blinded her. When they approached her car (or rather, Navy's squad car), she expected to be handcuffed and hauled off to prison. But that's not what happened. The moment she'd left Arie alone, he'd dialed 911 and reported that his father had tried to kill him and was going to kill his mommy.

When Police Chief Hicks arrived at the house, Arie went on to explain to him about Mr. Coffin disappearing, and how his daddy had done something bad to him. Sophia was taken away, but to a hospital by ambulance. And in the coming days, Navy's body was recovered from the aqueduct, and an autopsy was conducted on the corpse discovered by the Rogers boy. Conclusive identification of the teeth proved to be those belonging to Mr. Garnet Coffin.

And along with Navy's life insurance, Sophia and Arie were soon to find out their dear friend, Garnet Coffin, had signed everything in his will over to them, which not only included his property in Chapel Hill (and property up north), but also a small fortune. Although they were never to see his ghost again, Sophia and Arie could always sense his presence watching over them.

Flower Petals

1

A blue jay flew from one maidenhair (Ginkgo Biloba) tree to another, unable to keep its presence secret among the brilliant yellow leaves. Seventeen-year-old Flower Petals smiled at the sight as she stood at the front steps of Norbrook Secondary School. She then turned her attention to the double doors that led inside the school. Today was her first day of attending, not only Norbrook but school—period!

Having been home-schooled all her life, Flower's mother, Ronnie Petals, was hesitant to allow her daughter to enter the public school system. When begging her mother had failed to convince Ronnie that it was a good idea, Flower had to proclaim her independence and make the final decision for herself. Though still not persuaded, Ronnie had no choice but to concede.

With her class schedule in hand, she entered the building tremulous with excitement. The hallways were crowded with bustling students on their way to homeroom before the first bell. Everyone stared at her as she passed, some with curiosity, others with disinterest. Loud conversations were cut silent, then replaced with whispers and giggles. Flower barely took notice, her eyes rolling side to side, admiring the bright orange lockers, and wondering—hoping—that she would soon have one of her own to linger next to, door open wide, sharing secrets with some friends.

When she found her homeroom, as listed on her schedule, she was greeted by a handsome, blue-eyed, bearded teacher with dark, wavy, neck-length hair. With a trembling hand and sweaty palm, he smiled as he shook her hand. He put his right arm around her shoulders and stood at the front of the room with her. She'd already noticed the only empty desk available was right in the front row.

"Settle down," he told the students as they took to their seats.

Before his next words, the second bell rang, signalling the start of the school day. The teacher cleared his throat to gather everyone's attention. When the chattering ceased, he introduced himself to the new student.

"I'm Mr. Taff," he said, finally dropping his arm from her shoulders. Then, to the class, "Everyone, this is Flower Petals."

Snickers all around.

"Quiet! I expect you to behave like the young adults you are and not like a bunch of asses. Okay, Flower, you can have a seat right there," he offered, gesturing toward the empty desk.

"Thank you," she said in a sweet voice.

Flower smiled at the faces staring back at her as she sat down, rolling her long, dark, smooth hair over her shoulders. A couple of desks behind her, Jayden Rogers made a V with his two fingers and flapped his tongue between them for his best friend's amusement, but Declan Delany was not impressed.

"Asshole," he whispered to Jayden.

Declan was not a free agent, as they say, he was Tally Harper's boyfriend. Not because they liked each other, but because she said it was their duty as the two best looking students at Norbrook to be as such. He thought it was a funny statement, took it as a joke until they started dating. Turns out Tally Harper truly thought of herself as special and walked around with an invisible crown upon her multicolored hair (light blue on top, blonde in the middle, and cotton candy pink at the curled ends).

He'd been planning to break off their awkward relationship, but could never seem to find a moment when Tally was not surrounded by her three irritating friends Becky Foster, Nora Kees, and Casey Robinson. Prissy, stuck-up bitches just like their leader. He wondered as he watched Flower page through her English book if a girl with natural beauty as stunning as hers could be anything but a bitch.

A few desks to the left of him, Tally's eyes narrowed as she watched him gaze at the new girl. Her train of thought was interrupted by Becky, who tapped her shoulder from behind and whispered, "I bet she's a virgin."

Tally snickered through her pierced nose. She whispered back, "Bitch makes me wanna hurl. I'd like to dig my claws into those rosy cheeks of hers."

Next to Tally sat Nora, and behind Nora, Casey, so that all four of them formed a little square. Nora leaned over and said, "What's with that white flower in her hair. It's like, yeah, we get it, your name's Flower. Fuck off."

"Right. Maybe her parents are hippies," Casey added. "Hopped up on coke or something."

"Yeah, or maybe she's just a fucking cunt who needs that flower shoved down her throat," said Tally, glancing over at Declan.

"Ladies, you mind not gibbering while I'm teaching," chided Mr. Taff.

"Sorry, Gavin," Tally sneered.

"Cut that shit out, Tally," Mr. Taff said sternly, "or you'll be spending the afternoon in detention...little girl."

The four girls were giggling.

Declan was shaking his head, thinking, *I'm telling her today. Smartass bitch.*

Lunch hour finally came after what seemed to Flower like a very long morning. Again the stares and whispers were in abundance when she entered the cafeteria. Unbeknownst to her, most of the talk was about her staggering beauty. Even the younger students were taken aback by her appearance. Her full lips smiled at everyone, her blue-white eyes shone behind long dark lashes, and that luscious raven hair swept gracefully just above her waist. And watching her search for an empty seat to eat her lunch, was Tally's jealous squad, already plotting how they could take her down a few notches.

"Look at her. Thinks she's a fucking princess," Becky scoffed.

"And we're gonna rip that crown right off that meth whore's head," Tally spat.

The girls laughed out loud, making sure to draw Flower's attention.

2

Tuesday morning, just as Flower reached the school doors, Declan happened to be standing there waiting for Tally to show up (he'd spent all the night before gearing himself up to break off with her). When Flower approached, he felt his legs weaken and his breath quicken, a reaction he'd never experienced with Tally, or any girl, for that matter. He quickly opened the door for her, smiling like an idiot. Flower grinned, her sparkling eyes reaching out to his with magical effect.

"Do you always wear a flower in your hair?" he asked.

"It's to remind me of my father. He's the one who named me," she offered.

"Is he?"

"Dead? No. Mother says he's alive and well and thinks of me every day, but that's as much as I know about him."

"Oh. Sorry. I didn't mean anything by it. Just making small talk," he said as other students hustled in through the opened door behind Flower, several purposely bumping into her.

Fresh off a school bus, Tally and her friends stopped cold in their tracks at the sight of Declan conversing with the object of their disdain.

"Oh...my...perky...tits. Do you guys see what I see?" said Nora.

"That...*bitch!*" Tally groaned.

"Looks like she's got her batting eyes on your man," said Casey, fluffing her deep purple hair with her fingers, her matching purple lips smacking bubblegum. "Better watch out."

"Little slut doesn't waste any time," added Becky.

"And neither do I," said Tally.

"What are you gonna do?" Nora said excitedly, twining her faded pink hair ends around her fingers.

"You'll see soon enough," said Tally.

"Cool," Casey giggled, her pink bubble bursting with a Pop!

During first break, the four girls followed Flower into the girls' washroom. They waited for her to come out of her stall and approached her at the sinks. Tally stepped right up on Flower's heels and *Sssnip!* Flower turned with a start. Tally was holding a pair of scissors in her right hand and a large chunk of Flower's hair in her left. Flower gasped.

"What did you do?" she said with alarm, feeling at the back of her head.

Nora, Casey, and Becky were snickering on each side of Tally.

Tally held the lengthy piece of hair up before Flower's eyes and seethed, "Stay the fuck away from my boyfriend, bitch! Or the next thing I cut won't be your hair. Got me, bitch?"

Flower nodded as Tally waved the pointed ends of the scissors close to her throat. She ran out past the girls, the washroom door slamming with an echo behind her. The four girls erupted in laughter.

"Did you see the look on her face?" laughed Nora.

"That was fucking awesome!" Becky blurted.

"Yeah, but do you think the little slut's gonna run and squeal?" asked Casey.

"Not if she knows what's good for her," said Tally. "Someone give me a couple of elastics."

Becky handed her a pair of red elastics, which she then used to tie one end of the hairpiece, braided it from top to bottom, and secured the bottom. Smiling, she used the pink ribbon from her hair to attach the piece to her purse strap. Spinning around, she modelled the new adornment for her clapping friends.

"Maybe this will convince the little whore that I'm serious—dead serious."

"I think you already accomplished that, Tally," Casey reminded her.

The bell rang, sounding the end of break. Tally raised her nose and led the girls to their next class, swinging her purse with extra vigor.

After school that day, Declan waited with Jayden outside the front doors, hoping to walk Flower home.

"Just go, Jayden, I don't want her to get all shy on me because you're around. Besides, I don't need you to walk me, walking her, home," said Declan.

"Ditching your boyfriend for a girlfriend, eh. Fine. But when she blows you off—and I don't mean in the fun way—don't come running to me to hold your hand," said Jayden, laughing as he strolled off.

Declan waited until just about every student had left the building. And when Flower finally appeared at the doors, she immediately tried to rush past him. Declan chased after her, calling, "Hey! Wait up! What's the matter? Thought we were cool," he said.

Flower turned to face him, she huffed and said, "We were never anything. You have a girlfriend, so why are you bothering me?"

"I didn't realize I was bothering you," he said disappointingly. "And you're right, I do have a girlfriend, but not really. I'm gonna break up with her."

"Good for you. Now go bother her and leave *me* alone," she advised, turning from him and hurrying away.

Declan tried to keep up with her to plead his case. He argued, "No really. Look. The truth is I can't stand Tally. I never could. She and her girl pack are a bunch of bitches. Please, just give me a chance."

Flower stopped with another huff. "Listen, Declan, I think you're a nice guy. I even think you're cute. But this is my first time to ever attend a real school and I don't want to mess it up. So, if you really like me, you'll leave me alone."

Declan bowed his head, his shoulders slouched with disappointed. Flower touched his cheek with the palm of her hand just as bus #39 was passing by—Tally's bus!

("That fucking bitch!" she screamed, directing her girl-friends' attention to the couple on the grass by the trees.

"Guess she didn't take you seriously, after all," Casey snickered.

"Shut the fuck up, Casey, or I'll make the rest of your face match your hair."

"Like to see you try, bitch," Casey shot back, being no pushover herself.

"What are you gonna do now?" pressed Nora.

"Maybe you should cut off all her hair," Becky suggested.

"Bitch," Tally repeated under her breath as the bus drove on.)

"It's not about you," Flower said to Declan, caressing his cheek.

"Then what?"

Flower subconsciously reached to the back of her hair. She shook her head and sighed, "I can't tell you."

But Declan was wise enough to know that 'I can't tell you' had Tally written all over it. Anyone prettier than Tally was a threat, so he could imagine Flower being a high-level threat. Flower wouldn't be the first girl at Norbrook to suffer under her wrath.

"Is it Tally? What's she done?" he asked, fury building with every word.

Flower looked away, and that was answer enough for him.

"Don't worry. I'll handle her and her bitches," he

promised.

"No, Declan, please. Don't say anything to her or she'll come at me twice as hard," Flower said, turning to walk away once more. "Just leave it alone. Leave me alone. Please!"

Deccan's head was shaking as he watched her hurrying off toward the woods. There were no houses that he knew of in that direction, just the thick woodlands. The mystery of her intrigued him even more.

Later that night, while playing video games in his room with Jayden, Deccan's cell phone rang to the tune of Rush's "Tom Sawyer."

"Yeah?" he said.

"You back-stabbing son of a bitch!" shouted Tally's voice.

Declan cringed as he held the phone away from his ear, allowing Jayden to hear every word. Jayden shook his head and rolled his eyes. He whispered, "Ditch the bitch, man."

Still, Tally managed to hear him and shouted back, "Is that Jayden? Fuck you, Jayden, you little faggot!"

Jayden exaggerated his shock and began to laugh. This enraged Declan's caller even further.

"Wait till I tell all the boys on your team how your itty bitty dick gets hard for them in the locker room!"

"Calm your shit, Tally, and tell me what the hell you want before I hang up," Declan interrupted her rant.

"You know exactly why I'm calling, asshole. Flower

Petals ring a bell?"

Declan was silent.

"That's what I thought. Seems you've got a boner for the new bitch. When I'm through with her, she won't have anything you'll want," Tally threatened.

"Stay the fuck away from her, Tally, or so help me...."

"So help you what, Declan? You're a fucking pussy and you know it. Stay out of my way. Oh, and, asshole...consider yourself dumped!"

Declan looked at Jayden whose eyebrows were raised, mouth forming a perfect circle.

"How's that for luck? She broke it off without you even having to bring it up," said Jayden, chuckling as he maneuvered his digital man around the video game war zone.

"I have to warn Flower tomorrow before Tally tries to do anything. You know what happened to Debbie Deschamps," Declan reminded his friend.

Now it was Jayden's turn to cringe. He said, "Ooh yeah. Who could forget."

Debbie Deschamps, nicknamed Dirty Debbie by Tally and soon known only as Dirty Debbie to everyone at Norbrook, moved away from Chatter Falls after a failed suicide attempt. She'd been harassed by Tally's group for nearly a year before she'd had enough. The details of the bullying are sketchy at best, but Debbie's parent's had no doubt who to blame when they stormed the Principal's office, demanding justice in the name of their daughter. Unfortunately, Debbie was not willing to give the names of her tormentors.

One night while they were hanging out together, Tally felt comfortable enough with Declan to gloat about being the mastermind behind Debbie's demise. "Bitch had it coming," she'd said. And that was the beginning of the end of their relationship for Declan. Now, someone he truly liked was Tally's target, and he wasn't about to let her get away with it again.

3

First thing Wednesday morning, Declan raced to the school in hopes of catching Flower to warn her about Tally. He was too late. Before the first period, while gathering books from her locker, Nora drew Flower's attention while Becky and Casey poured four different shades of nail polish over her head and down the back of her baby blue mid-length sweater.

She didn't realize what they had done until she felt the thick liquid creeping into her hair. Nora, Becky, and Casey hurried away, laughing and pointing at her. She slammed her locker shut and ran for the washroom, tears enhancing the blue of her eyes. The first bell rang just as she approached the mirrors. Removing her sweater, she placed it in the sink and ran the hot water, trying to rinse the colors out.

Flower didn't notice Tally sneak out of the stall behind her. The girl gave a quick tussle to Flower's hair. Exaggerating her disgust, she mocked, "Ick! Don't you wash your ratty hair?"

When Flower swung around, her hair slapped the mirror, leaving streaks of nail polish.

"Get away from me, Tally," she cried, quickly wiping the tears from her cheeks.

Tally got right up in her face. "Or what, princess? You think I'm scared of you? You think you're tough, princess?" she jeered.

And without warning, Tally slapped Flower across the left cheek (and it felt so good to do it). Flower was in shock, holding her hand against her burning cheek.

"Hit me back, bitch! I dare ya," Tally hissed.

Flower just stood there, shocked.

"Yeah. That's what I thought. Watch your back, princess," she warned, walking out with her nose in the air.

Flower turned back to her reflection, Tally's handprint quite visible on her cheek, flaming red and outlined in white. She held back more tears and sneaked off home.

Thursday morning, Declan waited by the front doors once again for Flower. When Tally and the girls walked past him they snickered and whispered, making it obvious to him that they'd done something wicked to Flower already. Soon after came Flower, head down, shoulders slouched, hair tied in a thick braid and hanging over her left shoulder. Declan hopped off the railing he'd been sitting on and ran up to her.

"Flower! Are you okay?"

Flower nodded but her demeanor was one of defeat.

"You don't look okay. What happened yesterday?" he questioned. "I didn't see you at all."

"I left after the first bell. Tally's friends assaulted me at my locker with nail polish. When I went to the washroom to clean up, Tally was in there, hiding. She threatened me and slapped me in the face," Flower recounted.

"Fucking bitches. Why didn't you report them?"

"They'd only come back harder on me. I thought I would like going to school like a normal girl, but I don't know anymore. Maybe I should quit."

Declan took Flower by the arms, his hands gently sliding down to her wrists. Softly, he said, "Don't give up. I'll help you. Somehow we'll stop them. I promise. Do you believe me?"

Flower nodded.

"I really like you, Flower. I mean I really, really like you."

Declan leaned in and kissed Flower's cheek, bringing a delighted smile back to her face. Across the yard, Mr. Taff was watching the pair through his classroom window. His focus drew the attention of Casey and Nora as they entered the room. Their jaws dropped simultaneously. They turned on their heels and raced back out of the room, Mr. Taff none the wiser.

4

News of Declan and Flower's kiss reached Tally in a matter of moments. Though he'd only kissed the girl's cheek, Nora and Casey's version of events had him and Flower in a long and sensuous lip-lock. As much as Tally hated Declan she placed all the blame on Flower.

"Ooooh. That fucking slut! Time to put an end to little miss whore bag," she seethed, squeezing her hands in such tight fists her nails drew blood.

"Yeah and you should've seen Mr. Taff, I swear he was getting off on watching them," said Nora.

Casey nodded, adding, "That happy bulge in his pants wasn't for education."

The girls all laughed at that, except for Tally, she was fuming. Her heart was pounding in her chest and at her temples. No way was this bitch going to best her. No way!

Flower went nervously from one class to another all morning. But Tally and her girl tribe hadn't said or done a thing to her. This gave her reason to worry, and she would be just in her deductions. For during lunch hour, Tally and the girls were on a mission to obtain certain items for Tally's revenge.

While Becky stood watch for teachers, Tally, Nora, and Casey sneaked into the Auto-body shop class in search of any flammable products. One could tell instantly by the insane clown expression on Tally's face that she'd found what she was looking for.

"Got it!" she announced.

The four of them raced back to Tally's locker in a huddle of giggles.

"This is gonna be epic," said Becky.

"Right," Casey agreed.

The final bell of the day rang. Flower watched Tally's gang rush out of the classroom. She thought for certain she'd find them gathered at her locker, but when she got there, they were nowhere to be seen. She smiled at Declan at the opposite end of the hall where he stood with a group of boys. He wanted more than anything to walk her home today, but Thursday was basketball practice.

Flower placed her books in her locker and closed it. When she looked back down the hall, Declan and the group of boys were gone. The hallway was quickly clearing of students. In the distance, she heard doors closing, lockers slamming shut, and voices fading out. The school became a sort of eerie, abandoned ship. She was relieved to find no bullies were waiting for her outside the school, either. Seemed everyone was in a hurry to be somewhere else, including Mr. Taff, who was on his way to pay Ronnie Petals an impromptu visit.

Gavin parked his car at the edge of the woods, where a small kiddie park sat as empty today as it did every day. Parents in Chatter Falls feared the woods, and no one went near them after dark. Rumors of a witch roaming wooded areas in search of human flesh were not uncommon by any means. Movies like *The Blair Witch Project* helped raise the level of fear. But in Chatter Falls, the fear was warranted.

Hiking deeper and deeper into the woods, the day's light was already inching its way to the tops of the trees, and darkness pooled in around him. Colors were abundant: Poppy reds, crisp golds, sunflower yellows, and tangerine oranges. He knew he was getting closer to Ronnie's house when he passed through an archway formed of trees.

Next, he crossed a crooked bridge that lay over the green waters of a river. Tangles of red vines webbed along the wood railings and hung wild overhead. Once he crossed it, he passed through a patch of fog, and on the other side was Ronnie's house: An average looking, rundown shack perched high up on tree stilts. To the unknowing eye, there was nothing very unusual about it. But to Gavin, who could see through the illusion, there was no shack, but a giant ball of intricately entwined sticks like the nest of some monstrous bird.

Before he could reach the dwelling, he had yet to cross a monkey bridge over a fungus covered pool. *If the kids at Norbrook knew what route Flower had to take to and from school every day, they'd shit their pants*, he thought. He climbed the ladder up to the entrance of the nest and knocked on the door. On the opposite side of the door, a muscular gray-skinned arm reached out with a powerful hand and clawed fingertips. Ghostly green skeletal spirits screeched and wailed behind the demon witch. And as she opened the door the spirits fled in an instant, and the demon's appearance transformed into the beautiful, alluring goddess Gavin was more familiar with.

"Gavin. I've been expecting you," said Ronnie, smiling seductively.

"Then you know I'm not here for *that*," he said, glancing down at her ample cleavage.

Ronnie frowned playfully. "Then what is it this time? You finally ready to get rid of your wife?"

"No. I'm here because of Flower," he stated, looking around at the grandness of the place. Walls sloped precariously and at odd angles. The house and furniture alike were made from wood and designed organically. If one stayed long enough, one might see that the house was in constant change. Ever-growing and in motion, slowly, and accommodating to Ronnie's will and needs.

"What's she done now, Gavin? Drink?" she asked.

"Just water," he said, and watched her turn to fetch it. She always reminded him of Carolyn Jones (the actress who portrayed Morticia Addams on the original television series of *The Addams Family*). "I'm worried about her. There's a group of girls messing with her, and they're not a group to take lightly," he explained.

Ronnie handed him the glass of water, which he looked at with pause.

Ronnie chuckled and said, "Still doubting me?"

He drank the water down in one gulp.

"You know, Gavin, she's not a child anymore. This is what she wants to do. I tried my best to talk her out of it, but as you can see, I was unable to dissuade her."

"But hasn't she told you what they've done already? I can't help her, Ronnie. And you know if I interfere she may figure out that I'm not just Mr. Taff, English teacher; but that I'm Mr. Taff—father."

"You worry too much, darling. She won't know who you are until I allow her to. And as for these girls at school, I know exactly what they've been up to. Flower and I have no secrets between us. Well, except in the case of *you* that is."

Ronnie leaned forward and kissed him on the lips, and he kissed her back with just as much passion. He said, "Someday she'll pass on and then we can be together."

"And I'll be here waiting for you," said Ronnie. "Now run along, before Flower gets home."

As Gavin drove toward home, Flower was walking through the woods, humming to herself and admiring the foliage. Nora stepped out from behind the trunk of a Maple tree, and sang, "Hello, Flower."

Flower stopped in surprise. "Nora? What are you doing out here?" she asked, her voice on edge.

Nora walked toward her with a sinister grin. She said, "Oh, you know, just hanging around."

Flower backed away from the girl. "You probably shouldn't be out here alone," said Flower.

"She's not alone, I'm here," Becky announced, stepping from her hiding place in the trees.

Together the girls closed in on Flower, forcing her back against a tree.

"Boo!" Casey shouted, leaping out from behind the very tree Flower was leaning against.

Flower gasped and continued to back away from the three threatening girls.

"Why are you here? What do you want?" Flower asked with alarm.

"Tally's sick of your shit, and so are we!" Becky shouted.

"But I haven't done anything," Flower pleaded.

"'I haven't done anything,'" Casey mocked her.

"Not much. You're just a skanky whore," said Becky.

As she continued to back away from them, the three girls began to kick up the fallen leaves at her, chanting, "Skanky whore, skanky whore!"

"Stop it!" yelled Flower.

And suddenly, something wet splashed over her head like a bucket of water, only it wasn't water, it was gasoline! Flower coughed, her eyes and nose burning as she spun round to see Tally standing there with a gas can in her hands. "What...?" she started, but was cut off when Tally splashed more gasoline at her face. The other girls were whooping and laughing.

"Guess we found the witch of the woods," said Becky, clapping.

"Tally, don't!" Flower screamed, rubbing her eyes.

Tally tossed the can aside and pulled out a lighter. She nonchalantly lit a cigarette, smiling at her girlfriends. Flower was on her knees now, crying and using her jacket to wipe her face. The girls piled more leaves on her, laughing with elation. Tally signalled for them to step away.

"Let's see if Declan likes his girlfriend on the crispy side," Tally sneered.

"Burn the witch!" yelled Casey. "Burn the witch!"

Tally flicked her cigarette at Flower, igniting the girl in a *whoosh* of flames. Flower screamed as she rolled on the ground, spreading her circle of fire to the pile of leaves. Becky, Nora, and Casey ran from the screams, laughing.

Tally lingered, revelling in the moment.

"Guess now you're Declan's old flame," she jested. She waved her arms about and shrieked, mocking the girl on fire. "Whore," she seethed, then ran to catch up to her friends.

5

Six weeks later, one of Principal Collins's two secretaries, Mrs. Veronica Abby, knocked at his door and gently opened it to his, "Come in."

"Miles," she said, "the mother of Flower Petals is here to speak with you."

"Well, send her in," he said, quickly straightening the surface of his desk.

Mrs. Abby turned to the youthful-looking woman waiting patiently by the main entrance to the office. Never had she or her secretary in crime, Delores Reed, ever seen a student parent quite like this one.

"He'll see you now," Mrs. Abby told the woman, smiling awkwardly.

She and Mrs. Reed followed Ronnie Petals's stroll across the room to Mr. Collins's office. She was very beautiful, stunning in fact. Dark hair as long and lustrous as her daughter's hung loosely from a black broad-brimmed sun hat, roses like the ones Flower always wore decorated the brim. She walked with confidence in her high-healed, knee-high black boots. But most peculiar of all was the white mid-calf, turtleneck, flare long sleeve, lace dress she wore. She seemed to be from another era.

Both secretaries strained to catch Mr. Collins's reaction to his visitor but were not granted the opportunity as Miss Petals batted her eyes with a smile and closed the door behind her. Mr. Collins wasn't exactly a pushover in the looks department himself. A handsome black man of forty-two, his muscular physique was expressed through his tight-fitting shirt. Hair and beard tightly cropped. Golden eyes and a near-perfect teeth that gleamed when he smiled.

"Welcome," he said, standing to greet his guest.

When Ms. Petals turned around, he was taken aback by her beauty. However, Miles Collins was not one to lose his composure over a gorgeous woman. Ronnie acknowledged him with a slight nod as she sauntered up to him. As they shook hands, Ronnie spoke softly.

"Had I known my daughter's Principal was such a...charming man, I might not have waited so long to visit," she teased.

"Thank you, Ms. Petals, that's very flattering coming from a woman of your calibre."

"Call me Ronnie."

"Miles. Have a seat, won't you? Tell me, Ronnie, what brings you to our humble school, and might I inquire about your daughter's whereabouts?"

Ronnie sat down with grace and crossed her right leg over her left, hiking the skirt of her dress higher up her thigh. She said, "Flower is doing just fine. She took ill, I'm afraid. It was serious but she's recovering."

"I'm sorry to hear and also glad she is in recovery," said Miles.

"She will be returning soon. However, at her request, I'm here to pick up some work she might do while at home if that is possible," said Ronnie.

"Of course. I'll have Mr. Taff and Mr. Landry get a

package together and you can pick it up by tomorrow afternoon if that works for you."

"Perfect," said Ronnie, rising. She held out her hand once more to shake his hand. "Thank you for seeing me, Miles. It's been a pleasure."

"You're very welcome. Any time I may be of service, just call," he said, his voice deep, smooth.

Mrs. Reed and Mrs. Abby raised their buttocks off their chairs to watch the curious Ms. Petals exit the office. Then turned when Mr. Collins, who was standing in the doorway to his office, commented, "Nice lady."

Students were in the process of switching classes when Ronnie Petals was making her way down the hall toward the front doors. Everyone stared, including the teachers. Mr. Landry was standing next to Gavin between their two classrooms, watching the chaos when they spotted Ronnie.

"Woh. Wouldn't mind a piece of that ass," said Mr. Landry.

He didn't notice the expression of despise on Gavin's face.

"I'd better get behind my desk and hide this stiffy," Mr. Landry said, chuckling alone to his perversity.

"Yeah. You do that, Bill," Gavin said with disgust. When he turned back to the hallway, Ronnie was gone.

Just outside the front doors, Nora was sneaking a few quick puffs off her cigarette, when Ronnie exited the school. Nora gasped and let the cigarette slip from her fingers, hoping the woman hadn't seen. She coughed with embarrassment as Ronnie paused to smile at her.

"Hello, Nora," said Ronnie.

"Hello," Nora responded, before giving a second thought as to how this stranger knew her name.

"Feeling okay there?"

Nora nodded. "Yes. I was just heading to my next class," she said. Then, looking down. "Love your boots."

"Oh, thank you. Black. My favorite color," said Ronnie.

"Mine too."

"I'll keep that in mind. Gotta go. Don't be late for class."

Nora shook her head and hurried back inside. The moment the door sealed her in, she turned and looked out. The woman was nowhere to be seen. "'I'll keep that in mind?'" she echoed.

During Math class, Nora began to cough again. It started as just an annoying tickle at the back of her throat, then progressed to all-out hacking till her eyes teared. Students around her stared, giggling, but that stopped as the girl was unable to calm the cough down.

"Nora, honey, why don't you go and get a drink from the fountain," suggested an irritated Mrs. Ballard.

Nora nodded and raced from the class. She attempted to drink from the fountain outside the girls' washroom but was unable to stop coughing long enough to take a swallow. She burst into the washroom and stumbled to the counter. Cranking the cold water to full, she splashed her face, then stopped when she noticed something strange in the sink, something she'd hacked up.

Nora shrieked at the sight of the large black bloody hairball! She looked at her reflection, her skin now a pea soup shade of green, her cheeks undulating, looking as if they were about to tear apart. Stricken with unparalleled fear, she bolted out of the washroom, ran down the hall, and bolted out the doors, running crazed across the parking lot and into the woods.

Unable to scream through her clogged throat, Nora ran blind, arms flailing, deeper into the growing darkness of the afternoon. She fumbled over hidden roots and collapsed on her belly, crying hysterically. With difficultly, she breathed through her nose, clawing at her throat in desperation. Suddenly the wind steamrolled over her like an invisible wave. She fell back, eyes widening at the sight of something large moving in the tree above.

It was just leaves. Rust-colored leaves. But then that group of leaves snaked down around the tree trunk to the ground. Nora scuttled back. The leaves shuffled toward her, rose up in a giant fluttering funnel, then began to fall. And as they fell, the leaves took shape. And what they became was the most ghastly, horrific vision Nora could have ever imagined.

Standing no less than eight feet tall, the thing's head was covered by a hood of dark stretched skin and sticks. The leaves ruffled down its back and around its narrow shoulders, pooling at the ground, alive and crackling in the wind. Long skinny arms hung at its sides, no larger than the sticks that adorned its living gown.

As it approached, Nora watched as its face tore open to reveal a second face, and that face ripped open to reveal its third and main face; and she would have screamed had she been able. Its main face was an eclipse of moths! Some came and went, but the face always remained fully composed. This thing moving closer to her appeared to be feminine. And then it spoke to her, its voice a nauseating mixture of insects squirming and chittering.

"You have something I need, Nora. I'm here to collect."

Nora was coughing harshly and shaking her head as the thing raised its arms toward her, palms up, bony, gnarled fingers wriggling. And then she could feel something within her, something not of her, but alive within her. Suddenly she threw her head back and began to convulse, bones cracking throughout her body.

Abruptly, Nora's face stretched beyond its limit and black kittens came scurrying forth: three, four, five, six, seven, eight, nine; then several more escaped from her yawning belly: ten, eleven, twelve, thirteen! Immediately they began to feed on the girl's flesh. The demon witch was delighted with her work, watching the kittens enjoy their first feast.

She leaned over the corpse, dug her prong-like fingers into the bloody chest, and removed Nora's spongy lungs. After slipping the organs into a queer leather pouch, the demon was swept up into a leafy funnel and disappeared into the woods. And when the kittens had had their fill, Nora's body popped into flames and was turned to ash at once, leaving no trace behind.

6

Gathered at Tally's locker, she along with Becky and Casey were confused about Nora's disappearance that morning. None of them had seen her since Casey, who shares Math class with her, watched her leave class in a coughing fit.

"That bitch smokes too much," said Becky.

"Yeah. She probably used her cough as an excuse to sign out for the rest of the day," Tally ventured, shuffling the books about in her locker.

"Maybe I should have thought of that," said Casey, trying to check out her reflection in the mirror taped to the inside of Tally's locker. "Think I need a touch-up," she observed, noticing her purple hair color had faded slightly.

"You guys had better still be coming to my party tomorrow night. Don't bail on me like I know Nora's going to," said Tally, closing her locker door.

"As long as it's not lame like last year, Tally. I spent a lot of money on my costume and no one else was dressed up. It sucked shit," Becky complained.

"No, it didn't," Tally retaliated.

"Yeah. It did," Casey confirmed.

"Bitches," Tally said, laughing. "I promise this year will be different. No one gets in without being in costume. That's the rule. And this time my parents will be out of town for the weekend, so you know what that means—boys and booze."

The three girls high-fived each other with laughter.

The following evening, Casey phoned Becky just after dinner. "Hey, girl, wanna go with me to Lampman's Pharmacy? I need a few last-minute things for my costume and I don't feel like going alone," Casey explained.

"Fuck, Casey. You always do this," Becky whined.

"What?"

"Last minute things? Why do you always wait to get everything you need?"

"Well, it's not my fault. I was going to put off dying my hair but it really, really needs it. Please. Come on. We'll take the shortcut through the woods and be there in fifteen minutes. I swear I'll be quick," Casey pleaded with her.

Becky sighed with frustration. "Fine. But remember this next time I ask *you* for a favor," she said.

"Awesome. Thanks, bitch. Meet me in five," said Casey, ending the call.

Fifteen minutes later, the two girls walked briskly into the woods, following a well-worn path that worked its way from the south side of town to the north side where they would exit across the street from Lampman's Pharmacy.

"Tonight's gonna be a blast!" said Casey.

"It'd better be, or next year Tally can shove her party up her ass," Becky snarled.

"You ever wonder why we let her boss us around?"

asked Casey.

"Cause she's psycho."

"Yeah. She really is," Casey chuckled. "Think Declan will show his face tonight?"

Becky guffawed. "Are you nuts? Declan's a pussy. Now Jayden...mmm. All I have to do to get him stretching in his jeans is to say hello."

"Can you keep a secret?" asked Casey.

"Um duh."

"I once sucked Jayden's brother Rick's cock."

"Oh my god, Casey! You slut! What it taste like?" Becky wondered, grabbing Casey by the wrist.

"I don't know. Like guy dick, I suppose."

"And who is next on your dick list?" Becky said, giggling.

"Maybe Mr. Taff," Casey joked.

And as the two squealed with laughter, Casey suddenly hushed her friend when she heard something stir in the trees behind them. "You hear that?" she whispered.

Becky was nodding, looking around suspiciously. Then they heard the sound of boys laughing somewhere in the distance to their right. For a moment they're nerves eased off, then they heard the laughter again, only this time from somewhere off to their left, then behind them, closing in.

"What the hell's going on?" Becky said, nervously playing with her hair.

"Someone's idea of a Halloween prank," Casey presumed.

The laughter came again and again, from near and far, before them, behind them, then all at once surrounding them, ever nearer.

"How are they doing that?" wondered Becky.

Casey was shaking her head, confused.

The voices came louder now, only they no longer sounded like the laughter of boys, but unlike any voices they'd ever heard.

"This isn't funny anymore," sighed Casey.

All at once the voices leapt to the trees, a cacophony of shrill highs and rumbling lows, assailing their ears. The girls screamed and took off running back in the direction from which they'd come. They didn't have to look back to know that something was chasing after them. Becky soon took the lead, being the faster runner of the two. Neither could hear the other's cries of panic above the din.

When Casey lost her footing and tumbled forward, Becky had no idea she was leaving her friend behind. She raced non-stop till she cleared the woods back where they had entered. Finally stopping to look behind her, Becky, out of breath and dripping with perspiration, screamed, "Ca-a-ase!"

Meanwhile, Casey was out of breath, clambering to her hands and knees, when the woods broke to perfect silence. She looked around, sniffling. Before her, something camouflaged within the trees was watching her. Feeling her courage return, and her pride, Casey shouted, "Who's there? What the hell do you want?"

She listened intently but heard not a stirring. And

then a voice that crawled under her skin spoke a single word: "Fetch."

There came a loud rustling in the trees above like some concealed monkey was hopping from tree to tree, and when it seemed to be directly overhead, Casey turned and screamed. The creature pounced upon her with such swiftness, her mind had no time to elucidate what her eyes had seen. And so she perished under the undefined creature's savage attack.

In mere moments, all that was left of the girl was a few shredded pieces of clothing in a pool of blood. The demon witch approached, her living skirt brushing over the leafy earth. The creature placed the one organ from its victim that it was not allowed to consume—Casey's liver!—gently into the witch's hand.

When she turned to walk back into the woods, the creature leapt in great strides up the nearest tree and vanished. Behind the witch, flames gorged on the pulp that was Casey Robinson.

7

Becky stood in the middle of Woodlawn Road, screaming Casey's name. Part of her wanted to run back into
the woods to find Casey, but her survival instinct kept
her from doing so. Realizing Casey wasn't going to come
out, Becky turned and ran for home. By the time she
raced up the front steps of her house, she was spent,
her cheeks sunken with exhaustion. She bulled through
the front door and slammed it behind her, locking it
with shaking hands.

The house was dark, except for a single lamp on one
of the end tables in the living room. Ragged-breathed,
she called out, "Mom? Dad?" But no one answered.
She ponderously moved deeper into the house. Turning
into the kitchen, she found the overhead oven light was
on. On the freezer door, held in place with a magnet
from Lampman's Pharmacy, was a written note. Becky
leaned in closer to read: *Left early for the Hodgson's party.
Hope you have fun at yours. Try not to be too late. No drinking!
Love you. Mom.*

A sigh of relief slipped past Becky's lips. She opened
the fridge door and removed a carton of milk. As she
started to gulp the cold liquid back, dishes in the cupboards began to clatter, gently at first. Becky stood fixated
on the closed cupboard doors when she realized the
floor was vibrating beneath her feet. She gasped when
movement outside the window, above the sink, caught

her attention. Suddenly, the entire window imploded! Becky screamed, dropping the carton of milk on the floor where its white contents leaked forth.

A blast of frigid wind vomited into the room, whirling around Becky. She looked down with unbelieving eyes as the milk spill began to rise, morphing into a jiggling ball. Becky stepped back, captivated by the shifting sphere.

With a sound like a balloon popping, the bubble blew out into a tall female figure, with supple breasts and a noticeable navel. The head was faceless, and where her feet should have been, her ankles simply continued to the floor and were spread like the liquid she was. Splashes of her white flesh had jutted out from her shoulders, neck, and dancing arms, attaching to various spots on the ceiling, and stretched without tearing when she moved.

Becky subconsciously backed away, but not far enough. She was mesmerized. The room moaned as if sickened by the abomination. When the white demon extended its right hand to Becky, she couldn't seem to stop herself from reaching back. The demon's grip was gentle, icy, rubbery.

"What are you?" Becky whispered, her voice barely audible; and unbeknownst to her, her blue eyes had flushed white.

The demon's movements suggested a similar curiosity of her, slowly guiding her in closer. Becky had a dreamy expression on her face. Instantly, the smooth, pure white surface of the demon's face opened from chin to crown to reveal a devil's maw. With a single chomp, the demon removed the top half of Becky's skull! Blood streamed down its sleek figure. Becky's body convulsed limply in its arms. The demon then went in for a second bite. Becky's entire brain slid down its gullet for safe-keeping.

Then, letting the corpse drop to a pool of gore, the white demon spun into a blur and rode the wind back out through the broken window, taking Becky's corpse with it, and the window itself reconfiguring. All traces of blood—gone. The Foster's kitchen was once again pristine.

Three blocks down the road, Tally was sitting at her vanity, putting the finishing touches to her makeup for the party. She smiled at her reflection, fluttered her eyelashes, giggled, then stared just a moment longer. From within one of the vanity drawers, she pulled out a hidden pack of Next Blue Regulars and a lighter. With her parents out of town for the weekend, she could smoke freely around the house.

Her guests that night, which included Casey, Becky, a few boys from the basketball team, three girls from the cheerleading squad, and a couple of guys from homeroom, were expected to start arriving by 9 pm. She had about one hour to finish prepping. She'd already mixed a bowl of punch, consisting of fruit punch and vodka, and set an array of snack foods on the dining room table, atop a decorative Halloween cloth. She'd gathered all the CDs she wanted to play during the party and was presently listening to Lasgo.

She stepped out onto the wraparound porch where several pumpkins (carvings courtesy of her father), awaited her lighting of their candles. From a distance, she was a petite silhouette of a witch, with the backdrop of her parents' turn of the century Queen Anne Victorian house. As Tally stood there, her face now aglow from the candlelight, she breathed in the air. Prompted by a sudden drop in the wind's temperature, she went back inside, her skimpy black dress giving the night a peek at her ass cheeks, high heels clanking on the wooden floors.

She strutted over to the stereo and turned the volume up, lighting yet another cigarette while she waited. Dialing Becky's number on her cell phone, she waited impatiently for her friend to answer. The moment Becky's recorded voice responded with the typical I'm not available spiel, Tally hung up, infuriated. She didn't like when the girls ignored her calls.

"Bitch, you better answer," she said, now dialing Casey's number. When Casey's phone went on ringing with no response, Tally tossed her cell phone in a huff. "Where the fuck are they?" she shouted to the empty house.

And that's when she heard a startling boom.

"What the fuck?" she said, storming toward the staircase. A second boom, which seemed to emanate from the rooftop, gave her another start. She thought perhaps a couple of the guys might have sneaked in while she was in the kitchen, and were now up on the widow's peak, attempting to frighten her. Any other night, she would have torn them a new asshole, but tonight she decided she was going to be more tolerant, and catch them at their own game.

At the top of the stairs, a cynical smile narrowed her green lipstick lips. She removed her heels to better sneak up on whoever was behind this lame stunt. Bobby and Trey were well-known tricksters, and she was willing to bet a pack of smokes that they were the ones she'd find up there. "Assholes," she whispered, tiptoeing up the second floor stairs to the third landing. Here she became a little concerned, discovering the pull-down ladder already raised. Feeling less courageous, Tally gave up her plan and called out, "Okay, guys. This isn't funny. Party's gonna start and you're gonna be left up there all night!"

She listened for a response: goofy boy chuckles or the whiny exhalations of snooty girls caught in the act. Instead what she got was a third boom that vibrated down through the walls and floor. The large mirror on the wall behind her gave a twisting screech, pressure lines scratching over its reflective surface. Tally gasped out loud.

"Fuck this," she huffed, turning to head back down the stairs.

Just then, the pull-down ladder dropped from the ceiling and banged on the floor. Tally gave a mousy screech, spinning round to face it. *The boom made it fall,* she thought. *But what made the boom?*

Frigid air blasted her from the opening. Tally being Tally, well, nothing and no one was going to scare the shit out of her in her own house and get away with it. Stealthily climbing the wooden steps, a rush of wind blew the pointed hat from Tally's head and set her multicolored locks in a tantrum. Raising her eyes just above the landing, she peered out into the night, quickly surveying the widow's walk—no one! Not a soul.

She climbed up and out quicker now, discombobulated. Jostled by the wind, Tally stood alone on the walk, squinting out over the town under heavy dark clouds. When a long, low groan of thunder grew from the sky's belly, she slapped her thigh, infuriated with herself. "Oh my god. I'm so stupid!" she yelled at the night. "Fucking thunder!"

Suddenly, the pull-down ladder sprang back up and the trap door beneath closed with creaking force. Tally rushed to her knees to try and open the door, but it was jammed.

"No, no! This can't be happening. Fuck!" she screamed.

And just then, a powerful flapping sound like that of some arcane winged beast drew her attention from her current plight. Tally fell back on her ass, her face slackened. For her part in the sadistic, merciless assault on Flower, Ronnie Petals decided to appear to Tally in her true form (no cheap costumes from the local pharmacy). For no sight induced more respect, more surrender, more awe, or more terror than that of the demon witch!

Pulsating with an iridescent glow, the witch's sinewy arms moved almost mechanically. Large hardened breasts only half-revealed themselves from behind a long, pink, fleshy bib hanging down to her knees. Her legs, also flexing with muscles, did not end in a pair of feet, but rather spread out like the hem of a flowing gown.

As Tally lay back, propped up on her elbows in a frozen pose, her skin began to rot. Her eyes were protuberant and unblinking, despite the rain that now dampened her hair and dress. Her heart lurched with every subtle movement the witch made. She was unable to look her private devil in the eyes, for the witch's lumpy features did not give such secrets away. She could see no mouth or nose or ears.

Rolls like blood-soaked cloth were wrapped about the witch's wide neck. Only the bottom half of her grotesque face could be seen beneath the extended, shimmering, shell-like brim which drew to the top of her conical head. Fleshy skin ran over the edges of the brim like a garish table cloth. And when she moved, the weighty cloth swayed with hypnotizing effect.

"Wh-what...are...you?" Tally said in a shuddery breath. By now most of her hair had fallen out in chunks of dissolving goo (of this she was not even aware). She was, however, very aware of the tightening and blackening of her skin, the squeezing and stretching of her insides, and the overwhelming sensation of burning, burning like Flower must have burned!

"Wha...you?" she tried again, her bottom lip now melting into her chin.

She did not expect the voice that responded to come from such a far off place in her mind, clawing its way from the depths, shredding through her memories, devouring the very life she'd lived. And when it surfaced, she heard the foulest of nightmares vocalized:

Justice!

And hearing the voice caused Tally's eyes to burn white. The demon witch raised her hand, fingers splayed outward. Tally's rib cage burst wide open as if she'd taken a cannonball through the back. Her body shook from the unseen claw that dug through the useless stuffing and ripped out her heart!

Lying in her bed, surrounded by candlelight, wrapped in gauze from head to foot, Flower slept under the four pouches strung from the ceiling above her.

8

One week later, Flower kissed her mother's cheek before heading out.

"Look at you. My beautiful, beautiful girl," said Ronnie, lovingly.

Flower smiled back as Ronnie placed a fresh white rose behind her right ear.

"Love you, Mom," said Flower, accepting yet another kiss on her forehead.

"Have fun!" her mother called after her.

"I will!" Flower returned, in a hurry to meet Declan at the tree archway.

Ronnie lit a hand-carved pipe, gave it a few vigorous puffs, then retrieved the four pouches from her daughter's room. She sat down in front of the fireplace and began to hum to herself, pulling out the shrunken, rotted organs one by one, and placing them gently into the blazing pit.

And as Flower approached the archway, she hummed the very same tune as her mother. A broad smile replaced the song the moment she spotted Declan, waving to her from across the little bridge. They laughed as they embraced. Declan spun her round with the joy of seeing her again.

"Wow. You'd never know you were sick at all. You look...breathtaking," he said.

"Then why don't you kiss me?" said Flower.

So he did.

Michael René Dubé was born on October 27 1968.

He is the author of six self-published books including: *Quilth*, *Faun*, *Bag of Bricks*, and three books of poetry: *Fire*, *Different*, *You're Not People, You're Mikey*.

Michael resides in Welland, Ontario, Canada.